DOGS OF LONDON

DOGS OF LONDON

EMMA LEWIS-GALIĆ

First published by Emma Lewis-Galić 2021

FIRST EDITION

ISBN: 978-1-3999-1253-2

Cover design and typesetting by Chloe McDonnell

www.chloemcdonnell.co.uk

For Stevie, my Piper

Jackson, my Rhett

and

Saša, my Sebastian (sorry I killed you off)

DOGS OF LONDON

'...The bleat, the bark, bellow and roar

Are waves that beat on heaven's shore...

...Every morn and every night

Some are born to sweet delight

Some are born to sweet delight

Some are born to endless night...'

Auguries of Innocence by William Blake

'Until one has loved an animal, a part of one's soul remains unawakened.'

Anatole France

'You think dogs will not be in heaven? I tell you, they will be there long before any of us.'

Robert Louis Stevenson

MAIN CHARACTERS

RHETT / 'Doggy Dog' / 'Brown Dog' (a large Mongrel)

GREY (an Italian Greyhound) & 'Lady Human'

SARAH (a very old, yellow Mongrel) & Helen ('The Old Lady')

BEAGLE (a neurotic, miserable Beagle) & Audrey

NERO (a German Shepherd) & Neil

PIPER (a female, grey Poodle) & Lottie

SECONDARY CHARACTERS

ROLF (a black Working Cocker Spaniel) & Harold

Danny

KIP (a Border Collie) & Charles

LEXI (a white Staffordshire Bull Terrier) & Sylvie

OTHER CHARACTERS

The (3) Miniature Pinschers

LILY & LUKE (brown German Shorthaired Pointers) & Edward

JESSICA (a mongrel, RHETT's friend in the Serbian dog shelter)

Mick-the-drunk and the doorman (RHETT's friends)

Irene (shop manager at FARA)

Ophelia (Harold's sister)

Richie & Geoff (GREY's new humans)

Siobhan (Lady Human's cleaner and GREY's friend)

'The Old Man' ('RHETT's human')

Helen's brother Eddie, husband Ted (deceased), son George (deceased)

Lottie's boyfriend Sebastian (deceased)

ROMEO, PAQUITA, ARROW, PIKO (other park gang dogs)

A SKINNY GREY DOG

Two weeks from today, dusk

Somewhere in Kensington Gardens

GREY

He feels that night is coming, the sleek grey dog whose ribs show, whose limbs are impossibly slim. The shadows are lengthening, the air is cooling. The park emptied a while ago and the birds have stopped calling to one another, every last one. The little dog is called Grey. He curls up, cold and miserable.

He is feeling lost. Although his human, Lady Human, is mean, she has dictated his little life thus far and he feels adrift without her. He doesn't know where else to go, and he supposes that this hollow, at the base of this tree, is as good a place as any. Grey looks around, wide-eyed, pivoting his skinny, newly-naked neck nervously. He is trying to get familiarised with the dark; he's not used to it, not outdoors at least. The wind is still howling through the trees, and the space... so much space! He feels it, even if he can't see it. Now he understands what the tiny little sausage dog Paquita - one of the park gang dogs - had meant, all that space above and all around terrifies him. It's disconcerting and makes him feel exposed, vulnerable and powerless.

In the failing light he can't see much, so he strains his ears to compensate. There are sounds of rats, mice, worms, foxes, murmuring to themselves or one other as they scurry, patter, wriggle and trot past. He thinks he can understand something of what they say, snatches of their words, although he's not sure if he's imagining that. It's been a long day.

Grey has never felt more alone or more scared in his life and longs to see one of his friends. Lexi, ideally, or Rhett - but Piper or even Rolf would do. Just a familiar face, a familiar smell. Little things are burrowing into his fur, biting here and there. It unnerves him. The minutes pass and as they do, Grey becomes more accustomed to the new sensations. Aware that he can't stay as tensed up as he is indefinitely, he makes a conscious effort to relax his frame. It is a trick Rhett had taught him once, when Grey had asked him how he was able to be so brave.

'Fake it 'til you make it, Grey!' Rhett had told him, laughing.

Grey muses on his situation. He thinks about Rhett and what he would do. He feels emboldened, thinking of his friend, and valiantly gives himself a little pep talk. *It's cold, but not that cold.* Grey has heard humans say how awful it is to have to sleep outside, but it can't be that bad really. *There must be worse things than sleeping outside!* he thinks. *Boredom and living with a mean owner,* he thinks, *that really gets you down.* He calls to mind all the things he doesn't like about his life with Lady Human, all the things he doesn't like about her; he feels that it is a positive thing to do, under the circumstances. Eventually, the tiredness of the day gets to him. His eyelids droop and he dozes off.

The next morning

Grey awakes with a start from his dreams, which involved conversations with moles and foxes. He is shocked that he has slept through the whole night out here, exposed; at home he wakes often in the night, his mind racing. He looks around, and sees for the very first time the beauty of the dawn, the soft pink blush of it. The park, calm and peaceful, feels benevolent. It is quiet, devoid of people, the gates still locked shut. He hadn't realised before how much noise comes from humans and the persistent hum of their electronics. Without it, the park feels as if it is holding its breath. The dew makes everything sparkle. The smell of the grass is sweet and fresh and as he sniffs, Grey is overcome with emotion. He feels the weight and beauty of the world, the vastness of it, the sense of possibility and an intense feeling of joy, of love and of exquisite suffering.

Gathering his courage he stands up, thinking to get moving, but then sits back down, unsure. He has a scratch and thinks how lovely it is, not to have that damned thing around his neck. He feels gloriously naked. His leg aches, where he had hit the railings yesterday, but it isn't too bad. He stretches his body out, tentatively, placing weight on each leg in turn and checking that everything is OK. He ascertains that although his leg is bruised, there is nothing broken. His ear, though, there's a metallic smell wafting from it, and it feels strange, as if it's the wrong shape. It makes a funny flapping sound when he moves. He stretches, yawns, and then, uncharacteristically, jumps around a bit, like a spring lamb. He does it not only to warm himself up but also for the sheer joy of it, it feels instinctive. The grass is soft and damp under his feet. He feels a bit guilty, Lady Human hadn't liked him to 'leap around like a lunatic', so he's conditioned himself not to. He does it again a couple of times in defiance of her and feels rebellious and proud.

Grey wishes he could see Rhett to tell him how brave he's been. He gives himself a big shake, noting the lack of noise that his collar and tag would have made, and is surprised to feel invigorated. To think how terrified he'd been last night at the prospect of sleeping outside! Giving the ground a last little sniff, in homage to it keeping him safe through the night, he trots on across the park in the direction of the Round Pond. He is light on his feet and it only takes him a few seconds to hit his pace. He is hungry now, and thinks that he might find some food there - he's often noticed humans in groups or alone sitting and eating there during the day, whilst he's been dragged past by his dog walker.

A couple of crows sitting on a branch watch him, idly.

'Unusual to see a dog on its own here, in London,' remarks one.

'Yes. It must have lost its human,' replies the other.

'Hope it'll be OK,' says the first, 'they seem to be so dependent these days.'

Grey hears crows cawing. Perhaps they are hungry too, he thinks. Although he gets the sense somehow from the tone of the exchange that they are talking about something more sophisticated. He wonders if he really had understood the other creatures last night, and, if he had, shouldn't he be able to understand the birds, too?

Things look as well as smell different this morning from last night. Grey has only been in the park during its opening hours before and it feels magical to him now, so peaceful and still. A squirrel appears, suddenly, and darts past him, close enough that he feels the brush of its tail. It is followed by another, chattering manically. They sound frightened, their tails are flicking nervously and he hears their words:

'They're coming! Quick!'

'Get to safety, tell the others!'

'Have you seen little Peter?'

Grey doesn't know for certain, but they have heard rumours - about a morning culling that happens before the park gates are opened each day. Grey watches them as they shoot up the tree trunks out of sight. He pauses, one paw suspended mid-step, as more twitchy beings scurry and scamper erratically past him. Then peace resumes, and he carries on, placing his feet more delicately now, thoughtful. He wonders whether he really did hear the squirrels talking or if perhaps, he had imagined it again just.

He walks another ten metres or so, slowing down as he realises he doesn't really have a plan, except to find some breakfast, and now he doesn't even feel that hungry any more; the knot in his stomach is caused more by worry. The initial adrenalin of waking up free has worn off, and he feels deflated. He sits for a few seconds, uncertain, then steps his front paws out inch by inch in turn until he is laying down on the ground, but straight out like a sphinx - he doesn't feel relaxed enough to flop over onto one haunch. He crosses his paws and lays his head lightly down on the top one. Only his eyes move, crescents of white showing as they swivel this way and that. He is poised to bolt, to run like the wind, should it become necessary. His heart races and he can't quite catch his breath.

Grey's right flank thuds. It hurts even though there is no wound.

He looks at the big shape which he'd sheltered close to last night. Shrieking children climb up and run and jump around it in the daytime. His dog walker sometimes meets people near here, just outside the gates, they pass things back and forth, he's not sure what. Something at the top of the big shape is flapping in the wind. Waves of fear wash over him as he watches it, distrustfully, but he begins to trust that the flapping thing isn't going to do anything more unpredictable or worrying than that. He lays his head down on his crossed paws again and tries to think over what Rhett had said to him, about escaping.

The bottom falls out of his stomach as he realises the terrible mistake he's made. His head shoots up and his eyes widen with panic.

EVENING ROUNDS

Holland Park Avenue, dusk

RHETT

'Hiya, Dog,' the doorman at the Hilton shouts over. The rangy brown dog, Rhett, feels that it must be boring for the man, standing there for hours on end, waiting to let people in and out, so he often passes by to say hello to him. Rhett has known what boredom and waiting feels like. It's almost as crushing as cold, or hunger. Or pain. The humans tend to refer to the mental type of pain as anguish. Rhett shakes his head roughly from side to side, ridding it of thoughts of his best friend, Jessica, and trots over to the doorman.

Rhett barks a greeting, glancing up him, and then stoops to pull a sticky burr off his leg. He spits it out. The doorman crouches down to greet him. Rhett lets him smooth his head. He generally doesn't like to be touched - especially around the collar area as he is wary of being grabbed and detained. With those he knows are safe he tolerates it, but it still makes him uneasy and he is always ready to twist away if needed. Touch is a way of connecting, even for humans, and the allowing of it is a gesture of friendship on his part, a concession. In the cool calm of night-time, like now, when the frenetic rushing of things and people is to a certain extent suspended, it is easier to separate the strands of everything out and to identify energies and intentions. In the daytime when the whole city is alive, Rhett is jumpy - he fears being ambushed, as had happened to him once before. He'd been young then, and too trusting of humans; it was how he had ended up in that god-forsaken shelter in the first place.

The doorman takes his hand away but stays crouched, gazing at him. Rhett thinks that he is probably admiring the golden highlights on his face, the ones that everyone comments on. He shakes his whole body as the hand is removed and as he does, and the tension within him dispels. He likes the doorman, but is relieved that he has stopped smoothing his head. And vigilance aside, anyway he doesn't like to have human smell on him. Some dogs like it, he knows that, but he doesn't – it feels strange to him, repugnant even.

'I ain't got anything for you tonight mate, sorry,' says the man, shrugging, looking into Rhett's amber eyes, eyes that pool black when he is in a panic and turn golden in the sunshine.

'That's all right,' says Rhett, 'I just passed by to say hi anyway. I'm on my way to see Mick. D'you know Mick?'

The man doesn't answer, humans often don't. Instead he stands, knees cracking, the left one particularly badly, Rhett notices. His body generally smells healthy though, and Rhett is glad. It bothers Rhett when he smells sickness in humans; in decent ones anyway. Rhett, knowing that he won't get an answer, tosses his head at the man by way of taking his leave. The doorman nods back at him, smiling. Rhett turns away from the hotel and its guardian, and trots off purposefully, tail up.

The doorman looks after the big brown dog, wondering. He pivots back to the hotel doors and slowly walks inside to have a chat with Jeanette, the night receptionist. Jeanette doesn't like dogs much.

'I don't fancy all that mess they bring into your home', she'd told him the other night, when they had discussed it. They talk about a lot of random stuff, he and Jeanette. The nights are long and work to do, sparse. She may not like dogs much, but apart from that she's OK. Easy on the eye, and always happy to have a chat and a bit of a laugh. Makes the night pass faster. He finds that he daydreams about her sometimes, when he isn't at work, in a vaguely sexual but non-committal, benign kind of way.

Rhett goes on up Holland Park Avenue. He ducks into the second side street and to the inset garages, where his friend Mick can sometimes be found. Although he usually sleeps down near the river bank alone, sometimes Rhett keeps Mick company, curling up beside him on the concrete for the deepest hours of the night. Rhett isn't bothered by cold. It never gets really cold here anyway, not like in Serbia. Sometimes, if he is sober enough, Mick insists on preparing a piece of cardboard especially for Rhett to sit on.

'Hey, Dog!' shouts Mick, spotting Rhett coming.

Uh-oh thinks Rhett. Mick is drunk and garrulous, which can be a bit alarming as it makes his movements wild and unpredictable – he spills drink everywhere, falls over (even from a sitting down position) and sometimes gets into fights, or tries his best to. Rhett thinks that he prefers Mick hungover – although he smells even worse then and is even sadder, particularly after whisky which gives him the lowest crashes. Rhett doesn't understand alcohol and drugs, he isn't quite sure how they work. There's a lot of that stuff going around in their city though, that's for sure. He can sense the differing whirring and clicking and clacking of the brains and floating and rushing of the bodies; the euphoria, the blackness or the blankness, the strangeness of its oscillations.

Rhett approaches Mick and gazes into his eyes, eyes that are beginning to show the signs of drink and wear. Mick is sad, he can tell. Rhett is sad too sometimes, most often at night, when he's alone. The sound of the river soothes him, that's why he sleeps there. Rhett doesn't like his thoughts to be allowed to flourish as they always turn back to Jessica. His thoughts flourish when there is too much silence, that's why he has settled in London, where it's rarely quiet.

'So, Dog! What've you been up to, eh?' asks Mick, without answering Rhett. 'Chasing lady-dogs? Having a bit of argy bargy with other dog-dogs? Sniffing out naughty cats? What is it you do all day. Eh?' Mick sounds genuinely curious but his focus soon fades and he goes into a monologue about a friend he'd had back in his twenties, wondering out loud about what might have happened to him. Only half listening, Rhett wonders why humans talk so incessantly, seemingly just for the sake of talking. He sighs, discreetly, and lays his head down on his big hairy paws.

Mick is lonely, and nostalgic, although arguably less lonely than when he'd lived with his wife, who'd shut him out completely. Now at least he has the soup kitchen crowd, and the Thursday van; there are at least people who know his name, who look out for him and are kind to him. He hopes that one day he'll meet his daughter again, but he doesn't see how, and even thinking about it and how it might play out makes him feel ashamed.

He knows, in his heart of hearts, that he will never be able to give up the booze, even if the solution to him being able to build bridges with his daughter were as simple as that.

He looks into Rhett's eyes, shining amber under the streetlight, and smiles. This wire-haired, grinning brown dog is dependable, he checks in on him every few days. Mick-the-drunk is grateful for such things, these days.

He starts talking again, and loses himself in the ramblings and reminiscences which are a comfort to him.

Rhett tunes him out. Mick, like most people, talks a load of nonsense, but it's important for him to feel like he has an audience. He breaks off his story-telling momentarily with a conspiratorial smile to Rhett. With difficulty, he reaches back behind him into some sort of bag. Rhett wills him not to topple backwards. He does almost over-balance, but letting out a grunt manages to right himself, and draws out a shiny packet, which he unwraps. It has half a sandwich in it. It will have been retrieved from a bin, not that that worries Rhett. Mick momentarily wonders who had made it; that morning, or perhaps last night, in some kitchen, somewhere. A mother, a girlfriend, a dad, or a big brother? Mick had felt briefly sorry that it had been discarded, this small token of everyday love. The drink makes him more emotional. Or perhaps it's the loneliness that does that.

'Come on then, boy, come and have some of this, you must be starving!' Mick says.

Rhett isn't, actually, there's no need to go hungry in London, so much half-eaten food thrown away everywhere, strewn about. He rarely refuses decent food when he comes across it though, just in case. He has a fast metabolism and knows only too well how it feels to be hungry, it was some time ago now but he won't forget it in a hurry. He takes the half sandwich from Mick's outstretched hand, and makes a big show of chewing and then of gulping it down, hamming up looking ravenous. He licks his lips dramatically, in what he hopes is a grateful kind of way, because although he's said thank you to Mick out loud in his mind, he's not sure that humans actually understand their kind of speech.

'You're welcome, Dog,' says Mick, chuckling, and Rhett is glad that he seems to have in fact understood. It has been worth the deceit, worth the easy fakery, he thinks, to see this smile on Mick's face.

'Come on then, boy,' Mick repeats, and this time pats the cardboard he's managed to lay out wonkily next to him. Rhett doesn't much like the smell of the alcohol but he senses Mick's need for contact and he steps around to the side of him onto the cardboard and curls his big body up beside him and tucks his head in, like a swan; a big, brown hairy swan. Rhett feels Mick's big, cold hand patting and stroking him, in a sporadic non-rhythm, and half listens to Mick's ramblings, but he can't keep the other thoughts out of his head. He thinks how much Jessica would have enjoyed that sandwich that he hadn't needed. *If only he could travel through both space and time*! he thinks.The pain stabs at him, the anguish.

Rhett looks up into Mick's face. Mick smiles down at him fondly. Despite Rhett's highly developed sense of independence, he too finds comfort in small moments of connection with other living beings. He shifts his head onto his paws and sighs deeply. Mick's hand lays on him heavily, still now, and Rhett finds his touch unusually reassuring.

A clock somewhere not too far away strikes, slowly and lowly, twelve times. Rhett looks up at the sky. The moon is a constant in his life, he sees it as his friend. The clouds part and there it is. He greets it. Satisfied, he lays his head down on his paws again.

LOCKED IN

3 weeks from now, 3:35am

At Nero and Neil's home (a basement flat on Sinclair Road)

NERO

Nero paces up and down, and circles, restlessly.

Where is he?

His owner, Neil, has never stayed out this long before. He sometimes comes back smelling funny and crashing around, acting strange, but he always comes back. Nero starts to whine.

Something isn't right.

Nero bangs against the door with his shoulder, then does it a second time, now with the whole weight of his body. It should hurt his shoulder, the force with which he hits it, but he's a tough dog, a German Shepherd, and he doesn't even register the impact.

He strains his ears.

Nothing.

Nero sits down, unsure about what to do. Listens. He has particularly good hearing, even for a dog. He can make out the noise of the man sweeping the pavement across the road, trundling his cart along a bit, then stopping and starting up again. They pass the man sometimes, when they are out walking, and he pictures him in the moments between the sweeping and pushing the cart leaning on his brush, having a rest, tapping at something squarish in shape which is linked by small leads to his ears. He can hear the big people – female, mostly - screaming at the little people, who he can hear running, their little shoes slapping on the pavement. They are often told to slow down. He's heard Piper being told that before, he remembers, by Lottie. There's a building on the corner just opposite which all the little ones and a few of the bigger ones go into and come out of, a building that leaks noises of play at regular intervals but that is, in between, curiously quiet.

Just now there's nothing but the occasional screech of a fox. It's just after dawn, he thinks, before the early risers - joggers and the postman. The man with the cart usually comes later in the day though, which puzzles him. He hears the whirring of a bicycle, and he can tell from the rhythm of it, that the person riding it is doing so confidently, joyfully – hands-free, he imagines, not gripping the handlebars tight with tiredness or worry which is the other way he has seen humans do it.

Nero spends many hours home alone so he is accustomed to listening to the sounds of others' lives and has learnt to use his imagination in order to alleviate the boredom. But the empty silence in the flat, the not knowing when Neil is going to come back or what mood he will be in, and the rumbling feeling in his gut is all starting to get to him. Neil had left without a word some time yesterday.

Where can he be? Nero wonders. Laying prone on the floor, his head on his paws, only his eyes and eyebrows move, and his anxiety mounts.

Nothing!

It feels like forever.

His head jerks up as an idea pops into it. He places it back down on his paws almost immediately though, chastising himself.

Neil would kill me! he thinks.

Neil has a proclivity for anger.

ON BROOK GREEN

Brook Green (the Hammersmith Road end), 11:47am

HELEN

There he is again, sitting on the bench. Hunched over as if it is cold, even though it isn't. It makes Helen sad to see him - he always looks so defensive, so cross, as if he doesn't have a friend in the world. Every day when she walks past (*shuffles past!* she thinks, crossly) feeling a yen to speak to him, but she supposes that she ought not to. Maya, her daughter-in-law, is always scaremongering about how awful teens are today, how they all have knives and would sooner stab you than look at you. Helen thinks that this can't be true, but since Maya had said it, the idea won't leave the back of her mind, it lurks there. She smiles benevolently in his general direction now as she passes. *That can't antagonise him, can it?* she thinks. He doesn't look dangerous, he just looks miserable.

She oughtn't to listen to everything her daughter-in-law has to say, thinks Helen, poor Maya seems to be getting old before her time. A worry-wart, her late husband Ted would have called her. Still, it's understandable, having had her husband snatched away from her so suddenly. Helen wipes a tear away from her eyes, as she always does when she thinks about what had happened to her boy George, how his life had been so tragically cut short. It still makes her insides feel cold with shock and hits her afresh, several times a day. She hadn't held strong religious beliefs before her only son had been knocked off his bike and killed cycling to work one day and she sure as hell doesn't now.

Trying not to think about it, Helen looks down at Sarah who is also catching her breath before they continue.

DANNY

He sees her almost every day when he's wandering around the area, the old lady with her tired looking yellow dog. They often sit on a bench in the narrow end of Brook Green's triangle, or are walking, slowly, somewhere around it. It makes Danny feel anchored and comforted somehow to see them; as if at least this in life, that they are there, doing their slow rounds, is predictable. He watches them now, thinking.

Occasionally Danny checks in at school. Mostly not to go to lessons but to see the couple of mates he has and perhaps cadge a fag or two. He doesn't have any money to buy them; his parents had cut off his pocket money a couple of months back when they'd had that letter from the school. It hadn't been much anyway. They'd given him hell, his Pa had tried to force him to say he wouldn't skive off any more classes, his Ma had locked him in his room after tea. But they hadn't once asked him why he didn't want to go to school, why he couldn't handle sitting there in those stuffy classrooms. If they had, he would have told him about Sophie and Mia laughing at him from behind their hands, asking him to show them his work and then, when he was stupid enough to do it, mocking him.

The truth is, he can't make sense of it, everything gets jumbled up in his head and he starts to panic. Letters blur and just look like a load of squiggles and it all feels laborious. He likes the way that word sounds, his mind lingers on such words: Laborious. Despite the fact that he struggles with both writing and reading, he likes English lessons, and Drama too. He'd even been in the school play once. The whole thing had felt good, Danny had felt like he was part of something. He had been in the choir for it too; he had pretended to fool about, but he'd enjoyed it really. But that was all going back a few years when the teachers had had an iota of patience for him still. *Iota! There's another good word,* he thinks.

It all feels too stifling for him, school. He can't handle it, easier just to slink off out of the back entrance, hood up, slip down the cut through to Edwards Road and into the Springvale Estate with its *No Dogs* signs on the forlorn grass, looked out upon by so many eyes. And after that, to get lost in the human traffic of Shepherd's Bush. He feels safer there. Safer and more anonymous. Still lonely though.

Danny started training a few months ago, boxing. He really enjoys it, and when he feels lost or restless now he runs through the streets until sweat crawls down him. He feels like if he runs fast enough he'll leave his problems behind. He doesn't have decent trainers, but he doesn't let that stop him. He enjoys skipping too. All boxers skip, everyone knows that, whatever his Pa might have to say about it. He's mastered a lot of the different steps and it feels good, the rope turning fast but him beating it and counting, counting. It takes his mind off his school worries. He'd like to train outside their tower block, there's space, but he doesn't dare, people would give him grief.

He can do the skipping when he's in the gym though, they get it there. He loves best of all punching the bag, it makes him feel elated. He has to wait his turn though. The place he goes to is not really a gym, but a community centre on Masbro Road. It's free, but there are a lot of older guys there who want to use the bag too, and they give him fewer minutes on it cos he's younger. They're OK though, not mean. Danny had found the place himself. It had felt daunting, going through the registration process but he'd got through it, signing his name and writing out his address, painstakingly. He had smiled at the funny looking lady who had helped him and he had remembered, despite his nervousness, to be polite and to thank her.

Danny's small, but he's wiry, brave and fast, and he thinks that he can be a great featherweight boxer. It's a dream he keeps secret, he isn't stupid enough to tell anyone about it. Not his only real friend, Dom, with whom he doesn't have much in common except that neither of them seem to be able to cope with the parameters of school, certainly not his parents, and not even his little sister Kayleigh with whom he shares his bedroom at home.

That dog pops into his head, the brown, shaggy one that he sometimes sees on Brook Green. He looks out for it now. Is it a Retriever? No, Retrievers are yellow, aren't they. He doesn't know much about dogs, but he likes them. He'd love to have one at home, to be able to bury his head in its fur when his Ma screams at his Pa, at him, at Kayleigh. It isn't scared, that dog. *He* isn't scared, he corrects himself; it's a he-dog, Danny knows that, he's seen him cock his leg, and girl dogs don't do that. Brown Dog has guts, Danny can see that in the way he moves, the cocky sort of assurance he has. He bets Brown Dog gets into fights too, like he does with boys from the other school, the posh school. He feels a kinship. Brown Dog is always alone, too. He wills Brown Dog to appear, and decides that he'll follow him next time, maybe find out who the owner is, why he's allowed to roam around on his own.

Danny watches the old lady with her stick and her tired looking yellow dog making their way across the park, laboriously. (*Laboriously! That word again!*) She looks kind, like his Nan, who died a year or so back. His Nan had always given him a cuddle, even right up to the end, when he was almost 14 and his Pa had said he was too big for cuddles. Danny had thought that was stupid, but of course he didn't say it, and Nan had quickly learnt not to cuddle him when his Dad was around. She had always known instinctively how not to make things worse. His Pa had been a bully ever since he had come out of the womb, pumping his angry little fists, and of course Nan knew that - knew him - better than anyone. Sometimes you can't fight nature. He misses her, his Nan. She used to ask him how he felt, and she had waited for the answer, sat quietly and listened until he'd finished, if he ever got started of course. She had been on his side, he'd always been able to rely on that, even if he'd done something stupid. She had protected him, when she could.

Danny looks up and catches the eye of the old lady, who vaguely smiles at him. He half smiles back before looking down, embarrassed somehow. London's funny like that, all sorts of unwritten rules about eye contact, body language, facial expression - you have to be careful. *But it can't do any harm to smile at an old lady, can it?* Danny thinks.

MARCHING ALONG

Kensington High Street (near Waitrose)

HAROLD

Harold marches along Kensington High Street straight-spined, as his childhood doctor had always insisted upon, as if the deafness had something to do with his posture. He avoids all eye contact, and his eyes are fixed on a point far ahead, another suggestion hammered into him by that same doctor. It has caused him to stumble many times, but the habit is too ingrained to get out of now. Even after all this time he still imagines feeling the crack of a hard, wooden ruler on the back of his thighs or the top of his arm.

Harold is looking forward to his breakfast, which comes after his morning constitutional. He thinks about his dog, Rolf, who he hasn't brought with him this morning as he doesn't like to tie him up outside shops and he had needed to buy a couple of things. Harold feeds Rolf a raw diet and weighs the ingredients out fanatically. Mince with high bone content, sardines, eggs, offal, krill oil, flaxseeds, duck necks, lightly steamed vegetables, berries; Harold has a long list and ensures he gets the ratios right. He wears single use disposable gloves to mix up the twice daily meals and Rolf is nourished optimally, as is Harold who has his own meal preparation plan taped to the fridge. He follows it religiously week after week - turkey and vegetable stir fry with rice on Monday, salmon and broccoli with boiled potatoes on Tuesday, and so on.

Harold has been thinking lately about turning to a wholly plant-based diet. He turns over the term vegan in his head as he walks, uncertain how he feels about it. He wants to check that it isn't just some silly fad first. He will discuss it with his sister Ophelia when they meet for tea this week. Tea on Wednesdays is something they always do. Harold thrives on routine and Ophelia has always been understanding and supportive of his needs, his quirks as she lightly calls them. They share the tacit knowledge that afternoon tea - with scones and dainty little sandwiches with the crusts cut off them – is one of their only happy memories of childhood.

Harold is aware that he is different from other people, that he somehow falls short, but for the life of him is unable to emulate the normal behaviour of others. He stopped trying a long time ago. Harold turns into the mews and counts his way down the houses, as he always does. *One, two, three, four, five, six, seven, eight,* he counts in his head. *A pleasing number, eight,* he thinks. When Harold reaches home he opens the door with a key attached to his belt by a spiral cord so that it reaches the lock without him unclipping it. It had been a fad in the 80s and people regard it curiously now, but as far as Harold is concerned, nothing has bettered it. He is particular about such things and it pleases him. Such a simple, helpful invention.

In the hallway Rolf greets him, sitting calmly in a shaft of sunlight, swishing his tail gently on the wooden parquet. Harold thinks what a good dog he is. Harold wouldn't be able to sustain an ill-behaved, chaotic dog. He thinks about the Springer he had seen earlier in the park, spoilt and hectic, its owner frazzled and apologetic. He makes an irritated harrumph.

Rolf remains sitting as Harold takes his coat off, hangs it on a hook and walks past him. He only then gets up and follows him through into the kitchen, where Harold puts on the kettle for a cup of tea and retrieves a rabbit's ear from a ziploc bag in the fridge to give to him. Rolf wags his tail. He takes the proffered treat gently in his mouth and turns to trot outside, as he has been taught. He knows that after the rabbit's ear will come breakfast, so although it's a trot (Harold doesn't allow running at home), it's a fast one.

PIPER & LOTTIE

Kensington Gardens

LOTTIE

There's still a bite in the air but Spring is definitely on its way. Lottie, tall and slight, walks briskly, in a straight line and with her head down. Piper, a grey, unclipped Medium Poodle runs around haphazardly, enjoying the smells of the new season. She criss-crosses Lottie's path - now left, now right, now far away, now close. Lottie doesn't have to think about where she is, Piper always comes back. When her and Sebastian had first brought her home, Lottie had shuffled her feet along the floor, encouraging the tiny pup to follow her. Piper had delightedly followed, biting playfully at her socks. 'Piper has excellent recall!' people say. They seem to be surprised, as if it's something remarkable.

Lottie's parents watch their daughter closely when she visits, and discuss with each other at length after she leaves whether her relationship with Piper has, since Sebastian has been gone, become a little too intense. They adore Piper, of course they do, who wouldn't? But should your closest friend really be a dog, they wonder.

They come to the conclusion that whatever it is, it is preferable to the year that came before. A bleak, colourless year of Lottie not wanting to go out, not talking and being unable to cope with the simplest of tasks. A year of her washing rarely, eating minimally. A year of too much sleeping, or not enough. The signs of depression had been all too obvious. The awful twilight Lottie had lived in that they hadn't been able to lift. It had broken their hearts to watch her and be unable to take away her grief, to stop her suffering.

No, Piper had quite literally been a life saver, they think.

An hour later...

Lottie and Piper reach their building on Sinclair Road. Lottie puts the key in the lock and her heart sinks. In the park, she can forget. At home, it's a different story. Her stomach does its usual somersaults. She looks down at Piper's happy little face and feels the anxiety subside fractionally.

'Come on then, girl,' she says, 'in we go!' They enter the hallway of the Victorian building with its original tiles, cross through it and walk up the stairs. Their house neighbours will all be out at work now, Lottie thinks. She unlocks the front door to their flat, opens the door and bends down to unclip Piper's lead. They enter the small hallway and go on into the living room, which is clear of stuff. There are no mementos; it is bare, how Lottie needs it to be now there is no him. Lottie feels the familiar lump in her throat. *What would happen to Piper if something happens to me?* she thinks, but quickly pushes the thought away. She has to fight against the black thoughts, she knows that, and has got better at it. Is getting better at it.

'Breakfast, Piper?' she says.

Piper acquiesces, running through into the kitchen before Lottie and banging her paw down hard in the stainless steel food bowl, making it jump and clash on the floor. She looks back at Lottie happily, expectantly. Lottie laughs, thinking what a tonic Piper is. Today she will give her hard boiled eggs, rice, lightly cooked carrots and broccoli, sardines, and a bit of kibble. Lottie prepares Piper's meals first thing every morning so there is nothing to do now but take the clingfilm off. Piper licks her lips. Lottie lays the bowl down on the floor and Piper starts to eat.

Lottie takes a plate from the cupboard. As she does, she remembers a friend of hers, Hazel, being mortified seeing Lottie giving Piper human crockery. Lottie doesn't really understand why, particularly as she has a dishwasher. She shakes her head, irritated at the memory.

Since the trauma of losing Sebastian, Lottie has become less tolerant, less patient. Onto this, the prettiest of her collection of vintage side plates, as a snub to absent Hazel, she smears a knifeload of coconut oil followed by one of hazelnut butter. Lottie thinks to herself how awful it must be for other dogs to have to eat the same thing day in, day out, and is pleased with herself for being so inventive on Piper's behalf.

'For dessert!' she declares to Piper, setting the china plate down gently beside her, on a tea towel so it doesn't slip around as she licks at it. Piper wags her tail approvingly, head still in the first bowl, and quickly glances up at Lottie briefly as if to say thank you before putting her nose back into the bowl. Lottie smiles and reaches for a Nespresso capsule. She can't imagine her life without a dog. More specifically, she can't imagine her life without Piper.

PIPER

As Piper glances up into Lottie's eyes, she thinks to herself *Dear lord, what on earth have I got this time!* but sets to it with relish anyway. She is starving, and will generally eat just about anything anyway. She'd really prefer simpler meals though.

After twenty minutes sprawled together on the sofa relaxing, Lottie sighs deeply and gets up, sluggishly. She fetches her trainers and her coat from the hallway cupboard, perches on the edge of the settee to put the trainers on, stands and drags the coat on, seemingly reluctantly. She kisses Piper three times on the forehead as she always does before leaving, and exits, locking the door behind her.

Piper trots into the back of the apartment and neatly hops up onto the bed with its memory foam mattress and down-filled duvet. She likes her comfort. She curls up contentedly into the pillow on the side of the bed nearest the window, where the smell of Lottie is at its strongest. Sebastian had always slept on that side, but she can't smell him any more. She falls asleep within seconds and dreams happy dreams of chasing balls on ropes and of the endless, joyful retrieving of stuff. Sebastian is there with her, and Lottie too, they are both laughing and running around, hiding things and helping her find them.

REALISATION

Two weeks ago

Hammersmith Road (not far from Holland Park)

GREY

Grey is only half listening to his human, who is talking. On and on she jabbers. The pavement is warm and pleasant underneath him but still he sits gingerly, tail curled carefully around him as is his habit. He knows that Lady Human might be some time now that she is on the subject of foxes; she loves to wind herself up into an angry little frenzy about them. Grey yawns to himself, discreetly; she doesn't like to see the inside of his mouth. He rolls his eyes, thinking how ridiculous she is.

'I told her they're vermin! She was rude to me – very rude!' she is saying. Lady Human is not one of those people for whom seeing an urban fox is a magical, life-affirming experience. If one passes through their garden, as it sometimes does, she goes crazy, running outside with a broom, screaming and shouting at it. Their next door neighbour, who she is referencing, feels very differently. She is often outside, either gardening or meditating, and always talks to Grey if she spots him when Lady Human's cleaner, Siobhan, lets him out there. Sometimes he jumps and puts his paws up on the fence, so she can give him a stroke. Last time though, she'd been busy holding a funeral ceremony for one of their tropical fish. He had heard her chanting, and had seen her wiping her eyes as she had stooped to lay some flowers on the little grave.

There is talking to and talking at, Lexi had said the other day. Lady Human always talks *at*. She is getting herself all riled up with self-righteous indignation. Humans do that a lot these days, Grey thinks - he often sees them either shouting into or jabbing at their mobile phones, fretful and agitated. He thinks that telephones can't be a good thing and is glad that he and his friends don't have to bother with them. He tries to imagine a dog shouting into a mobile phone, and laughs. It's ludicrous. Human behaviour often baffles him.

The person Lady Human is talking at is trying to find her way to the Royal Albert Hall. She is an out of towner, Grey had smelt it immediately. She is down from Liverpool visiting her daughter. The woman is now looking at her watch surreptitiously, not wanting to be rude but desperate to extricate herself from this weird Londoner. She is regretting having asked her the way. Lady Human's rant shows no signs of abating. Grey can tell that the out of towner woman feels mildly on the subject of foxes and that she is somewhat perturbed by his owner's level of disquiet.

'They revolt me!' Lady Human continues, despite the lack of encouragement from her counterpart. 'They really do! Rooting through bins, biting babies! Making a nuisance of themselves, and looking so mangy!' she shudders, dramatically. 'Why don't they do something about it?!' She is all but screeching now and the woman is looking increasingly uncomfortable. Grey feels a sense of solidarity with her. He's used to Lady Human - she's all he's ever known as a life companion - but it doesn't make it any easier to be around her.

Grey gently swivels his head to look at the world around him. He knows better than to pull on the lead, he has learnt to sit patiently and quietly until Lady Human is ready to continue. She has a hell of a jerk on her for her scrawny size and had nearly strangled him a couple of times; he isn't going to make that mistake again. He lets his focus soften and feels as well as sees the little tiny bugs, dust mites, seeds and spores circulating around him in the air. It makes him think of the beautiful poem, 'Dust' by Rupert Brooke which Siobhan had recited to him the other day in her soft, lilting voice. Grey had liked it, though he didn't quite understand all of it. He had liked its wistfulness.

Humans are strange, he thinks to himself, not for the first time, as he tries not to listen to Lady Human gabbling on.

As a butterfly flutters past, he remembers what Siobhan had told him last week. 'Some species of butterfly live only one day, Grey,' she had said gravely - as if it were a secret to be guarded, or maybe a warning.

Imagine that! Grey thinks to himself now, just as he had when she'd told him. His eyes follow the orange, black and white wings flapping past his gaze. It's a rare thing to see on the high street, a butterfly. Although he isn't a pessimist by nature, Grey can't help but doubt its chances against the fast-moving London buses with their fierce, dirty slipstreams and the generally hostile urban environment. *Where can he rest, this delicate, fragile thing?* Somehow, he's sure that the butterfly is male, though he's not sure how he knows. Grey worries. Where can he get nourishment? What can he eat? How will he stay safe?

Grey hopes that what Siobhan had told him is true, all that about karma and reincarnation, and takes heart that the little butterfly will be back some day, even if his demise in this life is close.

'OK, come along Grey!' Lady Human says when she has finally exhausted her vitriol on the subject of foxes. She smiles tautly down at him. The other woman also looks down at him, for want of something better to do. Dogs are handy like that, people say, ice-breakers. He feels the Liverpudlian's relief and looks from her rounded, open face to that of Lady Human's, which is pinched and tight.

Lady Human flicks his lead. It's so unnecessary, that flicking of the lead; he hates it more than anything else. She sets off, at a brisk walk, down towards Kensington High Street, and Grey trots lightly on the pads of his feet beside her, nails clipping on the pavement discreetly.

Grey hears a girl behind them say to her companion, excitedly,

'That dog just rolled its eyes!'

He hears the second girl laughing her friend down. Then the first voice again, indignant,

'I swear it did!'

'Shaz, shuddup!'

'Honest to God!'

Both of them are laughing now, the first girl already doubting what she thought she knew she had seen.

Alongside them the traffic roars in bursts, and it makes him nervous and skittish. He manages to control himself now, he's learnt to, in order to avoid the yank, but he feels relieved when they reach the entrance of Holland Park. You can learn to repress fear and the outward signs of it but that doesn't mean it doesn't exist, it just submerges and hides inside, waiting till it can churn you up again, or explodes out of you and makes a big mess.

In through the gates they go, dispersing the pigeons into a temporary flapping cloud until they settle again. Lady Human's lips are pursed tight but Grey breathes a sigh of relief to be away from the traffic.

'Foul things!' she splutters with disproportionate venom to the sight of a group of pigeons pecking at the floor, minding their own business. Grey is unsurprised though, he knows Lady Human well. He has noticed how a lot of humans like her also seem to find non-humans pointless and irksome. Thankfully, there are those who take the time to feed birds, who crouch down to call squirrels to them, who speak to dogs and other fellow beings in a friendly voice. These humans give Grey hope.

He wonders suddenly, puzzled, why it is that Lady Human even has him, she seems like someone who wouldn't have a dog. He can't figure it out.

Sometimes here she lets him off the lead, and sure enough, she bends down and unclips it with her customary warning:

'Don't go careering around too much now Grey!'

He rolls his eyes for the second time that day and heads away from her, restraining himself slightly but still at a mild sprint, up to the border of the football field. He stops, cocks his leg for a pee, and has a sniff around. He notices a white Staffy a few metres away and she looks nice so he sidles over. Lady Human doesn't like him to socialise, but he can't always manage to suppress his natural urges, dogs are sociable by nature. The white Staffy has kind eyes and a stable, relaxed vibe. They greet in the customary manner, briefly at the front end, then a polite half circle and a quick sniff at the back end, finishing up with eye to eye contact.

The Staffy sits and scratches under her chin with her back paw. Grey sniffs at the grass, glancing up at her intermittently.

'Hi,' says Grey.

'Hi,' says the white Staffy.

'Gorgeous day isn't it!' he says.

'It really is.' He hears the smile in her voice. They both look around them for a few seconds. Grey decides to dive straight in.

'What's your owner like?' Which one is she?' he asks, and then adds 'Or he?'

The Staffy gestures with her head over to a slim, athletic looking lady, walking up the path, looking happy and relaxed.

'That's her, Sylvie.'

'Oh. She looks nice.'

Grey's voice comes out deflated. The white dog sniffs at the ground. He feels her willing him to feel comfortable enough to continue.

'I'm Grey, by the way,' he says, perking up, remembering his manners.

'Lexi. So who's yours?' she asks, gently.

'Over there,' he says, darkly, 'talking to the Chihuahua woman. She's a bit of a cow. My owner, that is, not the Chihuahua woman, I don't know her.' What he's said takes him by surprise, his eyes widen. It's something he hasn't expressed out loud before – or even, really, admitted to himself.

Lexi laughs despite herself, at Grey's expression. It's a very human expression, typically nonsensical as cows are everything but mean. He laughs too. He'd heard it said on the telly last night and had mimicked it, it had felt apt, shocking and irreverent - like something Rhett might say! Grey looks into Lexi's eyes and sees only kindness and openness there. He continues, 'She drags me around on the lead and barely ever lets me off. She's completely miserable and gives me awful food and she's always complaining, or being cross about something. Everything, in fact! It's just really dire living with her.' He tails off, again surprised at his own candour. But the torrent has started and he feels compelled to continue.

'I hate her home, our home – it's so quiet and lonely. And she's just horrible – negative and stingy and just... plain mean.'

As if on cue, Lady Human calls Grey over, urgently hissing his name, sounding stressed.

'I'd better go' says Grey, 'she freaks out if I don't come immediately.'

'I'll walk you,' says Lexi.

They start walking over to where Lady Human is standing but as they do she starts shrieking out loud and jumps up onto a bench.

'No! Shoo!' she shouts, hopping now from foot to foot, like a cartoon character.

'No! Shoo!'

She is looking genuinely panicked and they hurry over, but it only seems to make matters worse.

'Lexi!' Lexi's human, Sylvie, calls, sharply. Lexi turns to Grey.

'I've gotta go Grey,' she looks over at Grey's owner who is still up on the bench, and still hopping from one foot to another, 'but it was lovely to meet you. I hope your owner's all right,' she says, politely. 'See you again?' her eyes seek his. He nods. Lexi's brow furrows, he feels that she is worried about him. She touches his nose with hers and trots off.

'I really hope so!' he calls after Lexi boldly.

Lady Human stops screaming. It dawns on Grey that it had been the sight of Lexi coming towards her that had set her off.

Oh for god's sake! he thinks to himself in disgust and sits down in protest, mute, refusing to give her eye contact.

She fusses over to him, puffing and panting, and clips on the lead roughly, talking all sorts of nonsense. Grey decides during the monologue to which he tries not to listen that he can't continue to live with her. Not for a lifetime. On the way home, he drags at the lead, unwilling to return with her. He decides to try to get separated from her, somehow. He doesn't know how yet, but thinks he will ask Lexi her advice next time he sees her. Anticipating a better future and feeling detached from her, Grey sniffs at the air, feeling glad to have made his decision.

She, surprised at his sudden obstinacy and distracted behaviour, yanks the lead repeatedly and shouts at him, exasperated.

'Come on, Grey!'

His eyes glaze over as he sits down on the ground and turns his thoughts inward. From now on he won't expect anything good from her. In that way, she can't hurt him. He grits his teeth, feeling his collar being pulled up to his ears and almost even over them with the force. He braces against it and remains in position for a couple of heartbeats after Lady Human stops yanking, and then moves on. He feels he's made a point, and vows to do more.

Lady Human tuts and curses and mutters to herself, crossly.

SHEPHERD'S BUSH

Brook Green (Caithness Road)

RHETT

Rhett always feels conspicuous once he leaves the relative cover of Brook Green itself. There are a few tennis courts and a children's play park, but it's a glorified traffic island really. The local dogs and humans alike appreciate it though, as Londoners do any green oasis. The streets leading off it are rather empty and people tend to notice a lone dog around here, so Rhett is wary of do-gooders trying to capture him. They are almost without exception women. Rhett trots up Caithness Road as quickly as he can without breaking into a run, then turns right and takes the second left down Ceylon. Faroe is quieter, riskier. Then Milson, looking out for the Akita sitting in or just outside the dry cleaners. It's hard not to linger and have a long sniff on the little cut through with all its interesting smells, but it isn't a particularly safe place to do so, so he whips through it onto Hofland Road and then quickly after pops out up onto Sinclair Road where they are completing the Atelier development. It feels new and untrustworthy to Rhett, less solid somehow than the buildings that stretch up and down the street on either side of it. The windows seem just a little too reflective, something's a bit off, like there is no real substance to it. Like it is some sort of lie.

Rhett plans to do his usual trick and loosely affiliate himself mentally with someone walking in the same direction as him. He sniffs at a small clump of dandelions that have managed to grow at the base of someone's wall, waiting for a man to pass, then follows him, casually. If people even notice him, they will assume that he is just an off-lead dog. Slightly unusual, perhaps, but not alarming. Nothing to get *involved* over. Rhett lopes along a few metres behind the man all the way along Sinclair Road and up past the K West hotel entrance. The man doesn't even notice Rhett. When they get to the top of the little cut through ramp up to the Green the man girds himself to dart across the road before more traffic whilst there are no cars heading down from the roundabout. He is going to the tube, or to the shopping mall of course, like most of the humans do.

Rhett peels off from him, thanking him in his head for the safe passage and continuing along the south side of the Green, where the pavement is wide. It's interesting, Rhett thinks, how the smells of the streets change. His olfactory system always feels assaulted when the air of Shepherd's Bush Green hits him. The tired, dusty leaves of the trees, infused in relentless traffic fumes, dye from the plethora of hairdressers, fried chicken, coffee, the metallic, deadening smell of phones. A thousand different types of people, dogs, cars, foods, drugs. Smells of excitement, anticipation and stress. Smells of illness, happiness and depression. Smells of youth and smells of age, smells of poverty and of wealth, smells of innate goodness and of moral dereliction. The very pavements themselves smell dirtier and more interesting here on Shepherd's Bush Green: it is a microcosm of the wider city.

After walking for a couple of minutes, Rhett crosses the road and reaches the end bit of the Green where the grass is long and the wildflowers grow. He nearly choked on a chicken bone here once and he has been sure to leave them well alone since then. He turns to the right, past the imposing red brick Dorsett Hotel and past where the Post Office used to be. He waits patiently at the crossing for the green man, and exchanges pleasantries with an attractive female pit bull. She starts to flirt with him but is soon dragged, reluctantly, in a different direction.

On the Uxbridge Road itself, life is busier, louder, wilder. Rhett likes the urgency of it, the buzz. Sirens, testosterone, a certain desperation in the air. Wherever there are humans there is stress, but it's a different type here than down around Brook Green. Here, Rhett smells weed – the stink of it so potent that it makes him sneeze and move on quickly, out of the fug of it. There are abandoned syringes too, plenty of them, he can always smell the trace of evil in them and he steps over them only extremely carefully or, if he can, gives them a wide berth altogether.

He feels comfortable here, on the Uxbridge Road. In chaos he can survive, he can think on his feet, it's only containment that frightens him. He likes that the people here don't pay him any attention. People struggling themselves tend to feel less sorry for a dog. And why *should* they be sorry? He never really understands the distress people tend to feel when they see him without a lead, without an owner. Rhett sits and waits at another zebra crossing patiently, and a baby on his right, snug in her pushchair, shakes her rattle at him. He smiles at her and she smiles back. They say hello, inside their heads. *They are almost without exception good when they are young,* he thinks, looking into her innocent, smiling eyes. *She will soon forgot how to communicate with animals,* Rhett thinks, sadly, it happens earlier and earlier these days with humans.

When the light that the humans are watching changes hue and position, he first double-checks that the cars have stopped and then trots on. Rhett has excellent road sense, he has seen the consequence of getting too close to those brutal, malevolent lumps of moving metal one too many times back; they will destroy your body without even flinching, without a shred of conscience. In their own way they are formidable.

He trots on, the regularity of his legs a running stitch. He constantly looks around him, listens and smells, hyper alert. You have to be, when you're a street dog, there's no other way. His mind turns even further back to the days at the camp, that high wire fence. Now, he can go wherever he pleases. The novelty of that will never wear off. *Freedom.* It is essential to him as nourishment. He pauses, sneezes, shakes, and trots on, happy.

Rhett cuts down through Shepherds Bush Market. He likes it here because of the meaty and fishy smells, and the spicy ones that tickle his nose too. The memory of swiping a piece of fish once from a plastic tray when the fishmonger wasn't looking always sticks in his mind.

As he trots along he looks up to his right and left, at all the curious things that humans buy and sell and thinks to himself how strange they are, needing so much stuff. He emerges from the bottom end of the market with its falafel smells onto Goldhawk Road and heads west along it for a while before crossing. Trotting down Brackenbury Road he thinks about how the people he passes here take notice of him more than in the area he's just been through. The streets are a lot quieter too, there's no hustle and bustle. The dogs walking with the humans here are all well groomed. Some don't even smell like dogs and a few are even dressed in coats. Those that are dressed in coats are invariably a bit snooty, which makes him chuckle -he pities them and their lack of freedom.

There are demarcation lines in this city, he has realised, on either side of which people behave differently. Here, in Brackenbury Village and on the streets of Brook Green - Augustine, Aynhoe, Caithness and on the other side too – Luxembourg, Bute, Rowan, people notice him. He feels how unnerved they are, seeing a free-roaming, independent dog doesn't fit into their picture of normality. They question his right to be there and disapprove of him, or – at best - are concerned about him. Around council estates and on the streets where more people live in smaller spaces it is as if Rhett is pretty much invisible. Here or there someone tells him to 'shoo!' or chucks some food to him, or just calls out 'hey dog!' but mostly, he's ignored. He feels comfortable walking for example on the chaotic Askew road relatively safe from attention, melting amongst the legs, occasionally tripping someone up accidentally and making them curse or kiss their teeth at him.

Home for Rhett is rather a place than a human, a place where he is familiar with every nook and cranny, where he will be safe, stay safe. West London is his home. The river with its mud flats at low tide and his regular sleeping dens in the undergrowth on the banks of the river, close enough to hear it. The house boats with their off beat human inhabitants and the liveliness of the river path; King Street and Lyric Square whose fountains he sometimes cools off in in the summer; Hammersmith Road into Holland Park with its cast of regulars; Kensington High Street and Kensington Gardens where he most often meets his friends; Portobello Green market with its street food and Goldborne Road that he likes the vibe of; the Westway with its raw, fast, urban vibe; the haven of peace that is Little Wormwood Scrubs; Uxbridge Road and Goldhawk, and Shepherds Bush with its all-seeing angel and its chicken bones. He feels safe here on the streets and green spaces of West London, it's all that's familiar, all that's home.

BLACK THOUGHTS

Kensington Gardens (near the Henry Moore Arch)

NERO

Nero feels like there is a storm in his body. It's like that, some days are just worse than others.

Early memories plague Nero, they play on a loop in his head. He remembers being a puppy, playing with Neil, how exciting and how much fun it had been. He remembers being happy at first in his new home although he had missed the warmth of his siblings' bodies, and the big, calm, soothing presence that was their lifegiver. The nights after he had come to live with Neil had seemed strangely cold and silent; he still hates nights. He remembers feeling eager about life, positive about what was going to happen. He remembers looking up into the strange human face with big dark eyes and gleaming teeth that was to be his new clan. He had wriggled with anticipation, even though it had felt strange there only being two of them.

The dark-haired, dark-eyed being with the gleaming white, funnily shaped teeth had rolled him around on the floor, poking and smoothing and tickling him. It had been so much fun. He remembers thinking he couldn't catch a breath from laughing so much, like he might die from happiness. He had nipped a finger with his sharp, sharky teeth, and suddenly he had been flying through the air, whumph against the wall, crashing on the floor, the wind gone from him. He had been stunned. He had felt like the world had turned upside down and thrown him off it, then fallen in on his head! He had tried to melt into the wall but it had been hard, cold and unyielding, and his whole body had hurt.

Nero thinks reluctantly about the many times that had come after, peeing on the carpet by mistake and being half-drowned in the sink as punishment, that feeling of not being able to breathe, and the panic. Neil storming out and slamming the door behind him. The coughing afterwards, alone and sad on the floor, him both willing Neil to come back and dreading it. He remembers being shut out on the back patio in the cold and rain for hours until he had heard angry neighbours knocking on the door and shouting at his human. And being closed inside the washing machine, his neck beginning to ache and feeling not just uncomfortable but very, very uneasy – starting to scratch to get out but only slipping and sliding and panic overtaking him. He had quickly learnt to be scared of this person who had taken him away from his family, this person he had initially snuggled into, carefree.

So today, particularly, Nero feels like there is a storm in his body. Today, he feels as if, at any moment, he might flip. Flip is how his human Neil's friend Deano puts it. Nero doesn't like Deano; he smells awful, of greasy, stale fried food, and always wants to wrestle with Nero, which Nero finds disturbing. He had lost trust in that game a long time ago.

Deano has an unstable vibe, much like Neil, and Nero is beginning lately to feel it in himself, perhaps it is catching. One minute he can be walking along fine, no issues and then bam! something will set him off, even he isn't sure why or when it will happen, it's like a tide of rage that rises in him. Nero tries to think it through, tries to apply reason to it, but it makes his head hurt and his thoughts drift. All he knows for sure is that whatever it is, it is unpredictable, uncontrollable. He can't stop it when it comes and he can't even remember afterwards how he gets into the state he does, or why. All he knows is that he is suddenly snarling and lunging and wanting to hurt something, to really bite down, and hard, but at the same time and most of all he just wants to run away, as fast as possible.

The sensation is much worse when he's on the lead; being shackled to Neil and knowing he's unable to flee makes Nero feel even more jangly and anxious. Nothing seems safe, everything feels unpredictable. He looks up at the sky, fearing it might start that awful grumbling, splitting and crashing sound, as if it wants to wreak vengeance on the park and everyone in it. Nero's brow furrows. He sees a dog fifty metres away and growls under his breath. He feels as if it isn't him growling, but some inner alter ego, demanding to be let loose. He stops the growl and, somewhat taken aback to realise he controls it, whines, involuntarily.

It is certainly better not to trust that everything is okay, Nero thinks. *It is better to always be on your guard.*

Nero's body stiffens and his tail stops still as his eyes focus on the figure of the dog, some sort of long-haired collie mix. The dog is probably looking for a bit of argy-bargy. Its tail is loose, its posture is relaxed, as far as Nero can see, but still, he feels something in his gut, something he can't quite put his finger on. The dog has a certain air of cockiness, he imagines. Nero thinks that he had better warn the dog off, pre-empt it. He glares over, summoning wrath, courting it. His whole body stiffens even more and his eyes fixate now on the dog. His hackles rise, the stiffness turns into a freeze, his mouth is clamped shut. He is deathly quiet, barely breathing. A low growl starts in him, deep down, a growl that doesn't abate, a menacing growl that swells and recedes and swells again. He breaks the freeze and moves his limbs, stiffly, so stiffly that the front legs look like table legs, like they don't have joints in them.

The dog doesn't respond other than lifting a paw and looking over.

Even at that mild, non-inflammatory movement though, Nero snaps. He lunges and barks, frenzied suddenly, enraged. He froths at the mouth. It is almost like he is looking down on himself, he sees it happening, but doesn't know exactly why, because somewhere inside him he knows that the dog's glance was neutral. In the midst of this fit Nero feels detached from himself. He lunges but is held back by Nero and he snaps at the air, registering isolated images in his brain: of sky, of trees, of the dog's torso, of a person's face, of a section of the path and of a discarded takeaway coffee cup. He can't smell anything, but he can taste something metallic in his mouth and hear his own frantic barking and feel the pressure of thundering anger in his head.

The dog puts his raised paw down, averts his gaze and changes his path from the one he was on, to move in a direction away from Nero. Even though the perceived danger melting into the distance has proven to be unsubstantiated Nero finds that his adrenalin, now awoken, is loathe to subside. He can see now that the dog wasn't really a threat at all, but it takes a while for strength of his reaction to abate.

The dog could have been a threat though, couldn't it? Nero thinks to himself, fearing that he might be going mad. He hears Deano's voice sounds in his head: *Losing it!* it says.

Neil curses Nero, quietly, and pulls him in the other direction. Nero knows better than to resist, knows not to use his strength against his human, and skulks beside him, meek now.

THE GHOST OF SEBASTIAN

Kensington Gardens (near the Long Water)

PIPER

Piper looks at the branch overhead. She bets herself that she can catch it. She spots a Fox Terrier standing, watching her. She ignores him and trots back a few steps gamely, turns around and without hesitating, takes a run up and leaps. She doesn't quite reach it.

Damn it! she thinks to herself, as she lands.

It's then that Piper hears the voice inside her head, and she looks around for him, as she always does when it happens. She walks a few steps away from the branch and turns back around to face it.

Come on, Pipes! Sebastian says. He had always called her Pipes and he had been her running and jumping partner. They had had great fun together. Sometimes he had brought his bike so they could go really fast, as fast as the wind. Piper whines, almost imperceptibly, thinking about it. His presence is almost tangible, but it's not enough - she longs to feel his hand ruffling her fur.

Come on, Pipes! Sebastian's voice repeats itself, urging her. She steels herself, focuses on the branch, fixes it with a hard, determined eye. Runs. Leaps. *Yes! Got it!* she thinks. Just for a split second though, it doesn't want to come down, so she leaves it there. She lands, the thud of her four paws almost simultaneous, weirdly cat-like, and looks over at the Fox Terrier who she knows is still watching her, she can sense it. She sees that he is impressed, despite himself, and she preens a bit, thinking of that little Pomeranian her and Rhett so often see and laugh about. Then she looks away, easily pinpointing her Lottie, who she hears now calling to her from a distance.

Coming, Lots! she calls back, out loud in her head to Lottie. *Bye!* she says, hurriedly, to Sebastian. She is too late though; she feels the emptiness around her, he has already gone. She had found it strange at first, this not-quite-really-there presence of him, but now she is entirely used to it and is able to just enjoy it, even though she does still miss his physical presence. Sebastian had called Lottie *Lots* too, like Piper does now. She takes off and enjoys feeling the strength of her body – she doesn't think she will ever tire of running and chasing and definitely not of the game *Find It*!

Piper is always aware of Lottie's position relative to her, almost as if they have some kind of radar tracking system that links them. And she can always pick Lottie out, even if there are loads of other people around. It's easy to recognise her silhouette – long slim legs, big bulky scarf around her neck, the bag hanging across her body. The Bag has treats in it, as well as the Find It Things, sometimes even the Pullers that are lovely to carry and roll and bounce on the ground tantalisingly.

Piper races towards Lottie and The Bag, the branch that had challenged her, the Fox Terrier and even the not-quite-really-there Sebastian soon forgotten.

LOTTIE

Lottie sees Neil and Nero the German Shepherd, Piper's friend, across the water near the Henry Moore sculpture. She frowns, her heart going out to him. People have started muttering complaints about him, and she knows how that can end. *People can be real bullies about dogs these days,* she thinks, worried. *They gang up.* She is at a loss as to how she can intervene though; she can see that Nero wouldn't be much trouble given proper guidelines and a safe and stable home environment, but she suspects he doesn't have that currently. Neil is strict but he isn't physically abusive towards him, at least not in public. He doesn't even raise his voice to him. There's nothing tangible. And yet. And yet... Lottie has a bad feeling about

Neil and she has noticed Nero looking increasingly miserable, these past few weeks particularly. She fears it won't end well.

Sorry not to be able to give Nero a sneaky cuddle like she sometimes manages to when Nero is off the lead and Neil is distracted, Lottie rolls her eyes and huffs involuntarily. She resolves to do something about the situation, she just needs to work out what.

Lottie moves the focus of her gaze and smiles at the sight of Piper bounding across the grass towards her, tongue lolling. She wishes that every dog in the world, Nero included, could have Piper's life. Every single dog in the world. She'd home them all if she could.

'C'mon Piper, let's go!' she says.

DARK DAYS

Two weeks ago

A side street south of Kensington Gardens

AUDREY

Audrey sighs. She loves Beagle, but she hates that she can't just enjoy her walks now, that she has to duck and dive her way through the park, nervous and tense. She barely says hello to people any more, she can't spare the focus. She feels constantly stressed and embarrassed. What must people think of her, seeing Beagle looking so miserable and being so snappy?

Before, when she'd gone for a walk, she'd jumped on the bus just after Hammersmith and then off at Kensington Palace. Now, she gets Beagle carefully settled in his favourite place in the covered cosy cage on the back seat of the car and drives there, taking care to do it smoothly as he gets worried if the car jolts. She parks and checks the whole street for other dogs or anything else potentially frightening before coaxing him out of his safe place, and hurrying - whilst staying calm of course - across into the park and heading for the quietest spot. She now avoids the 'peak' morning hours, and goes at around 11, which of course cuts into her day but since she works freelance, as a bookkeeper, that is her prerogative. She would prefer to get started earlier but Beagle's needs are more important and she doesn't want to set him up for failure by overfacing him with too many dogs. The experts say that it is about setting your dog up for success and controlling the environment which frankly most days feels like an overly daunting responsibility.

The other day Beagle hadn't wanted to go out at all, he had just cowered in the hallway when she had gone to put his lead on, and pee had seeped out of him when she'd tried to pull him out of the front door; something had spooked him. Audrey had sighed and turned back around, taken her coat off, taken his lead off, cleaned up the pee and brought him back into the kitchen where he had wagged his tail at her slowly and mournfully. He had looked apologetic for existing. She had sank down then, onto the floor of the kitchen, and had sat with her back to the dishwasher door. She had cried. Sobbed. Beagle had hovered a paw up in the air, but had not come over to her. Steeped in misery himself, he had been unable to console her.

Audrey cries regularly these days. She isn't sure if she is depressed, angry, tired, lonely, run down or just overly emotional. She can't remember the last time she went out, it doesn't seem to matter, or she can't be bothered – she's not sure which. She feels detached from everything except Beagle and learning about how she can help him, everything else feels irrelevant, trivial. She's put a thunder shirt on him, she's prepared a cosy, covered cage stuffed with well worn t-shirts and socks (she drew the line at worn knickers), she's left 'relaxing music for dogs' on, the TV, classical radio, back to back piano concerto playlists. She's done counter-conditioning with filled kongs, given him all sorts of calming tablets and sprays, pheromones that are said to mimic a mother's milk, essential oils, flower essences. She's tried it all; nothing seems to make any difference.

Because of his crippling separation anxiety, Beagle soils the house whenever she leaves. Every vet, every dog trainer, every behaviourist she has consulted tells her the same. For such an extreme reaction, Beagle is in a state of pure panic. One vet has suggested that she could try him on something called Fluoxetene, which is basically Prozac. The vet has said that it is appropriate if the dog has deep seated, generalised anxiety that seems resistant to training, rather than specific phobias. Others on forums have suggested Zylkene, Alprazolam, Clomipramine. Audrey is considering starting him on one of these as she's getting desperate. She's even recorded him latterly in an attempt to get to the bottom of it, but after watching for a minute or two she had found it too depressing to continue.

She can't leave him, so she organises her life to accommodate that fact, and in doing so becomes totally isolated and feels herself slipping below the surface of normality.

She should invite people round more, she knows that, but she doesn't. She finds the phone calls she has to make to clients a trial and avoids verbal contact if at all possible, sending emails at random times of the night in order to communicate and messaging back claiming she is unable to talk if she receives calls. She knows that she ought to reach out to people, but she just can't seem to summon the effort. She feels that there isn't much to talk about except Beagle's behavioural issues, and not many of her friends are that interested in dogs - even normal, happy-go-lucky ones, let alone miserable, depressed ones. Even the ones that love dogs have tired of hearing about Beagle's problems and have lost patience with her. Beagle just isn't that endearing a dog, to other people. He shies away from cuddles and holds his tail down low, flicking worriedly. If someone approaches closer, he physically flinches and cringes away. Even the most ardent dog lover can't fail to feel insulted and disappointed by Beagle. It breaks Audrey's heart.

Audrey and Beagle scoot into the park and Audrey worries about how the walk will go. Her heart is racing and her breathing is fast. She starts her box breathing, and fights back tears.

STREET DOG

Aynhoe Road

RHETT

Rhett gets fed by street-cleaners and night-workers, by bin men and insomniacs, by drunks and night owls, by little old ladies and by toddlers. Getting enough food isn't an issue for him, nor is shelter. He doesn't sleep much anyway as he likes to be out and about in the night-time, it is cool and quiet and the interesting, raw sounds of wildlife are amplified, or at least no longer muffled by traffic and other man-made noises. He enjoys the absence of the overbearingness of humans and their gadgets, their shouting and their manic, self-obsessed energy. He feels it getting worse and worse lately, not that it's his problem - he doesn't have to live with one. He trots up Aynhoe Road, glancing in as always at number 30 where the glorious Red Setter used to live. As Rhett nears the end of the road he heads diagonally over it.

An old lady with a heart-shaped face has just turned the corner and is labouring down the pavement towards him, heavily relying on her stick, an old yellow dog beside her. The lady's eyes light up when she sees him ahead of her.

'Oh hello!' she exclaims as she reaches him, genuinely delighted. 'My, you are handsome!'

Rhett wags his tail. The lady doesn't seem at all surprised by the fact that Rhett isn't attached by a lead to a human.

'Hey,' says Rhett, to both the dog and the lady.

'Hey,' replies the yellow dog as her human stops. They have a sniff at each other.

'Sarah,' Sarah says.

'Rhett,' says Rhett.

'And this is Helen,' says Sarah, indicating her owner.

'Aren't you handsome!' says Helen.

Rhett stands facing them, wagging his tail rhythmically, like a metronome. Helen beams at him. They stay this way for an interlude.

What a wonderful dog! thinks Helen.

Life is made up of such beautiful moments! thinks Rhett.

'We're just on our way home,' says Sarah. Rhett feels her weariness.

'Nice day, isn't it!'

'It is.' Sarah agrees. 'Have a good walk, see you.'

'Bye now, take care,' says Rhett.

'Don't worry, we're not far from home,' Sarah gestures at a house along the street.

'Good good,' says Rhett.

They nod at each other and go their respective ways, Helen and Rhett feeling not insignificantly happier for this little interaction.

Rhett will always remember the yellow dog and her lady, although he will never remember which was Helen and which was Sarah.

A few minutes later, Rhett trots down the incline of Hansard Mews. The little houses, some with office fronts and pots outside are pretty and seem incongruously located, so close to the enormous roundabout at Shepherd's Bush. A train rumbles past on his left, then relative silence again, and birdsong. A cat is sprawled out on the cobbles outside one of the doorways, completely relaxed, sunning itself. It regards him impassively. Beyond the cat, some 20 metres away, Rhett sees a fox, crossing into the scrubby area beside the railway.

It freezes when it feels his gaze, and turns to look directly at him for a beat, then continues on its way. Humans seemed to be fascinated by foxes. Rhett can't understand why. Personally, he is disinterested in them as a species; he's not curious about their lives, their bin-ravaging antics, their foxy dramas. The fox disappears sleekly, noiselessly through a gap in the fence. Rhett hasn't broken his stride, he continues briskly, skirts the roundabout and heads East, along Holland Park Avenue.

As he's trotting along, Rhett mulls over something that Charles, Lottie and Sylvie had been talking about the other day - they had said that substance abuse and addiction was a purely human affliction. But dogs do get addicted to stuff too, he thinks. Chasing balls, especially here in the UK. Scavenging. Obsessive licking. Humping. Chasing down bitches on heat. Tail chasing. Biting themselves - that's a weird one. A couple of the dogs in the camp had done it, they hadn't been able to stop and it had been distressing to watch. One had become convinced that his leg didn't belong to him and had attacked it every time it moved. It should have been funny, but it hadn't been.

Rhett had seen some pretty odd neuroses in dogs, but he can't help thinking humans are still weirder, as a race. All in all Rhett feels lucky not to have one particular human to have to be worried about. Or one particular dog, for that matter. His thoughts turn back to Jessica, as they always do.

AN UNHAPPY HOME

Brook Green (Sterndale Road) 12:15pm

GREY

The minute they step through the door, the oppressiveness of the silent house starts to weigh down on Grey. Lady Human never plays music or has the radio on and only rarely, television.

Noise gives her migraines, she has decided. The truth is that she's always been sensitive to sound, always disliked a lot of noise. In the early years of marriage, it had felt tolerable, part of the set of compromises you make, those willing compromises that somehow always get less willing as the years pass, until you realise that you are suddenly absolutely no longer willing or even able to make them at all. These days, after one twist of life and another, her nerves are almost entirely shot and she is over-sensitive to even the slightest noise.

Grey lays unhappily on his thin bed in the corner of the stark, comfortless living room and stares into space. With his chin on his paws, he muses that there has to be more to life than this. Day-dreaming gets him through the long days - he wonders now what it's like at Piper's house, or Lexi's or Rolf's. Lexi's house sounds lovely - both grand and comfortable. He's not sure about Piper's, he can't picture it really - except that he knows it's a flat and that there is an armchair covered in deep purple elephant cord which catches the afternoon sunlight, Piper had told them about that the other day when they'd been talking about their favourite sleeping spots.

Rolf's home sounds comfortable even though Rolf has said that Harold is pernickety and too tidy.

Grey thinks about Rhett, about him not having a home. He lifts his head, concentrating on his thoughts. Rhett fascinates him. Grey wonders what he is doing right now. If only he could escape and join him. Imagine! Reflexively, Grey lets out a tiny whine. Lady Human reacts instantly, outraged.

'Grey! What's that racket? Stop it!'

Grey doesn't look at her, he just puts his head back down on his paws and rolls his eyes. He thinks about her jumping up on the bench in the park that day a few weeks ago and making such a fuss about Lexi. He's certain now, having replayed it in his head many times, that that's what it had been about. He's heard the chit-chat between people in the park about bull breeds and how they are perceived and so on but this is the first time he's really witnessed it. *Ridiculous!* he thinks, rolling his eyes again, even though there's no one there to see it. Just doing it makes him feel defiantly, rebelliously better. It's a quirk he's picked up from Rhett - expressive, dramatic, inimitable, confident Rhett! He's so happy that Lexi had introduced him to the others. Even though he only gets quick snatches of time with them his life feels fuller and he feels more connected, more sane. Before he'd met Lexi and the gang he hadn't really had any friends.

She had actually stood on a bench! The more he thinks about it, the more mortified he is - it had been so rude. He shakes his head, irritated. The metal tag clinks against the buckle of his collar.

'Grey! Stop that racket I said!' Lady Human says, sharply.

Life with her is unsustainable, he thinks. He tries to apply his brain to how he is going to escape but it all gets a bit exhausting and he ends up having a snooze instead.

HOME ALONE

At Harold and Rolf's home (a house on Kingsley Mews)

ROLF

Rolf, a black Working Cocker Spaniel, quite likes it when his owner Harold goes out. When Harold is around Rolf plays the game and acts the obedient little gundog, but when he's not at home Rolf likes to run riot. Haring around from the bottom to the top of the house and back down again he enjoys acting the fool and bumping gloriously carefree into things. Spinning around chasing his tail, he makes himself dizzy and flops onto the floor like a giddy child. He revels in acting crazy and zooms around with his tail tucked between his legs, changing direction as fast as he can, just for kicks.

Rolf spies a cat through the sliding doors and runs as if possessed, barking furiously, even though, in truth, cats don't especially worry him. The cat coolly pauses, paw up, mid-stalk across the garden. She turns her head to look at him, then pointedly looks away, puts her paw down unhurriedly, sits, lifts a paw again and starts licking it. She pretends to ignore him.

Rolf chuckles to himself. *Doesn't she know I have a hole in the door to get through?* he wonders. Quietly, sneakily, fit to burst with inner laughter, Rolf tiptoes over to the side door, praying she will stay where she is. Then, as fast as he can, barking and guffawing furiously, he shoots out of the dog flap, nails scrabbling on the patio slabs in his eagerness to catch her. She shoots off, jumping onto next door's brick wall and out of sight down the other side without so much as a backward glance. Rolf laughs out loud to himself.

He remains in the garden for a bit, having a sniff about and perfunctorily chasing a squirrel but, soon bored, he decides to go back inside for a little nap. Not on Harold's bed, he wouldn't go that far. But on the spare bed, that will do. Nice and comfortable, with a shaft of sunlight conveniently placed in an opportune spot. The cleaner won't tell, she's fond of Rolf and covers for him; he has seen her lint roller his incriminating hairs off the top of the quilt, which was made by his human Harold's paternal grandmother. She had been deaf and eccentric too, like Harold.

Rolf likes Harold a lot. He wouldn't say that he loves him, but then Rolf isn't an overly sentimental dog. Harold is a decent chap and a good owner. Sometimes he can be a bit fussy though, so Rolf enjoys the me-time that he gets at home alone. He hops up onto the bed and gets settled on the quilt, closing his eyes and soon falling into a light snooze. He's an uncomplicated dog and doesn't dream of anything remarkable. He listens out for Harold's key in the lock as that will mean breakfast.

FREE DOG

Kensington Gardens (somewhere near the Italian Fountains)

RHETT

Two of the park rangers suspect that the large brown dog is ownerless, but the first has convinced the second that it isn't such a terrible thing; the second isn't that bothered about dogs in any case so it wasn't hard. Why should they make themselves extra work by going out of their way to report a dog that may or may not be a stray? Too many rules in this country anyway, senseless annoying rules - and not enough pay to care about them.

Rhett trots past the park rangers, tail up, purposeful. Over to one side of him, he sees a German Shepherd that he recognises. He comes across lots of dogs like him - anxious and stressed out; there seem to be more and more of them in London lately. Rhett has got to know all types of dog characters on his travels. The problem in this city lately, Rhett thinks, is that dogs seem to have lost their self-belief, their sense of intuition and their ability to rely on it. They have been led astray by their humans, who are under the mistaken belief that they know best. Dogs here have completely lost their confidence. The number of times he sees humans misreading dog body language and making up issues between dogs that aren't ever there, until the dogs themselves even become convinced that they are... Rhett tosses his head, annoyed.

He thinks back to the city he's from, Belgrade. He'd lived there for a couple of years after he'd escaped from the vets after the camp, but it's over a year ago now and he finds that the details of the place have receded in his memory. He does remember a lot of busy roads, underpasses, trains and bridges, and that there had been multiple different groups of dogs roaming the city; co-alliances and bands as small as three up to packs as large as twenty five or more. One of these larger packs had been led by a Husky / Alsation cross and she had picked a fight with him for no reason, backing him into an alleyway one night. She had left a scar on him, all along the underside of his chin, a scar that looks like a shark's mouth. He had been lucky it hadn't got infected; he still remembers the pain of it, how it had been in such an awkward place that he'd had to sleep on his side for a week. He had scarred her too mind, since that fight she had walked with a limp and a misshapen left eye and had given him a wide berth.

Rhett knows that the German Shepherd walking with his owner is called Nero. Nero has clocked him, and stiffens. Rhett can't be bothered with fighting though, it isn't his thing, never has been. He knows dogs who like a bit of argy-bargy just for the fun of it, but it's not for him. He'll fight of course, if he needs to, but generally he avoids it; it seems unnecessary, and primitive. He shifts his trajectory slightly, towards Nero, careful to keep his body loose, non-threatening, but with no signs of submission. 'Alright mate?' he calls over neutrally, when he gets close. Rhett feels the other dog's confusion, wrong-footed by being addressed in such a casual tone. Rhett chuckles quietly to himself and trots past, close enough for Nero to lunge and reach him if he chooses to, now ignoring him entirely.

Rhett feels a pang of pity for Nero, his owner is a nasty piece of work. He doesn't spend too much time dwelling on it though - Nero gets fed, he isn't kept on the lead all the time or closed up in a cage, he gets out and about. If he wanted to, he could escape. Rhett shrugs to himself. It's to a certain extent the luck of the draw, isn't it, life. He can't help thinking about Jessica though, and about the camp he'd come from. Dogs upon dogs upon dogs, destined to spend their lives there. Them, and the ones on chains haunt his dreams, he'd seen plenty of them when he'd crossed through the lands on his journey here. He shudders involuntarily and then, rooting his four paws firmly into the floor to stabilise himself, shakes his whole body, vigorously, efficiently of these thoughts that he doesn't want to think.

Rhett hears the snarly growl of Nero's empty protests but he's already passed him and anyway he can hear that Nero doesn't mean it, how it's just noise. He trots on.

ON BROOK GREEN II

Brook Green (Hammersmith Road end)

DANNY

The old lady hasn't quite reached the end of the park when she stumbles and almost falls. Her dog stands beside her, doesn't move. It seems to be concentrating on staying upright itself. Before he can stop himself, before he can wonder if anyone is watching, Danny hops off the bench, and hurries over to her, that slightly lolloping gait he had initially consciously adopted now thoroughly engrained.

'Are you all right lady?' he asks.

She looks up into his eyes, a little embarrassed and visibly shaken but her eyes shine and she gives him a big smile, as if to reassure him.

'I'm all right my dear,' she says, 'just a bit wobbly on my feet these days. This damned stick!' She bangs the offending article on the ground twice, with a surprising flash of venom and takes his arm. He hardly feels it, she is as light as a feather. He notices that she is breathing a little heavily.

'Do you want to sit on my bench?' he asks her, concerned.

'Your bench?' Tinkly laughter emits from her and her eyes crinkle, looking deep into his.

He looks down at the ground, embarrassed, both at the teasing and at such direct eye contact. He isn't used to it. The lady pats his arm, the one she is holding, twice, kindly, and gives him an open, disarming smile.

'I'm only teasing my dear! I would love to sit on your bench, thank you very much, you're very kind.' Danny blushes and smiles, in spite of himself. The yellow dog looks up at him impassively.

They walk slowly over to the closest bench and sit down. The dog slumps on the floor and closes her eyes, gratefully.

'I'm Danny,' he says to the old lady.

'Helen,' she replies, smiling at him. 'And this is Sarah.' She gestures down at the snoozing dog.

'Nice dog,' he says, not knowing what else to say.

RESPITE

Two weeks ago

At Audrey and Beagle's home

AUDREY

Audrey is in tears again. She doesn't know how it has come to this, that her walks in the park have come to feel like something to be survived, that she feels guilty and traumatised leaving the house yet that it also feels wrong staying in all the time. She is in the habit of keeping the curtains permanently closed now. That way Beagle is less stressed by Things Outside, but it means also that their flat is permanently darkened and she finds that depressing. Audrey feels isolated, alone and cooped up being at home so much; and yet she feels unwilling to interact with anyone any more when she's outside and often catches herself rushing home, as if to safety. She is, as her mother would have said, at her lowest ebb, and having Beagle in her life has led her there.

Audrey had enjoyed her life with Tinks, an easy-going, long-legged, tufty, yellow mutt who had died of old age two years ago. She still misses him. Tinks had been laid back and calm, a friendly, loving, non-demanding dog. Audrey often thinks back to her old life of care-free walks in the park talking to people, meeting friends for drinks and the theatre, or for a meal in the pub with dear Tinks snoozing at their feet.

A new wave of sobs rocks her. Part of her feels that she is being a bit over-dramatic, and yet her gut tells her that her situation merits a dramatic response. How can a dog change things so completely, her friends wonder, it's just a dog. But Audrey feels it keenly, this existential change. Dogs turn plenty of people's lives around, just usually for the better. Aude used to be happy, but Beagle has made her unhappy, that's the nub of it. She is frustrated and depressed, and feels a deep and constant sadness, like the one she had felt a decade ago when her beloved Grandad had passed. Grief! It strikes her then that this period feels just like being in the grips of grief.

Audrey looks at Beagle's sad, frightened little face. If she just loves him fiercely enough, maybe she can protect him from being criticised or judged for not being normal, maybe she can save him from further emotional damage and repair the damage done so far. Her love for this being who is slightly-more-complicated but also slightly-more-precious than other beings grows daily, but it is also this love and the magnitude of it that drags her down. She wipes her eyes and stands up, decisively. She breathes in a deep breath and sighs it out, forcefully, then does it again. She thinks what she can do right now, in this moment, to help them both. *She will not go under,* she thinks. *They will not go under.* She wipes her eyes and heads towards the kitchen.

BEAGLE

His owner, Audrey, the one human of whom he is not afraid, re-enters the room. She walks towards him and places something down on the floor. He looks up at her, unsure what he's supposed to do. She smiles down at him and points at a square mat on the floor. He looks down at it, and back up at her, blankly.

'Come on Beagle!' he hears her say, although his left ear feels a bit muffled. *Perhaps it's the start of an infection,* he thinks.

'Yummy lickimat!' she says, encouragingly, 'Sardines! You love sardines!'

I do like sardines, Beagle thinks to himself, *but I haven't had them in ages.* He looks up at her, reproachfully.

She crouches down and beckons to him. 'Come on love,' she says.

He takes a few wary steps towards her, but sardine smell notwithstanding he still feels the oppressive darkness pounding in his head. He sticks his head out, mistrustful, and sniffs the edge of the mat.

It definitely smells of sardines... he thinks. *But it isn't a bowl, it isn't Audrey's hand, it's just a funny little mat. This can't be right!* Despite himself though, he takes a little lick. *Mmm! It is sardines! After so long*! Beagle feels his tail wag itself despite his sadness, and he takes another lick. And then another. And then he licks around his lips to get the delicious sardine oil off, his eyes half closing with the effort.

Audrey laughs and Beagle jumps backwards, startled.

'No, no Beagle, come on, it's fine!' she says, tapping the mat a few times and taking a piece of sardine between her thumb and first two fingers. She holds it out towards him. Again, he stretches his neck forward and takes the piece of sardine from her fingers. It tastes wonderful. He takes two steps forward and bends his head down and starts to lick.

Licklicklicklicklicklicklicklicklick.

He closes his eyes.

Licklicklicklicklicklicklicklicklicklicklick.

He licks right up to the edges now, exploring every millimetre of this magical little mat. *Why haven't I had sardines on a little mat before?* he wonders dolefully, feeling sorry for himself.

'There you go Beagle!' he hears Audrey say, happily, but it is as if she is speaking to him from far away. He hasn't felt this relaxed in ages. There is something soothing, so soothing about it. He likes this little mat. He continues to lick long after there isn't any trace of sardine taste left.

Audrey bends down and takes it away. Beagle follows it with his eyes and once it has been put away (*in the dishwasher, of all places!)* he flops his head down on his front paws, and sinks back into his usual depressive trance. He whines, sadly, and Audrey smoothes his head. The pounding darkness in it abates just a tiny fraction with her gentle, careful touch and as he thinks about the possibility that he might get to lick the magic little sardine mat again. Hopeful, he stares at the dishwasher until he feels his eyes droop, and falls asleep.

CONNECTING

Hyde Park (near The Dell)

NERO

Nero feels more confident off the lead. He feels vital, powerful, but doesn't know quite what to do with himself.

'Nero! Come!' It is a command, not a request.

Nero swerves to change direction and lopes back to Neil. It is instinctive, he can't ignore the commands any more than he can not scratch at the ground with his feet after he's pooed. Some people called them cues, but really they are commands. Neil and Nero both know that.

'Okay!' says Neil, as Nero touches his snout firmly, as he has been taught, into Neil's palm.

Okay is the release cue and it doesn't come often. Nero feels a small surge of adrenalin, of hope.

I'm free! I'm free to do whatever I want! I can run and run! he thinks. But he stops for a second and stands still, and it is only after this pause that he starts running, away from Neil, before he can change his mind. Nero is uncertain still and changes direction often. *What to do with this freedom, how to make the best of it?* He looks back at Neil but sees that he's deep in conversation with a pretty girl.

Nero throws himself on the floor on his back and rolls side to side, flopping his legs this way and that like the way Piper does - she makes it look really fun. He had met Piper when they were both only pups and they have remained friends. She's one of the only dogs he's allowed to play with, or at least up until recently. These days Neil even tries to keep him away from her. Still copying the way Piper does it, he curves his spine first one way then the other. It does feel nice, but he feels a bit exposed and vulnerable laying on the floor upside down so he gets up on his feet and gives himself a shake.

He spies that annoying Border Collie, darting around. Kip, he's called. He often hears the owner's lazy drawl, calling him. Nero's heart leaps with excitement. Driving his two back legs into the ground urgently, he launches off in the direction of the collie. *Strange name, Kip,* Nero thinks. *Stupid name!* Nero begins to channel all his anxiety and uncertainty into hatred of Kip. It feels good to be thundering along the ground, to have a feeling of purpose. He looks forward to connecting with Kip, he can almost feel it already, the fur in his mouth, the taste and smell of the blood as he breaks skin, the sound of Kip's yelps.

He will yelp, for sure, Nero thinks to himself. He hopes Kip fights back. Oh, the sweet release of the fight, when nothing else exists but action and reaction, the thrashing and clashing of bodies and power and speed and teeth. The *Adrenalin* surges in him and he drives himself forward faster.

He hears a voice resound in his head, it is solid, unshakeable, casual. 'No,' it says. His pace falters as he tries to place where it is coming from.

'Stop.'

The same voice again, male. It is a command, not a cue, even though it didn't come from Neil. Despite himself, Nero stops. The pleasure, the anticipation of connection drops away suddenly and disappointingly, a drug high on the wane. There is a tipping point, and he feels it. His stomach lurches, he feels it sicken. He knows he won't be able to get the high back. *Damn!* Nero feels angry at the voice and snaps his head around looking for it. He has stopped running now, and turns his body this way and that, looking, angrily. He finally pinpoints where the voice has come from, or rather who as his eyes lock onto a large brown dog, with a scruffy, wiry coat. About his size, maybe, although leaner, it is standing square and unafraid, and with its amber-coloured, unusual shaped eyes it looks into Nero's, calmly.

Almond-shaped eyes, Nero thinks. Something about the stillness of the dog disables Nero. He thinks it might be the one who had brushed past him just yesterday, cool as a cucumber, and said 'Alright mate?'.

He hears another voice now, this time a female one.

'Don't do that my love, it won't help.' The voice sounds sorry, and kind, and he thinks of his gentle, calm mother who he can barely remember. Tears prick at his eyes.

The amber-eyed dog looks over to where the other voice, the female voice, is coming from. Lying down relaxed in the shade of a tree is a stocky white Staffy. Nero can feel her gentleness. But although the wind has left his sails with all desire to chase Kip now gone, he still somehow feels a bit cross. His pent-up energy still needs something to do. It's out of the question to attack either of these two dogs. He can't say why really, the chemistry just isn't right, they don't call for it. He feels thrown and indecisive.

Just at that moment he hears his friend Piper call to him.

'Nero!'

Glad for something to do, Nero pivots. He spots her straight away - she is bounding across the park towards him happily with her distinctive, cheerful gait. He races towards her. Even though she is his only friend in life, when he reaches her he can't help himself, he lets out a roar of rage and grabs a mouthful of the scruff of her neck, and flips and flops her onto the floor first one way and then the other, like a wrestler. He hears Piper's human, Lottie, shouting at him, sharply,

'Oi! NO! Nero! No! Leave It!'

He lets go. He respects Piper's human and again, it's so clearly a command and not a request. Anyway he has done what he needed to, the action has exorcised his frustration and his rage is gone. Piper wastes no time, she leaps up and runs off, calling to him over her shoulder. She isn't phased, she likes a bit of a fight and Nero hadn't bitten hard, not really hard anyway.

'Come on then!" she teases, grinning. Nero glances at Lottie to check she's okay with it and sees that she is. Lottie likes him, he knows that, he's her favourite dog in the park besides Piper, he has heard her say it.

She has also said that he is misunderstood, not that he knows what she means by that. He launches forward again and pounds towards Piper, but it is different now, he feels happy. These are the best moments in life, by far, these moments of playing with Piper, even though they don't come along often. She is standing still now, but just as he reaches her she deftly side steps. He clumsily turns to make another approach but she is already a distance away, running, teasing him.

'Come on, slowcoach!'

She darts and veers and Nero chases, each time missing. She is athletic, Piper - fast and fit. He starts to feel tired and happy and laughs then, just for the hell of it.

'Piper!' He appeals to her to stop, which she does, suddenly, and flops onto the floor, long tongue hanging, tail wagging. He gets up, panting heavily, and lopes over. As he reaches her he sees her brace herself for impact and half close her eyes, but he just throws himself down beside her.

'Whatcha, Nero!' she says. Piper likes to pick up strange expressions like this from the humans.

He bumps his head against hers in reply, and grins.

Piper looks across at Neil and sees he is still busy talking.

'Come on Nero, come and meet Rhett and Lexi!' she says, running off in the direction of the large brown dog and the stocky white Staffy. After a moment's hesitation, Nero follows her, shyly.

'And leave Kip alone!' Piper throws over her shoulder, laughing, 'I saw you about to have a go at him!'

Lottie watches with interest. She notes Nero's loping, subdued gait. She hopes Neil will keep talking for some time. It's good seeing Nero being social. She holds her breath as he reaches the other two dogs. She observes. The meetings go well, circling, sniffing, loose limbs and happy, relaxed mouths. She smiles. It's good to have friends, she thinks, even though sometimes you think you want to be alone.

SHELTER DOG MUSINGS

13 months ago

A bleak dog shelter in the middle of nowhere, Serbia

RHETT

Rhett doesn't believe in the Dog God, but if he did he would think that He invented birds to keep all the dogs of the world who are bored, penned in or tied up from losing their sanity, because you can lose yourself in watching a bird, even if you're behind bars, or tethered. He watches the birds, longingly, wishing he could fly out of here. He's sure he could manage to take care of himself, find food and shelter, live on his wits, improvise. If only he and Jessica could somehow get through this fence! This inescapable, unabating imprisonment fills him with fear. *When will it end?*

He cocks his head on one side, thinking more about the concept of the existence of a Dog God. He isn't sure. He's heard the stories, of course. Some of the older dogs like to tell them to the new ones, to comfort them. Rhett likes to imagine there being someone up there looking out for them, able to change their fates. It gives him hope. Life in the shelter is grim and brutal, but there's always the chance of being taken out, maybe that's at the whim of the Dog God. Who knows, he thinks, sniffing at the air. Dirt and damp and rotting wood and pee, but something beyond that too, the unknown. If only he could get there.

Sometimes those crying, distraught ladies actually take a dog away with them. It's unclear how each dog is chosen and that makes it seem even more magical. It's like a lottery that you didn't know you'd entered. These extractions always bring an uplifted feeling to the whole camp, if only for a few days. They give those remaining renewed hope. The ladies don't visit often though, the stretches in between are vast. Whoever put about the myth that dogs have no concept of time was off their head, thinks Rhett.

He has tried to escape the camp a few times. Even though he'd known it was dangerous he had felt compelled to at least try. But even he has had to concede that it's hopeless. On his last attempt, the barbed wire had ripped a hole right down his right flank and he had nearly died a few days later, of blood poisoning. His body had been stubborn though, had not given in to Death, Death who came creeping, trying to claim it. Jessica had growled at it in the darkness and licked Rhett's wounds clean, tending him lovingly for days, even though her tongue had been dry and raw from the lack of freely available drinking water. There *is* a pond, they call it *the Rank Pool* but everyone knows that if you drink from it, it means certain death. She keeps herself away from it - mainly from devotion to Rhett. They all do. Until they don't of course.

During the fever, as he'd soared close to the edges of the world, he had imagined the Dog God telling him in a stern and booming voice to be patient, not to lose hope, not to just lay down and die because there was a whole new life ahead of him, ahead of a lot of the dogs at the camp. Here in this barren place with no comforts, it would be so easy to lose hope. But the Dog God had gone on to tell Rhett that even though he was now diminished by lack of food, regular clean water and restful sleep, he had to use his innate healing power, his vision and charisma to help others. Rhett had listened to this disembodied voice in his head and had inexplicably pictured the unknown deity as a black panther wearing an Adidas top and a chunky gold chain.

Scratching behind his ear with a back leg, Rhett thinks about the people who come to visit the camp, the ladies. They are so upset on the dogs' behalf. Some of the dogs try to cheer them up, jumping around barking, grinning, nuzzling up to them, licking them wildly or gently, but everything just seems to make them even sadder. They are so kind, the visitors, but Rhett can't help thinking that they would help more if they were positive and joyful, and just shared happy moments of companionship and distraction as opposed to all the sympathy and hand-wringing. That could be their real, albeit transitory, gift to the dogs of the camp, a few happy moments of play, of connection, of joy. Some of the dogs cuddle up to each other, but a lot of them still miss human touch. Some crave it. Rhett finds it distasteful, demeaning.

They work really hard when they are there though, the ladies, cleaning and repairing everything they can, working from dawn till dusk, and it makes a change to the dogs to have some decent humans around to watch and interact with. Rhett has noticed too that after they leave, changes happen. More pallets are brought, and even some gravel; these once laid down create more mud-free places to hang out. New, better insulated houses are erected, and despite the sour faces of the feeders, there is better food for a bit, biscuits instead of bread.

Rhett looks over at the dog houses across from him. One in particular is collapsing into the ground. A dog stands up, turns around a few times and settles back down with a big sigh, nose tucked into its body. Rhett feels stiffness in his joints so he gets up, stretches, and then jumps off into the mud. It's not that bad at this time of year. Jessica, next door, senses his movement and comes out of her house and jumps down onto the ground too and greets him, without words. In the winter they double up, even though neither of their houses are big enough really. Side by side, they trot off to do a round of the camp. *We might see my bird friends,* Rhett thinks, and makes sure to keep glancing up at the sky as they do.

IN THE WRONG LIFE

Kensington Gardens (near the entrance to the Pirate Ship)

GREY

Grey sits beside the bench, as far from Lady Human's feet as his short, fancy lead will allow. She hasn't let him off the lead today and he suspects that she won't. He feels glum. He generally feels glum when he's close to her. He stares across the stretch of grass longingly, watching Rhett, fifty metres away, playing with Piper. Grey feels a soft stab of envy; he's too fragile to play that rough, but he'd like to. He cocks his head, pensive. *Rhett doesn't even seem to move the same way as other dogs,* he thinks, *his movements seem more natural, or faster, or something.* Grey lays his front half down on the floor, resigned for now to his lack of freedom.

Sniffing absent-mindedly at the ground whilst watching the two of them playing, he mulls over why Rhett seems to be so different from the other dogs he knows. He pictures them in turn. *They are all dependent on humans, that's the difference,* he thinks. Rolf is generally either sniffing at the floor in a frenzy or looking up at his owner Harold, eagerly awaiting a cue, Rolf is definitely not independent. Lexi is always worrying about others. It's quite un-dog-like of her. Her owner, Sylvie, is the same and they help people as a team. Piper is a joyful, carefree character who lives in the moment, either fixated on fetching that stick or getting into that pond or leaping over that tree trunk. In-between though, she always orientates back to Lottie, as if they have an invisible string between them. Sarah is phlegmatic and level-headed and wholly harmonious with her elderly owner Helen, Grey can't imagine seeing one without the other.

Rhett is different. Proud, strong and brave, Rhett is unashamedly Rhett. He doesn't depend on or defer to anyone, he doesn't adore, idolise or emulate anyone; he just is. He doesn't have - and doesn't need - a human, and because he doesn't have a human he seems somehow purer. Dog in a purer form, undiluted by human influence and control. Grey watches Rhett's muscles ripple as he twists away from Piper. Rhett's teeth flash, he's grinning. Piper's belly is low to the ground and she charges at him, eyes gleaming. He's made her mad, Grey thinks, and smiles.

Grey's limbs twitch, he'd love to race over there. He sighs.

Yes, it has to be something to do with the fact that he doesn't live with a human, why he's so different, Grey thinks.

Lady Human crosses her legs. Grey glances up at her. He experiences her presence in his life as a slick of oil, an invisible but noxious toxin that covers and smothers, that threatens to choke the life out of him. Only the other day Rhett had told Grey how it makes him angry the way humans treat their dogs. Rhett talks often about how he thinks dogs should live freer lives, less dependent on their humans or perhaps even strive to live completely independent of them. Grey however isn't sure. He always gets goosebumps listening to Rhett; his heart starts to race imagining having such a life, but on the other hand, although he doesn't like Lady Human, he wouldn't in truth feel confident living entirely without her. He's always been so used to her deciding everything for him, so used to the lack of choice in his little life. It's dreary and frustrating on the one side, but on the other, it's safe, and doesn't make his heart feel like it's working dangerously fast. It would be hard, especially in the winter, to have to sleep outside, and he wouldn't fancy having to forage for his own food.

Grey continues to watch Rhett, still dodging away from Piper in and out of the dappled sunlight under the trees. Handsome, confident Rhett - how Grey wishes he were more like him, how he idolises him. Chin resting on his delicate, bony, crossed paws, he lets out a long sad sigh.

Since meeting Lexi, Grey has found that he hasn't been able to stop talking; he takes any opportunity he gets to discuss his predicament now. All these new feelings had come slowly at first, but now they tumble around inside him, jostling each other and threatening to spill out, in the form of 'bad' behaviour. He is finding it harder and harder to keep his cool and toe the line. His *insolence* as Lady Human calls it, is swelling.

In parallel with these feelings of bravery and frustration growing, Grey's life is becoming more miserable by the day. For Lady Human, the novelty of parading him around wore off some time ago and although she had employed a dog walker a couple of months back, she has recently decided that the chap is not to be trusted, so the future of Grey's walks and opportunities to socialise hangs in the balance. This worries Grey immensely.

That the walker is not to be trusted is a matter of rare mutual agreement between them though. He doesn't walk with Grey much at all, rather sits on a bench just inside the park for 45 minutes and reads his comic book or (more often, recently) jabs at his phone petulantly, belligerently, with stubby, grubby, bitter-smelling fingers. He rolls his own disgusting smelling roll-ups, and discards the ends on the grass when he is finished. He seems to eat only the most heavily plastic-encased food and drink that he can find and always leaves the debris behind, slyly and surreptitiously, like he's getting away with something. Why hadn't Lady Human chosen one of the other, pungently sweaty-smelling and exotically happy dog walkers who run and play and laugh with their canine charges? Trust her to manage to find the meanest, laziest, non-dog-loving dog walker out there! On the upside though, the dog walker at least doesn't shoo any of his new friends away when they come and mill around and chat to him.

Chin still resting on his paws, Grey wills Piper and Rhett to spot him and come over, wills Lottie to walk in this direction. Feeling melancholic, only Grey's eyes move as he watches his two friends larking about. It's awful, he thinks, to feel stressed and unsettled and not be free to run the feeling off.

Grey sighs again, his heart aching with longing for a different life.

THE ATTACK

A month ago, 11:16am

Kensington Gardens (the south side)

AUDREY

It is a spring day, with pretty cherry blossom on the trees and a soft, sweet breeze. Audrey exits her flat marginally less grim-faced, marginally more hopeful than usual. She had slept well last night, after learning on a webinar about a method that she thinks is worth a go, something about transferring calming energy down the lead by stroking it. It is exactly the sort of day upon which one would not expect something really bad to happen. Audrey has felt in her heart for some time though that at some point something really bad will happen, that it's inevitable, and she has been bracing herself for it, which is a constant strain. Audrey is chronically stressed. Today though, she isn't expecting it; she is fooled by that pretty cherry blossom on the trees and that benign, gentle breeze.

Audrey parks near the Albert Memorial. She smiles, uncharacteristically allowing herself to feel a moment of pride in what she has achieved: living independently in London, and walking her dog in, of all places, Kensington Gardens. She is a bright girl, but not brimming over with natural confidence and at 35 she is only now beginning to find her feet and feel properly grown up. Exiting the car, she turns her face towards the sun, enjoying its warmth. It is like a caress, she thinks. She and Beagle cross the road and enter the park. They start to walk along the path on the south side of it, near the railings.

Audrey observes her canine companion, and tries, as the webinar has taught her, to be objective, to try to detect how he is feeling from his body language. Could he really be in pain, she wonders, and makes a mental note to arrange a vet check. This though engenders a feeling of dread: a vet check is always an ordeal - for both of them. Determined to enjoy the day she shakes off the thought, squares her shoulders, breathes out and consciously relaxes her body.

After only a few seconds though, in her peripheral field of vision, Audrey catches sight of the Miniature Pinschers. Her heart gives a little jump but she tells herself calmly, as she starts to turn, *there's time... don't panic Audrey, they're far enough away.* Whenever she sees these three dogs they make her think of the precocious teenager mall rats she had used to avoid in Westfield. She never goes there any more of course, as she can't leave Beagle home alone. Now facing away from them, Audrey awkwardly strokes the lead and walks, briskly but without rushing, careful not to emanate a sense of panic, back the way they had come. Glancing back, she registers with an icy stab of fear that the main lead is slipping its holder's grasp. She can't tear her eyes away and sees as if in slow motion the woman fumble, try to grab the lead, fail. The woman drops her cigarette, curses, and stoops to pick it up, prioritising its retrieval over securing her dogs. They, gleeful and vicious, realise they are no longer tethered.

Audrey has been holding her breath all this time and lets it out in a rush. After a surprised pause, the three miniature hounds of hell start racing towards Audrey and Beagle, who are rooted to the spot, horrified. Audrey stares as the red, glistening mouths which are closing in upon them. Teeth flashing, jaws snapping, spit flying, the Pinschers' eyes are wide with excitement. The flailing, drooling trio seem to cover the ground impossibly fast, and are almost upon them in a flash. With a great force of will, Audrey tears her eyes away and looks down. Beagle has flattened himself into the ground. A horrible sense of dread rises in her.

Seeing Beagle close his eyes tight and be so utterly terrified, Audrey feels a sudden burst of outrage. Her protective instinct awakened, she steps in front of Beagle and squares up to the dogs, bracing herself for the impact, nails pressing into her palms. Time snaps forward and she registers that they have evaded her, despite the handicap of being shackled together and having to perform acrobats in order to disentangle themselves from each other they have swerved and run behind Audrey and Beagle. They are now on their second approach.

Time snaps forward again. It's as if the world is put on mute, Audrey loses her sense of hearing; only vision remains. One of the attackers makes contact and gets a firm hold on Beagle's left back leg. With great determination, in an impatient rhythm, he tries to drag him away. *Tugtug-rest, tugtug-rest, tugtug-rest.* Beagle just lays still, as if he is a rag doll or a soft toy. The dog that has hold of him reminds Audrey of a hyena and she remembers reading once that hyenas eat their prey alive. Appalled, a second fire rises in her, and blood again seems to whoosh around her body and flood right up into her head. The words explode out of her, and she bellows, 'LEAVE MY DOG ALONE YOU LITTLE SHITBAGS!!!!!!' She had heard the term 'shitbag' on some soap last night and had been shocked by the vitriol, the childish power in that one small, silly, made up word. Eastenders, that's where she'd heard it, she remembers. It's funny how your mind works under stress.

This vocalisation of fury feels like a great release, a rush of endorphins, but the euphoria lasts only seconds. The hyena-dog takes no notice of her and keeps going (*tugtug-rest, tugtug-rest*), Beagle even now still has his eyes firmly closed and is still as floppy as a newly dead rabbit. The other two dogs have started fighting each other. Audrey's heart skips with hope. She is just summoning the right moment to try to kick hyena-dog when out of nowhere she senses several other dogs running towards her. A white Staffy, some sort of big, brown, rough-haired one, and a Husky. Legs beginning to buckle, nausea rises in her and she feels overwhelmed. *This is it then,* she thinks, *the dog fight to end all dog fights.* Audrey frantically scrabbles around in her brain for what to do to break it up, she is determined not to be her usual passive self and the shouting has made her feel liberated, emboldened.

She doesn't have a heavy coat on to throw over them though, or a large bucket of ice-cold water handy. What else? Something about picking up their back legs like a wheelbarrow? As she is racking her brains, a surprising sensation spreads through her, a feeling of relief. This feeling of relief, of intense elation presents as an extended, attack of goosebumps, throughout her whole body but also, she feels, in her mind. Her hands, gripping the lead, unclasp involuntarily, and the lead drops to the floor. Hyena-dog has been tugging at Beagle and Audrey has been moving with them, so as not to make Beagle the object of a tug of war. Now she stands still, and meets the piercing, seemingly indifferent eyes of the Husky.

The white dog, a stout, muscular Staffy stands square and certain, with its back to Beagle, defending him. It exudes a sense of calmness and of authority as it stares at the Pinschers, soundlessly, solidly daring them. The Husky stands next to it and growls, menacingly, in the same direction. The brown dog lopes across effortlessly and takes the hyena-dog in its large mouth. With one extravagant and comic movement it throws it in the air, away from Beagle; it has gauged perfectly the exact moment that the hyena-dog's teeth were resting from its tugtug rhythm. This dog is happy looking, which should feel incongruous but doesn't. It glances at Audrey in passing, grinning, and its eyes are a liquid caramel. It's male, Audrey sees, and has the air of a cartoon dog. Audrey feels herself smile. The other two dogs have been yanked and dragged with it, such was the force of the dog's throw, and the threesome struggle about in a heap, disgruntled and out of their minds with fury. They turn on each other, making high pitched, sharp yaps and snaps and snarls at each other and at the air around them.

'Go, Rhett' Lexi hisses at Rhett, urgently. Beagle has now lost control of his bowels and is in a terrible state.

'Gotcha. See you, Lex, nice work!' Rhett says, grinning, and lopes off.

Romeo the Husky, an acquaintance from the park who finds London a bit warm and boring, is already running away from the scene of the fracas and Rhett catches up with him and gives him a shoulder bump. They slow to a walk, their body language friendly and loose.

'Nice work huh!' Romeo says, grinning, echoing Rhett, and Rhett grins back at him.

'Yup! Ach, what can you do - kids!' he replies. They both laugh.

'They'll think twice though next time, the little tykes!' says Romeo, in farewell, and heads off at a leisurely trot. His poor owners will be looking for him again; he escapes as and when he wants to for a bit of me-time and to alleviate the domestic boredom. Although he likes his human family, he feels in his blood that he was made for a different life than this, and yearns for it.

Audrey breathes out, incredulous that there has been no dog fight after all. Two of the dogs seem to have disappeared into thin air, only the white Staffy remains. The trio of attackers still look stiff and tense and poised to fight, they circle each other as much as their tangled leads allow, but with a few more air snaps and half-hearted growls their hearts seem to go out of it. They look back in the direction of Beagle, wanting to intimidate him, but the white Staffy demands that they avert their gaze. They sniff the grass, lick their lips, and back off a few steps, tails stumps lowering. Turning, clumsily, chastened, they run - tangling, falling, tumbling, righting themselves. In this haphazard, chaotic manner they run all the way back to their owner. She still has the cigarette in her hand and is taking deep, desperate drags, in between screaming at her dogs.

Beagle is cowering. Audrey runs the few steps over to him and crouches down to examine him. He's shaking and whimpering, but doesn't appear to be bloody. The white Staffy glances back at him, then flops to lay on one flank on the ground, panting, wide-mouthed, teeth gleaming, casually scanning the park around them. Something is bugging Audrey and she realises it's that she has the distinct impression that these dogs have been working as a team, communicating. Maybe she really is losing it, like her friend Mandy had said the other day.

Still crouching down on the floor, Audrey becomes aware of a woman running towards her. The woman is shouting across to her.

'Are you alright??' she is asking.

Audrey stares at her for a few seconds, feeling blank, or as if she is deep underwater. She has the sensation that she has not in fact heard the words, but only seen the lady mouth them. The woman reaches her and sits down next to her on the ground, putting her arm around her, without any hesitation or embarrassment. Audrey plonks down from crouching position onto her bottom. The woman gives her a big squeeze. Audrey doesn't remember in fact when she had last had any physical human contact and the feeling of warmth and solidity, the realness of this stranger takes her by surprise.

Mortified, but entirely unable to help herself, Audrey bursts into tears.

THE ATTACK II

A month ago, 11:21am

Kensington Gardens (the south side)

AUDREY

Once Audrey's sobs have stopped enough for her to be able to talk, she tells the stranger the whole story; how reactive and stressed Beagle is, how hard she's tried with him, how she can no longer even have anyone come over to her place because he pees on the floor when he gets nervous and whines and paces and annoys her friends, how she rarely goes out any more as she can't leave him alone. She realises whilst she is talking how angry she is with Beagle and that makes her cry even more. She wants to scoop him up and hug him to her. He, of course, doesn't like being hugged though, so she doesn't.

The lady listens quietly, without interrupting. She is attractive and wholesome looking, with a slightly turned up nose just like the one Audrey had always wanted as a teenager. She looks as if she'd be at home on a ski slope, or perhaps on a yacht. Only once Audrey has finished explaining and heaved a big, exhausted sigh does she start talking.

'Look,' her accent elongates the short word, 'this lady,' she makes such a disdainful, ugly face that Audrey can't help but smile 'this lady is a troublemaker!' She rolls the r of troublemaker and her speech is scattered with added 'a's and dropped 'h's. 'And her dogs?' she continues, 'well, they are poor, poor creatures who have to spend time with her and are going...' she makes a circling sign at her temple and contorts her face into another surprisingly gormless expression to indicate that she thinks that the dogs are going round the bend.

She smiles when she sees Audrey smile, and goes on. 'She is not a nice woman, and her dogs are not happy!' Audrey feels her chin wobble. 'Ah, no, no, no, no!' the lady continues, 'I see what you are thinking! I am failing, my dog is not happy, I am a... how you say it... terrible owner.' She has a sing-song rhythm to her voice and Audrey finds herself already feeling better. She gulps and half laughs and sighs all at the same time. 'You are not!' These last three words the lady says very firmly, very staccato, and the dark eyes in that tanned, healthy face bore into Audrey. 'You are not,' she continues firmly, 'because you are trying, you are trying your best.' She pats Audrey's hand in an old-fashioned, soothing gesture. 'I see it, yes, I see you every day, how you walk with him. He is a difficult dog, he is frightened, no?' This last question she asks very gently.

Audrey nods, looking at a tall, slim girl playing tug with a grey dog in the distance, some sort of Poodle, she thinks. She registers that all this time the lady has been completely ignoring Beagle. The white Staffy has stopped panting and is looking nonchalantly around, peaceful and relaxed. At no point does she even glance directly at Beagle, her gaze seems not to avoid him, but just to slide over him; just as Beagle would like the whole world's to do; no scrutiny, no demand to interact, no pressure. Beagle seems calmer than Audrey has ever seen him and he even nudges her leg and looks up into her eyes.

'It's okay, Beagle love, it's all OK.' Audrey says, softly, looking into his deep brown eyes, liquid with sadnesses. Once she's blown her nose and stopped wiping it with the man-sized embroidered (with a 'H') handkerchief that the lady has given her, she takes a big breath in and sighs it out, shakily but with determination. It feels like a turning point.

'Yes,' she says, 'he's really frightened.'

'So,' the lady continues, and then interrupts herself, 'Oh! By the way this is Lexi!' she gazes at her dog, who gazes back at her, then turns her head slowly to Audrey. Audrey looks at the white Staffy and feels as if she is looking into a human's eyes. 'Hi Lexi,' she says. Tearing her eyes away from Lexi's soft pools of understanding and kindness only reluctantly, she looks back at the lady.

'So, you are coming for a coffee, and you are going to calm down and tell me all of the whole story, and we see how bad he is, or not. It is,' she corrects herself. Audrey starts to protest, but the lady impatiently shakes her head and makes dismissive noises. 'You sit here, wait, under this tree, on this small hill where you can see around, you are out of the way a bit no? It will be fine, no? Stay! Ah?' she puts her hand out, palm out, like the hand signal for wait and again her kind eyes twinkle. She seems delighted to have this opportunity to help Audrey and Beagle, and indeed she is. With a small peal of laughter she walks off, but her dog doesn't follow. Audrey thinks that she might have seen a gesture pass between the two of them. The white Staffy, Lexi, smiles at her whilst glancing around, and she could swear that she holds Audrey's eye for just a heartbeat longer than a glance. Her presence feels comforting.

As the lady walks off, Audrey gazes round the park, feeling a bit numb. Beagle looks up at her forlornly. Audrey can't understand why he doesn't seem to be at all nervous of Lexi, it is so out of character. He doesn't strain to get away from her, doesn't lunge or snap at her. She puzzles over what has just happened in her head, and tries to remember the exact sequence of events. She can't shake off the feeling that Lexi and the other dogs - that big brown one and the Husky - had been communicating, it had all seemed so coordinated, so tactical.

5 minutes later...

Audrey looks up and sees the lady crossing the park back towards her. Audrey doesn't usually like busybodies, people interfering, commenting on Beagle and his fears and so on, and has begun to get quite defensive lately, but somehow this lady bouncing across the grass is different. She plonks herself down beside Audrey, completely unphased by the fact that, despite the soft spring gloriousness of the day, the grass is damp and muddy. She extends her hand (bronzed, slim, manicured, nails like the delicate pink insides of shells) saying 'Sylvie!' They shake hands firmly - someone had once told Audrey that her handshake was limp; she has always taken care for it not to be since - and Audrey hears herself replying 'Aude'. Everyone calls her Audrey and saying Aude is a spur of the moment decision.

It makes her feel as if she could be someone else which, quite frankly, at the moment, is a welcome feeling.

'So now have you tried a... what's it called, ahhh, animal communicator?' Sylvie asks, without any further small talk. The emphasis she puts on certain syllables, certain letters, how she draws them out and shortens them at will is charming and soothing somehow.

Audrey - Aude - catches herself laughing, surprised. 'No.... I haven't. I didn't actually know they existed.' Although she thinks it sounds like a strange idea, she feels intrigued, and somehow the demeanour of this Sylvie makes her put her natural cynicism, which has been mushrooming of late, to one side.

'Well... I know that there are many people who are doing it. Of course some of them they are... how you say it, crooks?' Audrey thinks the way Sylvie says crooks is marvellous, rolling the 'r' and over extending the 'oo' dramatically. 'But however, there are some who can be good and it is worth it, to give him – it! – a try - for your little dog, no?'

Audrey nods, and drops her gaze to Beagle. The lady, Sylvie is totally ignoring him, she notices. So many people immediately bend down to stroke Beagle, get in his face and are disappointed when they don't get the reaction that they expected. When this happens she can almost feel their disappointment rubbing off on Beagle, and on her, his failures compounding in her head, the bad experiences compounding in his. She knows she shouldn't care what other people think, but it's hard not to; sometimes she dreams of just moving far away from London, far away particularly from the people who make her feel like she is failing by having such an unhappy dog. Sylvie makes her feel quite the opposite of this, and even though she's only just met her, it feels to Audrey as if she could tell her anything, and that without feeling disloyal to Beagle. It is refreshing to hear Beagle being talked about as a character worth caring for, worth loving, worth turning her life upside down for. Anything that can help him, she's willing to try. She can feel tears welling up and is powerless this time to stop them, the shock is beginning to really hit her now.

'There there!'

Sylvie's adoption of this ridiculously British saying, and the incongruous accent in which she says it, almost makes Audrey laugh, and she inadvertently emits some funny hiccupping sounds.

'It's just, it's just...'

'I know, ahhhh? OK? People, they can be very... unkind.' Sylvie is rubbing Audrey's back, across the shoulder blades firmly, soothingly, and through her touch it is absolutely clear just what she thinks of those people. Finally, Audrey thinks, someone who is on our side.

Sylvie, not one to waste time, abruptly stops rubbing Audrey's back and, having got Audrey to unlock and give her her phone, starts messing around on it.

'Ah!' she says, and without checking with Aude, starts dialling a number. As it begins to ring, she passes the handset over.

Audrey takes the phone, hesitantly, taken aback – it was not a very British thing to do, and Audrey feels a bit affronted, but she puts it to her ear anyway. She realises that someone has picked up, but she hasn't quite heard what they said.

Audrey passes the phone back to Sylvie when she has finished. The kindness of two strangers in one day is almost too much for her and her eyes brim with tears, again.

'She will help you,' Sylvie says decisively, 'assuming she's not a crook!' She laughs. 'Worth a try, ah?' Audrey nods, mute. 'OK,' Sylvie jumps up to her feet, lithely, 'I go – am going' Sylvie rolls her eyes 'now, I have to see my husband before he leaves for Genève. I have to help him find his socks and his chargers and so on.' She rolls her eyes despairingly, comically. 'And then, I can relax!'

'We see each other again, not to worry. I see you before here, I'll see you again! Bye!' She shouts behind her, rushing now, waving, and is gone, just as suddenly as she had arrived.

GRIPES

Kensington Gardens (at the fallen tree)

THE PARK GANG DOGS

The leggy sighthound mix, Arrow, doesn't sit around to chat with them often but she isn't feeling her usual energetic self today. She puts it down to the full moon. Lily sympathises, saying she can never sleep a wink when the moon is full. Lexi looks at her askance, she hadn't thought of Lily as someone who would believe in the effects of the moon.

'So what gets on your nerves then, guys?' Arrow is asking, as Piper arrives.

'Hi, Piper!' she adds. Piper nudges Arrow's nose with her own and does a quick sniff at her rear end, then makes a round of the others. She bumps shoulders, sniffs more bottoms, circles, touches noses, and nods deferentially accordingly. Rhett she paws at playfully and in return he makes as if to bite her neck, grinning.

'I mean, with the humans,' Arrow continues.

'What do you mean?' asks Piper, throwing herself straight in to the conversation, quizzically. She can't imagine Lottie getting on her nerves.

'Well, you know, like it gets on my nerves that my human doesn't feed me until the afternoon. Am starrrrrrving after our run, and she's got it into her head that I should only eat once a day, in the afternoon. I mean, it's madness! She's eating all the time, literally ALL the time!

And there am I, starving! She never gives me food, she seems to think it's bad for me to have treats. Everyone else's humans seem to share with them. That gets on my nerves. I mean look at me! I'm skin and bones!'

They all laugh. Arrow's a beautiful shape.

'And she's not exactly wasting away! She eats treats - snacks - all the time!'

'To be fair there's nothing worse than a fat dog,' says Rhett, and they all laugh again, each thinking of one or other of the various overweight characters that walk in the park, most of them picturing Rufus-the-Bloodhound and Maisy-the-Whippet with the joint problems.

'Well there isn't, is there?' Rhett continues, 'Think of that old chap, the black dude, the one with the white blaze on his chest, he can barely walk he's so fat! His owner gives him rubbish all the time, pieces of cake and sausage rolls and cheese sandwiches and all sorts, I've seen him.'

'Jealousy'll get you nowhere!' jokes Piper.

'No fat dogs in Serbia though,' Rhett adds, suddenly dark. Piper looks at the ground, feeling silly, embarrassed about her ill-timed flippant comment which had missed the mark. The dogs variously mumble their assent, avert their eyes and sniff at the ground.

'No,' says Arrow.

'Fair point,' says Piper.

'Nor in Africa,' says Sarah, the only other dog present who has had some first-hand experience of living anywhere other than the UK.

After a less than reverent pause Piko, a not especially emotionally intelligent, tan coloured cockerpoo, chips in enthusiastically, 'Ooh yeah it gets on my nerves that mine forget to fill my water bowl, then they get cross and call me disgusting when I drink from the toilet! Or they fill the water bowl right to the top but haven't bothered washing it out and it tastes all stale... why would I want to drink from that? *That's* disgusting!'

The other dogs chime in their agreement.

'There's not much that gets on my nerves,' Piper volunteers, hesitantly, after a lull. She doesn't like to say anything bad about her girl, it makes her feel disloyal and a bit sick in the stomach. 'But,' she hesitates again, going on to finish in a rush, 'my Lottie keeps changing my food. She should know what I like best by now and stick to it, but she keeps changing it. Some of the things she gives me are really weird.' She shakes her head slowly, sadly, 'Really weird. I mean it's a good job I have a good stomach but...'

Rhett laughs, his black mood passed over. 'You're too spoilt you are, Piper!'

Piper looks coy. She is spoilt, and that's the way she likes it, frankly, she can't imagine it any other way and why should she.

'But really, Rhett,' Piper goes on, 'sprouts mixed with yoghurt and parmesan, and cooked sweet potato – all nice on their own, I grant you – but mixed with venison kibble?' Rhett licks his lips dramatically and the others laugh. Piper pulls a delicate, comic little moue of her mouth then laughs herself.

There is another lull, during which each of the dogs mulls over whether they consider themselves spoilt, or not.

'Don't even get me started' says Grey, sighing surprisingly heavily for his small frame, 'it's too depressing.' They all laugh and Grey is pleased to be considered humorous, even though it was unintentional. He isn't a naturally droll dog, like Piper, or Rhett. He doesn't often to get to hang out like this; he's lucked out today as his dog walker has stopped on a bench right next to the fallen log where they are all hanging out.

Kip startles them all by blurting out crossly, in his staccato, Border Collie way, 'Smoking! Drives me mad! Stinks even downstairs! Can't stand it! And the noise! Never silence! Always music, talking, singing. Jazz. Exhausting!' He tosses his head around and then flops it down on his paws. In another dog, it might be a restful stance, but Kip's eyes are alive and it's obvious he is ready to explode into movement at any second, if needed.

Piper cocks her head, thinking. She realises that up until now, aside from a vague feeling of annoyance when he chases her when she's chasing a toy, she hasn't paid Kip much mind. His outburst makes Piper wonder, not about the smell of smoke and how much it could vex you (her Lottie isn't a smoker) but about when she'd last even heard Kip's voice and if she's ever even had a conversation with him. You don't really think about it much on a day-to-day basis, but some dogs talk a lot more than others. And then some, like Kip, go through their lives in near silence, with little to no verbal interaction. How lonely that must be, Piper thinks, and resolves to try to bring Kip into the conversation more from now on.

The dogs each retreat into their own private thoughts about the difficulties of their various little lives. Rolf is thinking about the sheer weight of routine of living with Harold, it is all so predictable. Rhett is thinking how much better life is here than in Serbia, it gives him the shivers just to think about the place. The policy he tries to live by though is not to look back. As a wise old Lurcher had once told him: *There are no regrets in life, only lessons.* He gives himself a good all over body shake. Lexi is racking her brains but since she's a happy dog with a lovely owner, she can't come up with anything. Sarah thinks about the thing that's growing inside her, but doesn't want to mention it and put a downer on them all. It would certainly make their complaints seem trivial. And yet, she feels a wave of irritability wash over her. It is the pain and the tiredness, she suspects. Sarah avoids eye contact with the others and curls up into herself, tucking her nose into her tail, feeling peeved. Her heart races a little as it does these days at any snifter of stress. She's had enough of the conversation and closes her mind as well as her eyes.

Piper doesn't feel especially perturbed by the conversation. The crazy food concoctions are a minor inconvenience. It's true that Lottie is very different now than how she used to be - she is less fun, more sombre, but Piper doesn't feel it is something to complain about. Lottie still takes Piper for lots of walks and Piper is an optimistic dog both by nature and nurture. She has lost one of her human parents, yes, but although upsetting it hasn't overly distressed her, she has viewed the misfortune more as an opportunity to prove her love for Lottie, to ensure that she succeeds in pulling her out of the sad, hunched torpor and make her live again. And she is succeeding, with the help of the park gang, of course.

A BEATING

On Hammersmith Road

NERO

Nero slinks alongside Neil with a growing feeling of dread. He can smell the beginnings of Neil's bad humour stirring. As they approach home, Neil gets the massive bunch of keys out of his pocket. Nero wonders momentarily what they are all for. He knows one is for the low-ceilinged cellar space that runs alongside the end of the flat. He's been locked down there a few times and has heard the key turn in the lock. He knows that one is for a lock-up. He knows one is for Neil's mother's house, which is waiting to be sold. Neil's mother had died recently following a short spell of illness and at the end, incarceration in a care home. Neil hadn't visited her. Nero knows this as Neil rants about it often. Neil holds her accountable for all of it, the stinking mess of his life and feels that whatever she got, she deserved, every drop of the smelly carpets and horrible staff. He'd received no comfort as a child - why should she receive it now? Beside Nero, Neil glowers darkly - Nero doesn't have to look up into his face to know it. He doubts that there will be any dinner for him today.

Neil curses as he gets the wrong key and kicks the door crossly. When they eventually enter after all his impatient fumbling, he starts screaming at Nero. Or maybe it's at himself, Nero can't be sure. It takes only the slightest thing to set off Neil these days. He seems to be getting worse and worse and the explosions of anger are getting more and more frequent. The embittered, largely nonsensical monologues seem to be his way of purging his frustration, or of tending to it.

'Bollocks to them, they don't know who I am and what was done to me. Who do they think they are?' Nero has the misfortune to catch Neil's eye. Neil continues, 'and bollocks to you too Nero, ha ha Nero as if! What a stupid name, you're pathetic!'

With the word pathetic, a boot comes towards Nero and connects with his ribs. He lets out a yelp of pain and scoots behind the settee, only to be chased by Neil. Round and round they go - it would be funny if it wasn't so scary. Nero can feel his heart beating, he can feel manic, fierce stabs of adrenalin, and he smells the smell on himself, familiar now; he is starting to smell it a heartbeat before it hits his nostrils these days. Nero knows that the longer he makes Neil chase him, the angrier he will get and the bigger the beating that will result, but he can't act against his flight instinct. Sometimes he asks himself why he doesn't just run away from Neil in the park, never see him again. He suspects that others think the same, but are too polite to ask. That Staffy for example, the white one, Piper's friend, who had asked him all the pointed questions the other day. He remembers how the questions had made him feel. Confused, defensive, and bone-tired. And sad. It is a complex thing, this relationship between dog and human, a very complex thing, Nero thinks.

Nero, though terrified, makes himself stop. He holds his breath and rolls onto his back, bracing himself, his tail between his legs flicks nervously, anticipating the connection. His eyes are squeezed shut. Sure enough, it comes: Boomph! A kick in the head. His head swims. Neil stomps off. Nero scoots under the armchair, feeling relieved that the worst is over, but still cowering. He tries to focus on not wetting himself. That will only make Neil even angrier, if he sees it. But he feels it seep out. It's happening more often these days. When the trembling abates a little he curls up into a tight ball, and pushes himself into the back piece of the armchair for comfort. The pee cools underneath him. A feeling of utter misery and the dread of discovery overtakes him and he starts trembling uncontrollably again. He focuses on his breath and picturing Piper and Lottie, that always makes him feel better. He tries to shut his ears to Neil's angry noises. Gradually, the trembling stops and he falls into an uneasy, twitchy snooze.

AVIAN FLU

Kensington Gardens (near the bandstand)

THE PARK GANG DOGS

Beagle thinks about avian flu. He thinks that he might have it. The more he thinks about it, the more certain he is that he has it. His breathing just doesn't seem right, he has a persistent headache. He feels too hot, he feels off somehow.

'It's just the heavy weather, Beagle love, the air pressure,' Lexi tells him, patiently.

'Why don't you go and jump in the duck pond next to the Palace to cool off?' teases Rhett, who doesn't have a lot of patience for Beagle's hypochondria.

'What's it called, that pond?' Lily wonders out loud.

Rhett shrugs.

Lily sniffs.

'The Round Pond, isn't it?' Piper says, helpfully, in between spitting out pieces of bark, which she is vigorously tearing off a log she has found.

'The Round Pond? Are you serious?' Rhett says, with an expressive shake of his head. 'And they say we're simple!'

Lexi and Piper laugh. Lily sniffs again. She doesn't much approve of Rhett, or like him. He is far too irreverent and casual for her.

'But it's forbidden to swim in there!' Beagle responds, predictably, shocked, all his worry hackles activated.

Rhett laughs. Beagle turns his face away, a small sign of protest, but one nevertheless. Rhett notices, and chuckles to himself. Good for him! he thinks.

Lily nods, sagely. She is a righteous dog who believes in rules. Beagle likes that about her. He continues, feeling a bit hysterical now. 'Any dog that goes in there will be taken away and killed!'

Rhett scoffs. He doesn't mean to be mean but he can't help it, 'This is *Britain*, Beagle, that's not going to happen!' He rolls his eyes at Piper, who turns her head away to try to be discreet but chuckles nevertheless.

Last week, seeing Kip pelt over towards the Round Pond in chase of a Labrador in chase of a ball, Beagle had nearly had a heart attack thinking that Kip was going to continue right on into it and get carted away and killed. He isn't overly keen on Kip, he doesn't trust all that sudden darting, but still, he's one of the gang.

'Anyway,' he persists, sulkily, 'you can get awful diseases from duck poo, haven't you heard about them?' His voice has gone a bit squeaky with the outrage. Sometimes he is astounded by the frivolity of his fellow species; he feels the need to impress upon them the danger that is present around every corner. But faced with their distinct lack of concern, he feels completely impotent.

Piper and Rhett start an impromptu game of tag. The torn at log lays in the grass, ignored and forgotten, and Beagle feels the same. Even Lexi and Lily don't comment.

'Come on then Beagle, time to go!' he hears Audrey say, and he drags himself to his feet.

'Bye guys,' he says, forlornly.

'Bye love!' says Lexi kindly. The others don't seem to register anything and Piper nearly knocks him over as she leaps around him, away from Rhett. He feels stressed out and mournful.

REACHING HOME

Brook Green (Aynhoe Road)

HELEN

Helen and Sarah make their way along the path through the middle of Brook Green in increments; each step is a labour for Helen with her stick but even more so for Sarah, who stumbles involuntarily and often, as one leg or another fails her. They stop for rests frequently, Helen talking to Sarah all the while, about times long ago when Sarah was a younger dog and memories of even before that, before they'd met. Helen enjoys talking to Sarah about Ted, her late husband. She misses him still, every minute of every day, and it's worse at night, when she lays awake. What is that expression her daughter-in-law had used the other day, something about half oranges? Well, she feels like half of something without him, that's for sure, even after so many years. So much antagonism in marriages and relationships these days, she sees it everywhere and doesn't really understand it. It's simple, you fall in love, and love until that person is no longer there to love. And beyond.

A word that Danny had used recently springs into her mind: haters. 'There are so many haters these days,' he'd said, 'Hating on this, hating on that!' It had seemed to her a funny pronoun to use, on, but that was how you said it these days, apparently. She smiles momentarily, thinking of her new young friend, then her thoughts turn back to Ted, and their love. *Grief is the price you pay then,* for love, she thinks. *Yes, that's exactly it.* She sighs. It's hard, sometimes, without him; it's hard, the missing of him.

Whilst Helen has been pondering all this, they have reached Aynhoe Road and the house at the bottom end of it that is home. They reach it gratefully these days, and it sorrows Helen that she feels this yen to be home, to be secure, that she feels a creeping danger in being out, a vulnerability that she'd never felt before this year. She leans her stick on the wall of the porch carefully and fumbles around her neck for the key that hangs there on a deep purple lanyard (Wimbledon 2020) that her daughter-in-law had given her. That way, she always knows where it is. The trick to being old is to make things as easy as possible for yourself, Helen thinks, that's what it's all about. A constant fight to keep your head above water, yes, but usually, if you don't panic, if you take things slowly and calmly, you are okay. You need a bit of support, and that's irritating, but more than anything it's important to be sensible.

In flashes, Helen gets sick of being sensible and wishes to toss back glasses of wine like she used to, to dance herself silly at a party, or to jump on a horse and gallop about straight after she's washed her hair and it's still damp. To run and jump and skip without aches and pains, to not have to worry about catching a cold by sitting in a draft or about getting her shoes wet. But mostly, impatience aside, she is grateful for having made it to old age. After all, the alternative is so much worse. She thinks of her son, and the tears well up. It isn't right and she would give up her life for his in a heartbeat. Have given up. Helen sniffs her emotions back in before they spill out in the form of tears; she tilts her chin.

The important thing in life is not to let yourself get down about things, not to become a Victor Meldrew. Helen laughs. Danny hadn't heard of him when she'd mentioned him last week. Then next time they'd met, yesterday, he'd mimicked him perfectly, and Helen had laughed so much that she'd ended up clutching her chest with one hand and flapping at him with the other to stop. It heartens Helen to know that she and Danny laugh at the same things, that being old doesn't make you different. It's tedious, but it doesn't change you, fundamentally, if you don't let it. It's always a shock when you look in the mirror of course. You feel young inside, or at least if not young, then not old, but the mirror shows you something different.

It's *freaky*. Another one of Danny's words. She smiles. Helen feels as though she owes it to her darlings who have already passed over to be happy to be alive though, to make the best of it. Sarah stands by her side, stoically, on four tired paws, looking as though if she sits down she might never get back up.

Helen pushes the door open with a wrinkled, elegant hand and they enter. Slowly, everything goes so slowly these days. As always, Helen prepares Sarah's food as soon as they get in. This is Sarah's second meal of the day and after this, they can shake down, as they won't need to go out again, except for Sarah to pop into the garden for a quick pee before sleeping. Helen's friend Ada's words pop into her head as she bends down to put the bowl on the floor. 'Men get pompous, women get bitter.' Ada had said it just before she'd died, in a rare moment of lucidity. She doesn't know why it has come into her head just now, the brain is strange like that. Ada's husband had been pompous all his life and Helen had always been sorry that her best friend had married such an idiot. Helen isn't bitter, even though she might have become so, under the circumstances. It's a matter of strength of character, probably, she thinks. She makes herself a strong cup of builders' tea, with only a dash of milk and three sugars. Her Ted had always laughed about that, it didn't seem to fit her, he'd said.

Helen eats very little these days, she has lost her appetite.

'Like a fly!' her worried daughter-in-law often says.

SARAH

Truth be told Sarah doesn't have much appetite either, but she knows that Helen worries if she doesn't eat. She used to have such a healthy appetite. Particularly when Ted and Helen had first brought her home - she would wolf down any old thing. These days she struggles through to the end, not really tasting anything, battling to swallow each mouthful. She does this now, then gratefully stumbles over to her bed. She's more or less got used to the pain now, it is not more than she can bear. And she hasn't lost weight, unusually, despite the thing that is growing inside her and taking over. Sarah can smell it, of course. She'd smelt it the first day it had come, deep inside.

She had barked and barked at it then, to go away, tried to frighten it off, but it hadn't budged, and eventually she had come to the realisation that it wasn't going to and she had grudgingly accepted it to be a new part of her. It had replicated itself - insidious, pervasive, pushy - and had very quickly felt like something there was no point barking at, or trying to say no to.

Sarah knows that her time is running out, she feels it as surely as if it were a number counting down on a wall or an egg timer running out of sand. She lays her chin down on her paws, and racks her brains to find a way of making sure Helen will be all right when she goes. Sarah doesn't fear death but she dreads placing the burden she will inevitably place upon Helen, the impending loss that she knows Helen will have to suffer, and it saddens her immensely. She thinks to herself that she will ask Lexi. Kind, sage Lexi might know what to do. They often see her walking with her male human doing his steps around the streets of Brook Green, so Sarah will have an opportunity soon, she's sure.

Having formulated a plan, she falls into a blissful sleep, a state in which the pain mercifully falls away.

HELEN

Next to her, Helen sits in her favourite armchair, thinking to herself how odd it is that you never seem to have a favourite armchair until you get old.

REVOLT RISING

At Lady Human and Grey's home

GREY

Grey is dozing and dreaming of Rhett when he is woken by Lady Human calling him, her voice betraying growing irritation.

'Grey? Grey! Quickly now!'

Rising from sleep he patters across the wooden floor towards her, through force of habit. For now, she is the only way of him being able to get outside so there is nothing he can do but go along with her. She clips his lead on without another word, still cross with him.

Grey always feels better when they exit the house, the prison as he thinks of it. When he had heard that word for the first time, the house had jumped into his mind, even before he knew exactly what prison had meant. He always breathes a sigh of relief as he leaves its confines. Even if it is just to be dragged along on the lead peevishly by Lady Human, it is a relief. When he's outside he can take in others lives by smell, watch things in the short snatches he is allowed, listen to the interactions of others and he enjoys absorbing these fleeting vistas to mull over later at home, where it alleviates the tedium.

Not all dog-human pairings are like him and Lady Human, Grey had noticed that early on in life and it fascinates him still, all the more so now that he has proper friends who have their own humans in tow. He had broached the subject with Lexi a couple of days ago, hiding in the undergrowth, in order not to have a repeat performance of the bench-jumping debacle.

'Lexi?' he had said. She had turned to him, her soft eyes searching his.

'Yes, Grey?'

'Well, you know my human?'

'I do, Grey.' Lexi had had to make an effort to keep her voice even and neutral, he could tell.

'Well, do you think,' Grey had carried on, not even sure himself where he was going with it, 'do you think that I could change my human?'

Lexi had hesitated, she had been unwilling to disappoint Grey. 'I don't think so, honestly, Grey,' she had said. 'In my experience, humans are what they are. They're generally pretty stuck in their ways and they don't tend to change. And there's, well, just a certain... level in them.' She had spoken carefully, trying to answer the question to the best of her ability and Grey had appreciated the care she had taken. She had gone on, tentatively. 'Some humans are just not as nice, not as decent as others. It very often, so much more often than with us dogs, doesn't depend on their upbringing, their nurture, it's more about their nature. Us dogs are more forgiving, and we can change. What I think I mean is that humans hold grudges. So for example if they were poorly nurtured it's quite often liable to turn them into bad people. Even if they were treated kindly by their parents and by others around them, they can still turn out bad or mean, just like that.' She had shrugged, honestly, 'It's just more common for humans to be less good than dogs, in essence, I suppose.'

'Like Lady Human.' Grey had replied, sadly. He had thought then about Lady Human's sister, who he'd met once, and who had seemed really nice. Even though she'd looked the image of Lady Human, their smells had been totally different - Grey had noticed that instantly.

'Like Lady Human,' Lexi had confirmed.

Grey had looked sorrowful, but after a few seconds had perked up.

'But I didn't mean to try to change her. I meant to change her, as in not to live with her any more, but to live with someone else, to find another human. Or,' he had carried on then, sounding more unsure, 'to live without a human completely, like Rhett does.'

Lexi had cocked her head on one side.

'Hmmmm...' she had said. 'Hmmm.' She had sat down and scratched her left ear furiously with her back paw. Her left ear always gets itchy when she has a mental conundrum to solve. 'Perhaps. I don't know, truthfully, Grey,' she had said, hesitantly. 'I don't know anyone who's done it, to be honest.'

'That doesn't mean it can't be done though, does it.'

'No, Grey, it doesn't,' she had replied, equably.

Remembering this conversation Grey exits the house with Lady Human - for now still a pair, of sorts.

THE WHIFF OF FREEDOM

13 months ago

A bleak dog shelter in the middle of nowhere in Serbia

RHETT

Rhett has seen the odd dog being taken out before now but hasn't really thought much about it. He finds it best not to think about the future, about this present as it is stretching on, but rather just to focus on getting through the day. He also doesn't want to start wasting his energy daydreaming about something which is nebulous and unlikely, it doesn't feel like a healthy thing to do. It's all some of the dogs think about, especially the ones who've had homes before, the ones who weren't born here; the longing for it drives them mad. There's one little group of dogs who meet up and talk about it incessantly. Although escape is always at the back of Rhett's mind, he hasn't seriously considered a fairy godmother choosing him to be a viable exit option. It's nice when it happens, it lifts morale, but why should they choose him, out of all the hundreds of dogs that are there?

Suddenly though Rhett understands that that is exactly what is going to happen. He can't explain how but he catches the whiff of freedom, feels his impending rescue. He is going to be taken out by one of the women, he feels it, with growing certainty. *He is getting out!!!!!!* The news that has been borne to him on the wind becomes surer and surer as the ladies make the practical decisions and arrangements. They seek him out often, point at him and call him to them for a fuss.

He lets them, despite it feeling foreign and disagreeable to him. They are his way out, so he lets them. When they leave in the evening, he becomes restless and manic, impatient. He paces and whines, oblivious to the cold, and nuzzles Jessica frequently, distressed and filled with a sense of helplessness and frustration that he won't be able to persuade the humans to take her, too.

Despite this impotent sadness, the anticipation of freedom runs through Rhett, he shivers with the excitement of it. Needing to burn off some energy he dashes at other dogs and nips at them to chase, to play, goads even the genuinely dangerous ones. In the periods of calm that follow this letting off of steam he tries now to drink everything in. He sees a new found charm in the dilapidated dog houses and the little mound where they huddle up when the place floods, filled with a sense of solidarity and rage against the world for sequestering them there. Rhett shouts up to his bird friends, 'I'm getting out!'

They squawk back at him and swoop and dive, as if to celebrate his news.

Later

Life here has made Rhett mature quickly and his body is already fully grown, he is still only an adolescent, 15 months old. And as he curls up for his naps now with Jessica, he starts to feel melancholic. It is arbitrary, he thinks, who gets to leave and why. It enrages him that anyone would have such a lack of empathy as to hold them captive in the first place, he rails against it in his head. As a dog, one is sometimes awfully, horribly powerless in the face of humans and their decision making, their enforcement of what they decide must come to pass. Even if he'd wanted to, he wouldn't be allowed to choose to stay here, with Jessica. He begins to resent the ladies.

What right do they have? and *How can I leave her?*

Fraught, he gets up, circles, paces, whines.

FEARS

Kensington Gardens (at the fallen tree)

THE PARK GANG DOGS

'What are you scared of?' asks Beagle, mournfully. They are sitting together in the park by the fallen tree. It's a muggy day and no one feels inclined to run around too much.

Piper humours him. 'Ummm,' she says, 'not much, actually. I know a lot of our kind are scared of fireworks but I'm not, they don't bother me. Ummmmm,' she repeats. She really can't think of anything. 'Let me have a think, eh Beagle?' she says, turning to Rhett, trying to keep the conversation moving. She feels badly that she had laughed at him the other day, it hadn't been kind. 'Rhett?'

'Being closed in, being trapped,' he says matter of factly, with no hesitation and runs off, as if to demonstrate to himself and to anyone else who cares to see just how free he is.

Piper turns to Lexi. 'Lexi?'

'Hmm, I'm not keen on heights to be fair. My Sylvie took me to an agility class once. I was hopeless!' she laughs 'I wouldn't go along that walkway thing, I didn't know why all the other dogs were doing it! It seemed like madness to me, I didn't understand how they were enjoying it so much, it was really high up!'

'Oh I looooved that! Sebastian used to take me,' Piper says, 'It was great fun, we were really fast, everyone there said what a great team we were. Lottie said she was sorry, but that she couldn't face going, after...' Piper trails off and lays her head between her paws.

'Why, what are you scared of, Beagle?' asks Lexi, picking up the conversational baton.

'Oh well, I'm—'

'Flies!' Piper shouts out, loudly, suddenly, head popping up. 'I'm terrified of flies!'

Lexi laughs. 'You sound very proud of it, Piper!' she says.

'Ha ha, no, I mean, I really am – they freak me out, I hate them. You can never tell what they're going to do, urgh,' she shivers involuntarily and then does a dramatic whole body shake, 'they give me the creeps!'

'Sorry, Beagle,' she adds. Piper has innate good manners and everyone knows that interrupting is impolite.

They tacitly agree not to ask Beagle again though, Lexi had known as soon as the words were out of her mouth that she had made a mistake. She and Piper had exchanged looks, acknowledging what they were both thinking, that Beagle could go on for hours once he started, particularly on an issue such as this. So it was lucky that Piper had inadvertently stolen his moment. Beagle is itching to be asked again; he shuffles around on his bottom, restlessly. They deftly ignore him. Rhett returns and greets them all in turn, even though he has only been away a couple of minutes.

'Paquita?' Arrow asks. Paquita is quite notoriously a frightened sort of dog, that's why she gets carried around in a bag by Lottie, who is being paid to socialise her and build her confidence. They all listen intently.

'Oh – well, me,' she says quietly, thoughtfully, 'I'm scared of Space.'

'Space?' they all respond in unison, puzzled, forgetting their various intentions not to make her feel under pressure. Paquita looks embarrassed and stares at the floor.

'I feel vulnerable,' she explains, in a small voice. 'I know it's strange. But I'm only little. And sometimes things - like huge dogs or bicycles or running people - come hurtling through space. That's what I'm scared of.'

Everyone murmurs supportive words, assuring her that she isn't being silly or cowardly. 'I'm much better when I'm inside!' she says, 'I just like to know what's around.'

'Fair enough Paquita, fair enough,' says Rhett kindly. Paquita beams. She feels so horribly disadvantaged being so tiny. She'd love to be bigger, to have longer limbs in particular. 'It's quite a sensible attitude I would say really, quite a valid fear I mean.' He is thinking to himself how she wouldn't last five minutes in Serbia. He realises that he had been very lucky back there to be blessed with a certain brawn and long, strong legs.

'Not that you should be scared!' he adds, shaking his head a little over his clumsiness.

'The oven!' says Kip, abruptly, in that staccato way he has, not looking at anyone, following a running dog in the distance with his eyes. 'It hurt me once.'

They all murmur their assent that ovens definitely aren't to be trusted, nor the pots that bubble and spit from on top of them, even if they do smell nice.

Lottie beckons Piper, so she calls out her farewells to the others.

'Wait up, Piper, I'm coming with you,' says Rhett.

'Hi, Doggy Dog,' Lottie calls over to him.

AN ILLICIT SWIM

Kensington Gardens (near the Peter Pan statue)

PIPER

Piper gazes over at the body of water. She begins to pant with growing anticipation. If Lottie doesn't call her back before she gets to halfway, she bargains with herself, she will go for it, and just pretend that she can't hear her calling. She feels a pull to obey Lottie, but also, sometimes, not to. It's hard being a dog. Sly, wide-mouthed, tongue hanging out long, she lies on one flank, panting, and watches Lottie out of the corner of her eye. She is waiting until Lottie is distracted.

As she's waiting, she thinks about what Lily and Lexi had been discussing the other day. Piper had been absorbed in chewing at a stick at the time so had not joined in the conversation but it's true, she thinks now, that's the thing with being a dog, you can't really hide your true feelings, there they all are, in your smell, like a flash card summing you up. Beagle Lily and Lexi had summed up as *fundamentally damaged, terrified and pessimistic*; Kip: *neurotic, highly intelligent and easily bored*; Rhett: *confident, easy-going and independent*; Rolf: *shallow, aloof and physically gifted*; Piper: *joyful, mischievous and secure*. Lily had deemed Lexi *kind, sensible and warm-hearted* but Lexi had dodged the question when it had come to Lily.

Lottie has turned to greet Edward who is heading towards them, unbranded plastic bag swinging from his hand as usual. Piper is almost out of Lottie's sight line now so decides to go for it; she can't restrain herself any longer. She leaps up and races off within the fraction of a second, and determinedly doesn't look back. As she runs, she braces herself for the shout, a shout that doesn't come within the critical period. Nine parts glee to one part guilt she passes the little clump that she's singled out to denote the halfway point, and, knowing she is about to do something naughty (humans are sometimes strange about what they think is naughty, she thinks) but unable to help herself, she starts to imagine the feeling of the cool, fresh water on her skin. She races on, and hears Lottie shout now but as per her plan pretends that she hasn't. Her left ear has given a traitorous, telltale little flick though and Piper knows that Lottie won't have missed that.

She slows up only at the last minute before reaching the railings, so much so that even she herself thinks for a second that she might crash into them. In her rush to get into the water she pushes her way roughly past a podgy toddler with a fistful of bread in his hand. He nearly topples over but his mother grabs his arm just in time and rights him, protectively. The woman tuts and curses at Piper, who ignores her. The toddler greets her, smiling.

'Hi, Fast Dog!'

'Hi, Small Child!' she shouts, 'I'm going for a swim!'

Piper manipulates herself through the bars and gets into the water. *Ooh, nice!* she thinks. It feels as she had known it would. Piper heads out away from the shore where people are shouting and generally making a fuss. People seem to get themselves so worked up, she thinks. Especially about swimming. Piper swims towards a couple of ducks, who fly off. *Why do they always do that?* she thinks to herself. *I only wanted to say hello.* Nicely cooled off, she turns and swims back towards the shore, and her heart jumps when she tunes into the sound of Lottie calling her. She doesn't like to be separated from her human for long. She swims with all her strength, as eager now to get back to Lottie as she had been to accomplish her illicit mission.

AWKWARD CONVERSATIONS

On Brook Green (Hammersmith Road end)

DANNY

It's been a few weeks since they first met. They are sitting on a bench together, Danny's bench as they call it now, in Brook Green. He notices that Helen is shifting about a bit on the seat and looking nervous. This isn't at all like Helen. It seems as if she wants to broach something that she finds awkward. He hopes she isn't going to ask him about school and why he's not there, as he won't know how to answer.

'So, Danny James Connor,' she says. Danny likes that she calls him by his full name, not some shortened version or some stupid nickname like his friends do or *love, son* or the worst, *young man*. He draws his hand up to his mouth and starts to bite his nails, nervously.

'Tell me why is it you're hanging out,' Helen grins, pleased with her turn of phrase, 'here,' she gestures around them, 'all the time. Are you de-stressing?' She is teasing him but in a nice way, and he finds that he doesn't feel all defensive, as he might do if asked this by someone else. He usually feels so confronted by adults.

'I mean, not to put too fine a point on it and I know this is going to sound old-fashioned but to be fair I am rather old,' Helen's eyes shine with humour, 'but,' she pauses for dramatic effect, 'well... I won't pussy-foot around, better to be blunt: shouldn't you be in school?'

Danny finds himself laughing, he can't help it. But she doesn't let him off.

'Well?' There is a steeliness beneath her smile.

He sighs. Pauses. Realises he'd quite like to talk it through, it's been bothering him lately too. He tries to find the right words.

'Yes, I should. It's just that I find it quite... overwhelming. I get lost really early on in the lesson, once we have to write stuff down, and then I just get really bored and drift off and I can't take it. I feel claustrophobic, like I have to get out of there, at all costs. So I do.' He shrugs, apologetically. 'And the girls always take the mickey out of me. Last week they asked me to show them my work and then they passed it all the way round the classroom almost before Mrs Williams interrupted, it was so embarrassing.' He can sense Helen's compassion for him and feels vulnerable and tearful. He hopes that she won't try to give him a hug as he thinks that might make him crumble and he doesn't want that to happen. He feels the build up of snot and mucus in his sinuses. She doesn't try to hug him; she just sits, with her hands crossed in her lap, perfectly still, waiting for him to go on.

'I just get so muddled up and stressed out and it's so stifling, and the girls are so mean, they don't stop. On and on at me they are.' He shakes his head, looking both baffled and annoyed.

Helen listens calmly, head cocked on one side. She looks like a little bird, he thinks. She is reading his face as he speaks, he knows that, she does it all the time. She can tell if he's lying, although sometimes she doesn't let on that she knows he is lying, which makes him disinclined to lie to her unless it is absolutely necessary. He finds himself waffling on a bit then tailing off. There is silence. Birds chirp in the trees and a lone magpie in front of them – no wait, two! Good! - hop across the grass. Hop, hophop, hop they go, looking out for treasures with their beady eyes. Danny sneaks a look at Helen's face, curious to see what she thinks. He is grateful when she starts talking as he doesn't think he can explain much more right now, his head is pounding with the effort. He stoops and strokes Sarah's head, embarrassed at his rush of honesty, not able to look Helen in the eye but listening intently.

'Right,' Helen says, and pauses, reflecting still, seemingly getting her thoughts in order. He listens with all his might; he hadn't realised quite how thirsty for advice he is. 'As I see it,' she continues, 'there are a few-' there is a pause whilst she chooses her word, 'issues here. The first and the main one being that school doesn't suit you. But,' she looks at him sternly, demands eye contact. He gives it, laughing now, and she smiles. 'You are technically obliged to attend, and if you don't want to end up in some god-awful youth detention centre...' Helen waits for this to sink in, and he feels her eyes boring into his eyelids as he strokes Sarah's face. Sarah looks into his eyes, her expression neutral. He concentrates back on the tufty yellow fur on her head which he twirls in his fingers. Reluctantly, he draws his hand from her, straightens, and shifts uncomfortably on the bench. It is Helen's turn to reach down and stroke Sarah, telling her that she is a good girl. Danny realises that this isn't an easy conversation for her either. He appreciates her honestly, and her caring enough to bother with it.

She straightens in turn, and continues.

'So. You have to make sure that you play the game just enough, be there just enough, do just enough work not to get kicked out.' She smiles at him, conspiratorially. The other point is, and I may be wrong here, that you might be finding it difficult for a reason. You might, for example,' Helen says gently, 'be dyslexic.'

'Dyslexic?' he repeats, rolling the word around on his tongue. He's heard of it, vaguely. 'It just sounds like you might be, you're clearly bright but from what I can gather you struggle with understanding things from the page, or getting things down in writing.'

Danny nods.

Helen continues, 'So logic leads me to believe that perhaps you are dyslexic. Which by the way is absolutely nothing to be ashamed of and actually means that you can milk the system!' she tries to wink at him at this point, but she isn't very good at winking and makes a hash of it. It makes him laugh. 'A bit of extra leeway might be useful. A more minor issue in your life is dealing with things,' she makes a scornful face when she says the next bit, 'like those silly girls, Serafina and Mina.'

'Sophie and Mia,' he says.

'Yeah, yeah, whatever.' He grins. It feels good to have someone on his side. She dismisses him, and then, with a little flap of her bony, veined and elegant hand. He likes the way she speaks about Sophie and Mia, the way it takes the power out of them, he ought to learn that. Whatever! he repeats in his head, amused.

'OK.'

'OK what?'

'OK I'll try. And I'll ask about the dyslexic thing.'

'Good.'

He grins, embarrassed, and focuses his attention on Sarah again.

The rest of their chat is light-hearted and mainly based around analysing passing characters, guessing at their lives and personalities based on their appearances. It's a fun exercise and they like to argue their cases to each other. Like this they kill an hour or so before parting with a fist bump. A lady walking past pushing a pram looks taken aback and Helen and Danny both chuckle as they walk off in opposite directions.

UNBOUND SPIRITS

Kensington Gardens (near the Albert Memorial)

THE PARK GANG DOGS

'I don't have one,' Rhett replies. They are discussing owners and Arrow, a friendly sighthound mix who occasionally pops up at their meet ups, has just asked about his. Arrow is hanging out with them whilst her owner eats a packed lunch on a bench a few metres away, listening to a podcast. 'I tried having one on my way over here,' he explains, 'but it just didn't work out. He was a nice chap, but he had some funny ideas - he kept blowing a whistle at me. Seemed a bit frustrated by my lack of response.'

Rhett shrugs, or the dog equivalent of it, more the suggestion of a head shake than a shrug. He glances over and winks at Lexi. She knows very well what he thinks about humans who blow whistles, and for that matter about dogs who come running to them. 'My only human was the Old Man, I suppose,' he continues more seriously, 'but he was a companion, not an owner'. He says the word owner distastefully. 'He was... a friend. It was different.'

Piper is confused and looks at Lexi, who shakes her head briefly, dismissively,

'It's just words, Piper,' Lexi says to her, quietly. Piper looks at Rhett askance, as if she doesn't like his *just words*.

Rhett manages not to get caught out because he still has a soft rolled brown leather collar on him, a remnant of last year's interlude when he had lived, loosely, with the Old Man, himself also a wanderer.

THE OLD MAN

The Old Man had bought the collar for the big brown dog because it seemed too often to irk people that the dog wasn't wearing one, and it drew too much attention to them. He had bought the softest, narrowest collar he could find, for that size of dog. Weathered and wrinkled, the Old Man is a person of no fixed abode who walks the length and breadth of Britain over the course of any given year. When he had moved on from London this time he had asked the dog if he had wanted to join him, their attachment to each other having become quite strong over the course of the winter. Rhett, who had been pining for a glossy, strong-legged Red Setter living on Elsham Road, had felt disinclined to leave and anyway had made a promise to himself never to get too attached to a human, so in a way had even been relieved to see the back of his human companion. It had saddened the Old Man to part with the shaggy brown canine of whom he'd become so fond, but he's had similar reservations about getting too attached.

He and the brown dog had spent many happy hours along the river path between Hammersmith and Barnes. When the river tide was out, they could often be found mudlarking, one or other of them alerting their companion to anything interesting or curious, in order that they could inspect it together. And if the weather was fine and the sun's rays strong enough, they were in the habit of sitting under a particular tree and sharing lunch, the Old Man afterwards having a snooze, bundled up in his woollen jumpers, hat, scarf, gloves and overcoat. Probably, the Old Man thinks, they will hook up again later this year, in the Autumn, when he travels back down South. He hopes that will happen, but he vows not to get attached again.

The Old Man is on his way now up North, to see friends and to walk Hadrian's Wall, as he does every year. It's a sort of pilgrimage for him. He walks it alone, reliving happy memories of his girl, his sweetheart. He and she had walked it together once, before the war had come and she'd been in the wrong place at the wrong time. Helping one of her neighbours down in to the shelter she'd sacrificed her life, the bomb leaving only fragments of her and of the scorched red gingham from her hair ribbon, settling with the dust. But the Old Man remembers her, every line of her, and he enjoys the memories that play like a film in his mind, the many moments of happiness they'd had together. Perhaps it wouldn't have endured. This way she is destined to stay forever as he remembers her, perfect in every way. He can't imagine that it would have paled, their delight in being together, but you never know. At any rate he is happy to have the memories of her, of them as they were together, in their youth. Smiling, they had always been smiling, he remembers.

As he walks, he recites to himself over and over the words of the poem 'Dust' by Rupert Brook, as he often does when he thinks of her.

The Old Man is much like Rhett in many ways, a contented soul - naturally resilient and independent. He will no longer hold a woman in the warmth of a summer afternoon, a woman in a gingham dress with a matching hair ribbon. But he enjoys the sun's warmth on his face, experiences the universe's healing power and the welcome embrace of the soft ground which can always be relied on to be pleasantly cool in the heat of the summer. He takes pleasure from smelling the earth after it rains, from noticing the marvellous creatures and birds around him, from the feeling of grass tickling his face. Sometimes when he's still he feels insects actually landing on him, like he is just part of their environment, and that makes him feel honoured.

The Old Man mostly stays away from other humans but here and there he witnesses that they can be good too, and is touched occasionally by their warmth or thought. The meagre contact he has with strangers is important to him, if not entirely necessary. Unkindnesses don't often reach him - just like his friend the brown dog he knows how to disappear, how to make sure he is out of reach to those who might look for him, for one reason or another.

THE PARK GANG DOGS

'I love my two, I can't imagine life without them,' says Lexi simply

'Me too,' says Paquita

'Yes, ours is a lovely chap,' says Lily primly, 'I think it's only right that man and dog should live together.'

'Mine's all right, bit of a strange bugger but I can't complain. I'm all for it!' says Rolf

Piper stays quiet. She loves Lottie, but something disturbs her about the way Rhett had said the word *owner.*

ESCAPE FROM THE VETS

13 months ago

At a vet's office, Serbia

RHETT

The lady who had taken Rhett out of the shelter drags him into the vet's office. She smells nervous underneath the fragrance she is wearing. Rhett's on a slip lead so there's no escaping. She speaks to him soothingly the whole time and although he appreciates her good intentions, all he wants is to be free from the noose around his neck. They enter into the vet's inner office, and he is unceremoniously lifted up onto a table and restrained by eight firm hands. He finds it demeaning. They examine his ear and say that it is infected and that they will have to cut part of it off. He tries to thrash out of their grasp, but fails. Soon after, he's injected, he feels the needle entering and although he tries to jerk his leg away, he can't; the humans have him in a vice like grip from head to bottom and only his tail is free to move. The smell of something chemical which makes him feel nauseous and all the hands on him are the last thing he remembers.

An hour or so later...

Returning to consciousness, Rhett feels that he has something wrapped over one ear and secured around his neck; it makes him feel panicky and trapped like the hands did, and he longs to paw at it to get it off but he instinctively knows that he has to be smarter than to let the humans know he's awake. He keeps his eyes closed and listens out for the bolts to be drawn back, summoning his strength, willing whatever is pulsing through his veins making him sluggish to dissipate. He hears it, what he has been waiting for, but remains still; he knows that there are two bolts, he distinctly remembers seeing the cage on the floor of the room whilst he was being held down on the table. He has to be smart now, he has to escape. He is jumpy though, and doesn't feel he can keep up the pretence much longer - he yearns for action, movement, flight.

He hears the second bolt being drawn back and in one fluid movement flips up from his side onto his four feet, ducks his head and crouches his body low to exit. He manages to navigate himself straight out, even though his head swims a bit. He runs, skidding on the lino, out of the room and into the reception area he'd been dragged through not two hours earlier. Humans start to shriek and shout, dogs start to bark and whine.

'Go! Go!' says one gruffly, an English Bull Terrier who is not a fan of the vets. He's too old and lame to bother trying to escape himself, but he enjoys cheering Rhett on.

'Mum! Mum! Look at that dog!' a little pup squeaks at her human mum, excited.

'Stay away from me, or else!' growls a bulgy-eyed, bad-tempered chihuahua.

A person is entering the main door and Rhett takes the opportunity to scoot out, feeling hands on his back trying to grab at him, too late. He's relieved they seem to have taken the noose lead off him. He scoots off without looking back and the cries quickly fade into the distance and become a part of his past.

Only one thing is in Rhett's mind: Jessica.

KIP

Kensington Gardens

LOTTIE

Lottie watches Kip the Border Collie thoughtfully, curiously. She watches how he eye-stalks the others, how alert he is, how his crouched body trembles, poised always on the brink of action. Stillness, anticipation, interspersed with bursts of movement.

Piper watches him too. She hadn't paid him much mind until the other day and his sudden vocal outburst about the humans smoking. She runs towards the wooded part of the park, part of her knowing that her sudden, fast movement will incite him to follow. Kip immediately zeros in on her. He shoots forward then round to the left, eyes not leaving her form even for a split second, legs amortising the rough ground skilfully, without even once glancing down.

Lottie watches. She imagines he would have made an excellent working dog. She spots Charles, and raises her hand in greeting. He does the same back. Affecting to be tired out by the energy of his companion, he drawls, half-heartedly. 'Kip, man, chill out, will you?' He says it seemingly more to himself than to Kip. He pats at his top pocket and retrieves a box of cigarettes from there. He sits down on the ground, and draws his gangly knees up towards him, taking a cigarette out of the packet. He is over 50 but seems more like a teenager to Lottie in this moment. Resigned to wait, he leans back on one elbow, and his eyes lazily follow Kip, who is moving in arcs, this way and that, to herd Piper who is dodging, sprinting and doubling back erratically, clearly finding it amusing making herself unherdable.

Lottie sits down beside Charles, upwind of him. She used to smoke in the early days when she and Sebastian had been together, they both had, but she hates it now; the smell, the memories of being drunk and out of control, the connotations of loucheness and irresponsibility, of danger. She's become averse to anything that resembles danger since Sebastian was killed, the concept of things being life-threatening has expanded in her head. She often has to really concentrate in order to succeed in pushing the ominous feeling, which is ever present, away. It taints everything. Except, perhaps, her interactions with Piper.

'He'd really enjoy training you know Charles,' Lottie starts, tentatively, knowing she needs to tread gently in order to not make him defensive.

'Mmm,' says Charles noncommittally, the cigarette now squeezed between his lips. He cups his hands around the flame of the lit match he's just struck. 'I suppose he would,' he says neutrally. Lottie laughs and is rewarded with a slight, wry smile.

'How did you even get a Border Collie in the first place?' Lottie asks.

'Ah, well,' he lays his head back against the tree and closes his eyes, 'Now that was a weekend!' He has a deep, rumbling laugh. Lottie watches him. He has an interesting face, one which with advancing years will only get better, she thinks. She waits for him to take a drag of his cigarette and carry on.

'We ended up in someone's house in the countryside somewhere in the Wye Valley,' he continues, 'off our heads, naturally, it was a very creative weekend, musically. Some woman was getting in a tizz about a local farmer who'd drowned all but one of his working collie's pups, which he'd kept to wean. They didn't think it would be safe beyond that point.' He shrugs, opens his glittering, snake-like eyes and squints at her. 'I said I'd take it,' he shrugs again, and laughs. Lottie has the impression that he is laughing about something else entirely. 'I didn't really mean it, but that woman had been neurotic about it, wouldn't stop banging on about it. I said it to shut her up, really. I didn't think much more about it.' His gaze follows Kip. 'As I said, I was off my head. But just as we were about to leave she shows up in her flowery, mothbally dresses and cardigans,' he spits the words out comically, disdainfully and makes large, camp, arm gestures to illustrate. Lottie suspects he prefers his women naked, feral in a different way than this one had been, and laughs. 'With this little bundle in her arms. I didn't even see it at first. And she shoved it into the footwell of my passenger seat, along with one of her smelly woollen cardigans.' Again he makes a face and again Lottie laughs. 'I didn't think much of it at the time, to be honest. As I said, I wasn't really myself,' he chuckles again, 'and off I drove back to London.' He shrugs for a third time, with a half-smile on his face now, and a fond gaze at Kip.

Lottie thinks how different the beginnings of Kip's life with Charles was to Piper's with them. Piper had been cosseted and coddled and treasured at every turn.

'So you got back to London and then what?'

'Oh well, y'know,' he waves his arm vaguely, bored of the conversation suddenly, 'here we are,' he repeats, and sighs. 'Oh, and here he is!' Kip comes bounding up and touches his nose to Charles's hand, looks into Charles's eyes, and then heads off again. Charles looks surprised - checking in with him is not something he's taught Kip to do.

'Would you like me to do some training with him?' Lottie asks, abandoning her softly softly approach for a more direct one. Charles opens one eye and looks at her. The look is both lazy and shrewd.

'Mmmmm,' he says, neutrally.

Lottie goes on. 'I wouldn't charge you. It would just be interesting for me. Border Collies are so bright, Kip's so bright. And there aren't many Border Collies in London. You'd be doing me a favour really. It's weird, but I could swear that he's learning things without even being taught, I've been watching him.'

Charles has his eyes closed blissfully and is soaking up the sun's weak rays. Lottie thinks he must be mulling it over. She waits. She begins to doubt that he will bother to answer. She unties and ties the laces of her boots.

'Mmmmm,' he says again. He opens his eyes and looks at Kip, who is now annoying some young dog who is chasing after a ball. Kip is nipping at its back legs every time it moves. The owner is looking around crossly, to see who Kip belongs to.

'Well, okay, yeah,' he pronounces it more 'Yah' and Lottie wonders again what his background is. She suspects he is less proletariat than he makes out. 'Sure.'

'Great!' says Lottie, pleased. These days, she appreciates people who aren't too enthusiastic about life; she finds too much enthusiasm exhausting.

GOLDEN MOMENTS

Kensington Gardens

NERO

Nero takes advantage of the fact that his human, Neil, is trying to chat up a curvaceous young dog walker to have a proper romp with Piper and some cuddles with Lottie. Lottie is careful, she always makes sure to position herself where Neil can't see before calling Nero in to her. It bothers Nero that she has a sadness about her so he tries to cheer her up, licking up at her nose, at the delicious salty nostrils, and jumping up to give her a hug. She laughs, but pushes him down - not angrily, but firmly. She is surprisingly strong. How he would love to live with her and Piper! He and Piper chase around and tumble over, pin down and mouth at each other noisily, but not, in actual fact, hard. They love to goad each other. A man walking past glances at them nervously, and pulls his daughter to the other side of him, evidently scared. Nero gives him a scornful look and the rage almost rushes up in him but just at that moment Piper's Lottie calls him and Piper to her, firmly. A command, not a cue.

'Piper! Nero!'

They race towards her and both flop at her feet, panting heavily. Nero thinks about the idea of siblings. Piper and Lexi had been discussing it the other day. They had heard the word from the humans and been a bit confused about it, but Lily had clarified it for them: she had had many boy-siblings – brothers - and one girl-sibling, a sister, who had a couple of years later given birth to Luke. Luke had come to live with her and Edward as no one had bought him and he had offered him a home. Nero thinks that he and Piper could be that to each other - boy-sibling (brother) and girl-sibling (sister). Like best friends really, just with a more special bond.

He looks over at Neil who is still busy talking to the girl. She is gazing up into his face. He is handsome, Neil, apparently, Nero hears people saying it often, after they pass, sometimes giggling excitedly. Nero hopes he won't persuade her to come over to his place, Neil had brought a girl home before once and although the memory is a bit hazy Nero gets a bad feeling when he thinks about it. The girl back then had been uneasy as soon as she had entered the flat, Nero had felt it; even with dim lighting and candlelight there had been a bad atmosphere. He remembers, vaguely as if it had been a dream, her emanating a sense of panic and fear. There had been no anger in her, no fight - just terror. He remembers being shocked at the strength of the smell of that terror; this was all before he had started to detect hues of it on himself. He remembers the girl trying to leave and Neil not letting her, shaking her at the end. Viciously, gleefully. He had shaken her like Nero shakes that toy when he gets it, the one Neil only lets him play with occasionally, the one that has proper blood on it. That toy sends Nero into a frenzy, which in turn excites Neil and tells him to 'Kill it! Kill it!'. He can't remember what had happened after Neil had shaken her, and anyway he doesn't want to think about it any more. He gives his whole body a shake, trying to put her and what had happened to her out of his mind.

'Shall we?' he asks Piper, rhetorically. She, always game, runs off before saying anything, laughing over her shoulder at him.

At times like these, he could burst with happiness, but it is always over too soon. Sure enough, after just a couple of minutes Nero hears Neil calling him. He slinks back to him, cowed.

A RACE

Kensington Gardens

PIPER

Piper hears an altercation and looks across to see what's going on. It's over towards the far side of the park, about 200m away, but that isn't far for Piper. She sprints over to see what is happening, ignoring Lottie's requests. The requests turn into demands (Leave It! Piper, Leave It! and a more agitated Piper! Come!) but Piper catches more and more of the argument as she goes and somehow finds herself unable to turn away from the drama. A peevish little dog, a Pomsky, is screaming at another little dog, some type of Yorkshire Terrier, and as far as Piper can make out, it is an argument over some special ball. The first little dog has flown into a rage, screaming and spitting in anger. In between the verbal abuse, the Pomsky is physically attacking the other dog, who seems a little perplexed but is fighting back, since he is, after all, a terrier. One of the owners is shouting at them both, ineffectually, whilst the second is wailing, dramatically and unintelligibly. *Human really can be ridiculous sometimes,* Piper thinks, chuckling.

'Doggies, doggies, what are you doing! Stop it!' The shouting voice is irritating, reedy, desperate, and a crowd is starting to gather.

This could be fun, thinks Piper and moves further forwards, joining the fray.

'PIPER! COME! NOW!'

Drat! thinks Piper. She can't really ignore Lottie this time. *Shame.* She does a U-turn and races, grinning, back to Lottie.

Later, on the same walk...

'Dare you, Rhett!'

'OK, no problem Pipe.' Rhett says, coolly.

'You can't! You can't!' Beagle remonstrates, starting to shake with worry. His eyes are wide and bulge even more than usual and the familiar smell that he emanates when he is particularly stressed hits them in a wave.

'You'll catch a cold! You'll get arrested! Look! There's the Park Police!'

Lily chips in coolly, 'I don't think Lottie will be very happy with you, Piper.' She punctuates it with a sniff which leaves the others in no doubt as to what she thinks of their idea. Her nickname amongst the park gang dogs is The Fun Police. Piper puts her head on one side, and considers this. She doesn't like to upset Lottie or to disappoint her. Sometimes Lottie tells her off out loud but she can tell that Lottie is doing it for the benefit of someone else in the park, for some other human rather than because she is genuinely annoyed.

Piper had made Lottie cross a few times though. Once, when Piper just couldn't seem to help herself and had chased all the ducks and swans and made them panic and fly around and upset the tourists who had been feeding them. Lottie had been cross then, really cross. It had been winter and the birds had been hungry and Lottie had told Piper that they didn't want to be expending extra energy flying away from her. Another time when she'd given that puppy a little shake. It had been really annoying and hadn't wanted to leave her alone, it had just kept following her and launching itself onto her, and Piper had told it what for. Lottie had been cross then too and had given her a really long, really boring telling off. And the other time was when she'd bitten that child. Lottie had been furious then; it had freaked Piper out.

After she'd seen on the nannycam what had happened though, Lottie had been sorry and had apologised to Piper saying it wasn't her fault and had called the child an evil little tyke. Piper had felt both vindicated and absolved. The memory still isn't a pleasant one though.

Piper casts her mind back to the puppy episode.

Annoyed with the puppy who just wouldn't leave her alone and had kept launching itself at her, Piper had rounded on it and, taken it by the scruff of its neck, given it a little shake. It had squealed loudly and cried, 'Mum! Mum! She's hurting me!'

Piper had given it a withering look, thinking *Pathetic! What a grass!* and without giving it another thought had turned around to move off. She had been surprised to be confronted by the stiff, annoyed legs of a furious Lottie, who had had some awful energy about her. Sure enough, Lottie shouted at her, really shouted. 'Look at me!' Piper had looked up at her, trying not to laugh, trying not to jump and bound about on her back two legs.

'Whatthehelldoyouthinkyou'redoingdontyoueverdothatagain-mygirl! Never again!' Piper had stopped wanting to laugh, and had looked at the ground, unsure how to answer. She hadn't understood why Lottie had been quite so angry. She had put her paw up, and hung her head down, averted her eyes and tried all the appeasement signals she knew. She had felt like Lottie was really, badly overreacting and had misread the situation but had sensed that it wasn't the moment to argue. 'I do NOT like bullies! Do you hear me, Piper?' she had said, huffing and puffing.

Yes, Piper thinks, Lottie had been much angrier about the puppy than she had been about the duck episode which, Piper had sensed, Lottie had also found a little bit thrilling and not entirely a bad thing, seeing them all whoosh up in the air like that and all the tourists' gasps and oooohs and exclamations. Shaking the annoying little puppy had felt pretty good to Piper, but apparently it hadn't felt good for Lottie to watch. Piper's mind again moves to when she had bitten the little boy and a shiver runs through her, she doesn't like to think about it, even though in the end it had turned out fine. When she'd told Lily and Lexi about it the next day, still shaken, Lily had mumbled darkly something about *The Story of Gelert*.

Piper sighs. Although they are best friends and she'd choose Lottie over any of her canine friends any day, she has to admit that sometimes there are moments when Piper feels a disconnect. They are from two different species, after all.

Having thought all this through at speed, Piper decides that Lottie will only be somewhere between making the ducks fly up in the air cross and shaking a puppy cross, definitely nowhere near biting a child cross, and shakes herself all over. In doing so she throws off any doubts.

'OK, we race there and the first one who swims to the other side and the far path wins.'

Rhett looks at her, smiling, "k. On three?' Piper nods. Rhett counts, 'One... two... three!'

Piper is faster off the mark, her feet leave the floor before Rhett finishes saying three, but Rhett is longer-limbed and they reach the pond and leap into the air within a split second of one another. Lottie is a tiny fraction later as she has had to dodge around a sniffing Spaniel at the last minute. 'Oooooooh!' Piper hears a tourist say, admiringly, at the sight of her and Rhett leaping. Both of them are athletic and both are competitive, they have leapt far and hit the water with an enormous double splash. The ducks and birds scarper in various directions, diagonally airborne, horizontally waterborne, and everything in-between. The tourists exclaim to each other, chatter excitedly, and many instinctively lift their phones to video it.

It's cold, and Piper feels the weeds and reeds trying to tangle with her limbs. She kicks, strongly, fast, each of her legs working like the V11 cordless Dyson at home when Lottie puts him on surge. They call the Dyson *Bob*. She throws herself into the race like Bob would, with all her power. Piper feels Rhett to her right hand side and pushes with all her strength.

COME ON PIPES! she hears Sebastian's voice in her head, and it gives her a boost of energy. She has to stop herself scanning the banks of the pond for him, it seems so real. She's heard his approving grin in the words, and longs to smell his smell, to jump into his arms and to roll around on the floor with him. He'll always be with her sometimes, in spirit, she realises, and the realisation makes her happy.

Rhett reaches the other side a fraction before her. He heaves himself out, his muscles rippling impressively, and the barrel of his rib cage proudly defined. She knows he's won but she rushes all the same, Sebastian's voice in her head, telling her not to give up. Neither of them shake until they've reached the far path and when they do, they both laugh, exhilarated. They shake themselves thoroughly, to the sound of more tourists' exclamations and chattering comments.

They hear Lottie's screams. 'PIPER! PIPER! COMEBACKHERE - NOW!' Piper looks at Rhett and they race off back in the direction they had come. Piper feels the wind through her fur, the pull of her muscles, the air in her lungs. She is happy, who would not be? She screeches to a halt in front of Lottie and does her best sit, right up close to her, directly in front of her feet, just as Lottie likes her to. She looks up innocently. She feels Lottie softening.

'You'll catch your death of cold' Beagle says, sourly. Lily just sniffs. Rhett and Piper look at each other and grin. Lottie says words of crossness but Piper can't feel any crossness and snuggles into her leg. Lottie starts to laugh and says 'Oh get off Piper! You're wet! Come on, let's go, before you two get arrested! Come on, Doggy Dog!' Lottie gestures to Piper and to Rhett too to come and briskly walks back eastwards, away from the pond and all the tourists, who have stopped the chattering but are still gawping.

'There she is,' says one pigeon, watching Lottie striding across the park, 'she's the mustard seed girl.'

'That's her, yes, she gives good snacks doesn't she,' confirms another.

'She helped my friend Barry the other day, he was on his last legs and she took him in.'

'Ahhh, nice. He on the mend now? They take him over to that centre in Barnes?'

'Yup, he's doing all right I heard. Should be back with us soon I imagine.'

'Great. Good if he gets a bit more of an innings.'

The pigeons watch Lottie's arms keenly. They see one hand go into a pocket and they ready themselves but settle down disappointed when she just brings out a tissue.

A DILEMMA

Brook Green (a bench near the tennis courts)

SARAH

Sarah is a former street dog and comes from what was formerly Rhodesia. After being driven out to the middle of nowhere by a malicious human who had caught her begging in town and then being chased off by a pack of territorial dogs, she had fallen, head over heels, tumbling faster and faster to the bottom of a scree. Battered, bruised and emaciated, she had all but given up on life when she had been saved by Helen. More accurately, by Helen and Ted, Helen's late husband.

Following a quick, sudden illness and death of her Ted, Helen had had to move to the UK, and had insisted on bringing Sarah with her. She had refused to leave her behind. Now, six years on, Sarah's health is failing. She's ready and quite willing to go, to pass over, she's tired and feels she's had a good life and enough of it, but she's too worried about leaving Helen alone to let herself. How can she, after all the trouble Helen has gone to on her behalf? How can she leave her alone?

'I don't know what to do, Lexi,' says Sarah, sadly. 'I can't leave my Helen alone, I just can't. She adored her husband, so that was already a blow. But then to lose her son! It was tragic what happened to him, dying like that, so young. Lexi rubs her head against Sarah's, sympathetically. Sarah coughs a few times, then goes on.

'Helen's brother lives up in Glasgow. They haven't seen each other in years and his hearing isn't so good so they don't speak on the phone much, but they text and email a lot. She mentions him to me often. I'm sure she would love to visit him. I think Helen's worried about making the trip alone, or maybe she just doesn't want to leave me, am not sure. She would be so lonely without me, Lexi! I don't know. I can't hold on much longer though.'

Sarah has exhausted herself with this monologue and rests her head on the floor.

'Oh Sarah,' Lexi says sadly, 'I don't know what to tell you, I really don't. If only your Helen wasn't quite so proud. My human asked her over for tea the other day, I heard her. But Helen said no. She seems to think that she must be dull because she is so slow and old, as she puts it, and she doesn't want to be a burden to anyone.'

'I know, I know,' says Sarah. 'It's crazy. There's this boy though. A teenager. He sits on a bench and smokes,' Sarah makes a face, 'but he always stubs his cigarette out and stands up when we come along, and they chat. It was all very polite at first, but they have a real friendship now, they sit on the bench together and talk for ages. I wonder... The thing is, Lexi, these humans, they just want to be useful. And when they get old, they don't feel useful any more. It's not like us, we know how to just enjoy the feeling of the wind in our fur, lazing in the warmth of the sun, just the feeling of the earth underneath us, snapping at the odd butterfly,' she laughs, 'Although Grey told me off for doing that the other day!' Lexi laughs too.

'Age isn't so bad Lexi,' Sarah continues, 'If you have inner peace or can just relax. But they don't, they can't. They have to always be doing something, rushing somewhere. Helen's reasonably content compared to other people, but even she-' Sarah tails off.

Lexi nods. She knows what she means about the humans. They sit for some time in companionable silence, watching the various other dogs and humans walking in the park and enjoying the light breeze through their fur.

ESCAPE

At Lady Human and Grey's house

The wind howling through the trees always makes the dogs of London restless. It's the same the world over. The wind comes and it drives them to run, chase, howl, leap; to yelp, race, fight, love. It urges them to action. Humans watch, curious, and laugh, wondering just what's got into their dogs, but they would be wise to be careful as it's a primal urge that runs in the blood of canines on such days. Even in that of low slung Dachshunds and plodding Labradors, not always as amenable or as placid as one might believe. These blowy, wild days are the days of attacks, of fallouts, of change. The stillnesses between the gusts of wind are particularly dangerous.

GREY

As Lady Human bends down to clip his lead on, complaining as always, Grey grasps the opportunity and slips between her legs and out of the door. The spontaneity of his own actions takes him by surprise. He hears her screaming shrilly behind him and a great wave of relief and freedom washes over him. He races away from the house, the horrible dark-if-it-weren't-for-all-those-artificial lights house on the green, the prison, to the corner and turns up Aynhoe Road. He can't believe his own audacity! Adrenalin pumps through his veins. Grey takes a left past Costcutter, does a dog leg and passes the café with nice smells wafting out it as fast as his thin, brittle legs will carry him.

Grey feels a rush – fear, exhilaration and possibility. He thinks how proud Rhett will be of him and that spurs him on. He turns onto Masbro Road, on his right the school and its railings, the plastic chairs and the playground paraphernalia, empty of little humans now - they are inside having nap time. He sometimes feels little snatches of their funny, random little human dreams waft over, if he and Lady Human pass slowly enough, just at the right time.

Up, up, up Masbro Road, the corner shop on his left - more wafts of food, although nothing very interesting – cold, earthy vegetables, sanitised fruit. Past the vets and its steps to uncertainty. He feels the worry emanating from inside. They need to open it up and get a draft going through it, he thinks. 'Energy and feelings get stuck in places,' Siobhan had explained to him one time when Lady Human had gone out. She would be cross if she heard Siobhan talking to Grey of course, but Siobhan is always careful.

Grey runs across the road, missing a car by a whisker's width - he feels its hot, dirty breath on his neck. He runs fast, his little heart beating as if it might burst. Outside The Havelock there are people sitting at trestle tables or standing, smoking and drinking. They are talking too loudly, in piercing, braying voices, and they laugh even louder, as if it's a competition. Grey can't help but notice that most of them sound and smell a bit desperate. He glances to the side as he passes. A couple stand out, they have a glow about them, they are quietly talking with their heads bent towards each other over a pint of Guinness (she) and a red wine (he). The energy between them is palpable, beating. They emanate warmth, unlike the others. *Humans are a strange species,* he thinks, as he often does.

He soon finds himself level with The Bird in the Hand on the other side of the road and hears somebody exclaim as he passes, 'Look at that dog!'

A trail of discussion ensues in his wake, mostly women's voices.

'D'you think he's lost?'

'Oh poor wee thing, he looks panicked.' The voice takes on a plaintive tone by the end of the sentence. It sounds like a voice that is often plaintive. 'Brian can't you do something?' he hears it say. 'Brian?!'

'He looks like he's being chased, doesn't he!' and so on. A joke that he doesn't catch, a couple of male guffaws, one sounding uncomfortable and forced. It all fades out behind him, and spurs him on. Maybe he is being chased. A picture pops into his head of Lady Human, scrawny and spindly with her limbs flailing around, her mouth a graphite scribble – mean, set. Cursing him. He thinks his heart is going to explode with the exertion and the stress, and his legs are beginning to feel a bit wobbly.

Grey feels his resolve start to falter but pushes himself, tries to hang on to the boldness, to the astounding fact that he is free! He spies the dark mouth of the church off to his left. He wonders if he should hide in there, inside the big, still, dark building that smells musty and dusty and like it might be a safe haven for a little grey dog on the run. He isn't sure, and experiences the momentary panic of indecision, he knows that what he does now is likely to change the trajectory of his future. He can feel kindness there but something else too. Hesitant, he slows, then decides against it and runs on and around the corner, too fast, almost crashing into a bollard.

He is on Sinclair Road now and the tall, tall buildings exude all sorts of energies. He feels assaulted by the nearness of so many souls, the different lives and stories from all the homes beating, pulsing around and through him. He hears, inadvertently, a father and son arguing, a couple bickering, a woman crying. Like radio bandwidths they tune in and out as he passes so he only catches snatches. Grey runs and runs. He senses a Labrador exiting one of the buildings on his left, with a chap in a funny coat that smells a bit earthy, and a bit like wax. The man is carrying an umbrella and the plastic handle smells cheap, toxic.

Grey senses the harmony between the Labrador and the man, it is an old and solid friendship. The Labrador, an older dog, questions Grey, he is concerned for him, perturbed to see him bolting past. Grey shouts back in his head, loudly, unlike himself, too loudly, 'SORRY!' He doesn't like to be rude but he can't stop now to explain. He reaches a mini roundabout and crosses diagonally over it as he instinctively feels he has to go North. Suddenly he is flying through the air and he feels a searing pain in his back right leg and his left ear as they take the brunt of his tumble into the railings. The hard iron and the cracking, spiky paint are the least of his problems.

Grey quickly scrambles to his feet again, just trying to focus on what Rhett would do in his position. He starts running again, limping a little now and feeling as if all the bones in his body have been knocked out of kilter. Parked cars loom beside him and he scoots between them, across onto the other side, following the railings, swerving past a cat, giving it as wide a berth as he can. He has reached another roundabout. Smarter this time, Grey sticks to the pavement, turns right and registers a hotel entrance on his right, people hanging about looking at their phones, waiting, posing.

Towards the North Rhett had said, hadn't he? Onwards, then, although Grey can feel the vibration of traffic and with it, the fear in him rises and blood starts to thunder in his delicate, pointy little head.

THE SMELL OF FEAR

At Nero and Neil's home

NERO

Nero, ashamed and cowed, can smell it on himself when it comes. Fear. A sharp, almost sweet tang, it washes over him, drowning everything else out.

Nero is very familiar with it now, it comes whenever he feels Neil's displeasure, and before they cross the threshold from their flat out into the dark on their evening or nighttime walks. He can't help himself hanging back, even though that is guaranteed to make Neil mad and call him a coward and a pussy. He gets it when they cross the threshold coming back into the flat after walks, too. Neil often has a go at him then, it seems to be a habit that he has formed and Nero dreads it. At these times Neil's anger is not a fury but more of a tired rage, and his bullying Nero a way of self-soothing.

Once Neil has expelled his anger, punched Nero, thrown him against the wall, or just thrown something at him that Nero manages to deflect without much pain, Neil smells sated. Softer, kinder. Nero even approaches him sometimes then voluntarily, and feels a kindness in his touch, and a sorrow. He isn't all bad, Neil. Occasionally he absentmindedly rubs Nero's ears or strokes his head, even though that's only ever when no one is watching. It feels good when he does that. Nero loves him despite the scary moments. Nero loves Neil because he is his human, because Nero, being a dog, is full of love and has no one else to give it to. Neil is the only clan he knows.

Unidentifiable noises make him shiver, and it is at these times, when he is full of foreboding, that this smell within and around him is at its worst - cold, slick, sly. Noises he doesn't recognise such as an engine revving, a shout from a window or the sudden, piercing screech of some small animal set him off. Passing pass groups of people and feeling the heat emanating from Neil, the exuding of a type of challenge, the daring of people to take issue with them, the desire of Neil to let his feelings spill out onto something other than his long-suffering dog. Any whiff of a challenge from an unknown dog, verbal or physical, especially when he knows the dog is bigger, fiercer or stronger than him... Thankfully there aren't many about but that Akita that lives in the newsagents and walks in the area with its burly human is terrifying. Nero looks away, ignores him when they pass, much to Neil's disgust, but he always feels the cold voice slither over and reach him. The voice is similar to Neil's in its considered calmness, its quiet. It sends chills down Nero's spine.

'Come on then, mate' it always says, coldly, 'have a go will you?'

Something occurs to Nero out of the blue, and he cocks his head on one side, thinking. This smell he gets, he has smelt it on Beagle, too, and on Audrey. Not on any of the others though.

He tries to imagine living a life without the smell, without his fear. Lottie and Piper pop into his head. He savours their presence there and whines, softly.

BIRDS

Kensington Gardens

LEXI

Lexi shakes her head sadly as she watches Rhett in the distance, chasing birds in the sky. She's certain that some of the things he has been through have been quite traumatic. Rhett makes light of the time he spent at the shelter but she senses that there is more to it than he tells them. In a rare moment of serious reflection and candour as opposed to the vigour and drama with which he usually storytells, he'd once told her that the only thing that had kept him sane throughout those long, hungry days, days without food or human company, amongst the fights and depression and sheer hopelessness of it all, was the birds. Lexi had understood that he'd wanted to catch them to eat them as he'd been so desperately hungry. She understands, or tries to - who wouldn't, she can't imagine missing even one meal - but secretly it still turns her stomach a bit. Rhett's ears are both tattered, underneath the hair, Lexi has noticed. One, the right hand one, has a whole section missing. It feels a bit gauche to ask him outright what had happened to it though. She shivers, thinking about what he must have been through. And about the idea of him killing those birds. She wonders to herself exactly how he had caught them.

RHETT

Rhett still likes to play with the birds. Even though they are in the air and he is on the land, he loves the joyous liberating dance of running towards them and them seeming to continue on for him, scattering and soaring up into the sky, so free, then swooping back down towards him and them racing each other, him alongside or underneath them, running with their shadows. He remembers how back then he had loved to interact with them like that and had longed to join them. He remembers how they had seemed to rejoice when he had told them he was getting out. He always thinks of birds as his friends. He was happy, as he had moved from country to country, that birds were a constant. He could no more imagine a world without birds in it than a world without grass.

GOODBYES

13 months ago

At the border fence of the dog rescue shelter, Serbia

RHETT

In the dark, they meet at the fence. They have sniffed each other down easily, even though the camp perimeter fence is long.

Rhett's voice is gruff. 'It's hopeless, Jessica. I'm sorry.'

'I know Rhett, it's OK.' His eyes are cast down at the ground as if he is ashamed to look at her. She wills him to look up. He does. His eyes are red raw with emotion and his expression is one of complete despair.

'It's OK, Rhett, really. I'm at peace. My time here is done.'

Rhett knows by this that she means to go to the Rank Pool. He feels panicked with the imminent, overwhelming feeling of grief that wells up inside him.

'No, Jessica!' he blurts out, his voice now no longer gruff, but raw, searing. It cuts the air with injustice and pain.

'Yes, Rhett.' She is perfectly calm and steady, and he meets her eyes again. They are shining and he sees, with a sinking feeling in the pit in his stomach, the resolve there.

'I'm just so glad you're out, dear Rhett, so glad!' Jessica moves her whole body to the fence, as does he, they try to rub together. Oh, how I will miss her smell! Thinks Rhett. More than anything! For over a year she has been his constant companion, all through the freezing, icy winter. They have survived because of each other. She - her smell - is part of him. He sniffs her in and his throat aches, aches, aches with pain.

After some seconds Jessica stops rubbing her body on the fence and steps back from it.

'Enough, my dear friend. Go now Rhett,' she says.

He feels that she is somehow happy and is angry with her. He's angry with the fence, with Jessica, with humans, with the whole world.

'Please Rhett, don't be sad. I'm just so happy you're out. Live! Just live for me! And don't be sad, please!' Her eyes are shining now with tears. Rhett is crying, gulping, unable to catch his breath. He feels wrung out, like a husk. A torch light flicks on, sweeps in their direction.

'Go, Rhett! Please go now! Quickly! Please!' she says desperately, 'Live for me! And don't be sad! We'll meet again, in the next life! I promise you, dear Rhett. I'll wait for you, I'll look out for you! We'll have all those things we talked about. Remember all that? I'll be waiting. Thank you, for everything. I love you, my friend!'

She is gone, her final kindness being not to make him leave her, but to leave him. Rhett feels the future gap, the void where his soulmate should but will not be. He staggers, and drags himself away from the fence, into the undergrowth.

Despite himself his survival instinct kicks in, and he dodges the beam of the torch, slinks with his belly low to the ground.

'Live for me, Rhett!' resounds in his head. She had sounded ecstatic, elated.

'Don't be sad, please!' she had said.

He can hardly see for the tears, hardly breathe for the sobs.

As Rhett begins his long journey, crossing from country to country with an impossibly heavy heart, he ignores overtures from other dogs, he only snarls or snaps unintelligibly if he is spoken to. He feels outcast and rude and wild. He can only think about Jessica, about her goodness and about the unfairness of the world. He is furious. Grief-stricken, lonely, he feels like he will never regain his spirit.

Rhett knows what will become of her, and it is a source of great sadness for him, a burden he will always bear.

JESSICA

She has no chance of escaping, and no pleasure really in life, now that Rhett is gone. The knowledge that he is free makes her heart sing though and it is that thought which she clings onto throughout the hours following his departure. The very next morning, after watching the sun rise which is one of her favourite things to do, she drinks from the Rank Pool, knowing she will be released from pain and fear. She is glad for the certainty. The last eight years have been a struggle, and only the last one, spent with Rhett, has brought her any joy. It's time.

At least it gives them the option, she thinks. She has seen it happen a few times herself, some poor soul slinking there in the night, a small shred of dignity remaining, the dogmanity of not wanting the others to have to witness the Act. Reaching the edge, stooping down the head, taking the first few laps, tentatively, it even tastes of Death. More then, quicker, decided – drinking, drinking deep. And then the wait. Some say it comes quickly, some slow, but at least you can be certain that it means an end to it all.

She stoops her head down to the brackish water and tries not to feel the smell of it as she drinks.

ESCAPE II

Shepherd's Bush (corner of Richmond Way and Charecroft Way)

GREY

A strange building looms up on his left. What looks like a concrete slide comes out of the side of it. Ugly, imposing and seemingly abandoned, it gives out dead, neglected vibes. There is rubbish and dust swirling gently at its base, an area of concrete embedded with small pebbles, incongruously rustic in the urban setting. A few forlorn looking pigeons are pecking at the ground there. *Humans create such ugly things,* Grey thinks. Nature has to live, to survive, amongst all these ugly things, tainted by them; these pigeons that should be pecking at fat grubs are instead pecking at cigarette butts. It saddens Grey to see it.

Another row of houses, parked cars and people. Far more people now, he feels their eyes on him and instinctively knows it isn't good to be noticed. Magnolia leaves slimy and brown on the ground make him slip and curse. Grey heads up a ramp at the end of the road and dodges the hurrying people. He hears someone shouting, 'Hey doggie!' and 'Slow down!' into the wind after him. He is grateful for the concern of these humans who are clearly unlike Lady Human. There is a bar on the corner, with seats outside. People, mainly men, are standing outside, all bar a couple of them in shorts and flipflops, despite the cold and the wind. They are without exception clutching pints. Lively and loud, laughing and joking, they remind him of Jack Russells or Miniature Schnauzers. To the right of him, the traffic roars.

Taking the pavement running westwards would mean staying abreast of the awful noisy traffic and Grey begins to panic, it's all getting too much for him. Just as he is thinking about turning back the way he had come, the mass of vehicles slows and stops. It becomes distinguishable into individual cars, vans, motorbikes. Grey seizes his moment. He runs, scooting between the stationary cars across three lanes, so close that he can feel the heat of the tyres, smell the rubber and the petrol fumes, see materials squashed into the grooves of some of the tyres. It all frightens him. He holds his breath. He reaches the island between the two roads and hangs his head panting for a few breaths, then scoots on. Up the curb and onto the pavement, feeling like his heart is in his throat, he swerves left. There are so many people here, a mass of legs so dense that he has to slow his pace until he stops and starts his way along. Dodging, dodging, he feels his heart race, more from anxiety than exertion now.

Half the depth of the wide pavement is strewn with shopware, a cheerful display of plastic bowls containing miscellaneous cheaply made goods, and fruits and vegetables that don't smell. And then something different. Grey's head lifts, he sniffs in the direction of the doorway from which the smell is coming to investigate. FARA is written above the door. It has a homely smell, like how his cage smells when Lady Human goes away and Siobhan, who has dogs back home in Ireland, lets him keep the same blanket in there without washing it every other day. He is desperate to escape the noise and bustle of the street and hopes it will be quieter inside, so darts in through the doorway. He scoots around some metal legs, feeling the clothes brushing his back as he moves. There are the smells of lots of different humans here, but also of cats and dogs too. He heads to the area behind the counter and dives into a pile of stuff. Crouching his body down as far as he can, feeling protected by the fabric all around him, he peeps out, poised to bolt if needed.

Grey realises just how exhausted he is, the inside of his head is momentarily black with little stars. His head pounds, his body heaves. He hears himself panting loudly, so loudly that humans are bound to notice him, but he can't stop. He sounds like Beagle when he starts hyperventilating in the park and he almost laughs to himself; he is feeling a bit hysterical. Hide! he thinks urgently, trying to catch his breath, trying to slow it down, hide!

A woman approaches. He doesn't look, but he can feel her towering above him. She sighs, bends her knees, and groans as she squats down beside him. He is half hidden by clothes and he has the sensation that he must appear comic to her. She seems unphased though, as if it's every day that a random dog runs into her shop in a panic and tries to hide. She stays there, uncomfortably squatted, and waits. She doesn't ask anything of him, just waits. Grey's breathing is a lot less ragged now than before. He dares to peek, and sees that the woman has a large mole on her face from which a single hair sprouts. She still doesn't look directly at him, and Grey is thankful for that. She tells him to hide in the back. He isn't sure whether she has spoken out loud at him or what, he feels confused. He stays still, frozen. He hears words from her now, definitely out loud words this time.

'Go in to the back room, quickly little dog – hide somewhere, and stay as quiet as you can!' she tells him.

Grey's eyes widen. He looks up at her - she is upright again now, and statuesque. His eyes meet hers. She nods at him. This he is absolutely sure of. Perhaps he had imagined the rest. His feet catch up with him, he's been standing stock still after exiting from the pile of clothes, and he whips into the back room like a shot. Darting around, panicked, he jumps into a box of soft, perfumed scarves. Not the best choice in retrospect, he thinks, as he fights the urge to sneeze, but in a way he feels comforted as he burrows down, thinking of that fox he sees sometimes on Rowan Road, picturing her entering the churchyard, presumably on the way to her den.

He curls into a tight, tight ball, squeezes his eyes shut and listens with all his might. There is little oxygen down amongst the scarves and he soon starts to feel pleasantly heavy-headed. He breathes in the smells. Most are floral, but some are musky and woody. He likes those ones better and gently seeks them out with his snout. Once his breathing slows and his panic subsides, his muscles start to relax, and surprisingly he dozes off, his brain racing with manic dreams, snapshots of his escape. His body twitches, and he drops down the different levels into a deep sleep.

A little while later...

Grey, snug in his box of scarves, is twitching and dozing despite the stress coursing through his veins.

The shop lady, who is Serbian, looks in on him and decides that she'll give him some food before she sends him on his way, poor thing looks half-starved. She has known what that feels like, it's a hazy memory but one that gives her empathy with this poor creature.

Chicken wire and bare earth form part of her pre-human memories. Digging, desperation. Murky water, but if it is only murky you still take it, as much as you can get, anything that might help you survive. There's a thin line between surviving and not surviving, and any one thing can make that sliver of difference. Probably that's why she can't stop herself now. Greedy, some people call her. But she knows, knew, what it is like not to know when you will next get fed, she isn't stupid, she will always get her fill, nothing worse than having an empty stomach. She shudders, thinking of the feeling of it. She remembers, unwillingly.

She's never spoken to people about it, what's the point? In fact it's only now that she realises she remembers it. She's always just taken it for granted that she can work out how dogs feel simply by looking at them; she understands not only their body language but the vocal and the telepathic communication too. She understands it all instinctively, she just has to tune in.

Grey jolts awake. He smells her almost the instant the door opens, the atoms between them juggling and bumping each other urgently in order to alert him. She, Lady Human, has entered the shop. Ears pricked, Grey waits. He's poised for action, although some part of him feels assured that the shop lady will protect him.

The shrill, commanding voice of Lady Human reaches him. The smell of her, extreme cleanliness and cloying perfume, makes him start to tremble and pant. His lips draw back wide exposing his back teeth, the whites of his eyes begin to show and his tail curls right underneath him between his legs. Panic overtakes him. Paris, the perfume is called, she has worn it all the time he has known her; it sits on the hallway console table and she puts it on as she leaves the house, unfailingly. He hates all the notes within the smell of Paris, and will do for as long as he lives. He hears the voice of the shop lady now: deep, calm, unintimidated. He freezes, holds his breath, swallows down the panic he feels rising in him. He listens.

'No, no love,' he hears the shop lady say. Lady Human hates being called 'love' and will bristle at that, he knows, particularly at it being delivered to her in a foreign accent. The shop lady continues, 'no dogs in here!' She even laughs, and makes it sound genuine. She is mocking Lady Human. *How brave she is!* thinks Grey to himself, his eyes widening in the dark, his tail unfurling slightly - concentrating on the exchange is serving to dissipate his fear. Just like Rhett!

Lady Human starts up again, and Grey cowers back down, instinctively.

'A man swore he saw him run in here-'

'You must be mistaken love, no dogs in here!' Grey pictures the shop lady continuing to fold clothes, appraising them, sorting them into piles. 'A dog? Pfffft! Why would one come in here!' she scoffs, laughing. 'Who on earth told you that?' she asks, casually scornful. Grey imagines her barely glancing up from her folding.

'Err...' Lady Human says, flustered, unable to see outside the person who had directed her into the shop.

Lady Human realises she's been beaten. She finds that she hasn't the stomach for arguing with the formidable presence that is the General Manager of FARA's Shepherd's Bush branch. She recognises that here is someone on whom her bullying tactics won't work and anyway she feels suddenly exhausted from all the running along streets, screeching Grey's name. Short of demanding that the shop be searched, and she can't face the thought of breathing in all that second-hand dust - dead skin and all sorts, she thinks, shuddering - there isn't much she can do.

Grey senses that Lady Human is retreating. He hears the bell of the door go, and lets his breath out in a big rush. After a few seconds, the shop lady comes into the back room. He pops his head out from amongst the scarves, silent. She addresses him but doesn't seem to be moving her lips. Not for the first time he thinks: adult humans can't speak, can they? But now he thinks about it, he's seen Lexi speak to humans. Very young humans can definitely communicate, baby humans and the toddling ones - even some of those a bit older, too. The very old also, he remembers, thinking about it. It's all such a muddle in his head now, he's never thought about it so specifically before. He gives himself a shake to clear his thoughts.

'She's gone, little chap – you'd better move on, get far away from her.' The shop lady is brusque. 'Don't worry,' she adds kindly, 'it will be okay. You'll find your place. Just be careful of the traffic. And the bad humans. Don't let them catch you.' She gives him a stern look. 'You can run fast, use that. If in doubt, run!' She says with great urgency. 'And eat and drink whenever you can. Whenever.' He can feel her anxiety on his behalf and he feels touched.

She beckons for him to come to her and he does, cautiously, stiff-legged. He trusts her, but isn't really used to being touched much. She gives him a scratch and stroke and a pat all over, a bit too rough for his liking, and the scratching is unnecessary as he isn't at all itchy, but he can tell she means well. 'My, you're a skinny one aren't you!' To his surprise, with a rapid, fluid movement she efficiently unbuckles and whips off his collar. Her two colleagues, both young girls, are loitering in the doorway. Up till this point they have been mutely gawping, but now they spring to life and start to protest. 'Irene!' they say in unison but with various vowel mutations, to this day unable to pronounce her name the correct way. 'What are you doing?' one whines. 'You can't take his collar off!' the other adds. Irene stops them with a withering look. 'This is the best thing we can do for him; I'm only sorry we can't get the chip out of him too, if there is one.'

What are you doing? Grey also thinks to himself as she whips it off, but is not quite brave enough to address her directly. He knows it's important to have a collar on, and how important the shiny, clinky disc is. It enables people to return him home if he gets lost and the clinky thing is to tell them where home is. *Aaaaah,* he thinks, the penny dropping, and in his surprise turns full to Irene and looks up into her eyes. 'Yes,' she says to him. Again he's taken aback. She had talked to him, quite clearly, without moving her lips. He definitely hadn't imagined it this time.

This human, Irene, seems to Grey to have something of Rhett about her, as well as a touch of Lexi. It's as if they have the wisdom of a hundred lifetimes within them. He feels naïve by comparison.

She speaks out loud now, as humans do normally. It feels harsh after the softer, doggy-style telecommunication.

'Right, off you go, boy, go now, shoo! Shoo!'

The two girls start to complain again.

'Awwww, Irene!' One edges forward and crouches down, tentatively, evidently wanting to reach out and stroke him but also clearly very nervous. 'Can't we let her stay a bit?' she says. Grey is used to people thinking he's a girl.

Grey edges forward, paw up, and tries to lick Irene, to put his paws up on her, to appeal to her. He used to do this with Lady Human when he'd been a pup, before he had learnt that she was as hard as stone. His brain whirrs, thinking ahead. He doesn't know what to do out there, or where to go. And all those noisy cars moving so fast, he's scared of them, he'd smelt death on the wheel of one - of more than one...

Irene though is unrelenting. 'Shoo! Shoo!' she says with a finality that will not be argued with, ushering him out. He backs away, looking up at her, desperate, but soon feels the outside breeze on his fur and the metal tread of the shop entrance's step under one of his back paws. He stumbles, and turns to face the outdoors before he falls. He looks back and up at her again.

She looks into his eyes and with soundless lips, 'Yes!' she says, firmly but kindly. He sees the peaky face of one of the two shop girls craning around Irene's arm, watching him, worried. He bids Irene goodbye with a nod and thanks her, even as he is falling over himself and running away along the pavement, in the direction of Shepherd's Bush tube.

IN RECOVERY

Kensington Gardens

LOTTIE

The people of London, always keen to picnic, are doing it en masse now in Kensington Gardens. Some have just bought a few things from Marks and Spencer and spread out their coats or jumpers beneath them but some, more prepared, lounge on little rugs and have brought tupperware, cutlery and paper plates. Foreigners living in London, initially a little bemused by this practice, have caught the bug and the air is full of chatterings in several different languages. The sky is cornflower blue with little fluffy clouds and a light wind. It is not too hot to run around and not too cold that you absolutely have to. Piper spies Rhett over near the horse statue and races up to meet him as she hasn't seen him for a couple of days. They touch noses briefly, then Piper bounds back to Lottie. Rhett doesn't come with her though. 'Somewhere to be, Piper,' he'd said, enigmatically. Piper doesn't mind though, Lottie's all the company she needs really; her doggie friends are just a bonus.

Lottie likes to walk alone with Piper sometimes, not to talk to anyone. Today is one of those days. Lottie has her head down, to avoid noticing anyone she knows. She is heading towards the bandstand, and passing some waddling ducks. As Piper nears, she thinks about chasing them. The second before she is about to, Lottie's voice reaches her.

'Piper! No, Piper.' Lottie says sharply. Piper grins at her and obeys, veering off. When Lottie gets just past the bandstand she slows down, looking for leaves to press and enjoying not having to talk, or to listen. She loves her job, but sometimes it's a bit intense - not the dog training component so much but the communication with the humans, which requires great focus. She feels relatively unencumbered today, for the first time since Sebastian has been gone. She had always enjoyed exercising, before, and is pleased to feel some slight will for it returning. She stops where she is, and does some sit-ups, press-ups and planks. Piper potters around and comes back at intervals to nudge at her face. The third time Piper does it Lottie, laughing, gets up on her feet and walks over a few steps to a tree. She sits down cross-legged and leans her back against it, surveying the park. Piper lays by her side, touching Lottie all along her leg with the length of her body, relaxed but alert. Piper lays her head down on the floor and lets out a content sigh.

Lottie can't really remember a time before having Piper. She had brought a lightness with her to their household, even before everything that had happened. They had laughed a lot after the arrival of Piper, she and Sebastian, more than they ever used to, except for maybe when they'd first been dating. And after, well, after, Piper had been the only thing able to lift Lottie out of herself. She strokes Piper's flank, and thanks her silently, as she often does.

That evening

PIPER

Piper sleeps on Lottie's pillow. She feels the weight of grief in Lottie's head, and she tries to absorb it whilst Lottie sleeps. Piper wishes she could impart into Lottie her lightness of being. She's sad about them losing Sebastian too, of course she is, she had loved him - will always love him - but she sees no point in this dead, sad weight of pain that Lottie carries with her. Piper would like to be able to chase it away. She sighs, heavily, but within seconds she is fast asleep.

REACTIVITY

At Audrey & Beagle's home

AUDREY

Audrey now obsessively follows stories of other reactives like Beagle. It is a fascinating and terrifying new world. The RDUK Facebook group feels both like a lifeline and a dirty secret, as it does to so many others. She feels solidarity but also shame at being a part of it all; she can't shake the feeling that her dog's reactivity is somehow her fault. Being connected with similarly lost and overwhelmed humans makes Audrey feel less alone. She posts sometimes, feeling disloyal, late at night or in the small hours when Beagle is fast asleep, plagued even in dreams by terrors she can't begin to fathom. The supportive comments that are written in response alternately validate her concerns or give her a morale boost, but they don't of course ultimately change anything.

In his waking hours, Beagle's night terrors persist. His eyes bulge, his pupils dilate, he licks his lips. He pants, shies away from people, scoots away from other dogs or worse, tries to attack them. He is not a frustrated greeter, as one lady in the park had suggested some months ago - Audrey had looked up the definition of that and laughed, mirthlessly. He is fear aggressive, but she is at a loss as to how to fix it.

People have suggested various protocols with acronymic names like CARE and BAT, scentwork, massage and wrapping, building confidence through play, diffusing essential oils, getting into canicross or flyball or agility, doing parallel walks with trusted dogs, off-lead play sessions in secure fields, breed-specific doggie playdates. She had never had to think this hard about things when she'd had Tinks. Audrey has tried all the things that have felt open to them but with no impact and it is all beginning to seem hopeless. Her friends and family have started to suggest that she rehome him, have him put to sleep even. Their faces when they do so are screwed up carefully into expressions of mock anguish and empathy, things she knows they aren't really feeling.

Sometimes, she herself even thinks that it might be braver and kinder of her to end his life, given how much emotional distress he seems to be in every minute of every day. Turmoil is the word that strikes her when she looks at his face, she can almost feel his brain whirring and reeling and sweating with panic.

Audrey exits the house today, the morning after one of her regular nightly exchanges on RDUK, grim-faced and reticent. She feels like she might burst into tears at any second and knows she can't face trying to walk him today. She decides that she will just drive him around, and relief floods her with this change in the day's tactics. For his toileting they will go to that empty deserted industrial estate she has found, up near Wembley. The only thing that calms Beagle is driving around, smoothly, in the car, in his covered crate. They do it a lot. It calms her too, if she finds the right music on the radio, or a station that fits her mood. It is pathetic and nonsensical, Audrey knows, to have to just drive around aimlessly, wasting petrol and polluting the environment rather than being out walking in the fresh air, but it's worth it when she feels Beagle's stress ebb away. She isn't sure what it is that helps, perhaps the feeling of transition.

They cross over the road to her car and she unlocks it with the remote.

'Come on then, Beagle love,' she says, opening the back door.

He looks up at Audrey mournfully and she can't help thinking of Tinks, who used to leap into the car tongue lolling, right until the end.

AWKWARD CONVERSATIONS II

Brook Green (a bench on the grass)

SARAH

Sarah feels tired. She would be glad if she could just lay down and go to sleep and not wake up to the aches and pains and the pressures of living. She feels occasional flashes of crossness when Helen fusses over her, which is a new thing. Sarah can't be bothered with life any more, if she's honest. She would rather not, for example, have to bother to eat what is put down for her in her bowl. She would rather just slip away. She has no appetite any more, for anything. She mildly enjoys dozing in the sunshine if the conditions are right, but generally, she would prefer to simply cease to exist. It vexes her that she is so attached to Helen, and Helen to her. This co-dependence between humans and dogs is a double-edged sword, she thinks. It is too hard, having to leave her; Helen is all alone now, except for Sarah. So she struggles on. She makes an effort to eat, to get up, even to wag her tail. She sees that this gives Helen joy, and it is the least she can do after all Helen has done for her. She dozes off, half-listening to Helen and Danny's conversation.

HELEN

'So listen, have you thought any more about what I said?' she asks him, eyes boring into his and not giving him anywhere to hide.

'Yeah.' He looks down at the floor, starts scuffing it with his foot. 'No!' he admits.

She stops his foot with her stick.

'Alright, mafia grandma!' he says. He is half-laughing, half-cross, and she laughs at his expression.

'Well,' he starts, 'it's complicated.'

'Things usually are.' Helen says, drily, 'You don't like lessons, you don't like writing stuff down, and Laura or whatever she's called, and that other whiny little bitchface,' Danny laughs out loud at this, shocked, and Helen smiles, pleased with herself, and continues, 'make you feel uncomfortable, that po-faced teacher Ms Harris is always on your back, your head starts melting, blah blah blah.' She is quoting him verbatim and sounding dramatic and sulky and he can't help but laugh.

'Yeah, I know,' he shakes his head, still smiling, 'you're right. I'm trying. I went to most of my lessons this week.' Helen raises an eyebrow, turns her wrist gently, pointedly, and looks at her watch, then looks back at him, raises her eyebrow. He laughs again. 'Tuesday morning's my free period! Okay, I know, I know, okay. It's just I'm not sure... I'm gonna flunk the exams anyway, what's the point? I told my Ma what you said, about the dyslexia, and she said I was just whining and making excuses and that she didn't have time to be going up to the school and talking to them.' He shakes his head. Helen thinks he understands that his Ma is failing him and it makes her sad. Out loud, Helen tuts. 'Well come on Danny, use a bit of initiative! Speak to them yourself! That nice one, the young one, the teaching assistant, what's her name, Miss Connolly? What about her? Or Mr Flynn, the English teacher?'

He frowns.'Hmmm, maybe,' he says, but doesn't sound convinced.

She urges him. 'You could get some leniency on your exams. Or at least extra time to get more down on paper. It's important, Danny, I know it doesn't feel like it's worth all the bother, but it really is.' She says it quietly, seriously. He nods in agreement, but doesn't meet her eye.

'OK then,' she claps her hands on her knees, 'let's look at it from a different angle. You know I think that whatever you want to do it's smart to get some good GCSEs first, BUT the most successful people

I've known in life had an interest built their careers around their interests. There are jobs to be found in every area. Film, gardening, the outdoors, books, cars... you just need to pinpoint what you like. What really floats your boat.' He is leaning down and scratching behind Sarah's ears whilst she snoozes, head on her paws. 'I like dogs,' he says instinctively.

'Well, there you are then! That's a start! Let's think about that. What could you do with dogs? You could get a job walking them for a start, I've heard that's big business these days. You could start with that.'

'Yeah! I have loads of time I could - '

She interrupts him. 'Not whilst you're supposed to be in school you can't!' she says sternly.

He laughs. 'Oh yeah... well, when I'm 16.'

'Yeah,' she mimics him, 'yeah that's true. Not long eh? How old are you now?'

'15 and a half - well, three quarters, nearly...' Helen laughs, and he finds himself laughing with her, despite not meaning to.

REMEMBERING

On the riverside, near Hammersmith Bridge

RHETT

There is no wind tonight. The trees are quiet and the river too. There isn't anything to distract him from his memories tonight. Rhett lays his head on his paws, and looks up at the moon, the familiar moon.

He thinks about Belgrade. It seems like a lifetime ago. After he'd escaped the shelter, whilst he'd been trying to think how to rescue Jessica, he'd stayed in the city, to be close to her. After a few weeks, when the certainty that she was gone had settled into his bones, he had run away. He'd run a whole country before he'd even dared to look back, at which point he'd stopped running and discovered train travel. He'll never tire of that feeling of getting on a train in one spot and exiting from it somewhere entirely different, the air full of exotic and intriguing smells.

In Belgrade, it had been almost more normal for dogs to live without humans than with. For those without their own humans there were plenty of them who would help you if you asked for it, but mainly, you lived on your wits, independent. Rhett thinks about the ladies who worked in the bakeries, he had liked them, most of them had gone out of their way to give all the stray dogs bread early in the morning, and last thing at night, when they were closing. Sometimes pastries too, with cheese or even meat in them. They gave you stomach ache, but it was worth it. Rhett's mouth waters, thinking about those pastries.

There had been a lot of violence out there, in Serbia, but a lot of warmth too, a lot of fun and spontaneity. Summers had been hot, oppressive and engulfing, with nothing to do but sleep and try not to die of heatstroke, the mosquitos next to the river had been as big as bees. Winters had been brutal, hard, glittering with snow. Many street dogs were taken pity on in the winter and got moved into the foyers of shared buildings at that time, or given warm, soupy meals by kind hearted humans. Rhett's mouth waters again. Some dogs simply froze, or died of infections, or got hit by cars and died of their injuries, unless they were lucky enough to get picked up by the many humans who found they couldn't bear not to help.

Here it's different, dogs have different problems. Rhett might go back one day, he thinks, he's a bit sick of London and of the fact that the dogs seem to be losing their dogginess here. He finds it odd that almost every dog you see on the street or in the park in London is attached - mentally, if not also physically (*if not carried!* he thinks) - to a human or humans. The dogness of dogs here feels somehow less, it feels as if they are becoming humanised, diluted somehow. He finds it a bit sinister.

Dogs shouldn't really have complexes except for those based around lack of shelter, security, food, should they? But it seems to Rhett like dogs are developing human traits these days - guilt, anxiety where there should be none. Fear also, and aggression. Rhett puts it down to the frustration of having to mould themselves to fit into human society. He can see that it must be hard to resist the effects of humankind's persistent anthropomorphising, to not to start to play the role that is expected, encouraged. He tuts, scornfully. *What's wrong with them all!* He doesn't want to become dependent or enmeshed, and will never attach himself to a human, or allow one to attach themself to him. Thinking of the Old Man though, he whines, softly. *He's different,* he tells himself. He had enjoyed sleeping next to him here, next to the river. He's only ever slept next to the Old Man, and to Jessica.

He does get lonely sometimes, even though he wouldn't ever admit it to the others. He wouldn't want to be so attached to a human but it does feel tempting sometimes, when you meet ones like Lottie and Sylvie, and Edward. Even Charles. Rhett sighs.

He looks up at the moon, and lets himself remember Jessica, even though it makes his heart hurt.

ALABAMA ROT

Kensington Gardens

BEAGLE

Beagle and a few of the other park gang dogs are lounging on the grass around the fallen tree. Audrey, Sylvie and Lottie are sitting on it having a good old chat, they often convene here. The park rangers have allowed the fallen tree to remain; they say it will encourage beetles to thrive, that there will soon be a colony there. Piper diligently listens and looks out for this imminent, important beetle colony, but she hasn't been able to smell or hear or see them yet.

'I've got some bad news guys.' Beagle says in a sad voice. 'I'm pretty certain I have Alabama Rot.'

Piper snorts and disguises it as a cough, and Rhett looks away to hide a smirk.

Beagle carries on, 'Yes, I caught it over there,' he says, gesturing to the wild, muddy area of the park that he has never ventured into, 'the other day. There's no cure.' He waits for a reaction, but as he gets none, continues. 'I'll die a horrible, painful death, and the vet won't be able to do a thing.' He looks around for the smallest sign of engagement, of encouragement. But even Rolf who is usually quite easy-going and tolerant exudes an air of impatience. He exchanges a glance with Rhett and as if by tacit agreement they race off to have a game, tearing around after each other. Beagle's sure he catches the words 'monologue of gloom' in Rolf's head as he moves away. Rolf had tried to hide his thoughts, but unsuccessfully.

Lily and Lexi murmur sympathetic, wordless sounds, but even they seem to be quite non-committal, and Beagle has the impression that they are only listening with half an ear each. He feels like stamping his paws on the ground to get their attention. 'My kidneys will shut down and I'll get sores all over my body. And in my mouth. I'll die in agony. Actually, Audrey will probably have to put me out of my misery with a lethal injection.'

Beagle is incredulous that no one is responding. Piper looks bored, she is busying herself gnawing at a stick and zoning out. Luke is absorbed in licking some mud off his privates and doesn't appear to have even heard what Beagle has said. Lily has flopped onto her side, and dozes in the sunshine. Lexi is watching Rolf and Rhett, shouting encouragement. Beagle isn't sure what he expects them to say in response to his grave news, but he feels that it really demands more attention that it is being given. He tries to find the sore on his leg that he had found last night in order to show them, but realises to his annoyance that he can't locate it.

A FEELING OF FOREBODING

At Lottie and Piper's home

PIPER

It's the day before the anniversary of Sebastian's disappearance, Piper recognises it from last year. Lottie is especially jangly. She feels to Piper spiky and unpredictable, she even smells strange - sour, somehow - and she is prone to fits of bursting into tears. When they had walked in the park earlier, Lottie had put her head down and stuck to the area within the cover of trees, avoiding even Sylvie and Edward, both of whom had passed within 100 metres of them. Sylvie had looked for her, having spotted Piper who had run across to greet her and Lexi, but Lottie had purposely stayed out of sight. Piper hears her now on the phone to her parents, answering their questions in a fake, light voice. When she puts the phone down she heaves a massive sigh and bursts into tears, hiding her face in her hands. She is sitting on the floor with her back to the sofa. Piper snuggles her body into Lottie's as hard as she can and licks at her hands and her face furiously, trying to help. Lottie just pushes her away though, half-heartedly; she is not in a good way.

That night - the whole night - Lottie doesn't sleep, so Piper tosses and turns with her, and pads after her when she goes into the living room to watch TV. Lottie seems strangely unaware of her, unusually detached.

Piper, worried, sits by the settee, hovering her left paw up in the air uncertainly. She lick her lips and whine, softly. Getting no reaction,

Piper hops up and lays on the settee beside Lottie, not knowing how to help. When Lottie gets up and goes back to bed Piper gets up too and follows her. Piper senses that Lottie is very fragile.

LOTTIE

Lottie feels Piper nosing at the duvet so she lifts it and Piper gets in. Piper has started doing this lately. She has always slept on the bed on and off, but now, she actually gets into the bed. Lottie had thought it strange at first, but she doesn't any more. As Lottie knows will happen, Piper throws herself into the curve of her body, pushing herself in as close as possible. Lottie shifts slightly to accommodate her and settles into a restless doze, her hand on Piper's fur. It's comforting. She doesn't know how she would have been able to survive the grief of losing Sebastian without her compact, joyful little side-kick. Sometimes she imagines that Lottie is part of her, the good part, the core, where the life is. She feels herself to be a dried out husk. She wishes she could lose herself, disappear somehow and just Piper remain. So to remain, but inside Piper somehow, for them to be one; she doesn't feel enough to be whole on her own any more, it's as if Sebastian has taken some of her with him.

PIPER

In the morning, after a cup of tea but nothing to eat, Lottie clips Piper's lead on. They go out but not to the park, just around the streets, and as soon as Piper has finished doing her business Lottie leads her straight back home. She doesn't say a jaunty, cheerful hello to any humans that they pass, as she usually would, let alone stop to chit-chat. At home, Lottie perches for a few minutes on the edge of the settee, with her head in her hands, then gets up and leaves the apartment, stroking Piper sadly, thoughtfully. She says 'Bye, Piper darling, see you later,' and kisses her three times on the forehead as usual, but doesn't look her in the eyes before exiting. Piper feels uneasy.

That evening

When Lottie comes back it is late in the evening and she immediately gets out Piper's lead. Despite the black atmosphere that Lottie brings with her Piper jumps about happily as Lottie clips it on, wiping the tears from her face. Piper wonders how she has any tears left, after how much she'd cried last night. 'Let's go, Pipes,' says Lottie quietly, sadly.

Down the stairs they go, out of the front door, Piper waiting patiently as Lottie double-locks it behind them. Lottie looks left and right down the street, up at the moon, and down at Piper. She seems distracted and she can't seem to even decide in which direction to walk. Knowing that movement will help her - it always does if one is feeling unsure or nervous, they had discussed it in the park the other day - Piper pulls her. Left, down towards Olympia. It is a decision that will change the trajectory of their lives, or at least that of the next week.

AN ARGUMENT

Kensington Gardens (near the bandstand)

RHETT

Rhett loves days like this, windy and cool but with a warmth in the sun that can warm your body up nicely if you lie in a sheltered spot. He feels the sun to be healing, as he does the moon and the forest, and the very earth itself. The feeling of soil or grass beneath his feet pleases him. As he roams the streets, he notices grass growing in the cracks in the concrete, against the odds, and takes heart in seeing it. Most man-made things don't feel healthy, Rhett thinks. He despairs of humans, with all their electronics and their plastic gadgets - they even drink from them, which he finds disgusting. Rhett drinks directly from the earth, from the rivers, from the puddles, the little brooks that no one notices any more but that still tinkle and have life in them. He shudders thinking about the stagnant pool from which his best friend Jessica had chosen to drink her death. Planting his four feet firmly on the floor he shakes his whole body and head vigorously, trying to rid himself of the painful memories which always dwell too close.

Sylvie is lying on a blanket in the dappled sunshine, reading a book. She doesn't seem in any rush to leave. Lexi and Rhett have covered several topics already, and are now getting into a heavy one.

'But don't you think,' says Rhett, panting a little, 'that sometimes, in some situations, for some dogs, it's just preferable to put an end to it all?'

'Suicide, you mean, Rhett?' Lexi twitches a little, involuntarily, as she says the word. She has used the word expressly as she can't be doing with euphemisms, but it has still made her flinch. 'Nope, I don't. There's always hope.' She says it somewhat tartly, an unusual tone of voice for Lexi.

Rhett reacts before she has even finished the word *hope* with a growling, angry sound that comes straight from the core of him and manages to express without the use of words exactly what he feels: he thinks what she has said is ludicrous, naïve and offensive. Sylvie looks up from her book, surprised. He shakes his head around, looking for all the world like he has a wasp stuck in it. He doesn't want to be rude, but he can't help shouting, and physically getting in Lexi's face a little, swiping his head against hers and connecting with a bump.

Sylvie has laid her book down in her lap and is watching this interaction between her Lexi and Doggy Dog, intrigued.

'What do you know about it?' Rhett shouts, 'You who's always lived…' he swipes his head around at the park, 'here! With her!' he gestures at Sylvie, crossly. Sylvie is exactly the type of owner he would have chosen for Jessica and he feels sadness filling his head. *It isn't fair!* The words of that poem - he doesn't even know how he knows it - run on a loop in his head:

Every morn and every night, some are born to sweet delight.

Some are born to sweet delight, some are born to endless night.

It isn't fair. It isn't fair, Rhett thinks. It isn't fair.

Lexi remains neutral. She isn't phased by the head bump, or the shouting, she understands that Rhett is struggling with an issue close to his heart and thinks that it is good they are talking it through. And she knows what Rhett means, she *is* privileged and entitled. She is probably amongst the luckiest one percent of canines across the planet.

Lexi waits, still. Out of respect for Rhett and what he's been through, what he's seen, she tries to resist using words this time until she has fully thought them through. She seeks his gaze but is careful to stay mute until he stops huffing and puffing. She knows that there is more to Rhett's background than he is letting on and forgives him any lack of manners. Some dogs are anyway over-sensitive about body contact, Rhett's head bump had been little more to her than a human giving another human a shove, and the little ones – particularly before they get the grasp of words - do it all the time. It's natural, instinctive.

Lexi wants to show Rhett that she is sorry for upsetting him, that she apologises for her thoughtlessness, and approaches him gently. She licks his muzzle, twice. He lets her.

She sits down, gently, her movements purposefully soft and placatory. 'I just like to think that there's always hope, Rhett,' Lexi says, carefully, 'what can I say. Maybe you're right. I just don't think I could do it, however miserable I was. I think I'd always have hope that my situation would change. But then I guess I've always had a coddled and fear-free life. If I had a different history I'd probably feel differently. But don't we have like – an instinct for survival? Wouldn't that be stronger than anything else?'

'Mmmph! It's just,' Rhett says gruffly, 'sometimes dogs have such awful lives that it's unbearable.' He turns away, not wanting her to see his eyes. 'If you'd seen some of the things... it's not... it's not like this everywhere Lexi,' again Rhett gestures to the expanse of the park, its green goodness emanating a happy, peaceful atmosphere as if to prove his point. He shakes his head and lays it down on his paws, sadly. He thinks of Jessica. He has been ruffled by Lexi's words. Of course the idea is abhorrent, if you think about it logically. He does still think that drinking from the Rank Pool had probably been the right choice for his friend Jessica – the camp was no place for an old dog without a best friend and Jessica had been getting on in years - but it will haunt him forever.

Rhett doesn't really believe in the afterlife but he tries desperately to, tries to picture Jessica running free somewhere, being showered with treats and comforts and love, playing all day long with other dogs and all the right type of humans.

Sylvie, satisfied that the dogs have resolved whatever disagreement Lexi and Doggy Dog had had and that peace once again reigns, returns her eyes to her book.

ESCAPE III

Uxbridge Road, near Shepherd's Bush tube station

GREY

On the street again, Grey starts running. He feels Irene and the two other shop girls watching him. It's like a warm glow of protection and he's sorry when he no longer feels it. He hears the shriek of brakes and turns his head sharply towards the source. He locks eyes through the windscreen with the eyes of a human who looks like she finds the Shepherd's Bush roundabout a trauma at the best of times. Grey sends over his apologies, feeling an empathy with her; she looks as frightened as he feels. Without knowing it, as if he has a homing chip implanted in him, he has somehow crossed to the East, onto Holland Park Avenue. He hurries, a fast trot now, nails clipping the pavement in a regular rhythm up the gentle incline of the pavement. He continues past a pub with tables outside, past a place smelling of pizzas, past a butchers, a deli, a bookshop, past the dark mouth of the tube, on and on, crosses the road during a lull in the traffic, up and up, until he passes the entrance to a car park and hits the western end of Kensington Gardens, at which point he cuts a right, and slips between the railings easily.

Slowing to a gentler trot and then a walk, his body cools rapidly but the adrenalin in him keeps pumping. It is still daytime, the park is open although it won't be for long and there are people milling about. He sees no one he knows, except Neil and Nero over on the space beyond the main path, but he doesn't feel inclined to approach them; he's scared of Nero and that glazed look he gets. It strikes Grey that he doesn't feel nervous now. He is usually on the lead when he sees him, that's the difference, he thinks. Grey feels a spark of mischief. He could run past Nero, tease him, see how fast he can run. He knows he can outrun him! The flare of the idea dies out quickly though, why on earth would he want to provoke Nero? He sits down, one paw suspended in the air, and watches the pair curiously. As he watches, it dawns on him that Nero wouldn't be allowed to chase anyway; his owner would just call him and he'd go slinking back at the first sound of his name.

It occurs to him now that maybe Nero is as miserable with his owner as he'd been with Lady Human. Musing on this, he continues to watch, his head cocked on one side. Nero doesn't look happy it's true, he doesn't feel happy. Grey realises, with a jolt of surprise as he tunes into Nero's energy, that Nero is scared. He is able to see it now, observing him coolly, calmly, from a distance, stationary and not scared himself. He's never done that before, it throws a totally different light on things.

He keeps watching, glad of something to do, glad for this link with someone who is at least vaguely familiar.

He thinks about Lexi, how soothing he finds her presence, how sensible and wise she always is, just like this shop lady. He longs to see her, or Siobhan, or one of the others. Even just something familiar would do, like his cage in the hallway at Lady Human's house – although far from cosy it had still been a comfort of sorts. Out here... He isn't sure if he is made right for Rhett's sort of adventure. Maybe he can track down Siobhan and go and live with her. She'd been talking only the other day about pet-friendly rental agencies, she wants to get a cat. Well, he isn't much bigger than a cat, is he? Certainly not that fierce, universally feared Bengal one that allegedly terrorises Brook Green and has been made famous on local social media chat groups. The one Siobhan laughs about and says she wants to meet and shake the paw of as it sounds like a right character.

He thinks he might be beginning to understand what Rhett means about the effect that humans can have on their dogs and the power they have over their lives. He watches a few other couples and family groups, observing particularly the interaction (or lack of) between the canines and the humans. *Interesting,* he thinks to himself, *interesting,* and almost forgets his predicament.

A NIGHT IN THE PARK (A SKINNY GREY DOG)

Somewhere in Kensington Gardens

GREY

He feels that night is coming. The shadows are lengthening, the air is cooling. The park emptied a while ago and the birds have stopped calling to one another, every last one. He curls up, cold and miserable.

He is feeling lost. Although his human, Lady Human, is mean, she has dictated his little life thus far and he feels adrift without her. He doesn't know where else to go, and he supposes that this hollow, at the base of this tree, is as good a place as any. Grey looks around, wide-eyed, pivoting his skinny, newly-naked neck nervously. He is trying to get familiarised with the dark; he's not used to it, not outdoors at least. The wind is still howling through the trees, and the space... so much space! He feels it, even if he can't see it. Now he understands what the tiny little sausage dog Paquita - one of the park gang dogs - had meant, all that space above and all around terrifies him. It's disconcerting and makes him feel exposed, vulnerable and powerless.

In the failing light he can't see much, so he strains his ears to compensate. There are sounds of rats, mice, worms, foxes, murmuring to themselves or one other as they scurry, patter, wriggle and trot past. He thinks he can understand something of what they say, snatches of their words, although he's not sure if he's imagining that. It's been a long day.

Grey has never felt more alone or more scared in his life and longs to see one of his friends. Lexi, ideally, or Rhett - but Piper or even

Rolf would do. Just a familiar face, a familiar smell. Little things are burrowing into his fur, biting here and there. It unnerves him. The minutes pass and as they do, Grey becomes more accustomed to the new sensations. Aware that he can't stay as tensed up as he is indefinitely, he makes a conscious effort to relax his frame. It is a trick Rhett had taught him once, when Grey had asked him how he was able to be so brave.

'Fake it 'til you make it, Grey!' Rhett had told him, laughing.

Grey muses on his situation. He thinks about Rhett and what he would do. He feels emboldened, thinking of his friend, and valiantly gives himself a little pep talk. It's cold, but not that cold. Grey has heard humans say how awful it is to have to sleep outside, but it can't be that bad really. *There must be worse things than sleeping outside!* he thinks. *Boredom and living with a mean owner,* he thinks, *that really gets you down.* He calls to mind all the things he doesn't like about his life with Lady Human, all the things he doesn't like about her; he feels that it is a positive thing to do, under the circumstances. Eventually, the tiredness of the day gets to him. His eyelids droop and he dozes off.

The next morning

Grey awakes with a start from his dreams, which involved conversations with moles and foxes. He is shocked that he has slept through the whole night out here, exposed; at home he wakes often in the night, his mind racing. He looks around, and sees for the very first time the beauty of the dawn, the soft pink blush of it. The park, calm and peaceful, feels benevolent. It is quiet, devoid of people, the gates still locked shut. He hadn't realised before how much noise comes from humans and the persistent hum of their electronics. Without it, the park feels as if it is holding its breath. The dew makes everything sparkle. The smell of the grass is sweet and fresh and as he sniffs, Grey is overcome with emotion. He feels the weight and beauty of the world, the vastness of it, the sense of possibility and an intense feeling of joy, of love and of exquisite suffering.

Gathering his courage he stands up, thinking to get moving, but then sits back down, unsure. He has a scratch and thinks how lovely it is, not to have that damned thing around his neck. He feels gloriously naked. His leg aches, where he had hit the railings yesterday, but it isn't too bad. He stretches his body out, tentatively, placing weight on each leg in turn and checking that everything is OK. He ascertains that although his leg is bruised, there is nothing broken. His ear, though, there's a metallic smell wafting from it, and it feels strange, as if it's the wrong shape. It makes a funny flapping sound when he moves. He stretches, yawns, and then, uncharacteristically, jumps around a bit, like a spring lamb. He does it not only to warm himself up but also for the sheer joy of it, it feels instinctive. The grass is soft and damp under his feet. He feels a bit guilty, Lady Human hadn't liked him to 'leap around like a lunatic', so he's conditioned himself not to. He does it again a couple of times in defiance of her and feels rebellious and proud.

Grey wishes he could see Rhett to tell him how brave he's been. He gives himself a big shake, noting the lack of noise that his collar and tag would have made, and is surprised to feel invigorated. To think how terrified he'd been last night at the prospect of sleeping outside! Giving the ground a last little sniff, in homage to it keeping him safe through the night, he trots on across the park in the direction of the Round Pond. He is light on his feet and it only takes him a few seconds to hit his pace. He is hungry now, and thinks that he might find some food there - he's often noticed humans in groups or alone sitting and eating there during the day, whilst he's been dragged past by his dog walker.

A couple of crows sitting on a branch watch him, idly.

'Unusual to see a dog on its own here, in London,' remarks one.

'Yes. It must have lost its human,' replies the other.

'Hope it'll be OK,' says the first, 'they seem to be so dependent these days.'

Grey hears crows cawing. Perhaps they are hungry too, he thinks. Although he gets the sense somehow from the tone of the exchange that they are talking about something more sophisticated. He wonders if he really had understood the other creatures last night, and, if he had, shouldn't he be able to understand the birds, too?

Things look as well as smell different this morning from last night. Grey has only been in the park during its opening hours before and it feels magical to him now, so peaceful and still. A squirrel appears, suddenly, and darts past him, close enough that he feels the brush of its tail. It is followed by another, chattering manically. They sound frightened, their tails are flicking nervously and he hears their words:

'They're coming! Quick!'

'Get to safety, tell the others!'

'Have you seen little Peter?'

Grey doesn't know for certain, but they have heard rumours - about a morning culling that happens before the park gates are opened each day. Grey watches them as they shoot up the tree trunks out of sight. He pauses, one paw suspended mid-step, as more twitchy beings scurry and scamper erratically past him. Then peace resumes, and he carries on, placing his feet more delicately now, thoughtful. He wonders whether he really did hear the squirrels talking or if perhaps, he had imagined it again just.

He walks another ten metres or so, slowing down as he realises he doesn't really have a plan, except to find some breakfast, and now he doesn't even feel that hungry any more; the knot in his stomach is caused more by worry. The initial adrenalin of waking up free has worn off, and he feels deflated. He sits for a few seconds, uncertain, then steps his front paws out inch by inch in turn until he is laying down on the ground, but straight out like a sphinx - he doesn't feel relaxed enough to flop over onto one haunch. He crosses his paws and lays his head lightly down on the top one. Only his eyes move, crescents of white showing as they swivel this way and that. He is poised to bolt, to run like the wind, should it become necessary. His heart races and he can't quite catch his breath.

Grey's right flank thuds. It hurts even though there is no wound.

He looks at the big shape which he'd sheltered close to last night. Shrieking children climb up and run and jump around it in the daytime. His dog walker sometimes meets people near here, just outside the gates, they pass things back and forth, he's not sure what.

Something at the top of the big shape is flapping in the wind. Waves of fear wash over him as he watches it, distrustfully, but he begins to trust that the flapping thing isn't going to do anything more unpredictable or worrying than that. He lays his head down on his crossed paws again and tries to think over what Rhett had said to him, about escaping.

The bottom falls out of his stomach as he realises the terrible mistake he's made. His head shoots up and his eyes widen with panic.

ABDUCTION

Holland Park Avenue

GREY

Grey exits the park, Rhett's words thundering in his head. 'If you ever escape from her you'll have to be very careful never to go back to any of the places you've been with her before!' he'd said. Grey can't believe he's been stupid enough to forget. He fast-trots along the pavement, anxious, blood rushing about in his head. He is oblivious to the car coming up behind him, slowing to a crawl, so absorbed is he in his thoughts about where to go, the mistake he's made, and how to rectify it. He is loathe to head into completely unfamiliar streets, that's the problem, he longs in this moment only for the familiar. Grey suddenly becomes aware of a large human presence behind him. He cries out, but before he can galvanise his feet to break into a run he feels himself lifted up into the air by two strong arms. Another pair of arms help bundle him up into some sacking material. The smell is strong, sharp, malevolent, frightening. Woodsmoke and a sweet, cloying, floral sub-scent, as well as male, stale sweat. The woodsmoke smell is on both, cigarette smoke too on a female, and something chemical as well, something that hurts the inside of his throat and makes him want to stop breathing in. The first pair of arms hold him now alone, vice-like, and he hears the click of a car boot. He knows that noise even though it is slightly different from Lady Human's car boot. He hears muffled voices.

'Nooooooo!' he cries out in his head, frustrated and angry that he has been so stupid. He feels himself being thrown onto a surface, not as hard as the pavement but hard just the same. His bruised leg hurts as it makes contact but although he registers that it is painful, he barely cares. He struggles to get to his feet, he knows that these moments are critical, that they are his best chance of escape. Wrenching his head around desperately trying to find his way out of the sacking, he feels the thud of the boot slam shut. Sensing the space above him close in he is aware of the limited amount of air, and the darkness, like last night, freaks him out. It is all too much, particularly after yesterday's high drama and his night outdoors. His heart beats like fury, all he can hear is the hammering of it in his chest.

The engine starts up. They are moving. He thinks he is going to have a heart attack. *Chickens die of fright, don't they.* They'd talked about it once, in the park, the humans, he'd heard them, he remembers thinking that it was a curious conversation. *Can dogs?*

IN SHOCK

Kensington Gardens

LOTTIE

Lottie is beside herself. She is bereft, and incredulous. The fact that Piper isn't there is affecting her physically as well as emotionally. There's a sickening, dull, constant ache in her stomach, an itching, crawling sensation all over her skin, a pounding and gushing in her head. Her extremities feel frozen. She feels like her soul has been cut out. The not knowing where Piper is, the anxiety of wondering if she is safe – or even alive - manifests as a physical pain. It reminds her-no, she can't let herself think about that. This is a time for action, not for slipping away as she had then, when there hadn't been anything she could do. She has had 500 posters printed with a happy smiling picture of Piper, some contact details, and REWARD FOR RETURN! Some people have advised her against that (it encourages dog-napping, they say) but Lottie is too desperate right now to care about how she gets her Piper back, just as long as she does. She's kicking herself for not putting a bandana on her this morning. Piper usually wears one but she'd rolled in fox poo yesterday so Lottie had taken the whole thing off and replaced it with a spare, plain collar. A bandana would have made her more noticeable. If she gets her back she vows to kit her out in the most garish bandana she can find, every single day.

In putting up posters, Lottie is relieved to at least have something to occupy her. She stops at every other tree, careful to face the posters in different directions, roughly at eye level, winding the end of the tape round and round. She doesn't know how long they'll need to last so she winds round each whole tree twice, top and bottom, then with the clear wide tape round (twice again around the tree) in the middle of the poster. It has become a sort of obsessive habit to touch her hand to Piper's face three times as she leaves each poster, willing it – the poster, and Piper herself - luck. She prays as she walks, even though she had last prayed as a child. 'Please God, bring her back safe. Please God, bring her back safe. Please God, bring her back safe.' She now understands why the adverb fervently is so often linked with the word prayer.

In her distraction, Lottie almost walks past Edward.

'Lottie!'

She looks up.

'Edward,' she replies, flatly.

Edward looks around for Piper. He reads the poster Lottie has just put up.

'Oh my dear.' Edward sounds baffled, thrown.

'Oh that's just rotten, poppet, really rotten!' He screws up his face into a pained expression that she's not seen before. He's usually so unruffled.

'Have you eaten?' he asks, suddenly and energetically. It seems such an incongruous question.

Lottie puts her head on one side, thinking with a stab of distress that this is a habit she's picked up from Piper. She realises that she hasn't, not for a while, not since yesterday evening in fact, when they'd taken Piper, grabbed her lead and hoicked her up in the air and thrown her into a van, pushing Lottie over and driving off almost before she could scramble to her feet.

'Errrr - no, no I haven't actually,' she says.

'Oh good, GOOD!' he beams, inappropriately pleased.

'I'm going to get you something then, from the caff!' You can tell he has children, Lottie always thinks, from his language.

'Bacon butty alright? I'm quite partial to them myself,' he says with a twinkle in his eye and a wink which she almost misses seeing. She has an urge to hug him. She nods and tears prick at her itchy eyes. 'Thanks, Edward,' she says.

Lottie sits on a bench, head in her hands. She has a splitting headache. She didn't sleep at all last night, she had been making up the posters, working out what to do on the internet, where to log her 'lost/stolen pet', writing up the incident, not that there is much to say. She had also messaged people cancelling today's appointments. Her clients will for the most part as well as being upset for her, be annoyed; most people who pay for her one-to-ones in Kensington Gardens are of a certain type and although largely lovely, they are used to getting exactly what they want, when they want it. But Lottie can't waste any headspace on thinking about the business she might lose. She runs through in her head the people she knows from the park, thinks who could be of help. Funnily enough, even though she regards many of them as friends, she has no way of contacting most of them. It hasn't been necessary. She sees them more than her non-park friends already, without the need for formal arrangements. She has Aude's number, and Sylvie's, as well as Charles's. She must contact them, at least. She takes out her phone, snaps a photo of the poster and types a quick message. She sends it to each of them in turn.

Lottie hasn't told her parents yet. She can't bear them to be anxious too, about Piper or about her; she can't carry that burden too. Piper had always stayed there when Lottie and Sebastian had needed to travel somewhere and they are very fond of her. She can't face worrying about them worrying too, it would be too much. Tears threaten to spill out again when she thinks about how kind and lovely her parents are, how supportive they had been when... How worried they would be... *No,* she thinks to herself firmly, and musters all her strength to shake off her tearful mood as Edward approaches, smiling, handing her a bacon roll in a napkin. He reminds her of her Dad. She would love to see her Dad right now, to get a little strength-giving hug from him.

'Oh – thanks – thank you Edward – I really am hungry.'

He beams.

And as she says it, she realises how ravenous she actually is and starts to wolf down the bacon bap gratefully.

Twenty minutes later

'Oh darling...'

Sylvie is striding towards her; she has followed the trail of posters Lottie has left in her wake. *Unusually early for her!* Lottie registers, despite her agitated state of mind.

'What happened?' she asks.

Lottie tries to talk but the look of pure sympathy and compassion in her friend's face is too much and sobs heave up in her. Sylvie walks with her to the next tree where Lottie repeats the actions, well-rehearsed now, of taping the poster onto the tree. Lexi follows them, discreetly, worried. She feels that something is very wrong. She feels that Piper is nowhere near, and Lottie smells funny.

'They took her!' Lottie says, with a strangled gulp. Sylvie is the first person except for the police and Edward that she has told. She has never seen Sylvie pale before now.

Lottie's face feels dirty and her mouth horrible, she hasn't cleaned her teeth since yesterday. Her skin is hot, as if she has a fever. She puts the pile of posters and tape on the ground and rubs her face and eyes with both hands, roughly. She adjusts her rucksack and bends down to pick up the posters and the tape. Sylvie follows her, frowning, and waits for more. It is disconcerting seeing Lottie without Piper, she's never seen one without the other.

'They took her! They just grabbed her and pushed me over and before I knew it they were gone. It was a transit van. Lottie feels the panic rising when she remembers Piper's excited looking face looking back at her. Piper had pulled back when they had tried to drag her into the van but one of the men had just scooped her up and thrown her in. Lottie had seen him flinch backwards a second later, perhaps Piper had bitten him. That would be a very Piper thing to do, under the circumstances.

'Oh Lottie, darling.' Sylvie says sadly. Lexi approaches Lottie and snuffles at her hand. Lottie crouches down and strokes her, brings her forehead down and rests it on the top of Lexi's broad head for a few seconds, breathing her in. But she has a different smell from Piper and although comforting, it also feels wrong. 'I can't believe I was such an idiot!' she says in a choked voice. Sylvie rubs the top of her back, firmly.

'There there,' she says, soothingly.

Lottie can't bear thinking about where Piper is now, yet she finds she can't stop. She imagines her being used as a bait dog, or locked in a small, grotty cage. She feels like howling with impotence. She feels like punching something, or smashing her forehead against the tree. A flood of sobs threatens to breaks out inside her and she makes a strangled noise, then hiccups, loudly, exhaustedly. She rubs her hot, grubby-feeling face again.

'I went to the Police but they said there's nothing they can do. They logged it onto the system but they said they don't really have the resources to follow up. I talked to that policeman at Holland Park, you know the nice one? And he promised he'd keep an ear out, but... There's so much of it going on these days, apparently. I've put her on Doglost.' Again the tears threaten to spill out. '...and I've posted everywhere I can on Facebook. But,' she stammers, 'it doesn't look good as I know she was stolen, she's not just lost. They either stole her to use as a bait dog, or to breed from. They wouldn't know she was spayed as we had it done laparoscopically, there's no scar...' Lottie is as white as a sheet now.

Sylvie smiles at her, reassuringly, 'Ah come on now! You think they would be able to use Piper as a bait dog? Everyone loves Piper, you know how she is, remember we call her Magic Dog! She bewitches everyone, even the most aggressive dogs. Remember that one last week? The one the man warned us about but she had him rolling around on his back like a puppy playing? Ah? No one will harm her, for sure,' Sylvie says decisively, 'she would have them licking her ears for kicks, not biting at her, you know her! She's too smart, our Piper, you know that!' Lottie feels Sylvie's eyes drilling into her and willing her to be positive. She watches a small ant on the path.

Lottie feels that Sylvie believes what she is saying. 'No, no, no - it is not that.' Lottie thinks that Sylvie sounds like Poirot and feels a small smile somewhere in her mind. She will tell Sylvie later on, she thinks, when all this is over, and it will make her roar with laughter. If they find Piper. She can't imagine life – anything – if they don't.

'Please,' Sylvie says gently, putting her hand on Lottie's arm, 'don't worry huh? Is for selling, for sure, she's a pretty dog - looks cute, neat, just the type. No,' she says firmly, 'they try to sell 'er. She looks young, no?'

'She's two years seven months, but she does look young doesn't she, maybe they think she's younger, a Standard Poodle puppy?'

'Yes, could be.' Sylvie says and falls silent for a few moments, thinking.

'Now, we have to be really clever about how to find her, and quickly. Let's sit down and have a coffee and think, ah?'

'No, no, no - I have to put these up.' Lottie says defensively, waving her pile of posters and sounding simultaneously panicked and firm. Lottie doesn't want to sit down for a coffee, she won't sit down for a coffee, not for a hundred years, not for a thousand. She won't rest, she resolves, until she finds her Piper. And then she won't let her out of her sight.

'Of course, darling,' Sylvie knows better than to try to stop her, 'you keep going, I bring a coffee to you, we – how you say it, walk and talk, huh?' Sylvie smiles warmly, and Lottie is grateful for her presence, out of all her park and non-park friends. It calms Lottie a little, and she feels for the first time that there may be a glimmer of hope.

Money is what they'll be after, she thinks. Well, they can have all of hers, just as long as they give Piper back. There must be a way. She heads over to the next tree. 'See you shortly.' Sylvie calls after her. Lottie nods, distractedly. Sylvie and Lexi exchange worried looks. Lexi stays with Lottie as Sylvie heads over to the coffee hut.

RHETT'S GUILT

Kensington Gardens

RHETT

Lexi is an idealist, Rhett thinks, she believes that kindness begets kindness and that one simply has to educate people, or dogs, as appropriate, or appeal to their better nature. Rhett, conversely, is a realist.

When he'd by chance come across one of the Feeder Humans a couple of days after his escape from the vets, he had attacked him and let his rage fly. Had anyone been there to bear witness they would have thought Rhett a rogue, aggressive dog as the attack had been entirely unprovoked. It had been no more than what the man had deserved though, to be bitten on the arm and then chased, all the way along that country lane. He had been cruel, peed on their dog houses for fun and done a lot worse things than that too. No, Rhett thinks, giving himself a thorough shake all over, he doesn't regret for one second what he'd done, unpleasant though it had been. He hadn't liked the taste of blood in his mouth, and he sometimes dreams of it, curled up in his hideout amongst the leaves, whimpering and barking, waking himself up with his own voice. But he doesn't regret it.

Despite this, something has made Rhett stop short of telling Lexi about it. They discuss all sorts of things at length but she has peculiar views about things and has led a sheltered life, it would be hard for her to understand the level of badness of that Feeder Human and Rhett doesn't want her to think ill of him.

When they had first seen Lady Human scouring the park, screaming for Grey, a stone had settled in Rhett's stomach. He has looked everywhere, he hasn't stopped looking, but he hasn't been able to find their friend. Everyone he asks says the same, that they haven't seen the skinny grey dog for a couple of days, maybe three.

Rhett knows how much Grey looks up to him and he feels dreadful. Lexi blames him as much as he blames himself, he can tell, she can barely look at him whenever she sees him she's so cross. He's never even seen her really cross before, even that time when they'd defended Beagle during the attack by the Miniature Pinschers. He sees her now, near the horse statue in the park, and she finally breaks her silence. Rhett finds that he feels strangely relieved, like when a storm that is brewing finally hits.

'You encouraged Grey to run away, Rhett!' Lexi says, exploding 'you with all your talk of Cusco and how all dogs should be free and blah blah blah!' She bumps his head with hers. He steps back.

Sylvie watches, bemused. She's seen Lexi and Doggy Dog argue before but this seems to be instigated by Lexi who is generally so mild mannered. Last time it had appeared to be Doggy Dog who had been provoking her, Sylvie remembers.

Hanging his head, he stays silent, and by his apologetic stance accepts the blame she has apportioned him. He shouldn't have said all that to Grey, he thinks, he should have got off his soapbox, not riled Grey up so much. The sad fact is that a lot of dogs these days need protection. For all the frugality and coldness of Lady Human, she had provided Grey with shelter and safety. Rhett feels like bashing his head against a tree. What if they never find Grey? he thinks, and shivers. He feels chilled to the bone and for the first time in his life longs to have someone who could soothe him, tell him what he should do. Grey isn't cut out to be on the run on his own. Rhett is terrified they won't find him in time.

'I know, Lexi, I know,' he says sadly.

'What's up, Doggy Dog?' asks Sylvie who notices that he doesn't seem himself. He ignores her and moves on, away from them.

'I'm sorry, Lexi, really I am. I'll keep looking.'

He trots off slowly, sadly, to do another round of Kensington Gardens, Holland Park, Brook Green and all the places in between that he's ever seen Grey.

That evening, after dark

Sarah has been under Rhett's care for some time. He had discovered back in the camp, quite by chance, that he has what is termed by some as the *healer gene*. What Sarah has he can't heal, only stall. That's all she wants though, she says, that's all she needs. It is very human of her, Rhett thinks, to need just a little more time to make things right, just a little more time to sort things out. That's another reason he doesn't want to get too involved with humans, they get themselves in such a muddle over everything, make such a mess of things - you can feel it tangling them up inside and somehow their dogs get sucked into it all.

Most evenings, at some point, Sarah goes to lay by the back door. Helen assumes it is because of the coolness of the floor there, the slight draft. She would be surprised to see the big brown dog from the park lying mirrored on the other side, leaning against the door, still, seemingly focused on a certain spot in the air in front of him, as if he is in a trance.

The neighbour in the flat upstairs next door often wonders why that long-legged brown looking dog comes so frequently, lays down there for a while, and then leaves again, all for no apparent reason. He doesn't ask Helen though. He isn't one to talk to his neighbours. Rhett looks up at him now and the man could swear that the dog is trying to talk to him, but he quickly draws the curtains in a panic. He is very easily embarrassed, and any potential interaction, even with a canine, causes him distress. He would be diagnosed with agoraphobia as well as borderline personality disorder, were he able to face the waiting room of the doctor's surgery. Ironic, really. He ought to call a helpline but even that is too much for him, he only just about manages to speak to the Waitrose delivery man on the intercom.

CAPTIVE

Under the Westway

GREY

The cage Grey is in is vile, it reeks of fear as well as dirt, other dogs have been in here before him. He can smell some kind of acrid smoke, horses and sewage; the stench of the whole place fills his nostrils. He never thought he'd yearn for his too-clean dog bed or the pristine floors of his former home. That already seems like a lifetime ago. Here is terrifying, much more so than being at home alone with Lady Human when she was cross. He is angry with himself for having let himself be trapped, and disappointed he has been such an idiot. He feels sick thinking about Rhett finding out what has happened to him, how stupid he has been.

Grey is just turning around and around and curling himself into as small a ball as possible when he hears the humans coming in, the ones who had picked him up off the street. He cowers and faces the wall, praying for them to leave without touching him. He hears bumping and cursing from them, it sounds like they are carrying something. The surface his cage is on vibrates as a heavy object is thumped down onto it. The humans leave. Quiet descends.

Wait! He can hear breathing! There is someone in the cage next door, he thinks. Grey can't see as there is some tarpaulin between them, but he can feel a presence, which he thinks is canine, and somehow, that is comforting. It gives him courage, even though really, it could be anyone. It could be Nero. He clears his throat before he loses his nerve and nudges at the side of the cage with his muzzle. He senses the presence cock its ears up, alert.

'Ahem, errrmmm, hello?' says Grey, his voice sounding thin and sticking in his throat a little from lack of use.

'Hello!' comes a silky, feminine, young voice. He didn't expect that, but he's relieved. The voice makes him think of a King Charles Spaniel. He feels he ought to take the initiative in the conversation, since he started it, but finds that he can't really think of what to say. In the end it is she that goes first. Before she speaks though, she yawns, delicately, for effect, he senses. Almost languidly, drawing out the first word, she asks, 'So, how did they get you?'

He thinks, then replies. 'I don't know, I didn't see them coming. The last thing I remember I was running along the pavement and I got grabbed and I had the feeling I was being scooped into a bag thing, and I kept thinking of Paquita who travels around in a bag ... oh, you don't know Paquita do you... well, she's a dachshund, a tiny one – I mean, even smaller than, erm, normal ones... anyway, I was thrown into the boot of a car, and then I must have blacked out. When I came to, the car was bumping along some rough ground and eventually it came to a stop. They lifted me out and manhandled me out of the sack thing, and into this cage. I couldn't see much, it was dark, they had a torch but it just dazzled me. And then this, I mean they moved the cage here earlier. I wasn't far away before, just next door maybe.'

The dog next door gives a small sigh.

'Grey?'

'Yes!' Grey says, surprised.

'It's me, Piper!'

Grey's heart feels like it will explode. 'Oh, Piper! Am so glad it's you! I couldn't place your voice, isn't that the strangest thing?'

'Yes – weird – I recognised yours immediately. Couldn't you smell me?' she asks.

'I'm all over the place to be honest Piper. It's a bit of a shock all this'

He feels her nod. 'And yes of course I know Paquita!' she says.

'She's one of my Lottie's client dogs. Brown, bulgy eyes, Lottie calls her Millipede as a nickname? Carries her in a bag?' Grey nods. He knows she can't see him nodding but also that she will know that he is nodding.

'Were you alone? Or out with your human?'

'Alone. It's a l-l-l-long story.' The way she had said 'your human' so fondly (had her voice cracked, just a little bit?) makes him feel bad about divulging the fact that he has willingly run away from his human.

'I was with my Girl...' He definitely hears the catch in her throat this time. 'We were just going for an evening walk around the streets when they grabbed me. I barked and barked and I struggled and struggled but I couldn't get free. I bit one of them too. I... well, here I am.' She sounds quite flat when she says the last bit. Disappointed with herself too, he imagines. Piper is like Rhett, and like his new acquaintance, Irene - confident, and brave.

'Do you think... well... what do you think they plan to do with us?'

'Huh! Sell us, of course!' she says, with complete certainty, apparently surprised and even slightly amused by the question.

Grey tries the idea out in his head.

'Sell us?' he says out loud. That hadn't occurred to him. He hasn't really thought up till now about why he has been abducted. He thinks about the stories he's heard of dogs in Asia being stolen and sold for meat. He tries to shut off those images, he'd seen things on Siobhan's computer, horrible things, shocking things, things that made her sob. She has regular direct debits going to animal rescue charities across the world, even though she can barely pay her rent each month.

'To who?' he asks thickly, slowly.

'To people who want to buy prize dogs!' she laughs. So not for meat then, at least not that.

'It's either that or for fighting, to use as bait dogs.' Funnily enough when she says this she has less of a catch in her voice than earlier.

She seems to be less worried about their fate than the concept of not seeing her human, her Girl, again.

'But I don't think so...' she muses, pragmatically, 'as they mostly use Staffies and Terriers and whatnot for that. What are you exactly anyway, a Whippet?'

'I'm an Italian Greyhound-' Her laugh starts before he has finished the word, and he feels a little put out.

'Sorry, no offence, but thinking about it – look at you - I definitely don't think we're here as bait dogs!' Grey wishes he could laugh but he can't help but feel offended.

Piper's grey snout is nosing at a gap in the tarpaulin. 'Hey, help me move this cover will you?'

He gives her nose a polite touch with his. Between them, they manage to shift the tarpaulin back a bit, clearing wire square by wire square between them so they can see each other.

'Hello!' he says brightly, temporarily forgetting about the smell, and their predicament. It feels good to look into her eyes, it feels grounding. 'Of course it's you! Sorry, I couldn't place your voice. Weird.'

'No worries,' she replies. We could use it to our advantage you know, the fact that they don't think we're fighting dogs. The fact that they think we're weak, vulnerable, scared. Meek!' This last word she says with a grim determination, it seems, to prove their captors wrong. He can also detect in her words a touch of humour and of scorn.

'I d-d-don't know – I don't think we're a match for them.'

'No, no of course not! I saw the two brutes who took me, remember!' She shakes her whole body, crossly. 'But, well, we might take them by surprise if we try to make a run for it. We could hide...'

'How fast can you run?' she continues.

'P-pretty fast, I th-th-think,' says Grey, pleased by the question but not wanting to boast. People often say he would be one of the fastest in the park if he only dared to run when he was let off. Only bigger sighthounds were faster. He'd felt pretty fast when he'd been running away...

He wants to reassure her. She is trying to be brave, he can see that, but still.

'L-l-listen...' he says. It comes out all wrong, his voice has gone all funny, and he keeps stammering. The stammering is something he'd done a lot before, before he'd got used to chatting, with Lexi and the others. He hadn't had much opportunity to practise speech before that, Lady Human had kept him quite isolated.

'They'll find us, the others, I'm sure of it. Rhett will find us and come and rescue us!' he says proudly.

'Oh Rhett, he would be handy to have around right now, he'd have a trick up his sleeve for us...' Piper muses.

'You know him?' Grey asks, surprised. He doesn't remember seeing Piper and Rhett together before and hadn't known they knew each other.

'Of course!' says Piper, breezily, and Grey feels the delight ebb, in its place a little pang of something that he can't place in his stomach. Of course he is pleased Piper knows Rhett too, but he wonders why he feels a bit off, suddenly. Grey suddenly remembers, he had seen Rhett and Piper playing once, in the park, before he'd met Piper.

'Well,' she says, dismissively 'it would be great if they come and save us, but I think that in the meantime maybe we ought to work on a plan ourselves.'

'Just in case, you know?' she adds, kindly but firmly.

'Errrr, o-o-okay.' Grey wonders about the stammer coming back, he hasn't had it in some time, he'd even almost forgotten that he'd had it before. His tongue feels thick in his mouth. It has been a long day. All this bravery and daring is pretty new to Grey.

'So ermmm, what do you think we should do?'

'Well, I've already been thinking about it for some time. Since they took me really. But of course I'm really glad you're here now, I feel braver already now that there's two of us.'

He likes her more and more, this pretty grey Poodle with her delicate grey snout and her lovely feminine smell.

'How are your teeth?' she asks, suddenly.

'My teeth?' Grey exclaims, taken aback and a little bit horrified.

'You know – biting?'

Grey detects a smile in that last word but thinks he must be mistaken.

'Ermmmm,' he is a bit embarrassed and doesn't know what to say. Doesn't everyone know that biting is a faux pas? He's heard his Lady talking about it to her friend, the unfriendly one with the two Labradors, the only other dog walker that she talks to. They'd agreed that all Staffies and Rottweilers and Dobermans bite, or will bite, or have it in them to bite. They had seemed to be quite sure about it. Grey hadn't met any Staffies or Rottweilers or Dobermans who bit, but he had still got the gist of the conversation, what they thought should be done to dogs who bit. He remembered their voices, shrill and excited.

'And should!' his human had said.

'And should, indeed!' the Labrador lady had agreed.

'I bit someone once,' Piper goes on, continuing to shock him. He begins to suspect that she is doing it on purpose now. He watches her as closely as he can.

'Yes,' she goes on, quite matter-of-factly, 'it was a horrible little boy who kept poking me and being mean to me and pulling my tail and sticking his fingers in my eyes. On purpose!' she exclaims, dramatically.

'I mean I know some children can be a bit unpredictable - rough even - but most of them are quite fun to play with. But this one, well, he was just rotten!' He feels her outrage. He wishes he could see her better but it's not easy, in the rapidly falling dusk and because of the angles, too. He adjusts his position, standing up and curling his body around the other way. That's better, he thinks. It's quite dark in the room but he can catch the dark gleam of her eyes.

'So,' he prompts her. She seems to be itching to tell the story so he might as well indulge her. It's not like they're going anywhere.

'What happened?' he asks.

'Well,' she starts, with relish, 'I'd just had enough. I'd tried to get away but a big wooden thing was blocking the exit. It had toppled over and brought a load of other stuff with it, I don't know how the humans didn't hear it. They had told us to play nicely now – ha! - and he was chasing me round and round. A real terror he was, a real nasty little tyke. Only four and a half, apparently, I heard them talking about it all after. Anyway, thankfully,' Piper goes on, 'they had a thing called a Nannycam. I don't know what that is but apparently it saved me. My girl was crying afterwards and I heard her talking about it to her mum. She was saying that they would have tried to have me put down! Am not exactly sure what that means either, but I don't think it can be good...' she trails off.

'Where did you...' Grey wonders if he is being indelicate, but finishes anyway, 'bite him?'

'Oh!' she says, not phased by the question in the slightest, 'On his chubby, little hand. The fleshy bit below the thumb. I gave it a good old bite, sank my teeth right in. He tasted horrible! Of course, all hell broke loose - he screamed blue murder and started crying. My Lottie and her friend burst into the room. I was waiting at the door, where all the stuff had fallen over, wagging, quite pleased with myself to be honest, but I saw my Lottie go all white and she had ever such a funny energy about her. I was so relieved to see her and I jumped up on her and tried to show her that I was sorry but also to explain about him poking me and chasing me and everything... I knew she'd believe me,' Piper reflects, looking sad. 'But she was so upset and cold towards me, it was awful. She was quite rough when she pushed me off her, I was trying to lick her and say sorry, but... it was awful!' she repeats.

'I felt like all of a sudden,' there was a long pause, 'she didn't love me!'

Grey hears the hurt in her voice and he finds he likes her all the more for this little flash of vulnerability.

'Anyway,' Piper says brightly, suddenly regaining her natural good humour, having remembered the end of the story, 'they rushed him off to the hospital - the hospital, for goodness sake! Bit dramatic, I thought! - and I was bundled unceremoniously into the car.

Lottie didn't even let me sit in the front like she usually does. It was all very weird. Apparently it was a good thing the boy's owner is honest, I heard my girl say that to Grandma on the phone too, as she later looked at the Nannycam footage and saw exactly how it happened and even she, the mother said she couldn't blame me, that he was being a little terror to me. So that was that!' Piper stops, and seems a bit lost.

'And now I can't even remember why I was telling you that story. Ah yes! Biting! So I know I can do it but I'm not sure I could get my jaws round those arms of his.' She pauses, and then continues, sounding mildly surprised, having just remembered a fact. 'Actually,' she goes on, 'thinking about it, I've bitten a few times... ears and that. Dogs of course, the little boy is the only human I've bitten, and I'd almost forgotten about that! It was some time ago. But yes, it's easy if you're in the mood, biting – Miller and I do it sometimes. And I gave Nero a nip once and he nearly killed me, ha ha, you can imagine! – you know Nero, right? He's often in Kensington Gardens. He's a good friend of mine.'

Grey is impressed.

'I know of him, yes' he says, non-committally.

'Anyway - it gets quite a reaction I can tell you! That's all we need really, to give ourselves a few seconds of space to bolt. A little sharp nip, a finger maybe. Don't think I could get my mouth round anything else – they're hefty people. And you're not any better.'

Piper is examining his delicate jaw openly, and Grey feels self-conscious. She has a very direct way about her, for all the initial impression of femininity and softness.

'No offence,' she adds, as an afterthought.

'If we could get to his face of course, that might be a bit easier. Nip him on the nose...' she muses out loud. He thinks she is teasing him now, but he isn't sure, it's hard to get the measure of someone's sense of humour that quickly, he's only ever really said hi in the park before or chatted in a group. He finds he is beginning to get cold feet about all this escaping business.

'No' she says firmly, more serious now, 'Run. We have to run, that's our best chance. I'm good at faking and swerving if we need to, I practise a lot with my friend Miller, she's got some teeth on her when you get her riled up and I've learnt to avoid them.'

'Miller? A girl?'

'Yes,' snaps Piper, defensively, go through whole thing and check when continuing speech capital letter or not? 'Why not? She's a German Wirehaired Pointer,' she says, proudly, 'and she's really good at dodging - and wrestling.' Piper shakes her head, appreciatively, and Grey can feel her pent-up energy. She's clearly a very active dog and it must be hard for her to be caged like this.

'The one you b-b-bite. And bites you?' Grey asks, starting to get amused now.

'Yes! And they say mine's a boy's name too!' Piper is defiant now. It's Grey's turn to have a private little chuckle. Piper couldn't look more feminine if she tried. 'And you?' she sizes him up as much as is possible through the gap they have made, through the wire squares. 'You can run,' she says confidently. 'You're an Italian Greyhound. I just registered that, sorry, I know you told me before -' she shrugs, 'so of course you can run, and marvellously fast. You sighthounds...' she shakes her head again in that way she has, 'We go up to Wormwood Scrubs a lot and peow, gone like the wind you lot!'

A funny feeling washes over Grey. He isn't used to receiving direct compliments, he certainly hadn't ever received any from Lady Human. Piper's human probably constantly tells her how capable and wonderful she is, what a good girl she is, how she is the cleverest and most beautiful dog ever. Grey has heard other humans talk to their dogs in such a way. Piper is an optimistic dog, that much is clear; life has clearly taught her to believe in herself.

'So that's what we'll do, run.' Piper says calmly, having apparently forgotten about the issue of how they will escape from their stiff wire prisons. She turns herself around and around, for all the world as if she were up on the bed at home not in a cold, comfortless cage at the hands of madmen. Abruptly, somewhere between two and three turns, she flops down decisively and tucks her head into her tail.

'I'm having a snooze,' she says, yawning again, delicately but this time Grey feels, more genuinely. Her yawn displays a fine set of gleaming white teeth albeit with bluntened canines, and a healthy dark-pink tongue. He wonders at her sense of calm, but notes that even he doesn't feel quite as frightened as he technically should, given the circumstances.

'We always have a nap in the afternoon, me and Lottie,' Piper says. Again that sadness, he can feel how much Piper is missing her human. 'No point rushing and getting it wrong, the food's actually not bad here. Chappie, can you imagine! They must have bought it in for us special, aren't we lucky! And the woman does come to clean the cage, she did mine before they moved me here.' Piper says, a little bashfully. Grey has been wondering what will happen when he needs to toilet, which will be soon. He's not used to squalor. Piper's obviously been caged slightly longer than he has, he's been holding it in and she probably had too, as long as she could. He wrinkles his nose up. Lady Human's obsession with being clean has brushed off on him.

'And before you think it - no we can't get out when she does that. We can't risk angering her.' He feels her fear then, and an involuntary shudder runs through him.

Grey settles his head down on his paws, drawing strength from the presence in the cage next to him.

PIPER

Even Piper, brave little dog that she is, feels much better for having an ally in this adventure.

LOCKED IN II

A basement flat on Sinclair Road, 3:36am

NERO

Neil would kill me! Nero thinks.

Neil has a proclivity for anger.

Thinking about Neil catching him makes Nero's ears go back and his tail tuck close in underneath him, between his legs. Despite this fear, the urge to do something proactive is strong, he can't just wait any longer. He stands up and trots decisively into the kitchen, to the cupboard that he knows has food in it. Happy to have a task, his tail unfurls and almost wags. Then it stills, neutral. He very gently grips the knob between his teeth, and with deep concentration manages to pull it out, almost an inch, but then it slips, and bangs closed. It's an awkward angle, but the knob is made of wood, and he thinks he can do it. He keeps trying. It's an extremely old kitchen and there's dirt in the grooves, he can detect the appealing, sharp stink of it. Neil isn't particular about cleanliness in the flat, even though he's fastidious about showering. His natural smell is sour, so he washes it away every morning as hard as he can, then masks it with other smells, so strong that they make Nero sneeze. It builds up though, quickly, Neil can't hide it successfully for long.

Nero keeps working at pulling the door open, but each time, his teeth lose their grip and the door snaps back into place. After the fourth unsuccessful try, he backs away and sits down a few paces away, uncertain. He cocks his head, listening. Whines. Circles a few times, paces to the door and back, then down the other way along the hallway and back again. For want of anything better to do, he decides to try again. He looks at the knob, tries to work out where he might have gone wrong. He can't. He just needs to be patient, go slowly, be more precise, he thinks.

He reaches his head forward, positions his body carefully.

Slowly. Slowwwwwwly. Careful.

He steps his feet back, gently, gently, as if he's trying to walk backwards on a tightrope. He feels the pull of the door close mechanism against his grip, but he persists, ever so gently. Millimetre by millimetre he wins the battle.

There!

Nero holds his breath momentarily, fearing that letting it out will break the spell. He has managed to pull it out enough now, pivoting his body backwards and to the right in fractions of movements. He freezes, still holding the knob in his teeth, gingerly. Saliva starts to pool in his mouth, and he needs to breathe, to swallow. He feels claustrophobic, all of a sudden. He holds his nerve though and lets go only gently, closing his eyes for a second. No noise, no creak, the door remains open. He swallows, and continues to watch the door for a few seconds, distrustful, half expecting it to swing shut. It doesn't. He has almost forgotten what he wanted to do, and then his eyes fall to the contents of the cupboard. His heart leaps and he pounces in, like a fox after a mouse.

With action, Nero's stress falls away. He thrashes around in the cupboard, his body almost fully inside. He pulls things out as best he can, indiscriminately, and scatters the contents. His teeth clamp satisfyingly on a packet of biscuits. He wrenches it out, steps backwards, drops the object on the floor at his feet and towers over it, securing it with his paws. He rips frantically at the packaging, tears at it with his teeth in rapid, upward motions. The muscle memory of his ancestors guides him. The packet bursts and lets out its chocolatey, biscuity smell.

Mmmmmmmm!

Nero's mouth waters as he leans into the job in an awkward bow, spitting pieces of biscuit wrapper out left and right, impatiently wolfing the biscuits down as he gets to them, extracting them roughly and ingesting as fast as he can. The crumbs make his mouth dry and get stuck in his gullet as he tries to gulp them down. He has to cough some up, momentarily losing his breath. He rights himself from the choking, swallows a few times impatiently, then greedily puts his nose towards the floor again, seeking solace in the gorging.

Nero has never tasted human biscuits before, and thinks they are delicious. Neil doesn't share his food with him. When Nero used to look at him beseechingly when he ate, Neil would say things like 'This is too good for you, you're just a poxy dog!' It had made Nero feel ashamed, and now he slinks away whenever Neil prepares himself food. Nero rips his way through and wolfs down a few more packets of things, some tastier than others. The hunger pangs abate but he barely notices. After some time, when he realises he has finished off everything that seems to be edible, he stands still, and surveys the mess, the remains of the contents of the cupboard scattered around him.

Thirst hits him.

There's no water in the bowl, it's long gone, though he keeps returning to lick at it in vain. As the kernel of fear of what Neil will do when he comes back returns, Nero's tail starts to creep under his body again, and his ears flatten. Remembering how Neil gets really vicious, how the ugly fury in him rises, Nero cringes and whines, involuntarily. He tries to reassure himself. *It's OK, it will be OK, tomorrow it will be okay, he'll be cross but I can handle it and he'll be sorry afterwards, he'll give me extra food and fuss and some of those stick treat things. He'll regret it and be sorry, and he isn't bad. He'll be back, and it will be okay, after a while...*

Nero, surprising himself, lets out a howl. Even though he's so often scared of him, Neil is his human, and he suddenly misses him, it's been too long. Nero has never done a howl before and it feels good. He does another one, a longer one. It makes him feel a bit better, it soothes him. He feels that if he howls long and hard enough he might be able to make something happen, so he tries, but before long it starts to just feel futile and lonely. A neighbour stirs in her sleep, hearing him, but thinks she must be dreaming, she pictures wolves in her head. It's a shame Nero is not a barker, that could save him. But this is the only time he will vocalise, the only chance for someone to hear his call for help. The quiet feels more oppressive to him now, after the howling.

Nero wonders how long it has been, if it is light yet outside, or still dark. He pads towards the front of the flat. It's still dark, though it is sometimes hard to tell in their basement dungeon, especially as Neil often keeps the curtains closed, as they are now.

Oh no.

Nero feels in his bowels that he will soon need to defecate, so probably morning is near. Sometimes when they exit the flat to go out for a walk he is shocked by the light and feels disorientated as it is so dingy in the flat. He looks up to where he knows the top of the curtains is, where the light comes in, when the light comes. Nothing.

His head jerks up as he remembers something. *The human pee place! In there is water!*

He trots purposefully along the short hallway, hope in his step. He enters the bathroom. The lid is down. *Dammit.* He tries to push it up, but can't manage to further than a fraction, it's too heavy.

Dammit!

He whines, frustrated. Now he needs to pee too. With poo he can hold it, he's learnt to do that, just to breathe shallowly, not to move too much, and the feeling will pass after a while. But peeing, that's harder. And it will make Neil really mad if he pees in the flat. He whines again, and cowers at the thought of the beating, the chain that Neil will wrap round his fist to make it hurt more. Thinking about it just makes his need to pee all the more urgent though. The more he worries about the repercussions of his scavenging session, the more he feels it coming. Desperate now, he paces a few steps one way then the other, and circles, unsure what to do.

The bedroom door is in front of him. He has an idea. He pushes it open with his nose and enters. There, near the big sound machine thing, the plant, that will hide it! Hope rears its head again; Nero is a hopeful dog, still. He will try really hard not to get it on the carpet. Maybe Neil won't notice. He hurries over to it and cocks his leg. It takes his bladder longer than it should to release, the fear of the beating stops it despite its desperation to empty its contents. Finally, the flow starts.

Ahhhhh, better!

It's a long pee, and Nero enjoys it. He holds his leg in place for a few seconds after the flow stops, then places it down. He looks at the floor and sees there is a pool of pee there, soaking into the carpet, even though a lot of it has gone into the plant pot. His heart sinks. Ears down, tail under, he slinks away, back into the hallway, and through into the living room. He tries to put the mistake and the feeling of guilt out of his mind. Physically, at least, he is relieved. The thirst plagues him but there is nothing he can do about that, he can't get water whilst he is locked in here alone.

Nero lays on the hard floor, his place. It doesn't occur to him to go anywhere else. He feels quite drowsy now. He curls himself up as tightly as he can, he always feels safer like that. He tucks his head into his body and surprisingly quickly drifts off. As he does, his body unfurls slightly. He finds comfort in sleep. Sometimes, in his dreams, he's living with Lottie and Piper.

This time though, it's just dark.

BAIT DOGS

Under the Westway

PIPER

Piper and Grey hear two humans talking. They are standing at the entrance to the outbuilding, they can make out their shapes in the moonlight.

'There's one next week, on Monday,' one of them says. 'They need some to encourage the Rottie's blood lust, he's not fighting yet.' The voices both laugh, harshly. 'Too used to sittin' on a sofa, no doubt. They haven't fed him for a few days, so he should be getting keen. Those two would be perfect. The Poodle might be game, she might have some fight in her, she bit Rog on the way into the van.' They hear a short laugh. 'I tried to get twenty quid each for them but he said the scrawny one was barely worth bothering with. We settled on £35 for both and we'll have to deliver them by Friday. He won't last two minutes that skinny one. Probably die of fright!' They both laugh. 'He'll probably need a couple more too for over the weekend - preferably spaniels - nice and wriggly he said, gets 'em going. We can go out this afternoon for a look, if you like. Get them from outside the supermarkets is the easiest. Dress nice!' An affirmative grunt from the one that sounds like she might be a woman.

Both dogs' eyes go as wide as saucers in the dark and even brave little Piper feels a chill run through her. Dog fighting? They'd heard that it happens, Rhett had told them, but they hadn't really believed it. They are shocked. Grey starts to tremble uncontrollably, and to pant, fast and loud. His eyes roll about in their sockets, Piper can see the glints of the whites of them.

'Grey!' she says, sharply. 'Pull yourself together! It just means we have to get out before then, that's all.'

'Grey!' Piper hisses in the dark. The humans have walked away from the entrance, but she isn't certain they aren't still near.

'Grey!' she tries a third time, 'Let's think!' she appeals to him, feeling panic lapping at her edges.

There's no answer from Grey. He seems to have lost the power of speech and can't stop trembling. Piper gives up hissing at him to get a response, he is clearly freaking out and there isn't much she can do about that. She makes herself breathe, slowly and calmly, deep belly breathing it's called, Lottie does it sometimes when she comes back from that place that smells of oranges. She hears Sebastian's voice in her head. 'Come on Pipes, you can do this!' he says. A fire ignites in her belly. They will escape. They have to. She thinks about Lottie, and her stomach swoops. She thinks of the last time she'd seen her, how her face had gone completely white. Just before she'd bitten the man that threw her into the van. Rog. She wishes she'd fought harder, managed to wriggle loose. She thinks back to that awful primal cry Lottie had emitted when she had heard the news about Sebastian. She has to get back to her, she just has to. Piper racks her brains trying to think what day it is today, she goes over things in her head and works it out: Tuesday, it is Tuesday. She calculates that they have two or three days in which to escape.

She hisses at Grey again but gets no response. The cage is vibrating he's shaking so much.

LOCKED IN III

A basement flat on Sinclair Road, 4:14am

NERO

Nero wakes up and doesn't feel too good. His head is muzzy and he's lost track of time. He can't be bothered to get up and check the cupboards again. He knows that he's finished every last scrap of edible food. In the throes of boredom and in his desperation to alleviate it, he's even eaten some pieces of Neil's shoes. Tired now again, his head hurts and he feels woozy. His stomach hurts, too. His head is pounding and he lays it back down on the floor, drifting in and out of consciousness.

The smell of fear, which had brought with it as it always does a dirty, scratchy feeling to Nero's mouth and an anxious buzz, has for a while now been replaced by something else, a nagging, cloying smell and an ugly, dull accompanying feeling that bypasses his stomach and heart and goes straight into his bones – despair.

Nero hears Neil's key in the door and almost jumps out of his skin. He scrambles up, desperately, his body a rush of mixed emotions. He is on four paws briefly but then sways and falls. He tries to focus on the front door but it is shimmering, like a mirage. He feels hyper-aware, anxious, a little sick. His head pounds but he lifts it just slightly, a centimetre perhaps, to watch Neil coming towards him down the hallway, his angry, heavy footsteps making the floor vibrate. But they fade out before they reach him, as does Neil and Nero feels compelled to lay his head down, to close his eyes. It was a hallucination, he thinks, relieved - but the realisation that he doesn't actually wish for Neil to come home makes him feel blank. He's past caring. He just wishes, if anything, to fade away.

Outside, after some time, the sun rises.

The day passes.

The sun sets.

The night passes.

The sun rises.

The day passes.

The sun sets.

The night passes.

The sun rises again.

Nero lies throughout, deathly still now.

The breath comes still, but barely; it is slow, and shallow.

Nero is dancing across the clouds, weightless; he is looking for Piper.

POLICE RAID

Under the Westway

PIPER

'Something's happening Grey!'

Piper's heart is in her mouth. She can hear the approaching sound of two vans. She can feel that people nearby are rushing. She can hear clattering, running. One of the humans runs in to the rickety wooden building they're in. He pulls back the locks of their cages, and says 'Scram! Scram!'

He sounds panicked. Piper looks across at Grey, whose eyes are wide. He is pressed up against the back of the cage.

The man runs out.

'Come on Grey, let's go!' urges Piper. She jumps down onto the floor and turns and puts her paws up at the entrance of Grey's cage. 'Come on Grey, let's see how fast you can run!'

She turns and runs off, looking over her shoulder to check he's coming. She sees the shape of him jumping to floor in the dark. Her heart races. *Now this is an adventure!* she thinks.

'Coming, Piper!' says Grey.

THE ANIMAL COMMUNICATOR

At Audrey and Beagle's home

AUDREY

Audrey has tried all sorts of supplements and calming remedies with Beagle. You name it, she's tried it; and sometimes she feels like she might as well study to be a dog behaviourist for all the time she spends reading training books and discussion threads on forums. Beagle's level of fear, his paranoia and the depth of his depression seem to make him resilient to every antidote. Sylvie had mentioned the animal communicator the other day after that awful episode in the park, Audrey's heart had leapt, instinctively, as it always does when she hears about something that might help her companion. The animal communicator, Joanne, explains in her bumph online that sometimes just feeling heard makes a difference to some of her clients. Audrey thinks it's lovely that she calls the animals she helps clients. Joanne's website says that she has worked with clients of various species including macau parrots, rabbits, horses and donkeys. It even mentions her having worked with a rat.

Audrey decides that she had better give it a try or she will never know, and transfers her money to Joanne's account via Paypal. She books the session online. She walks across the room and takes a couple of appropriate photos of Beagle in portrait mode, including one of him looking straight into the camera dolefully. Still standing, she sends them over to Joanne by email. She then sits at her desk and meanders around the internet trying to find out more about dog confidence issues, animal communication and any vaguely related matters.

The whole thing is a rabbit warren, and whilst she's in it, she drinks three quarters of a bottle of white wine. She then abandons the computer, shifts herself to the sofa and, still scrolling around the internet, now on her phone, finishes the bottle. Feeling guilty but high, she opens a second one, and feels briefly garrulous, and then doesn't. Whilst Audrey is feeling garrulous she thinks of phoning a friend, but she realises she doesn't have anything to say to them, and she can't think who she'd like to talk to anyway, so she doesn't. The moment quickly passes, anyway.

The next day...

It is the morning of the Zoom call with the animal communicator and Audrey finds herself feeling nervous and more than a little bit stupid, as well as horribly hungover. Hangovers always manifest themselves for her as anxiety, on top of the headaches and sickness. 'Aude.' She says the name out loud as she lays in bed the next morning trying to work out how bad her headache is. She likes that Sylvie and Lottie call her that, it is a name that Audrey had picked herself, it had been her choice. Most of her school friends and people at her previous workplace had called her plain Audrey or even worse, her childhood nickname, one that had stuck from a phase she and her girlfriends had gone through of trying to 'extend' their names – Audriana. It would be pretty if it were the more Italian 'Andriana' - but Audriana, she thinks, just sounds extraordinarily woeful.

She sighs, sadly, and wonders for the hundredth time why Beagle is so tormented. She has read every one of Joanne's online reviews, many of which claim that she has *changed all our lives* and *made a huge difference*, some going into greater and more specific detail, stating how she has *uncovered underlying health or pain issues their animals were suffering from*. These were allegedly animals that vets had examined and found nothing wrong with. Audrey is sceptical, particularly this morning, but she's committed now. She scrolls through the news online and then social media in order to kill time before nine fifteen, the start time of the call. So many dogs with Inflammatory Bowel Disease, who knew! There's even a special Facebook group for them. At least Beagle doesn't have IBD.

His toilet habits are perfectly normal, although even there, Beagle finds something to worry about, sniffing back behind him despondently after he toilets.

Audrey looks down at Beagle. He looks up at her, sadly. The familiar ring tone of Zoom makes them both jump. Aude's stomach lurches. Lately she has become nervous about conversing with people, in person or on the phone. She answers.

'Hi, Audrey Brown?'

'Err yes, that's me.' She coughs to clear her throat - it had come out all squeaky.

'Joanne. Joanne Smith. Good to meet you. Do you want to put the picture on just for a minute or two?'

'Err, OK...' Audrey clicks the camera icon and sees herself pop up on the screen. She fidgets, unhappily, seeing her face, and starts smoothing her hair. Joanne has an open, unlined face, a broad smile, slightly crooked teeth. Audrey feels herself smile back.

'Hi!' she says, attempting to come across as confident, but failing. She doesn't find the telephone a comfortable medium. 'Do you want to see Beagle?' she blurts out, feeling awkward.

'Sure! I don't need to – but if he's there, why not!'

Audrey angles the computer so that Joanne can see him.

'Hi Beagle!' Joanne says, perkily and without a trace of irony, as if talking to dogs were as sane as eating ice cream on a hot day.

Audrey angles the camera back to herself.

'You didn't name him yet or...?' asks Joanne.

'Oh! Well no – I mean – yes and no. I couldn't find a name to fit him and somehow Beagle stuck... I know it's a bit silly...' Audrey tails off apologetically.

Joanne jumps in quickly and says reassuringly, 'No no, it's OK, it's just that sometimes - occasionally, not always - names can be important to animals. Google Anna Breytenbach and Diabolo,' she says. Audrey scribbles it down diligently, curious. Maybe this is the key! she thinks to herself, and as quickly admonishes herself – she needs to keep hope in check, there are no easy fixes with Beagle, she has learnt that much.

'Anyway- doesn't matter. So!' Joanne says, brightly, 'Anything you want to tell me about Beagle? I mean some people prefer not to - they think I'm a crook, they like to check if I am! I totally get it,' she laughs openly. Once again, Audrey finds herself smile. She thinks of Lottie, who has tried to hide her cynicism from Audrey to be kind but obviously thinks that Joanne is a charlatan. Joanne answers her own question as she can see that Audrey is struggling to answer politely. 'How about we go straight into it, that way we can have a chat afterwards when I've told you what I've got from Beagle.'

'OK!' says Audrey, relieved to have been given an out from an awkward dilemma but still feeling slightly rude. Lottie had lectured her quite strictly just yesterday about not giving too much away before the session. Lottie obviously thinks that this whole thing is a bit like going to a fortune teller. Audrey hopes that Sylvie is right, not Lottie. Sylvie who had said 'there are more things in heaven and earth...' wagging her finger comically at Lottie. Audrey smiles, thinking about her new park friends, who she feels like she's known forever.

'So, Audrey, just give me a moment to tune in to Beagle will you?'

As Audrey is about to ask her does she want the camera on Beagle or on her, Beagle walks off and settles, somewhat unsurely, as always, on the other side of the room.

'Oh!' says Audrey, embarrassed.

'Don't worry about the camera being on Beagle now, I don't need it to be. And don't worry if he goes out of the room, or falls asleep, or does the wall of death round the room for that matter!' Joanne laughs, 'It doesn't matter at all. The sessions have differing effects on them, you can never tell how they'll respond and no response is wrong.'

'OK,' says Audrey hesitantly. She has a sinking feeling, a feeling that Lottie is probably right. This all seems a bit beyond credible.

'I'm tuned it to him, I can't really explain how it works and there's no point wasting time on that. But it's a bit like Reiki, if you're familiar with that, in that it can be done from afar - as long as you request the subject's permission. With animal communication that part isn't quite as clear but I need to 'dial in' - that's the only way I can describe it.

'OK, am trying now, just keep quiet for this bit, if you don't mind.' Audrey nods. There is silence from Joanne's side, which lasts twenty seconds or so. Audrey waits. It feels like a long time. She feels awkward and doesn't know where to look.

'So,' Joanne starts. 'Beagle seems to be very... how to say it...' Audrey laughs, grimly, she realises that Joanne is trying to word it kindly and muses that perhaps there is something in this after all.

'Disturbed.'

This is Audrey's first taster of how precise Joanne will be with her words, how frank. She is taken aback, and feels tears prick at her eyes. It is all she can do to nod, curtly. She feels affronted, and defensive, she can't help it. Joanne doesn't seem to need any kind of verbal confirmation anyway, it seems like she is totally confident in what she is saying. She doesn't give the impression that she is fishing for clues or feeling her way, and anyway she doesn't seem to be focused on Audrey but now on some middle point in the air in front of her.

'He's holding a lot of pain in him.' She pauses and shakes her head slightly. 'I don't mean physical pain, I mean emotional pain.' Another long pause. 'He thinks he's ill, he's preoccupied with that, he worries about it night and day. But he's not - I can't see anything on that side of things, nothing at all in fact, he appears to be totally healthy. It's just that he's scared – terrified. He never had a safe place until he came to you and he hasn't yet been able to shake off the fear. And it's manifesting itself in him feeling pessimistic about absolutely everything, including his health. Which, ironically, is stopping him from enjoying the life of a perfectly healthy, fit dog. It's unusual...' During this next pause, Audrey watches Joanne. She has her head cocked on the side slightly, and seems to be listening. Again Lottie's reservations pop into Audrey's head.

'I'm trying to get that across to him, that he's not ill, that he's perfectly healthy, and that he's safe now, but he's... he's very... resistant. Very stubborn. Well, of course, he is a beagle after all!' Joanne laughs, seemingly trying to lighten the mood. She seems to have broken off her mental communication with Beagle and turns now to look directly into the camera, into Aude's eyes.

'I'm giving him a breather now, Audrey. This can be quite intense for them the first time, quite a shock, feeling someone witness their inner thoughts. Not unpleasant, I'm sure, but certainly strange. Some dogs – well, animals, birds, whatever, find it quite hard to communicate, to either express or absorb anything, to open their mind. For others, it comes entirely naturally. I've seen this a lot, traumatised beings tend to live in a permanent state of flight, all I can really tap into is that they want to run away, that they are petrified.'

'Oh,' says Audrey, disappointed.

'No, don't worry, it just means it sometimes takes a while to break through. Some dogs get chatting immediately, some dogs warm to the experience.'

Audrey thinks of the others in the park, she'd bet that Lexi and Piper would be immediately chatty dogs, that brown dog they always see on its own, Doggy Dog, as well.

'OK, just give me a second Audrey.'

Joanne's eyes drift away. Audrey looks over at Beagle. He is curled up in a ball now, like a cat. He lifts his head to give a huge yawn, then tucks his nose back into his back legs.

'OK, I can see... Even though he's not exactly telling me, he's letting me inside some of his memories. He can't help it, they're so intrinsic to him. It's his past that's hurting him... he grew up in a place where his mum didn't feel safe,' Joanne's voice sounds sad and Audrey thinks that if she's a fake she's a damned good one, 'and he's never really got over that. I'm trying to get across to him – it's difficult to explain how, but I'm trying to get across to him the concept that it is in the past, that it is behind him, that it is not current, not real, now, and that he needs to let go of how he felt then, because it is colouring everything for him.' Joanne pauses and takes a big gulp of her tea. 'I'm describing it in images, I think, it's hard to nail down exactly how the communication works be honest, even for me, but images seem to be a big part of it.' She sounds far away, unfocused, and Audrey realises that she is in Beagle's world, in his mind; her talking out loud is just in order to keep a thread between her and Audrey. A fine thread, but one that she knows Audrey needs.

Audrey looks over at Beagle again. He doesn't appear to be listening, he appears to be sleeping. Joanne continues, 'Was he kept in a small space with quite a lot of other dogs? I can see lots of cages and other mums and pups, not just his litter, his mum. Is he scared of other dogs?'

Audrey almost laughs. 'He's scared of everything,' she says, honestly.

'Yes, am getting that.'

Audrey realises that at some point her cynicism has dropped away. Joanne sounds a bit traumatised, her voice has gone low and a lot quieter and less bubbly.

'As for where he was kept,' Audrey says, 'I don't know. I was under the impression he was kept just with his mother and his litter mates in a home but...' the horrible and now glaringly obvious realisation is dawning on her that the lady who had sold him to her had not been telling the truth.

Joanne's briskness is back. 'I'm trying to get across to him that he's safe now, that you won't let anyone attack him, that he's safe with you, and that he would feel better if he could relax a bit. He's very highly strung.'

Audrey nods vigorously.

'Do you mind telling me where you got him from? I'm wondering if he could be from a puppy farm. That's what it looked like, to be honest, the image I saw.'

Audrey thinks back to the advert she'd seen on Pets4homes and the woman she'd met; her taut smile, the stressed vibe. She'd been insistent that Audrey not come to her house, that they meet up halfway. 'More convenient,' she'd said briskly, when Audrey had said it was no trouble, that it was only just over an hour's drive away. The penny drops for certain as Audrey remembers her casual, 'How about we meet up in a car park?' Audrey groans, feeling duped.

The seller woman's words resound in her head, 'The only male in the litter left, a happy go lucky sweet little thing.' She had been tautly smiling again, you could have heard that even over the phone, if you'd been listening. And Audrey had brought cash with her, as instructed. She rolls her eyes at her own idiocy, and clenches her jaw, at the malice of people. What a sucker! But then again, who wouldn't fall for a puppy!

'Yes, it's quite possible,' she says, feeling stupid.

'Well, good he's got you then!' Joanne says, positively. 'He does like you, you know, more than he likes anyone else, he'll just take some time to trust. He's asking for patience. Or, he would if he could communicate that.' She changes tack. 'Is there some white dog that you know? Stocky? Some sort of bull breed maybe?' she asks. 'He feels safe with her.'

'Yes!' Audrey says, astounded, 'That's Lexi! My friend's dog' she says, blushing slightly at the word friend. 'She's lovely, very calm. She's a Staffy, a white Staffy – a very stocky one!' Audrey feels tears pricking at her eyes. But then Lottie's reservations surface in her. 'But Sylvie, Lexi's owner, she's the one who told me about you.' She pauses. 'She just found you on a google search though, I think.' She shakes her head, confused, not sure which voices in her head to listen to. Joanne seems unphased.

'Well, it's good for him to be around that dog. Beagle feels at his least fearful,' Joanne gives a short, mirthless laugh by way of acknowledgement that it is all relative, 'around her.' Audrey nods as Joanne is saying this, and thinks about how Beagle is when he's alone in contrast to how he is when some of their park gang friends are around. It's a subtle difference, but noticeable. Harold had remarked on it the other day, in fact.

When they ring off five minutes or so later Audrey is surprised to find Beagle snoring softly.

As long as she's known Beagle he has never slept deeply enough to snore. Audrey tiptoes past him and makes herself a cup of tea then sits down to text Sylvie and Lottie. 'Park in the morning? Had the session with the animal communicator, need a debrief!'

After a few seconds she hears the ping of a return text.

'Great! 10am - ish usual place!' from Sylvie and then one a few seconds later, from Lottie, 'Should be in KG@11 - will text u once there - hope went well! xx'

Audrey smiles at the exclamation mark, at Lottie trying to be positive despite her cynicism. She is happy she has these two new girlfriends to talk to. Maybe, just maybe.. she thinks, and watches Beagle, who is snoring.

Joanne tries her best not to get too emotionally involved; she'd worked hard on that when she was doing her training. She could see early on that the job would quickly start to deplete her otherwise... but she still sighs when she finishes the Zoom call with Audrey and Beagle. Sometimes this job can be heavy, she thinks, some of the images you see. She shakes her head and pulls Mickey in for a hug, if she could she would save all the animals in the world. Not for the first time, she thinks about the human capacity for evil. She knows about puppy farms, but she had felt it – really felt it – through Beagle. She shivers. She isn't sure what is harder – cases like these or ones where the subject is in pain, real physical pain, pain that sometimes can't be cured with drugs. She can feel the pain, when she connects with them – the emotional pain and the physical pain. Happily, most times she can help, and she generally loves her job, but it's not always easy. She stands up and glances through the window to check the weather. She decides to go for a walk. She often does that after a difficult work session. She purposely schedules breaks in between clients, otherwise her job becomes too intense.

She picks up Mickey's lead and he jumps off the settee where he'd been fast asleep and rushes over to her, giving himself a big, happy shake. The joy he takes in the simple things always brushes off on her.

'Come on then boy, let's go!' she says. He smiles up at her and wiggles around, panting, impatient now to be out there.

KING'S CROSS

The day after the police raid

King's Cross train station

RHETT

Grey and Rhett hang around at the back of the train station. Rhett still can't believe that Grey had found him and not the other way round. Piper and him had known that Grey slept on the river near Hammersmith and had headed straight there when they had fled from under the Westway, Grey had been adamant that they find Rhett. Rhett is impressed that they'd managed to find their way and track him down, very impressed. Piper had agreed on the proviso that she go straight home afterwards, she had been desperate to get back to Lottie.

Rhett is experienced in the drill but Grey has to fight his nerves, which are clearly trying to get the better of him. The fast train approaches. Keep away from the platform, train not stopping at this station! Terrifyingly noisy for a few moments - thundering, juddering. Then it passes, and peace descends. There is birdsong, and drifts of conversations float by. A mother and her daughter, talking about making lampshades and getting material from Goldhawk Road, or maybe Berwick Street in Soho; a lady on the phone to her friend, talking about where to meet later; a couple of work colleagues on their way to an off-site meeting discussing how to deal with a difficult client.

It will be soon now, Rhett thinks, he can tell by the way the people waiting on the platform exude an impatience, they want to board the train, ensure they get a seat, settle to their newspaper or coffee or to the mindless scrolling of social media. They want to move on with their day, waste it in other ways than waiting for a train. Rhett can sense that Grey feels impatient. He needs to get on this train in order to start the next chapter of his life, but Rhett senses that he feels somehow wrong about leaving London. He understands, it is all Grey has ever known and anyway most dogs aren't big travellers. London has always been his home and such uncertainty lays ahead. Rhett is sorry that Grey has to do this, but it's the only way. The park gang have all seen, smelt, heard Lady Human looking for him. Grey can't be allowed to fall back into her hands. Who knows how she might punish him? Anyway, now that Grey has had this taste of adventure and of freedom he'd find his former life even harder to bear. *Long are the days for those in chains,* Rhett says to himself, one of the mantras that repeats in his head. It is a sadness that is almost more than he can bear thinking of all those he had seen along the way, been unable to help. He is determined to make things right for Grey. He is so thankful to have been given the chance to help him.

'Soon,' Rhett says, under his breath, 'but calmly, remember. Imagine you are invisible. Don't make eye contact. No running. We find a nook, we curl up, we sleep. Easy as that. Be relaxed... Grey!' Grey is looking around nervously. Rhett waits for him to return eye contact and when he does, he nods at him, encouragingly. Grey nods back. Rhett is proud of him, he thought he'd be a bag of nerves, much worse than this. They wait another couple of minutes, as the train arrives, pulls in, and its doors open.

'Now!' Rhett says it almost under his breath. They trot across the platform from their hiding place behind the ticket machine, Grey's shorter legs moving more rapidly than Rhett's. It is surprisingly easy to be invisible, the humans are all so busy and mostly - helpfully - glued to their phones. In through the doors they slip, winding themselves between the various legs and vanishing before anyone can notice. As luck would have it they've entered at the doors where there is a bike rack and since there are already two bikes there as well as two large rucksacks, they just slip in behind them and fit into the spaces their shapes have created. As planned during the night, they curl up and close their eyes. There will be no food or water for the duration, no peeing. Rhett has warned Grey about this, it would be too risky and could draw attention to them.

In fact, no one notices the two four-legged bodies, it is dark outside now anyway, only when the toilet door opposite them opens is there a risk of them being illuminated and discovered. Grey at first squeezes his eyes shut, he dreads being found out, dreads being shouted at, shaken, fuss. Rhett knows that Grey dislikes confrontation. He thinks back to the camp, how the different types of dogs responded to drama. The terrier mixes quite liked it, but the sighthound types like Grey were hopeless with it, the Great Danes too. Some breeds suffered more than others under shelter conditions - pointers for example seemed to desperately miss humans and were consequently amongst the unhappiest there. Rhett watches over his little companion who is soon dozing. The movement of the train, the muffled noise, the warmth is comforting, and Grey is bound to be both mentally and physically utterly exhausted after his ordeals over the last three days. It's no wonder he's fallen asleep, Rhett thinks. Grey sleeps and dreams and twitches his way to Edinburgh. Rhett remains wide awake, but closes his eyes in order not to inadvertently draw attention to them. He peeps occasionally at Grey.

Almost six hours later

Rhett wakes him.

'We're here, almost. We need to be careful to get out of the station fine, just. Stick close to me, and move fast.'

THE SMELL OF THINGS AFTER RAIN

Kensington Gardens

PIPER

Piper loves the smell of the park after the rain. She zips around with her nose to the floor, tail wagging furiously. She is deaf with smelling, high, she gives herself over to this one sense and her eyes glaze over, she isn't using them. The pictures in her head that the smells engender are psychedelic, marvellous. Like that time she had licked a bit of ketamine off the table when she'd been at Lottie's friend, Beth's house. Lottie had freaked out when she had seen Piper lick the table and grimace. Beth had told her not to be stupid, that there was nothing there, nothing left, but there had been - oh there had been! Lottie had watched her closely that day but the little trip Piper had been on hadn't had any outward signs. Only perhaps a slight, almost indiscernible glazing of the eyes, a certain stillness of her body as her mind had departed it for its adventure.

This feels a bit like that. Colours exploding, a riot in her imagination, senses completely overwhelmed. Piper doesn't know where to go next and zigzags erratically. When it's dry, she can smell her way along the lines of the squirrels' tracks, the foxes', and even, she thinks, along those of the birds, although those are very, very faint, almost like echos of tracks. But now, after the rain, the most wonderful, overwhelming, rich, pungent, earthy mixture of soil and nature and goodness is everywhere! All the various smells merge and hit her nostrils; her brain is assaulted and it makes her lose herself, she can't discern any individual tracks now, the whole is too rich, too delicious.

'Piper! Piper!' she hears Lottie call, as if from a distance, but she can't stop sniffing, drinking it all in, the smell of happiness exuding from her in turn and adding to the joy of the day. She ignores Lottie's calls, she has been neurotic since the episode and keeps calling Piper back when she's not at all far away. 'PIPER!' she hears Lottie scream and the urgency in her tone is such that Piper forces herself to lift her head from the ground, just in time to see one of the park's machines bearing down on her. She registers the noise of it, and, a split second after, its foul smell. *Why does everything man-made smell so awful?* she thinks. *Especially when it's new and especially if it involves any sort of electricity.* Piper feels Lottie's relief and smells it too, as Piper jumps out of the way of the machine and bounds back towards Lottie, jumping up on her just as she isn't allowed to do. She can't help it, she just has to give Lottie a double high five.

'Piper!' Lottie groans, but Piper can tell that she isn't angry, she senses only the love Lottie has for her.

Ohhhh, that smell, that smell, what is it?! Piper thinks to herself when the machine has gone and Lottie has released her. She has to find the source. It is intoxicating, pungent. Yeasty. Piper sniffs frantically, tracking back when it gets fainter, following it again, trying to find the exact spot where it is at its most intense. When she finds the place she gets more precise, her sniffing rhythm changes. She positions herself to flip and roll her neck into it, just where you put perfume if you are a human female.

'Piper!' Lottie screams at her. Piper looks at her for a second, wide-mouthed, then fully committed, flips and rolls and wriggles about, grinning at Lottie from her upside down position. Her teeth gleam in the sunshine. The canine ones look like they've been sawn off - they are worn down by carrying things. The vet had commented on it on their last visit. Sebastian had laughed it off and ruffled Piper's head fondly and called her a silly fool. Piper half hears Lottie groaning. She'll probably get put into the bath tonight, but Piper doesn't concern herself about that as she wriggles and writhes on the floor and tries to get as much of the delicious smell on her as possible. This is well worth having a bath later for.

Piper sniffs the air and knows, although she doesn't know how she knows, that Lexi is on her way. She grins at Lottie, who smiles back.

CHANGE

At Audrey and Beagle's home

AUDREY

Audrey's phone beeps and she picks it up. It's Charlotte. She reads the message and, unusually for her, taps out of it without replying. She lays her phone to the side of her on the settee, face down. Charlotte had annoyed her the last time they'd met, with her bitchy comments about this and that, her constant prattle about their joint school friends and indiscreet chat about their various dramas and disasters. Frenemies, Sylvie had said people like Charlotte were. Sylvie had rolled the word around her tongue dramatically as she had said it. One should avoid Frenemies at all cost, she had said. Audrey finds herself following a lot of Sylvie's advice of late. Sylvie is only maybe a decade or so older than her, but she is very wise and seems able to reduce everything down to its simple equations, always making you wonder why you'd never done it before of your own accord. Audrey now relies on a little game she has made up to help her make decisions. In her head she calls the game *What would Sylvie do?*

Sylvie's voice pops into her head now: *How did receiving that text make you feel? Did you think,* (and Audrey smiles, thinking of Sylvie saying it) *ahhhhh, Charlotte! How delightful!* (pronounced dee-light-fooool) *and did it bring a smile to your face? Huh? Orrrr did it make you think 'argggh, Charlotte! And how would you feel if you did see her, would the evening fly by, would you laugh a lot, would you feel happy and energised?*

Or would the smile on your face be forced, would you feel totally drained by the time you went home? All these questions Sylvie would ask. Audrey decides, upon pondering them in her head, that Charlotte will have to be cut out of her life. She feels proud of making the decision. It feels like another turning point. She leaves the phone where it is and makes a conscious decision not to reply (the valour!) and settles back to the episode of House that she has been watching. She has a secret crush on Dr House, she finds the similarities between him and Harold striking.

The next day...

Audrey strides out with Lottie and Sylvie through the park, laughing. Piper and Lexi romp alternately ahead and beside them, happily, also saying hello to other dog and human acquaintances they pass. Audrey has left Beagle at home with a dog sitter, part of the action plan they have formulated to rehabilitate Beagle and to rescue Audrey from the downward spiral that she has got into on account of Beagle and all his issues and that will otherwise end in total depression (Sylvie's words). Lottie and Sylvie have convinced her that it will be impossible to even have a chance at changing Beagle's outlook on life if she herself is on a right downer (Lottie's words). Is it having a reactive dog that makes you anxious, Audrey wonders, or is it being anxious that makes your dog reactive? Probably a bit of both, she thinks. In her case it had definitely been the former. She'd never suffered from anxiety during the era of Tinks. Well, not unusual levels of anxiety, anyway.

Audrey is in good spirits with Lottie and Sylvie flanking her. She's made a conscious decision not to feel guilty any more about leaving Beagle at home, and to just enjoy her time with her friends. Her new friends. Truth be told, she's got a bit fed up with her old ones. Despite owing her nothing, despite not having any shared history, these new friends seem to be there for her unconditionally, and it just feels easy. They don't need to meet up for a whole evening or for lunch out in some fancy restaurant. They can just bump into each other and chat for a couple of minutes, choose to have a long walk together, or to grab a coffee and sit together on a bench or a fallen tree;

there's no pressure, no pattern. In the six months before meeting the park gang, Audrey had thought that she was going a bit stir crazy. She had retreated into herself and had no longer talked to anyone if it weren't strictly necessary. It had been her dog walking friends who had saved her, not her old friends, not that that had been their fault particularly, it's just how it was. She probably hadn't been there for them either, in their darkest hours, she thinks.

The Miniature Pinscher incident, although traumatic (she still shudders when she thinks about it) is what had led her to them all in the first place. Sylvie and Lexi were first of course, but quickly after had come Lottie and Piper, and all the others too: Harold and Rolf, Edward, Lily and Luke, Charles and Kip, and others, too. Of these, she remembers the names of the dogs more reliably than that of the humans. She can't now imagine her life without the regular interaction with these park people and their dogs. The nights in the pub from years ago feel loud, forced and aggressive, and they pale in comparison with the gentle, eclectic talks she has in Kensington Gardens every day. The days of dreading walks have also passed with the help of her new gang; Beagle's behaviour is slowly but perceptibly improving, and with friends often around to amortise potentially stressful situations, Audrey feels more confident. She is well liked in the park. It's funny, she thinks, how a clique can be a good thing, once you are in it - if it's the right clique. *Tribe,* she thinks, *that's what it's called, finding your tribe.* She'd read about it in a magazine a while back. She feels that at long last, she has found her Tribe.

A LAST MINUTE REPRIEVE

At Nero and Neil's home

NERO

As if in the distance, he hears a big bang, a muffled crash, feels a vibration through the floor. His mind drops back into his body with a sickening thump.

What the hell is that!

Is he back?

Feeling relief and fear, in equal parts, he is so exhausted that although he is aware something is happening, he can't move, can't wake. He drifts away again; it was probably only his imagination again anyway, he thinks. He feels so very tired. Nero thinks he hears someone shout, 'In here!' but they sound far away.

He feels hands on him, probing his mouth, his gums, his eyes. He feels kindness in the handling. Even if he hadn't, he wouldn't have any strength to resist, to fight. Sleep is coming back, he can't stop it any more, has no will to.

'Oh god, Bob, poor thing.'

'Yup. We'll have to get a drip into him – as soon as we can - it's touch and go, just look at the poor thing, strewth. He's been in here for days. No water, probably... and,' there is a pause, 'he ran out of Hobnobs.' The second voice laughs, grimly. The first voice doesn't laugh.

Nero feels himself lift up, away, his mind is out of his body now, looking down

Woah! Something is wrong... *Is that me?* He looks so weak, so fragile...His head is spinning now, and he feels himself whoosh back down and into his body, a thump and then the familiar queasiness. It is too much, he welcomes the fall into sleep, he surrenders.

Peace.

CONFESSIONS OF SORROWS

Brook Green

HELEN

That Helen lost the love of her life some years ago is a pain that is always lodged within her, and part of her is looking forward to seeing him on the other side. She's not ready yet though, despite the relentless missing of him. Helen plaits her long grey hair every morning carefully and puts it up into two buns, which she unplaits every night. She loves nature and the feel of the wind on her skin. 'The earth delights to feel your feet and the wind longs to play with your hair' she tells Sarah. She loves life - the sound of birdsong, the sight of children or dogs playing and of people laughing, of young lovers holding hands. Tattoos and piercings notwithstanding it's all the same, young love, she thinks, you see it in the eyes, and in the way the young lovers create a bubble around them that excludes everyone else. Helen watches all this from her bench on Brook Green.

Violence and conflict, of which there was much in Africa, has taught her to be mindful and to appreciate the calm days, the beautiful days when nothing much happens. She is astounded by how ungrateful people are when they complain of being bored. 'Do they not see the news, families fleeing their homes, devastated by loss and grief?' she asks Sarah, often.

She feels like shaking people who say they are bored. 'What so many others would give to be bored!' she exclaims to Sarah, often.

Helen's body is failing her, and that makes her frustrated, though she tries not to get bitter. She has to use a stick, much to her shame and frustration. The stick is helpful and benevolent, but Helen hates having to use it, she bangs it on the ground crossly when she is safely sitting down on her bench, and stows it as far as she can away from her, which Danny teases her about. Helen hates being frail, she hates that her son was taken too soon, but she loves life and she appreciates every day she is granted, every new season.

Helen and Lottie are sitting on a bench in Brook Green, with their backs to the tennis courts. Lottie is having a break between clients and drinking a coffee. Since Helen had first talked to Lottie, when she had, because of young Danny, approached her with a view to understanding more about the field of dog training and how to get into it, she has recognised in Lottie something of the reflection of her own pain; she saw the shadow of it immediately, etched on her face, felt its presence. She senses it in the moments between the words, in the faraway looks between action, in the fleeting, painful moments that Helen sees desperation holding Lottie in its grip. She isn't sure whether Lottie will tell her, but it feels right to ask, so she does.

'What was it that happened dear?' Helen asks her softly.

'My... my boyfriend,' Lottie starts, and stops. Takes a deep breath.

'My boyfriend was killed. A stupid accident, someone driving too fast, undertaking in a bus lane.' A pause.

'Fast!' she spits the word out. 'It wasn't fast, even. No one can drive fast in London. It was just unlucky. He clipped him, the... the man who...' Lottie takes another deep, shaky breath. Helen looks down at her hands folded in her lap. She feels pale, bloodless hearing these words. The same had happened to her George, cycling to work. How many young lives are claimed like this?

'It was just how he hit him, apparently. It was instant, they said. They probably always say that. What's the point of saying anything else?' Lottie lifts her eyes and gazes across to the children's play park, her eyes on a young figure swinging backwards and forwards, angling its little body this way and that, eager to go faster, higher.

Its parent is standing beside the swing, texting. The little body doesn't seem to care, although perhaps it is crying out to be watched, to be pushed, Lottie can't tell, they are too far away for her to make out their expressions.

'Maybe it was the truth?' ventures Helen gently.

'Yes.' Lottie frowns. 'I don't know how instant it could have been, honestly. Could it?' she looks into Helen's eyes. Helen finds herself shaking her head, looking down at her hands in her lap again.

'I don't know' she says, plainly, quietly. She takes a deep, unsteady breath.

'Am so sorry.' Helen says, seeking Lottie's eyes, trying to push away thoughts of George flying through the air, hitting the front of that lorry. This is not the time to wallow.

There is nothing else to say. They sit in silence. Piper nuzzles Lottie's hand, trying to take the pain away. Sarah snoozes on the floor.

'I... I don't want them to know, the rest of them. The dog people.' Helen knows who she means. Friends they meet, dog walking, some of whom they hold in common. 'Please don't tell anyone.' Lottie looks at Helen. Helen nods, she understands. 'I can't bear for it to always be there, you know, like people can't laugh, that they ask me how I am all the time. How can I be?' she looks into Helen's eyes and in an instant sees the grief, sees how exactly she understands.

'You lost someone too!' she says. 'Your husband?'

It is Helen's turn to look away. 'Yes, my husband,' she says, in a faraway voice. 'Nine years ago. But...' Helen hesitates, not wanting to add to the mountain of sorrow, but sees she can't avoid finishing now without lying. 'My son, too.'

An involuntary sound escapes Lottie, a feral cry. 'Oh Helen. I'm so sorry.' The tears brim over, unstoppable now. Helen's revelation has a cataclysmic effect on Lottie, she starts breathing heavily. It is a panic attack, or nearly a panic attack. Lottie has started having them about three weeks after it had happened. She only nearly has them now, since she has started going to a lady who has taught her some breathing and mind exercises to do when she feels it coming on.

She stops it now, slowly gets herself under control, not worrying about making Helen wait. She shakes her head from side to side, violently. 'It's just so unfair!' she says, angrily, 'Horribly unfair! I'm so sorry, I can't imagine how you feel. They say that's the worst thing. I can't – I don't have children so I don't know but...' she turns her whole body to face Helen and looks into her eyes. 'I'm so sorry, Helen.' she says.

Helen reaches for her hand and squeezes it. She doesn't look at Lottie but keeps it there and, with her thumb, rubs it, over and over, soothingly. They stay sitting like that for some minutes.

Helen clears her throat, breaking the silence.

'Right dear, I must get on. Pass me that awful stick will you?'

PROGRESS

Kensington Gardens

AUDREY

Audrey's heart skips as she walks to the park, Beagle's customary hangdog expression notwithstanding. She looks forward to her walks now, they have become totally different since she and Beagle have started going with Harold and Rolf. Harold had suggested it one day out of the blue and Audrey had jumped at the idea. It helps Audrey's confidence having Harold beside her and Rolf's presence helps too, he doesn't put any social pressure on Beagle, and Audrey's heart is touched when she sees them walk along harmoniously side by side or sniffing at the same spot. Harold says that dogs learn from other dogs, and Beagle has a few now in his circle of trust. It is making all the difference. He is fine with Lexi and Rolf, Piper, Lily and Luke and even that big brown dog, the one with no owner, the one Sylvie calls Doggy Dog. He has got used to Lottie's most regular charges too, Paquita and Gatsby and Spartacus. The latter two are giant breeds, but they are so gentle and calm and low energy that even Beagle has realised that he needn't be nervous of them. He's also getting more confident around the humans too – Harold, Sylvie, Edward and Lottie.

She spots Harold, who shouts across to her - 'Audrey!' She smiles and waves at him, holding her pepper spray aloft and waggling it. They don't kiss when they reach each other, they don't touch at all. It's hard - unless you are Sylvie - to make the transition from a park friendship to a real friendship; one where you might, for example, kiss on the cheek, or both cheeks, every time you meet. It is particularly hard with Harold. He has an awkwardness about him that only Sylvie is continental enough to ignore. Sylvie kisses him anyway. Sylvie kisses everyone.

'So, you got it then!' Harold says, looking distinctively owl-like, in his funny little glasses.

'Yes, you're right Harold, I feel better now I have some action plan for if he gets attacked. I mean,' she fiddles with her black bum bag which serves as a treat pouch, 'I'm unlikely to actually use it,' she looks up into his eyes bravely, but finds, disappointingly, that his are on Rolf, 'but it's there, isn't it!' she says, brightly.

'Indeed, dear Audrey, it is!' Harold says, looking into her eyes briefly. She thinks to herself not for the first time how unusual they are, green-brown with flecks in them. Warm eyes, for all his otherwise stand-offish exterior. She would say gruff but he's too posh to be gruff. She wonders about his use of the word 'dear'. It sounds incongruous coming from his lips, it is the sort of thing Edward might say, and Edward is older, roughly by a generation.

Calling people dear is something that Harold has been taught by his sister who tries to school him in the art of social interaction whenever the occasion arises. She had used it once as an example of what it might be nice to say to someone, what might sound warm, and he's never forgotten it. He tends to over use it. It is a curious, impenetrable world, the human social one, for people like Harold to whom such things don't come naturally.

Harold does a half circle around Audrey in order to walk on her left hand side. It is a quirk of his, seemingly to actively choose which side he walks on beside any given female. Audrey has seen him do it with Sylvie too, and with Lottie. Audrey always wonders why, and decides to just ask him. He is unphased by the question and seems surprised by her even needing to ask.

'I choose to walk on the side of you from which danger is more likely to come, Audrey. It is one useful thing that my father taught me himself.' Audrey looks confused, so he goes on. 'For example, if we were walking on the pavement I would walk nearest the road, to protect you from the passing cars. It's the correct thing to do, as a gentleman.'

Audrey doesn't know what to think about this, she has a brief urge to giggle. 'Aha, I see.' It feels a bit archaic, even to Audrey who is naturally rather old-fashioned. But there's something quite touching about it.

She changes the subject by saying, neutrally she hopes, 'How did you train Rolf, Harold?'

'Ah, Rolf, well, he went to gundog school, one in Kent, so I can't take all the credit. But,' he frowns, 'I noticed that he wasn't quite... alright when he came back, I think the chap's methods were a bit suspect. He was a bit - what's the word?' Harold stops and closes his eyes, head tilted up towards the sky. Audrey has the opportunity to study his face closely, and uses it. He's older than she'd thought; middle age is just beginning to show in it, as it will soon in hers 'Cowed,' he says. 'Yes, that's it, that's exactly it, cowed.'

'Oh dear.' Audrey says, concerned. She looks at Rolf. He doesn't appear to be cowed now. 'Cowed isn't good,' she says hesitantly, wanting to acknowledge the doubts Harold has expressed but also not wanting to appear rude.

He looks at her as if she is mad. 'Well he's only a dog, dear.'

Audrey feels her hackles rise, both on behalf of dogs and of feminists everywhere, but she doesn't respond. She takes a breath, and looks at him askance, she has learnt not to be too quick to react to some of the things he says, not to hold some of the silly things he says against him.

He notices the look, and seems to realises that his comment has come across as somewhat odd.

'I mean - what I mean is - well, yes, it was perhaps not ideal but as dogs go, he fits in well into our human world, no?'

Audrey mumbles an agreement. Harold looks into her eyes with an unusual intensity. His are bright, there is a passion beneath. He goes on. And as he does, he holds her gaze, demands it even. It is most unusual. Audrey forces herself not to look away, even though she can feel the blush creeping up her neck, into her face.

'It's awful not to fit into the world properly, you know,' Harold says, sounding hesitant and a bit flustered.

She can tell that he is offering her a part of himself up and, despite feeling awkward, she wants to respond in kind, so touches his arm gently, meaningfully, and looks back into his eyes and says, 'Yes, Harold, I imagine it is.'

Harold is thinking how lovely Audrey's hair is, how lustrous, how shiny, how chestnutty, and how it looks as if it smells clean and fragrant. Despite himself, despite his awkwardness and his aversion to touch, he is tempted to lean in towards her and breathe in the smell of it.

They are walking slowly, neither of them is in any hurry for the walk to be over. They turn by mutual agreement up one of the paths leading to the Rondpoint des chiens, as Lottie and Sylvie, both skiers, have coined it. It is a large horse statue that has 4 paths leading off it. A leggy, boisterous Doberman runs across the path fifty metres in front of them. Audrey stiffens automatically. Harold has seen it too. 'Don't panic, Audrey,' he says, quite firmly. She can tell that he is looking at her but her eyes don't leave the bouncing form of the Doberman. He continues, 'remember what we worked on.' Audrey squares her shoulders, straightens up, breathes deeply. She calls to Beagle, and to her relief her voice comes out sounding confident. Beagle looks up, and moves towards her. He is on a five metre long training lead – she doesn't dare let him further, or off completely; he scoots away from anything that moves and she's terrified of him running onto the road and getting hurt, or simply of losing him. So many lost dogs these days. He looks up at her and she bends down and passes a treat to him. Surprisingly, he takes it. He is not feeling overwhelmed then, if he can focus on taking a treat. She beams at Harold but he looks stern. He is concentrating, looking between Beagle and the Doberman. 'I don't think he's clocked him yet, Audrey. Watch him.'

Audrey watches, and sure enough Beagle's body position changes as he notices the young, large dog. Beagle's gait is permanently crouched

- his walk a creep, his stand a stoop - but it gets more pronounced now, his ears angle back and his brow completely crumples. His tail disappears underneath his bottom, Audrey feels her blood pressure rising. She does as Harold has taught her though, slides her hand down the lead and calls to Beagle in an upbeat, casual voice, 'Let's go!' she says, doing a brisk 180 degree turn and walking calmly but decisively off in the other direction. Beagle keeps rubbernecking, eyes wide; the whale-eyed expression would be comic if it didn't betray such anxiety. With the change in direction though he starts to look marginally less miserable. Harold has turned with them and whistles to Rolf, a confident, enormously loud wolf whistle which makes Audrey's heart do a little jump. She smiles to herself, wishing they could bump into one of her old friends right now. It is such a long time since she's had a male friend, she's almost forgotten what it is like. She ought to look up Scott, her good friend all through high school. They had made it through the traumas of adolescence together: spots, puberty, bullying, exams. She wonders what has happened to him, she ought to call him and check he's OK. It's easy to go under these days, and he hadn't been the most robust of characters at the best of times.

'You see, it's better when he's moving!' says Harold, 'Dogs who are anxious can get blocked and more stressed out if they are made to stand still. It's not natural to be on a lead you know!' he admonishes her, looking at her over the top of his glasses. 'Dogs – particularly dogs like Beagle - like, no, need to feel like they have a choice. Agency, it's called. It makes them feel nervous and stressed when they feel like they don't. Have a choice I mean.' Harold has a theory that Beagle would be less reactive without his lead on, but Audrey isn't willing to risk it and has dug her heels in on that point. They pick up the pace a little. Not rushing, not panicking, just walking with purpose. Audrey forces herself to look towards the horizon, to keep her breathing steady and to make sure her limbs stay loose and relaxed.

'It's ironic me giving you lessons on comportment, after all the ones I had to do as a child.' Harold says, smiling grimly to himself. 'Ophelia, my sister, used to help me, she made a game of it, it made it all less painful; I was always stumbling and being told off. In the evening when we were alone in our playroom she used to walk around with books balanced on her head, mocking Mr Thomas. He was my teacher, I was home schooled. She tried to create his booming voice, it made us laugh a lot. We were anyway relegated to the west wing of the house, far away from Mother and Father, and Nanny Dora wouldn't tell on us - she didn't like Mr Thomas either.'

'It must have been difficult, having to do comportment lessons as a child. I was hopelessly clumsy too!' Audrey says, thinking about the few mortifying lessons of ballet she'd attended before she'd been allowed to give them up. They continue in companionable silence for some time. After a few minutes, Audrey starts telling him about the daycare centre she has found, about all the services and asks him if he thinks it's a good idea.

'Sorry, Audrey?' he says.

Audrey blushes, embarrassed. Had she been wittering on, boring him, she wonders.

'I was just saying' she says, scolding herself in her head for being apologetic and squaring her shoulders, 'I was saying that I've found this place called Nine Trees, it's a doggy daycare place, but it's a bit different. They do socialisation programs and that sort of thing for reactive or anxious or aggressive dogs. I wondered if perhaps they could arrange to put Beagle amongst some...' she pauses, unsure of how to say it, 'non-threatening dogs. In a safe enclosed space, where he could be off the lead,' she smiles at Harold, 'and see how he gets on with it. I'd want to be there, I wouldn't just drop him and leave him, but they might allow it. I mean, I'd insist on it and I'd be paying so...' she finishes bravely. She will call and ask, she resolves to herself, Sylvie's voice sounds in her head says Good! If you don't ask you won't get! And Audrey's own voice in her head repeats over and over her mantra: golden limbs, golden limbs. Sylvie would approve, a mantra is definitely a Sylvie sort of thing, even one manifesting dubiously non-feminist aspirations.

'Good idea Audrey, very good idea. He needs to have more and more positive moments with his own species, good experiences. Dogs can build new neural pathways, they can change. You can't change their past but you can change the past of their future, if that makes sense.'

He laughs, evidently tickled. Harold finds the oddest things funny, Audrey thinks, but finds it endearing.

He turns to face her and beams. 'Yes, that's a really great idea!' he says. Audrey feels a warm glow. She reaches down and strokes Beagle. She's frightened to push their friendship, but it feels like the right moment.

'How's your sister?' she asks. 'Ophelia isn't it?'

Harold seems a bit thrown and Audrey immediately worries that she might have hit a wrong note, and berates herself for being so pushy. Too personal! she thinks, Drat! Just as Audrey is scrabbling around in her brain for something else to say, he continues.

'Fine,' he says shortly. Small talk obviously doesn't come naturally for him, either. 'Well, actually,' he goes on, quieter, as if he is sharing a secret, 'she's not fine. She's leaving her husband. And I'm glad!' He says these last sentence loudly, almost triumphantly.

HAROLD

Harold is determined - determined! - that he will not be ashamed of it. He knows exactly what his parents' reaction will be: deep sighs and furrowed, cross brows: *Shame on the family!... Oh, Ophelia!... Darling, can't you just make it work?! Percy's a complete poppet, what's wrong with you? Really dear I don't know why you expect so much out of life!* and so on and so forth. He can imagine Ophelia's darling face turning away from those of her parents, wilting like a flower. Are they both doomed to perpetually disappoint Mother and Father? Once again it will be Ophelia and Harold turning only to each other for validation, for comfort. Dear Nanny Dora is long gone. Well, so be it, he will hold his head high telling people his sister is divorcing. He is glad! Percy's anything but a poppet, he's a bully and an entitled, boorish, horrible prat.

AUDREY

'Oh!' says Audrey, not knowing what else to say. 'Is she, um... is she unhappy with him?' she asks, gently.

'Very!' Harold answers, with a frown. 'He's not a nice man, at all. And she should have made the decision sooner but... well, you know how it is.' She doesn't, actually, and nor does he - neither of them have had much in the way of functional relationships, but that is something they leave unsaid, there is a limit to the exchanging of confidences at this point in their friendship.

'He's...' Harold seemed to be searching for the right word, he does that, he likes to be precise. He finds it. 'Undermining. He undermines her. Always. It's horrible. I'm very glad she's leaving him, very glad.' He says it proudly, decisively. To Audrey's surprise, he goes on.

'She's always protected me, Ophelia, it's just how it's always been. But lately I've been feeling protective of her too. No one but a sibling knows the whole truth of a childhood, what you take into your adult years.'

Audrey vigorously nods her assent, even though she herself is an only child. She has often wished that she weren't, and she often wishes there was someone to share the overwhelming and at times stifling love of her parents with. She notes that he glances at her as she does nods and seems satisfied with her reaction. They walk on in companionable silence.

'Do you like Earl Grey, Audrey dear?'

Audrey nods her assent, although she can't help a gentle smirk crossing her face. Somehow whenever she's with Harold she feels like she's in a Jane Austen novel. She's always liked the Austen novels, mind.

'Of course I do, Harold.'

Harold thinks to himself what a pleasure it would be to see Audrey more. He suddenly feels very positive about his future. Ophelia will be free of that awful monster of a husband, and he pictures the three of them drinking tea on Wednesdays. Maybe they could even go out for dinner somewhere, like Ophelia had suggested once. He can deal with a bit of change, maybe, it's not beyond him, he thinks, bravely.

SAFE BEHIND BARS

At a dog shelter, South London

NERO

Nero wakes up, ravenous. He opens his eyes, and lifts his head.

I can do that again! he thinks.

Head lifted just off the floor, only his eyes move, taking in his surroundings.

What was wrong with me before? he wonders.

Where is Neil?

Where am I?

He looks around, not moving his body yet but craning his head. He is in a small area, 2 metres square, with concrete walls and one side barred, looking onto a corridor, again concrete. His sense of hearing returns with a whoosh and all of a sudden the voices of all the dogs in neighbouring runs crowd in on him. Barks and shouts and conversations, whines and yaps and nonsensical whimperings, arguments and laughs and demands for food and attention. Questions, appeals and laments - lots of laments. He looks around, panicking, but realises he is alone.

What's going on?

Who are all these dogs, what are they doing here?

What am I doing here?

Why am I behind bars?

Nero drags himself up onto his feet with a sense of urgency. He stumbles, weakly, and then realises that he has some tubes attached to him and jumps away, freaked out. He tears at them with his teeth.

Jesus! He says. It's a word he's picked up off his owner, Neil, who particularly enjoys blaspheming because his mother had been religious and he had despised her.

He stoops instinctively with his mouth to get to the sharp feeling in his leg. He tears at the patch.

Ouch, ouch!

He tugs, again and again. Something gives. He spits out the thing in his mouth, although it takes him a few tries, it's sticky.

That's better.

What is this place?

He goes towards the bars, sniffing, interested now, he smells there is food.

Food! He thinks, longingly.

He opens his mouth and tries to bark but only croaks, pathetically. Someone happens to be walking past, just at this point. Fortuitous.

'Oh, 'ello boi! You woke up!'

The someone approaches and looms in front of the light, beyond the bars. Nero instinctively backs away. The voice softens, and the man now crouches down, slowly, a little way back from the bars. He speaks softer. 'Lucky boi, anuvva few aahs and I reckon you'd'a been a goner! Close call, no mistake. 'Ere, 'old on a minute, yer starvin', I know.' The man straightens up, knees clicking, and Nero whines, desperate for food. He stops himself vocalising, even though it takes a great effort of will. Neil hadn't liked him to whine. 'Wait, just 'old on, I'll be back,' says the man, holding his palm out in the universal sign language for wait. Nero knows it from the park and watching other dogs and their humans, but Neil had been against using hand signals. Nero had envied the dogs in the park whose owners had communicated using hand or body gestures, they were much easier to understand than words.

The man starts to walk away and a piercing cry of a bark escapes from Nero, a sound like nothing he's ever heard before, it startles him. It happens again, followed by a cat-like, anguished yowl, again a noise he doesn't think he's ever made before now.

Where's Neil?

Why am I in here?

Will that man come back?

Will I get some food?

I'm starving!

When will that man come back?

He might never come back.

He might just leave me in here forever.

Who are all these dogs?

Are they going to come and attack me?

Nero starts to panic and throws himself against the bars, but he finds he is quickly out of strength. There's water in the room, he spies it out of the corner of his eye, and runs over the few steps to the bowl and laps at it, desperately, eagerly. It's something, it brings relief, just the motion of drinking. He doesn't feel thirsty any more though, he registers, that awful thirst that he'd had, back at home. How so? He hadn't drunk, since then, had he? He doesn't remember. He looks at the snaky tubes he has disentangled himself from. He lifts his head lightly, looks up slightly, at an angle, without seeing – he's focussing on listening. The man is coming back, he hears the steps. Nero snaps into action, sits his bottom on the floor so he's in a sit. His posture is alert, straight, he sits like a Good Boy, like he's been taught, and shifts his front paws, shuffles his bottom.

Wait, waaaaait he tells himself.

'OK boi, good boiii, it's comin' it's comin'...'

The man bends down and opens a hatch and slides the bowl through it.

Don't spring up and knock the bowl before it hits the floor, that makes the humans angry... waiiiiit...

'There!'

Nero can smell what's in it and the salivary glands in his mouth explode into action, his mouth fills with drool. It seeps out and drips onto the floor.

He licks his lips, they make a smacking noise.

Wait...

He is licking his lips, again and again, involuntarily, and his paws are working up and down.

'You look like yer kneadin' bread, boi!' the man laughs.

Nero focusses on waiting, control. He doesn't take his eyes off the bowl.

The human stands up, and Nero feels its confusion. His confusion, it's a he human, he can tell. The human is laughing, Nero doesn't know why, it doesn't sound mean like when Neil laughs at him and makes him wait for his food, sometimes not even giving it to him at all but just removing it and tipping it into the toilet and flushing it away. Nero is filled with sadness when he does that, and it even makes him hate Neil, momentarily. Nero cocks his head on one side and looks at the man, trying to work it out.

The man is laughing now, but kindly, and his laughter soon dies out.

'Yer owner was a dis'plinarian, huh?' he says, and tuts. 'I'm more used to bein' mobbed an' jumped all over t'be honest! Yer a sorry sight boi, skin an' bone.'

Wait...

Wait... Nero tells himself in his head.

'Go on 'en boi!' The man gestures with his head to the bowl, making some movement with his arm that Nero doesn't understand, Neil had been economical with hand gestures, demanding that Nero understand everything through verbal communication, even though he knew that's so much harder for dogs.

Nero doesn't move a muscle except to cock his head. Sometimes Neil makes him wait for hours. He can't work out what the man wants from him but thinks he'd better be careful.

I'll get beaten if I go for it before I'm allowed and he'll whip it away anyway and not let me have it, he'll take it away to the pee place...

Nero wonders, suddenly, if some dogs don't have to go through this process. The man seems to be just telling him to eat. Without waiting. Without complication. Nero's brain hurts. *It must be some sort of trick,* he thinks. But he's so hungry...

'Go on boi!' He feels kindness emanating from the man, who gestures with a nod of his head towards the food bowl again, then with a small, sad sigh puts his hand through the hatch and pushes the bowl further in towards Nero.

Oh god I can smell it...

Does he... Nero strains and strains to understand the man, who is staring at him. The man does nothing, just waits, looking at Nero.

Does he mean....?

He doesn't want to get a beating, but on the other hand it will be worth it if he can bolt it all down before the man reaches him.

'Yes, go on boi, eat! Eat!' The man urges. Unable to restrain himself longer, Nero surges forward and wolfs it down, as fast as he can. God it feels good, he thinks. He isn't able to get it in fast enough, gulps it back, bolts it down, the food barely touching the sides, quickly after hitting his empty, nervous tummy. It takes about 10 seconds for him to empty the bowl.

He hears the man walking away, chuckling and saying

'That's a Gooood Boiii!'

Nero licks the bowl obsessively, he licks the floor, he licks his chest and his front paws, in case something fell there as it does sometimes. He whines involuntarily. After he's licked at the empty bowl and the floor and himself for a long time he lays down, suddenly exhausted. He can hear barking and shouts and conversations all around, and it is a little distracting, but that there are multiple voices makes him feel less pressured than if there had been just one. He feels relatively secure. He lays on his side and sleeps.

As he sleeps, one particular dog keeps up the same lament, on a loop, for hours. Its voice is hoarse, cracked, raw.

Let me out of here! I want to go back home! Let me out of here! I want to go back home to my people! Where are you, my people? Why did you leave me? Where are you? Let me come home!

And another howls, the sadness palpable.

Why?

Just that one word.

Nero twitches in his sleep. He's looking for Piper and Lottie.

A NEW START

Edinburgh train station

Rhett and Grey slip between the legs of passengers largely unnoticed, except by a twenty year old student who is staying on the train beyond Edinburgh. Her seat faces the exit doors and she stares after them. She rolls her tongue around in her mouth playing with the piercing in it, thoughtfully, wondering. She notices the section missing from the brown dog's ear and the lack of a collar on the skinny grey dog. Something fishy, she thinks, about these two dogs, but since it is none of her business she turns her mind to something else, her tongue still playing with its piercing.

GREY

Grey is nervous. The butterflies in his stomach won't stop and he's queasy. He feels such a long way from everything that is familiar, even the air itself is different here: denser, damper, with a sharp sort of cold in it. He hadn't expected that, somehow, that the very air could smell different. It unnerves him. Sniffing, trying to identify the differences in it, he thinks of space, of places impossible to picture but certainly completely unlike his home city with its grey, familiar pavements.

'It's... different here,' he says to Rhett, tremulously.

'That's the point, Grey,' Rhett replies firmly, 'we had to get you far away from there. We couldn't have Lady Human finding you.

She didn't chip you, which is a good thing, and that woman in the shop who took your collar off did an amazing thing, I'd like to meet her one day. I have a feeling we'll be lucky Grey. The Dog God will help us.' Rhett winks. 'We need to find someone to take you in up here that's for sure, and soon.' Rhett frowns. 'It's too cold here to live outside. And you're not the type anyway.'

Grey feels offended but Rhett gives him a pointed look, and he can't help smiling back. It's true. 'OK, OK.' His little sighthound life is in his friend's hands and, even though he's scared, he has faith in Rhett.

'We just need to pick well,' says Rhett, scanning around him. They had wandered around a bit after exiting the station and found a little square not far from it, where they are now sitting. Grey notices that Rhett looks extremely focussed and serious, not at all like his usual loose-limbed London self. He is sitting upright and still, his front paws tucked back tight into him. He looks for all the world just like a dog waiting patiently for its owner, his head turning intelligently, serenely, this way and that. He has the air of an entirely different dog. Grey can't help stealing furtive glances at him.

'What is it, Grey?' Rhett asks, distractedly.

'Oh, nothing Rhett, nothing.' Grey says, smirking slightly. He looks in the direction Rhett is looking, even though he doesn't really know what he's looking for. They sit like this for maybe twenty-five or thirty minutes, watching the various people. Huddled up in coats, they pass by singly, in pairs, in groups. Grey looks up into the faces, as many as he can. They seem slightly different from London humans, but he can't place how. Grey starts to get really, really cold. He doesn't want to sound like he's complaining but he's shaking hard now, in bouts. He's just about to say something, when Rhett says, quietly, 'Hmmm. Interesting.'

Grey follows his gaze to the shop entrance opposite, a bakery, where two men have exited, laughing, one rather large and hirsute, the other slighter, fairer. Both have beanies on, and overcoats. Rhett barks, once, loudly, and Grey gives a start. He doesn't think he's ever heard Rhett bark before. Rhett barks again, again once, again loudly, and to Grey's astonishment the hairier of the two men looks directly over at them, and a smile floods his face.

'Ahh look at the wee pooches!' they hear him say. Without hesitation he moves towards them and Grey goes to stand up. Rhett though doesn't move from has statue like position and hisses at him, urgently, 'No Grey, stay still, sit down, let them come to us!'

It makes Grey less wary that they are men, he is more scared of women.

'Och,' the first man says, crouching down and stroking Rhett gently, after first politely letting him sniff his hand. Grey watches, completely stunned. Rhett doesn't let people pet him, it's just something he doesn't do. In fact Grey doesn't think he's ever seen him even touch a human, except maybe Lottie, but even then, it has definitely happened only rarely.

'You don't have a home you wee dogs, eh?' asks the man, his voice low and kind. He looks into Grey's eyes, then back to Rhett.

The second man crouches down and softly reaches his hand out to Grey, slowly and unthreateningly, as the other man had done with Rhett. Grey sniffs, tentatively. He smells of apples and bacon, and something Grey can't put his finger on, something a bit woody. It smells a bit like Harold, and Edward. They are all intoxicating, appealing smells and certainly very different from Lady Human's perfume, Paris. Grey decides that he definitely prefers men humans.

'Ahh you poor wee thing,' the bulky one says, turning his attention to Grey, 'Y'er freezin' eh?' He looks into Grey's eyes. Grey looks longingly at the man's chest, at the soft looking jumper underneath his big coat. He'd like to climb in there and get warm. The man turns to his partner,

'D'you think they have a home Geoff?'

'Well, I dunno Richie dear, I dunno. What if they're waitin' on someone?'

'I don't think they are,' the other chap says doubtfully.

'This one looks half starved. And so cold.' He rolls his 'r's, but differently from Sylvie. He gestures at Grey who is now shivering uncontrollably. 'And the other one isn't much better.' Rhett is doing his best to look pathetic, his head hanging right down although his body is in a proper full upright sit. Grey almost laughs, and thinks I wish I could tell Piper and Lexi about this! Rhett is a real actor!

'Why don't we take them home and then go from there love?'

Geoff looks at him, he knows what is about to happen.

'OK, OK, Richie, if they follow us,' he says, gently 'but no encouraging them.'

Grey looks at Rhett, whose face betrays no particular emotion. But when the men walk away Rhett springs to his feet and takes his place by Geoff's side, just like Rolf does with Harold. He trots right beside his leg, perfectly in sync. The man called Richie laughs, and winks down at Grey, who feels suddenly overwhelmed, but in a good way.

SARAH DREAMS

At Helen and Sarah's home

SARAH

Sarah feels the tang of it in her mouth, it's always there now. It saddens her. That life should end, it just seems wrong. It seems wrong to leave Helen, it goes against Sarah's every instinct, it's so cruel this life, this getting attached to each other only to be ripped apart. She barely remembers the time before Helen and she can't imagine them not being together. She does though understand that that is how it has to be, she accepts the inevitability of it. Sarah is resigned to and reconciled with the fact that she must soon die. She hopes however that now, with Lottie's help and Danny's friendship, Helen will have the strength to move on into another phase. Helen is already talking about going to visit her brother Eddie up in Glasgow, and it is something that heartens Sarah, to know that once she has gone, Helen will be free to do it. At least one good thing will come of her passing. Sarah knows what a hit it will be for Helen, her going, but she clings on to this positive thought. Eddie, people had used to call him apparently. By all accounts he is a big character, large of heart, loud of voice, bursting with energy and sparkle. Sarah will never meet him now of course, at least not in this life, but she feels she would like him if she did. Ted had, and that's good enough for her.

Sarah likes to play a game as she falls asleep at night, or when she goes for a snooze during the day, for that matter. She imagines Helen making the journey up to visit Eddie. Sarah can picture her stepping up onto the train from the platform carefully, walking along the carriage a little way then sitting down next to someone, another lady perhaps, or maybe a clean-shaven young man in a suit. Helen always takes care to ask, in Sarah's imaginings, before she sits down. Sarah knows that Helen would do that. She knows all of Helen's mannerisms and tendencies, she knows just how she will ask, with what cadence, with what expression, body movement and inclination of her head. Sarah imagines the young man, the clean-shaven one, smiling back at Helen and saying, 'yes of course,' and engaging in some polite small talk before returning to the work he had been doing on the computer. They sit in companionable silence. The young man is happy that some smelly yob or loud obnoxious person talking on the phone hasn't sat next to him, and Helen is satisfied with her choice of seat and neighbour.

Or perhaps, Helen will choose a young man to sit next to, a young man who looks troubled and has thick, dark stubble and one ankle crossed over the other knee, claiming space. She asks the same question in the same tone to this youth, and he responds, less gracefully but in the affirmative and as he does so he shifts his body slightly, to give her more room. For all his swagger he knows his mother would kill him if she were to see him do anything else, and he has always been aware of her presence in the ether since she passed over last year. Helen seeks out this youth's eyes and ekes some conversation out of him. He starts to soften and to free himself, in spite of himself, in spite of his anger at the world, of his not knowing where he is to fit within it, of not having his mum to run home to and in spite of all the responsibility that is falling on his little shoulders now.

Or perhaps, Helen will sit on a four-seater table opposite a harried young mother. The mother within Sarah's imagination gives Helen a quick, apologetic smile, and Helen's nearness will serve to soothe the fractious child, who will fall asleep. Quickly afterwards the frazzled mother does too, gratefully. Helen smiles and doesn't attempt conversation throughout all this, she just quietly reads her book.

When they get close to Glasgow Helen will start to get butterflies, Sarah knows. The Helen in Sarah's imaginings excuses herself and asks her hypothetical male travelling companions to watch her bag (small, she will pack light) whilst she goes to the ladies. Or if she is on the four-seater with the mother and child she carries it with her and manoeuvres it on to her lap as she gingerly sits on the rudimentary metal toilet seat and tries not to breathe through her nose (but not really through her mouth either). She returns, swaying slightly with the movement of the train but gripping the tops of the seats tightly, sensibly, and the butterflies inside her continue their fluttering all the way until the train draws in to the platform. After that, Sarah knows, she will have no time to pay them any attention and they will disappear. She will spy Eddie as soon as she gets off the train, he will be larger than life and just the same as she remembers him, looking up and down the platform with concern on his face. She will see that great, familiar and to her ageless face break into a wide smile as he sees her and spreads his arms (even though she is still 20 metres away from him) to give her a hug.

Sarah likes to imagine all this, to feel the certainty of the ending of it. It is how she gets to sleep, when the pain starts to gnaw at her. It soothes and distracts her, thinking about it. She always falls asleep at that point when Eddie spreads his arms wide, or even before, heartened. She has made up now hundreds of train travelling companions for Helen, but the welcome at the station is always the same, just as it will be when it comes to be.

HELEN

'Jesuschrist, girl, get a grip!' Helen shouts at the telly irreverently, and then chuckles. Danny would have grinned and rolled his eyes and laughed out loud all in one, hearing her say this. *Get a grip!* is one of his more regular expressions, as is *jesuschrist!* Even though he always clamps his hand over his mouth half way through saying it. He probably thinks Helen is religious because she's old. She laughs. Helen is pretty sure that God won't strike her down, even if her dead friend Ada's late husband would have pursed his lips and shaken his head hearing her blaspheme.

Helen thinks about Danny. She loves seeing him laugh. Young adults are under so much pressure to act cool these days, and it's nice to see him able to let his guard down. She hopes she'll live long enough to see him turn into the fine adult she knows he'll become. She turns the channel over. She can't bear a lot of what's on telly these days. Cocking her head on one side, a habit she has picked up from her Sarah, Helen thinks about how life has dealt Danny an unfair hand giving him the parents it has. She is sure he will get on fine in life though. He's such a genuine, endearing, kind, droll boy. She smiles to herself thinking about some of the conversations they've had, amused. He doesn't treat her like an old person, and she loves that she feels younger when she's with him. Perhaps she should try the micro-dosing thing he had told her about last week. Or that marijuana oil stuff, oHHo. That would give her daughter-in-law something to really worry about, she chuckles.

She wonders why one is expected to be so sensible when one is old, shouldn't it be the time to let oneself throw caution to the wind a bit, she thinks. She remembers that poem about wearing purple in old age; she isn't keen on it as prefers sombre, serious poetry but she has to admit that the writer of it has a point.

HYPOCHONDRIA

BEAGLE

Beagle also thinks that he might have a B12 deficiency. He doesn't know how to get Audrey to have him tested and has been obsessing about it for months. His four little legs get pins and needles whenever he is still, his tongue feels too big in his mouth, he feels not right – tired and a bit dizzy, unfocused. The more he thinks about it the surer he is that he has it. His body just feels like it isn't functioning properly, like something is off. He worries and worries about it.

Ironically, Beagle picks up a lot of knowledge about illnesses from the radio which Audrey always leaves on in order for Beagle not to be unsettled by silence

He also thinks that he might be suffering from that personality disorder where you hear voices - he's heard about it on the radio. Schizophrenia it's called. Apparently around 5% of those who have it end up killing themselves, which makes him worry not just about dying but also about how on earth he will manage to do it when the time comes that he needs to. He keeps hearing strange sounds, outside of the house and in. He finds it impossible to settle at home and scuttles with his tail between his legs, cringing, from memories of half-remembered moments, an atmosphere of threat. He cowers away from imagined, faceless demons, malevolent presences, and from the torment that is his own brain.

He slinks from one bed to another, now into his crate but finds it oppressive, now onto the beanbag by the window but finds it too exposed, now out of the room, quickly scooting through the scary, high-ceilinged hallway through into the utility room and onto the memory foam mat. The mat has a cosy topper, and it is placed on a raised hiK9 bed, which is mounted on legs, for ventilation. But now Beagle worries about this. Surely drafts are dangerous? he thinks. He'd heard Audrey's mother tell her that, and she had seemed particularly earnest on the subject. So back he goes into the living room, into the corner where he has a full vantage point of the whole room and feels relatively protected by the wall on the left of him, and by the wooden piano overhanging him. He waits a few seconds, but this isn't right either. He slopes across the room and into the basket by the door. He's not very comfortable and thinks he can hear a fly. If even Piper is scared of flies then they must be dangerous. Finally, exhausted by all the indecision and anxiety he hurries back over into the crate and settles into an uneasy snooze, popping his head up every few minutes for a nervous little 'woof'. He spies with his one open eye Audrey, who sticks her head around the door as she is passing to go to the loo.

'Oh Beagle love,' she says to him gently, 'you don't have to stay in there all day.'

It seems to Beagle that the sentence might have a question mark in it but when, not knowing how to respond, he ignores her, her head disappears and she pulls the door to a little. He hears her sigh and feels even more mournful. He knows on some level how difficult he is to live with, and hates himself for it.

SAFE BEHIND BARS II

At a dog shelter, South London

NERO

The man is sorry for him, Nero can tell. He isn't sure why at first as he feels almost happy here, the barking doesn't bother him too much and he's quickly come to learn that he has regular food, four times a day even, every day! He is on extra portions as the shelter has assessed him to be dangerously underweight. And water he gets as much as he wants, whenever he wants it and never any punishment for taking it! Neil had liked to withhold or extend sustenance to Nero on a whim, and it had been tiring not knowing when you would have to suffer the gnawing feeling in your stomach, or the thirst, always having to be frightened whilst you ate or drank because you were anticipating the potential crack of his belt on your back. Nero can pee too, any time he wants, there's an exit to an outside space that is obviously meant exactly for that, it makes him happy. He drinks some water, trots out to pee, trots back in, drinks some more water, lays down, listens to his neighbours, and repeats the whole exercise.

Nero doesn't talk yet, even though his next-door neighbours on both sides and the one two doors down towards where the humans come from have all sent questions his way. He stays silent as he doesn't know how he feels about the camaraderie, chatting with other dogs is not something he's had much experience of, except for a bit lately with Rhett and Lexi and a couple of the others. He's only really chatted at any length with Piper, who was his first and only real friend.

It isn't bad here, he thinks. He doesn't suffer too much from the lack of freedom as anyway Neil hadn't let him run freely much and has, by necessity grown used to being held captive. When he hadn't been, and had protested, at the beginning, Neil had nearly broken his jaw with a beating he would never forget. Here he feels safe. He likes knowing that he doesn't have to fear any of the people who come to feed him or to clean his living area. There are three of them: two men, and one woman. He likes the woman best, but he thinks of the first man he had met, the one he had seen when he first woke up, as his. For him Nero is extra obedient. He hopes, shyly, hardly really daring to hope, that the man will take him home with him. All three of the humans fuss him and scratch his head when they come in. Sometimes they take him out for a short walk. Sometimes there'll be another dog on a lead nearby. But Nero just puts his head down and avoids eye contact. The humans always tell him enthusiastically what a Good Boy he is, walking so nicely on the lead. He's surprised by that. It wouldn't occur to him to pull.

The humans are always in a hurry though, which makes him sad. He feels that they are always a bit sad too. *Is it because they don't have more time?* He wonders. He thinks that it must be. Humans are strange creatures, always so busy. He wonders why one of his three carers doesn't stop and have a little nap with him, he's heard about humans doing that with their dogs, and it sounds nice. Piper and Lottie do it, he knows, as well as Sylvie and Lexi. Dogs and humans acting like siblings, like litter-mates, that's what life should be all about, he thinks - how Piper and Lottie are together. He thinks about them often, it makes him happy. He had used to watch them in the park when he'd been on the lead and hadn't been able to go and greet them. They often play together, more like dogs do than humans, oblivious to everyone else around them. Lottie and Piper had included him, when they could, in the rare moments when Nero was off lead and Neil was distracted. That hadn't happened often though. He misses Piper, and looks forward to telling her all about all this, about everything that has happened. It feels like a long time since he has seen Neil, since they had been for a walk. Kensington Gardens feels like a different life. He wonders where Neil is and gives a little whine, unsure of how he is feeling, unsure of whether he wants to be reunited, or not.

Nero hears them talking beyond the bars, his man, and the lady.

'There's not much hope for 'im really,' the man is saying ''e's a young dog, a fine dog, but Germ'n Shepherds, well – pound a penny aren't they. He's got prey drive too innit.' Nero wonders what that is. He pricks his ears up to the max as the man continues. 'Won't be able to be trusted wi' the Fifis, 'e'll need an experienced owner. People don't like to take 'em on unless 'ey're pups do they, scared, innit. Anyway, they only seem to wanna take Mals these days – f' pets and f' security both. Easier, innit. Smaller, easier to train too, that's what they say anyway. Not sure it's true mind. Maliga'ors they call 'em. Not good in the wrong 'ands. Like any dog I s'pose. No, I'm not holding out much hope for 'im. I'll ask our Kelly to stick 'im on the breed rescue site though, you never know – werf a try innit. She can be determin'd when she puts 'er shoulder to it!' he chuckles. Nero has met Kelly, she'd told him his name when she'd come round one lunchtime to meet all the new dogs. She's got several different colours in her hair and a pale, round face with lots of piercings in it, and a pale, round body to match – a body always sheathed in the bizarrest outfits the woman part of his threesome of carers had said once, Nero had heard her. His man puts one hand through the top bars to give Nero's head a fond ruffle. 'Y' nevva know, y' nevva know boi, y' might get lucky!' Nero presses his head into his man's hand and wishes for the contact never to stop. But the man moves away, he has work to do.

Nero puts his head on his paws and whines, properly now. He feels quite unsure about what is going to come next for him, and he longs to see Piper and the others in the park. Well, Rhett and Lexi at least. Even though Neil hadn't allowed him to socialise much with them he had managed to exchange at least a few words every time in passing one or both of them. Even short conversations sometimes, when Neil had been distracted. Piper, had always run over to get some time with him whenever she'd seen him, and Lottie had always let her. Lottie had sent Nero good vibes from afar, he could always feel it. Neil had often had to physically chase Piper away, or shout over to Lottie to call her. Sometimes Lottie had affected not to hear so they could have a bit more time together, she knew that Piper was easily capable of dodging out of Neil's reach if he had tried to grab her, annoyed that she'd been hanging around.

Nero had felt that he was beginning to become friends with Rhett and Lexi, and he'd even exchanged a few sniffing pleasantries and so on with a few others in the group, Lily, Lexi, Rolf, and even some snivelling wreck of a dog called Beagle. Those moments had given him a warm, proud feeling. That Border Collie friend of theirs, Kip, had always annoyed him though. Nero begins to daydream about how he will have a good go at him if he ever gets back to the park. If Lottie isn't watching, of course, or Piper.

CONNECTION

Kensington Gardens

LOTTIE

Lottie feels the weight of the world on her shoulders. She knows she is over-reacting, she knows her anger is disproportionate, that she should shrug it off when people are idiots, when they throw litter or bitch about dogs for no reason, but she just can't help it, she's furious. Since losing Sebastian, things bite at her that didn't bite before. It's a sign of grief, apparently, of trauma. Some woman had just had a go at Piper for running through her son's football game.

'I don't know, Harold,' she says, as they walk down the path towards the Italian Fountains, 'I feel...' she looks into his eyes and notices how kind they are. She thinks about Audrey, who she thinks has a crush on Harold. 'I really feel like I can't live around humans much more, they...' she shakes her head, desperately, 'they just drive me mad. They're so angry all the time! Me included!'

'Ah Lottie, Lottie,' Harold smiles and although he sounds a bit patronising, now she knows him better she can tell he means well. 'Can I tell you something?' He stops as he says this and turns to face her. 'I have had a long struggle with living amongst humans. I have... how can I say it... some differences from others. I had a lot of problems as a child. And it continued, persisted into adulthood. I began to hate people, at one point, really hate them. I tried to stay away from them completely. Well,' he looks her directly in the eyes and says, 'you know.' In this moment of candour, Harold is referring to the time before they had become a friendship gang. Proud, tall and awkward he had marched about the park, isolated and aloof, his well-behaved little gundog Rolf at his side. Until dear, kind Sylvie had noticed and brought him into the fold.

'My only real friend was my sister, Ophelia. She was the only human being I talked to. For years! And long after that, after I started being able to talk to others, she was still the only one I really trusted. It isn't the answer, Lottie, you have to...' he searches for the words. 'Let people in!'

Saying this he grins at her and she laughs back.

'Seriously though. You just need to surround yourself with the right people. Like my Ophelia – and now, you lot. People who will see you right.' He looks struck by something in what he has just said. 'And who see you right,' he adds, softly. Lottie feels she wants to hug him but thinks he wouldn't like that so she touches his arm.

He smiles at her, and reminds her of an owl. 'Come on, there's Beagle, let's see if we can't make him a bit less miserable, huh?'

'Yup!' Lottie says, 'Audrey deserves it.' She looks at Harold as she says Audrey's name to see if he will give anything away but his face has reverted to its usual indecipherability.

'Audrey!' he barks, sharply, and Lottie laughs to herself. Audrey looks up and smiles at them. Blushing, she gives a little wave.

RESTLESS

An estate somewhere in the countryside near Edinburgh

RHETT

Rhett is getting itchy feet. It has been a peaceful, calm interlude, living with Richie and Geoff. He likes Ginger, the one-eyed Tomcat. He's a feisty character and makes sure to let him and Grey know who he thinks is boss. Rhett is beginning to find life a bit too predictable with Richie and Geoff and Grey though, not to say claustrophobic. Rhett sleeps on the flagstones downstairs, not the warm ones near the hearth but the cold ones near the back door. Grey sleeps in a smart tartan basket by Richie and Geoff's bed upstairs. They'd got one for Rhett too of course, matching, the perfect size for his big frame, and put it on the other side of the bed, but he isn't into all that. Geoff had known he wouldn't be but he had indulged Richie.

Grey doesn't understand how Rhett feels, he knows that, Grey himself is delighted to be discovering the joys of a proper relationship with a human. Richie is Grey's human, rather than Geoff even though Grey is very fond of Geoff too, and vice versa. There's no point discussing it with Grey, and anyway Rhett wants to protect his friend from understanding his limitations as a dog. But Rhett knows that the time is fast approaching when he will need to extricate himself from the whole set up. He has already taken to staying out all night some nights, and shuns any food that is put down for him - even black sausage. He prefers to catch his own food, early in the morning or at dusk rabbits, or the ground nesting birds. He likes not having to eat handouts or scavenged human food as he had in London, or food that is served to him in a bowl.

Rhett feels his limbs strengthen from the increased exercise, he feels his lungs clear and his blood run fast and healthy from the carnivorism. All those half-sandwiches he'd used to eat back in London had made him feel a bit sluggish. Grey too is stronger, healthier, Richie and Geoff feed him top quality food and a wide variety, to keep his microbiome healthy Richie says. Richie enjoys preparing meals for Grey and Ginger, adding sardines, raw eggs, powdered superfoods, chopped liver, seaweed and all sorts of other nutritious things. Grey has put on weight and muscle, but he is still not a dog that relishes the cold and he is no good as a nocturnal hunting or adventuring companion. Not only that but Rhett is beginning to tire a little of his adoration. As much as he is fond of Grey, he longs to leave and vows to himself to do so, very soon.

SARAH'S FINAL JOURNEY AND A REUNION

At Helen and Sarah's home

HELEN

Helen sees Sarah's tail wagging. It is just an irregular, faint flick at first, then gets faster, stronger. It's beating properly now, thumping, and it makes Helen smile through her tears.

SARAH

Sarah is walking down an enclosed passage made of foliage; flowers bloom all the way along it, their scent sweet and heady. Sarah looks up and around her at the flowers, some of which look impossibly large and beautiful. They are a bit like rhododendron flowers, but pinks and whites instead of purple. Birdsong fills the air, and beneath her feet is grass. As she walks, everything seems to be getting brighter, as if all her senses are sharpening. She feels the dewy grass softly caressing her hot, cracked paws, and the tiredness in them starts to ease. The angry fever that had gripped her for so long is melting away out of her body. She breathes in the freshness of the air and feels invigorated. All the things she has lost are being returned to her. Her sight, which hasn't been sharp for some time because of thickening, dulling cataracts, is altering rapidly; with the passing seconds it sharpens, and Sarah soon feels as if she is seeing in technicolour. She doesn't remember seeing colours this vibrant, even in her youth.

Scents are starting to hit her now thick and fast, she breathes them in as hard as she can, revelling in the intensity of her restored sense of smell. A welcome, familiar smell enters her nostrils; her head snaps up and she whines with excitement. She sniffs at the air. The scent plume comes from somewhere beyond the path of flowers, and she rushes on to uncover the source of it. It is the recognition of this odour that is making her tail beat so hard back in Helen's living room - she can smell him! She wonders that she could ever have forgotten this dear, familiar whiff; this inimitable, delicious aroma of honesty, hard work, compassion for all beings, ridged nails, tobacco and dry skin, bristles of a thick moustache, deep wrinkles around the eyes. He is there, she can feel him, and all the glorious olfactory traces of him engulf her.

She sees him now and he spreads his arms wide as she runs towards him. Oh the joy of feeling the strength in her limbs again and no aches, no pain! She bounds towards him faster and faster and jumps right up into his arms, into his embrace. He, Ted, her long-lost and much-missed favourite person. Sarah isn't thinking about Helen now. She has passed over into the other realm. She leaps out of his strong arms down onto the floor, back to full youth and strength - she had forgotten what that was like! She, young again, leaps about sniffing the earth here and there in glee, looking back up at him frequently, to check he is still there. He grins at her, his eyes creased up, delighted to see her, to be reunited. He looks beyond her, as if looking for something. Not seeing it, he nods to himself slightly, looks back at Sarah, and smiles.

'Come on then, girl,' he says, and leads the way.

HELEN

All the while, Helen is talking to Sarah, she finds it soothes her to talk. 'Do you remember, Sarah, when we found you? When my Ted climbed down that scree and saved you? Do you remember? How he carried you up? He was old himself then, but he was always a fine man, a hero. He wasn't scared of the other dogs, the wild ones. He wasn't scared of the people either, telling him not to do it, of that horrible man who was mocking him, do you remember him? I remember him shouting, I remember his voice, it was so harsh.

He carried you all the way back up in his arms – you were too weak to walk - and from that day we kept you close to us, you never left, we loved you, and you loved us. And we'll be together again, all together. Before too long, I promise.' The movement of Sarah's tail is only a little flicker, she is under heavy medication now. For three days she has barely been able to make it out to the back garden, and Helen has known that it is time. It won't be long now, Helen is sure of it.

Helen can't really bear it, but she knows how important it is for dogs to be able to leave without feeling that they are letting down those left behind. So she is brave. She's had to be brave, very brave, twice before, and she can do it again, she has to. Her voice faltering, tears that she will soon cry gathering in her sinuses, she buries her face in Sarah's fur, breathing her in.

'Do you see him Sarah?' she asks, with sudden urgency. She feels that Sarah does, and has experienced a sudden rush of elation. 'Is he there?' Sarah's tail, which has been only faintly flicking, starts beating hard now, despite the medication. A feeling of pure joy fills Sarah. She gets goosebumps all over, and laughs, in delight. Helen feels through Sarah that bolt of recognition and gives a little involuntary cry, 'Oh!' One hand still stroking Sarah, the other hand flies to her throat, feeling for the necklace that Ted had given her so many years ago, the one that she always wears.

Sarah's tail abruptly stops, and something changes in the air.

Helen feels tears pouring down her face, and she is both reassured and desolate; she knows in that moment that Sarah is gone.

Helen had thought for a while that it would be this way. Anything else would be too cruel. Some people believe there is nothing, after death. But now she knows for certain. Helen had felt Sarah slipping away from her, had felt her breathing getting shallower, slower, until it was barely there at all. Until it wasn't there. She has crossed into another realm, that is all. Ted had met her and she had moved over. That was all. It had been peaceful. It is over. Sarah is there now, waiting for Helen - along with Ted and George. Her parents too, though their smiling faces are blurry in her mind, like in the old photographs she had of them. She remembers the way they were with her, always kind, always loving, and the happy times they had had together.

She looks forward to seeing them all again. She feels overwhelmed with joy. Exquisite pain, of course, but it is joy that underlies it, she feels that.

The elation passes and Sarah is momentarily sad that she herself can't go just yet but then shakes her head and admonishes herself. She can be patient a while longer, she has to be. Surprisingly clear-headed, Helen sits, her head bent over Sarah, still stroking her. The tears have ceased now, she feels bereft but somehow comforted. She had known she was right, that he was waiting. She knows now, Sarah had seen him, Helen had known it in that sudden beating of the tail, the defying of the drugs that were shutting her physical body down. Sarah had always loved Ted best, out of the two of them. That beating of the tail is proof for Helen, all the proof she needs. She feels immensely relieved. Now she just needs to wait. She can do that, wait a little bit longer, then they'll all be together. She cradles Sarah's head, strokes her gently. It seems that they stay that way for a long time.

The vet is in no rush, these are things that no good vet would push. She has lost three dogs herself and it had broken her heart each time; she knows exactly the importance of the moment, that it has to be softened as much as possible.

It is Helen who breaks the spell and straightens up, bravely.

'OK,' she says, letting out a long sigh, 'you can take her now. I'll never be ready. But after all, it's just a body now, a shell, isn't it.' The vet nods her agreement and smiles, yet she too bends to stroke Sarah's inert body and Helen sees a tear drop. They both stand.

The vet speaks gently, suggesting that Helen call for her daughter-in-law and go with her into the other part of the house, whilst she takes Sarah away, in a bag. It wouldn't seem right for Helen to see that, nobody should see their loved ones being zipped into a bag, even when they know that it is just the shell of them. Helen does, and her daughter-in-law gives her a cup of tea.

After that day, Helen switches to Earl Grey. She can't face the taste of normal tea any more as it tastes to her of goodbye.

POSSIBILITY

At Audrey & Beagle's home

AUDREY

Audrey has recently changed her diet, on the advice of Sylvie who said that her diet is doing her no favours whatsoever. Sylvie is blunt when she wants to be and has told Audrey that she will feel better if she eats more sensibly - something about blood sugar and mood. Audrey is plump. Always has been, always hated being. She is torn – you are told to love your body and embrace your curves, but you are also told to ditch the carbs and shift the weight. She is confused. She doesn't want to be anti-feminist and go on a diet to conform to someone else's ideal of perfection of form (waif-like, ridiculous), but on the other hand, she would love to have longer, leaner limbs (golden limbs!) and a flat tummy. Just once, and maybe only for a while, just to see how it feels. She'd also love to have a tan and highlights in her hair, for it not to be boring, sensible chestnut brown. Charlotte - her friend from junior school - has a golden tan and highlights in her hair and has done for as far back as Audrey can remember.

As she sits drinking her coconut milk latte, Audrey replays to herself the conversation she'd had with Harold earlier that day. To fit in in the world, that's the way Harold had somewhat curiously phrased it, she remembers. Yes, she thinks, it's important if you are not one of those brave, pioneering sorts like Rhett, or someone like Charles who simply doesn't care about others' opinions, who has no desire to conform. For some people, social interaction and being amenable comes easily. For Lexi. For Piper, Lottie, Helen too. For Beagle, not. And Grey, too, had been more like Audrey, she thinks, uncertain of himself and looking to others for validation. She wonders what had happened to him. They never see Lady Human in the park now, not that they had often except in the ten days after he'd gone missing. They hadn't seen Grey with the dog walker again either, after that. *He can't have been found,* Audrey thinks, sadly.

Beagle looks up at Audrey, a little less mournfully than usual and she pats the space next to her, as she often does. Her Tinks had always sat beside her on the couch, and patting it as an invitation is a habit she hasn't got out of yet. It is hard though for her to have her advances shunned so consistently. To her amazement, this time Beagle clambers up. Dramatically laboriously, and with a big sigh. He curls himself into a ball next to her, nose tucked in, the configuration of him making her think of a fox. She beams to herself. Beagle isn't exactly relaxed, but he is markedly better than he had been six months ago. And before that there had been just a miserable plateau, for a long time, after the initial hopeful but disturbing year that had followed getting him. It's funny, Audrey thinks, she'd heard from a few people now that just when you get really desperate, just when you think you'll crack, that you can't take it any more, the universe gives you something. It has been true for her, just when she had been at breaking point, Sylvie and the rest of the park gang had exploded into her life, and the impact of knowing them had changed everything, both for her and for Beagle.

Harold had also been put in her path. Her thoughts skirt around the idea of him, his funny quirks, his eyes. Absent-mindedly she strokes Beagle, who doesn't even flinch.

SUNSTROKE

BEAGLE

Beagle has sunstroke. They'd been out too long in that fierce sun yesterday. It had been nice, he has to admit, hanging out with the others on the bank in the sunshine with a view of Kensington Palace, but he had known even then that he would pay the price for it. He pants, miserably. He is certain he has a temperature, he feels hot then cold then hot again, all within the space of a minute. Not only that but he aches all over. It had been fun, he has to admit, running around with the others yesterday. But he shouldn't have exerted himself so much. Plus, that Rhett had knocked him over. Not by mistake, he realises that, it's just that he's so big and clumsy, so cavalier about everything. Beagle envies his fine health and vitality but thinks he ought to watch where he is going a bit more. Restless and uncomfortable, he moves from one place to another, and gazes at Aude reproachfully, he feels like the sunstroke is her fault. Aude gazes back at him, at a loss.

Beagle looks away, and heaves a big sigh. *There's so much to worry about in the world,* he thinks.

BOARDING THE TRAIN

London Euston train station

HELEN

Helen boards the train. She is a bit puffed out, but happy with herself. Her eyes shine. The past few weeks without Sarah have been extremely painful, coping again with loss. First her husband. Then her son. Then Sarah. It has felt hard, but Helen is stoic. There is really no other option, after all. And she is so looking forward to seeing her brother Eddie. He will be a tonic, he always has been. Even when they were little he had always made her laugh. She is to stay up there for three weeks but who knows, maybe they will work something out. The weather is harsh up there of course, she'll have to get some cashmere jumpers, but that's easy enough.

Helen's beginning to feel like it might be time for her to move on from London. Everybody rushes about so fast. It would be fine if she could keep up, she has always loved the buzz, but now, as she can't, it only serves to frustrate her. Helen will miss her park friends of course, if she doesn't come back. Particularly young Danny, Lottie, and Hugh, Sylvie's husband, who she sees often doing his daily walking laps of the area. But she thinks that she might enjoy the company of some people more her own age too. Eddie has said that his local friends are looking forward to meeting her. He's never suffered fools or bores gladly so she's sure she'll like them. If not, they might at least be interesting. Sometimes disagreeing with someone is as interesting as agreeing with them on everything, after all; although she adores her one remaining old friend, since their outlook and opinions are so similar it always feels a little like talking to herself.

She'll miss the boy, Danny, most of all. They'll stay in touch though, he's already shown her how to message him and has connected them so that she can tell him how she's getting on up there, what dudes she's hanging with, who her new bff is and all that. She smiles, thinking about him, about their friendship. People think it's funny, them making friends with almost a seventy year gap between them, but it doesn't feel funny to Helen, it feels completely natural. He's changed a lot over the last few months, Danny, since they've known each other. He no longer sits hunched on the bench in Brook Green like he used to when they had first met. He goes to school more or less every day now and has started shadowing Lottie too, learning from her about dog training and behaviour. He reads blogs and watches vlogs in his spare time about the different theories of dog training, even listens to whole books on his headphones. He has hacked into Helen's Audible account, with her blessing of course; she never uses all her credits in a given month so allocates one to him. He always spends a long time choosing his book and is very grateful to her, especially as he knows that she is, like him, far from loaded.

Helen likes using the word 'loaded', it makes her feel young when she says it. She smiles to herself. A text pings on her phone. She smiles, and puts on her reading glasses.

GOODBYE

An estate somewhere in the countryside near Edinburgh

RHETT

Rhett is not generally an overly emotional dog but he finds that the sight of Grey shivering on the edge of the moor and pretending not to be cold in the early morning mist gets to him. This little slip of an Italian Greyhound who he'd barely registered when they'd first met has thoroughly worked his way into his heart, and he will miss him. But he knows how sensitive Grey is, and he doesn't want to make it harder for him.

'Right then Grey, this is it! This is where I turn around and go back!' he tries to sound light-hearted but he sees that Grey isn't convinced. He can see that Grey is himself desperate to lessen the pain of their parting and trying not to crumble under the emotion. Rhett knows how Grey looks up to him, and how he's been instrumental in this whole debacle. He's so relieved it has worked out okay. Grey replies reasonably evenly, trying hard to hide a wobble in his voice, 'Yup, give my love to the park gang will you? I miss them, but it's good to think about them there, I can feel them, you know? Lexi and Piper and co. Even Kip. And those funny humans. I wonder how Harold and Audrey are getting on!'

They both smile.

'And Beagle.'

Rhett nods, rolling his eyes a little. *Beagle is a typical London dog,* he thinks.

'Somehow I feel that they're alright.'

'Yeah, course they are Grey, course they are.'

The name Sarah hangs in the air between them. Would she still be alive?

'Don't worry Grey. I'll send word. I've got my ways!' Rhett gives a cocky little flip of the head towards the hills. Grey nods.

There's an awkward pause.

Their breath is visible in the cold morning air. Rhett and Grey move towards each other. Instinctively, they rub their necks together. Rhett feels Grey's warmth and he breathes in his friend's smell and rubs his neck on Grey's, as hard as he can. He will miss his smell. That's the thing you miss the most, he remembers that with Jessica. Tears prick at his eyes, and he turns away abruptly. He starts to trot off, and calls over his shoulder, gruffly, 'You did so well, Grey, you know, you really did so well. You left that awful woman behind for good now. You were so brave, you've been so brave this whole time. I'm really proud of you.'

He doesn't want Grey to see his tears so, voice cracking, he throws the words over his shoulder without properly looking back, 'See ya!'

GOODBYE II

An estate somewhere in the countryside near Edinburgh

GREY

'Thank you, Rhett!' Grey calls after him. It sounds thin and inadequate given everything Rhett has done for him, but Grey feels a surge of warmth inside knowing for sure now that Rhett is proud of him. He sits, shivering, and watches the wiry, athletic figure of his friend and mentor move off. He watches Rhett as hard and as long as he can, trying to imprint on his mind Rhett's inimitable gait. He knows he will miss seeing that confident lope, that endearing swagger Rhett has and he anticipates the pain of the loss. The lump in his throat feels like it's the size of an egg. He strains his eyes until the mist completely swallows up the figure of his friend.

How I will miss him! Grey thinks.

Grey whines then, gently, without meaning to. He realises he is holding his left paw up off the floor; it's something he always does when he is uncertain, or worried. He places it back on the floor, looks around him, and does an enormous yawn. It is all very exhausting, emotion, he feels bone-tired. The yawn makes him feel a bit better. It also feels like a dividing line. The air around him feels empty - too empty. He feels bereft.

Grey fervently hopes with all his sighthound heart that Rhett will reach home safely. He hates to think of him travelling alone, even though he knows Rhett has made longer journeys than this and that he will be unphased by it. Reluctant to leave the spot, as part of him hopes to see Rhett lope back into view saying he has changed his mind, Grey sits for some time. Eventually though, heavy-hearted, he stands up, and walks slowly back up, over the field towards the house. He crosses through a gap in the hedge into the garden. Thoughts of breakfast cheer him. He has put on weight, thanks to his new diet. The dew is fresh, cold and wet on his paws and when he reaches the bottom of the garden, after one last, longing look behind him he hops onto the path thankfully. He delicately trots up to the back door and inside, using Ginger's catflap.

Grey will miss Rhett desperately, he will miss having his hairy, warm, dependable form to snuggle up to when it's cold in the daytime and the fire isn't lit or even, when it's not cold; to touch toes with him when they are both stretched out on the flagstones having an afternoon nap. He will miss his presence and the feeling that everything will be all right, because dear, solid, brave, wise, worldly Rhett is there. He will miss his smell, the very essence of him. The lump in his throat is still enormous. He swallows, sad.

'Ah there he is!' beams Richie, reaching down to ruffle Grey's body with the large hands that always smell so earthy and delicious. 'Where's yer partner-in-crime, eh? Out huntin'?' Richie is unconcerned, and Grey wants to shout at him, but on the other side he understands why he's not worried, Rhett often goes AWOL for a few days, he is that sort of dog. 'You like yer comforts though don't you!' Richie chuckles to himself, and turns back to the frying pan where, Grey knows, sausages and a delicious thing called black pudding are being cooked, as it is the weekend, and Richie and Geoff always have a big fry-up then. They share it with Grey and Rhett and Ginger. Ginger gets the second portion when it becomes clear that Rhett won't partake.

As he waits for his breakfast, curled up in his basket on the raised platform, out of the draft, Grey thinks back to the time he had first spoken to Lexi about whether she had thought it possible to change your owner. Geoff has sat down in the armchair by the fire waiting for Richie to finish off the breakfast and Grey feels his big hand stroking him, rhythmically, absent-mindedly.

Grey feels relieved to no longer be living in that still, sinister, ticking house and tucks his nose into his paws and sighs a heavy, long sigh that is full of all sorts of feelings.

HOME IN LONDON

At Harold and Rolf's home

HAROLD

Harold returned last night from his annual summer holiday *en famille*, a tense fortnight with his stiflingly uptight family. Usually Harold feels a certain indifference about his life but this morning he is filled with an inexplicable jauntiness. He is happy to be back home, feeling a lightness that he's not felt for the past two weeks, nor even possibly ever before. Before he'd left, he realises now, something had changed, but he'll need some time to process what it was. Harold had felt quite emotional yesterday when he'd picked Rolf up, this is a first for him. He doesn't agree with talking to dogs. Lottie and Sylvie are always doing it and he has told Lottie many times in no uncertain terms how ridiculous he thinks it is, not that she takes any notice. To his surprise, he catches himself doing it this morning.

'So, Rolf,' he says, looking down at his housemate, 'to the park, eh?' He has finished reading the paper and is drinking a cup of coffee, made with his new Nespresso machine, a gift from Ophelia. The machine would be much easier than using a coffee press, she'd said, much more practical, less washing up. He'd told Ophelia that he wanted to make some changes in his life, but he had not been exactly sure which ones. She had thought that a coffee machine might be a good and not too overwhelming way for her brother to start. She had been right. It had put a subtly different spin on his morning and pressing the buttons pleases him. His sister, Ophelia, had been a support this holiday as always, but only when she had managed to snatch some focus away from her demanding, clingy children.

As he looks down at Rolf, who is sitting by his feet, Harold thinks about how he and Ophelia might both have lived very different lives had they had a different upbringing.

Ophelia has changed this year, he thinks. She now has a defiant tilt to her chin in the face of her husband's frequent barbed comments, and a distinctly less adoring expression when she looks at her children, both the spitting image of their father. He seems to be just another incarnation of their father and Harold is surprised to realise with a sudden clarity that he hates them both. It's strange to feel such a strong emotion, especially for one's own father he imagines, but nevertheless he feels it keenly, this newly defined hatred for his father and his silly, pompous bully of a brother-in-law.

Up until this holiday, Ophelia had never stood up to her husband, to Harold's knowledge. And ever since he could remember, Harold had always been aware of the relentless comments made by him specifically designed to undermine his sister. They had always bothered him, these derogatory comments. The more company there was, the more his brother-in-law seemed to feel the need to belittle his wife, and so, the worse the comments became. It wasn't that Ophelia had stood up to him this fortnight vocally, she hadn't, but there had been a subtle shift. Instead of her previous sad-faced attempt to pretend not to notice or stoic refusal to register the slights, there has been this new tilt to her chin and the quiet settling in of a glittering, stubborn look in her eye with each new casually-barbed comment.

Ophelia is building up to something, Harold feels sure of it. He is pleased with himself for gleaning this emotional stuff, it's hard for him but he thinks that he is getting better at it with age and experience. He now even almost enjoys applying himself to the puzzle that is other people.

'To the park to meet the gang?' Harold says to Rolf, who wags his tail eagerly in reply, trots off to the hallway and retrieves his lead, carrying it with a gundog's soft mouth back to Harold to deposit it into his long-fingered, pale, softly-cupped palms. This time, though, Harold has come to intercept him and crouches down in the hallway. He accepts the lead gently and looks into Rolf's eyes, and ruffles his head fondly after the deposit is made. It is the first time Harold has noticed the flecks in Rolf's irises, the freckles on his lower eyelids.

'Come on then boy!' says Harold and experiences a feeling of camaraderie. Rolf wiggles around happily, excited about the imminent opening of the front door, the front door to another adventure Outside.

Were Harold able to articulate it, he would say that what has changed this holiday is that, partly thanks to Ophelia's change in attitude, partly down to his own changing perspective on things, he all of a sudden no longer feels like a little boy terrified of upsetting Mother and Father. That he has felt come upon him an unbidden but welcome sense that all their rules and regulations, their traditions and their sense of decorum are slightly ridiculous. Were he able to dredge it from his subconscious, he would also be wondering what they'd think of Audrey. Audrey is not well-bred, she is a normal girl, pink-cheeked. Not groomed, not cool, superior or aloof like the casual, entitled, ego-driven females he's been introduced to all his life. She is, though, to Harold, just perfect. She is like Ophelia in that she is fundamentally kind, warm, honest and not seemingly indifferent to everything, like most of those tall, weak-chinned posh girls he knows from their family social circles.

He is certain that Ophelia will like her, and that she will like Ophelia, and that is all that is important. His parents won't think that she is perfect, and that makes her all the more perfect to him.

ROLF

Rolf notices that there is a definite new cheerfulness about his human lately, since he's come back from holidays. Rolf senses that Harold is thinking about seeing Audrey in the park and he finds he is happy for him. He's a good owner, Harold, and he'd like for him to be less lonely. He himself doesn't have any special attachment to anyone – Rhett and Piper are fun to race around with, Luke too when he joins in - he likes his uncomplicated, masculine energy. He finds Kip a bit irritating as he nips at Rolf sometimes when they're running about. He can't help thinking that Lexi and Lily are a bit boring and heavy. Rolf hasn't seen Grey in a while, he realises. Rhett neither, thinking about it.

Rolf doesn't really mind who they see there, in actual fact, he is just looking forward to the smells and freedom of the park. His fortnight at gundog kennels has been, rather like Harold's, oppressive, and he is glad to be back home.

HOME CHECK

At Lottie and Piper's home (a first floor flat on Sinclair Road)

LOTTIE

The 'officer' from the rescue centre, a stout, pear-shaped lady smelling of liquorice, goes to take off her shoes at the door.

'Oh, no need!' says Lottie.

'Are you sure?' asks the lady.

'Absolutely!' Lottie replies. She would feel funny making a mature woman take off her shoes and have to walk around in tights. It would seem too intimate, somehow. And aside from that, she really isn't fussy.

They walk through into the living room. She suddenly sees the flat objectively, as if through the officer's eyes. It is bare. It hadn't occurred to Lottie till now that she might not pass the home assessment. She begins to feel nervous. There are no dog things per se. Piper lives as she, Lottie, lives. She sleeps on or in Lottie sleeps, or indeed wherever else she fancies. There is no outside space, only a little balcony that isn't really much good for dogs and that Lottie only now uses for hanging the washing out on when it's warm enough. She and Sebastian had got very drunk there in the early days, when they had first bought the flat. They had been delighted with their outside space and they'd had great plans for it. They had been delighted with everything, back then.

Lottie blinks back tears; she needs to focus now, for Nero's sake. She thinks about him waiting somewhere in a concrete pen with bars and her heart races, uncomfortably. She tries not to think about all the dogs in concrete pens, and worse. Her previous therapist had urged her dismissively not to worry so much about every living being on the planet. Lottie had stared at her coldly, she had found what she had said harsh and heartless. The therapist said she was 'hostile' and 'overly emotional' Lottie had changed therapist shortly after that. The one she goes to now seems to be more amenable, and to better understand her concern for those in the animal kingdom. She feels that this is important, since it's such an essential, integral part of her, always has been since she made homes for woodlice when she was a young child.

The woman gets a clipboard out of her bag. Lottie fights the urge to laugh. A clipboard of all things seems so old-fashioned these days. She gets these inappropriate urges to laugh randomly, at the most inconvenient of times, since the loss of Sebastian, it had started at his funeral.

'Would you like a cup of tea? Coffee?' asks Lottie, trying to get a handle on her nerves.

'Oooh, tea please,' the woman replies, looking grateful and frazzled, 'strong, with lots of milk.'

'Coming up!' Lottie replies and thinks to herself that it must be the first time she has ever said that; it doesn't feel like something she would normally say. The pressure of the home check is making her feel slightly hysterical.

'Feel free to have a nosey around,' she says to the lady, gesturing to the back of the flat.

'Are you sure?' asks the woman for a second time.

'Of course!' says Lottie, and laughs. 'I don't think we have anything to hide!' She feels nervous. But unbeknown to her that little pronoun will in retrospect decide in her favour in the lady's mind, once she realises Lottie lives alone with Piper.

Lottie addresses Piper, 'Go on Pipes, show the lady the rest of the flat!'

Piper wags and walks to the middle door, looking back at them.

'Come on then!' she says to the lady.

The lady laughs and the tension goes out of the air. She follows Piper's wagging tail out of the living room.

When they return, Piper is still wagging happily. The lady is also still smiling. She picks up the clipboard and pen and addresses Lottie, who hands her a cup of tea. The lady takes a grateful gulp and then sets it down carefully on a coaster.

'Lovely cup of tea!' she says. Lottie grins. They'd talked the other day in the park about how hard it is to get a cup of tea right for someone you don't know.

'So, you live with...?' she leaves the question open-ended. Lottie realises that it is quite a big flat for one person. She swallows and looks out of the window, feigning not to have heard, buying time. She feels tears pricking her eyes. This is important though, she has to save Nero. It is the first time she has said it, actually said it.

'It's just Piper and I now. I had a boyfriend, but he was killed,' Lottie says quietly, plainly. 'A year and a half ago.'

The woman's hand flies to her mouth. Lottie wonders why that happens. For some reason she feels compelled to explain.

'It was a bike accident.' she says.

'Oh I'm sorry!' the lady says. She had assumed that Lottie was single.

Lottie shakes her head and shrugs. She reaches down to stroke Piper.

'It's okay.'

The lady looks at her candidly.

'I have to be honest, Charlotte, the only issue I can find is that you live in a flat.' She looks down through the sheet, turns it over. 'That's not ideal, but given your work is flexible and you already have a reasonably high-energy dog...' Her forehead is creased; she looks tired. 'And obviously your profession works in your favour...' She puts down her pen, takes her glasses off, looks into Lottie's eyes, with a direct expression. 'Full disclosure. Nero's not a dog we would home with just anyone. He's... tricky. He could go either way. He'll need structure, leadership, management, training. Time. Patience. And he's already had a few incidents logged against him, so you'll have to be very careful. Sadly, people are all too ready to jump on a bandwagon about a dog, particularly a breed like Nero's. But my gut feeling is that in the right environment he'll thrive. The staff tell me he's a really sweet dog.' She smiles. 'And it's good to hear that he already knows Piper here. I'd suggest we set up an introduction within the home. Piper might act differently on her own turf, and he's likely to too, inside. We don't really know how he was treated at home but we can imagine it didn't feel like a safe environment to him. Bottom line, he might be more reactive in a home environment than in a kennel, or out on walks. But we can try, if you're willing. If that meeting goes well, the next step is an overnight stay, a weekend stay and if all that goes fine... well, he's yours. We're grateful that you came forward. It was,' she says, delicately, 'difficult. People will do anything for a slice of fame and his former owner has become quite notorious.' She shudders involuntarily. 'The Kensington Killer, they're calling him'.

Lottie thinks of Neil, of those dark eyes. She still can't believe that he'd done what they are saying he did. Time will tell. She hadn't liked how he'd treated Nero, but she can't help feeling a spark of sympathy for him, . He'll be separated from his dog forever, she thinks. She remembers how she had felt in the days after Piper was taken. The feeling of dread she had had during that time lays heavy in her stomach. Poor Neil, she thinks, privately.

'Poor Nero,' she says out loud. 'He's a lovely dog, we know him. It'll be fine, I have no doubt. But we're happy to take it as slow as you say. We'd love him to come and live with us.'

They both look at Piper, who wags, and they laugh.

WINDS OF CHANGE

At a dog shelter, South London

NERO

Nero lifts his head. He feels something has changed. He feels something is going to happen. He can't explain it. He has butterflies in his stomach. He whines. His man is approaching along the corridor, whistling. He sounds happy. When he reaches Nero he stops, looks at Nero, shakes his head and smiles at him.

'Your lucky day boi, innit! Your lucky day!'

MEETING OPHELIA

Kensington High Street (a cafe near the station)

AUDREY

'Audrey!'

'Ophelia!' Audrey smiles and sticks out her warm, friendly hand. Ophelia smiles back and takes it. Ophelia's own is bird-like and cold, but has a surprising strength in it. They shake hands gently, warmly. Harold beams.

'I've heard so much about you!' Audrey says.

'Me too you!' Ophelia replies, laughing and looking at Harold, who is flustered and fiddles around with Rolf's lead. Audrey blushes.

'And this must be Beagle!' Ophelia says, to diffuse the awkwardness, and gestures loosely, elegantly, taking in the quivering dog who is sat right next to Audrey's feet.

'Yes, I'm afraid so!' Audrey laughs, shaking her head. 'You'll have to excuse him, he's not very good with new people.' Somehow Audrey knows that Ophelia won't do the things that people usually do. She seems to have in her a grace, an emotional intelligence; she has probably soaked up all that had been meant for her younger brother. As she could have predicted, Ophelia only very discreetly glances at Beagle and doesn't stoop to try to fondle him.

'I know, I've heard all about him. Don't worry, I'll just ignore him. He'll get used to me!' Audrey finds that she likes the certainty that they are to become part of one another's lives that is present in Ophelia's wording. Audrey thinks to herself that she has never before met someone who comes across as simultaneously so modest and so confident. She instantly likes Ophelia.

They are standing in the outdoor area of the cafe opposite the big hotel at the south-western corner of Kensington Gardens and Ophelia smiles at Audrey as she sits down on one of the pretty iron chairs. Harold and Audrey do the same.

'Your brother's been amazing,' Audrey tells Ophelia, blushing. Harold, who pretends not to have heard, can't help smiling, though he turns around to hide his face, ostensibly to look for the waiter to ask for menus. 'He really has. He knows such a lot about dogs, he seems to get them, you know?'

'Shame he's not the same with people!' Ophelia laughs a tinkly, gentle laugh, including Harold in her joke.

He smiles at her indulgently, happy to have a reason to let the smile that had already been on his face show, and says 'Ha, ha!' drily and then turns to Audrey and says, 'Ophelia is the one who tells me how to act around people.' He looks at his sister and smiles fondly.

'It's... it's not as easy for me with humans as with dogs. You might have noticed.' Audrey is surprised – not for the first time - by Harold's candour. She can see how he draws strength from his sister, they clearly adore each other. They all grin and Audrey gets goosebumps.

Audrey thinks to herself how wonderful it must be to have a brother. Or, even better, a sister! A sister like Ophelia. She feels comfortable with her immediately, even though she is fiercely pretty and clearly extraordinarily posh. She is dressed in an inimitable, quirky way that suits her petite frame perfectly - all vintage, Audrey suspects. Her thick, lustrous hair is cut into a bob that sticks right out dramatically from her slender, alabaster neck. She has scars on her face from acne she'd had as a teenager, but she has covered them cleverly with make up and has the prettiest, twinkliest eyes that Audrey has ever seen. Pure green, both mischievous and kind, with flecks in them, like Harold's.

Audrey picks up her coffee and smiles shyly. She feels ungainly next to Ophelia but also, comfortable. She feels Beagle leaning against her leg, and relaxing. Ophelia gestures to the waiter, who has been studiously ignoring Harold but for her comes straight over. She has that effect on people. She smiles warmly up at him, and he blushes. Harold beams, looking from Ophelia to Audrey, and bends down to ruffle Rolf's head happily.

'Yes!' he says to him happily, goofily. Both Ophelia and Audrey laugh with delight.

THE END

In Sylvie and Lexi's garden

SYLVIE

'There appears to be a large brown, swan-like dog curled up in our garden' says Sylvie's husband as he looks out of the window.

'Oh! I thought I saw him the other day! That's Doggy Dog! He'd disappeared, we haven't seen him for ages!' Sylvie says, rushing to the window to look, 'Yes! That's him! Great. I thought he might come in one day; he walks us home sometimes, me and Lexi, and I took a few bricks out of the wall some time ago so he could get over if he wanted to. I was worried about him.' She laughs, apologetically. Hugh raises an eyebrow and smiles.

She smiles back at her husband, then down at Lexi, who grins her wide Staffy grin back and trots out through the back door.

LEXI

'Rhett! Where've you been?'

'Ah, long story Lex. I found Grey, and had to get him out of here.'

'Oh! Am so glad! We were so worried about him! About both of you... you just disappeared! He's OK?'

'He's fine, yup. More than fine.'

'Tell me all about it Rhett.'

The two dogs settle down for a long chat. Sylvie watches them from the kitchen window, smiling. She picks up her phone to text Lottie and Aude to tell them that Doggy Dog is back, and safe.

EPILOGUE

MEETING FOR CLASS

Kensington Gardens (near the horse statue)

THE PARK GANG

Sylvie is unfailingly late and today is no exception. Always in a good mood, she is extraordinarily well balanced and unstressed, for a Londoner. Her dark hair is decisively, professionally highlighted and she wears it in an elfin cut that suits her neat and pleasing features. She dresses expensively though casually, and clutches a coffee in one hand, today and invariably a double espresso with three sugars. In the other, precariously, she holds her large phone and some keys. Her stocky white Staffy, Lexi, trots beside her jauntily, smiling widely. Lexi walks without a lead, even on the pavement; Sylvie doesn't even carry one. It would be perceived as strange in her native Switzerland, and it is here in the UK too, but such things don't bother Sylvie, who has an air of amenable yet steely self-assurance.

Charles never stands when he can sit or recline. He arrived some 5 minutes ago and from his prone position on the grass raises a hand, languidly, in greeting. He likes Sylvie. Everyone does; she is attractive, confident and kind. Charles is a jazz artist. People are amazed by this fact, as if they disbelieve that such a vocation still exists. Tall and mumbling, he always smells of cigarettes and often of alcohol. Through his smile perhaps, or because of something in his bearing, he also exudes the suggestion of other, less olfactorily detectable vices. For him, night is often day and day, often night. As Sylvie approaches and stoops to give him her delicate, pale hand in greeting, Charles guffaws, gently. He has just made a joke to himself; half inside his head, and half out. Sylvie smiles at him as their hands touch, she knows better than to ask for an explanation. His thoughts, just like jazz, are erratic and hard to follow. Charles takes his sunglasses off to smile up at her, and squints in the sunshine. Wrapped around his elegant neck is an Arabic scarf, which juxtaposes flamboyantly with the sunglasses. His impossibly long, lean limbs are clad as always in skinny, scruffy black jeans and they hang down low on his non-existent bottom in a manner that belies his 50 odd years. Laying a few feet away from Charles is his dog Kip, a Border Collie who is also somewhat aloof and self-contained. There though the similarities end, Kip is as neurotic as Charles is laid back. Kip loves these meet-ups, his brain craves learning. His body position - a permanent, poised crouch – doesn't reflect this though and Kip isn't a communicative dog - he doesn't greet any of the other dogs arriving, or their humans. He is just intensely focused on Lottie, itching for things to start.

Hurrying up the path waving, blushing and flustered, is Audrey. Shy and round-shouldered still but markedly less than before, the psychological burden that she has been carrying is starting to lift. With her, her dog Beagle ducks and darts, cringes and slinks, reluctant and tormented. Audrey holds onto the lead firmly, smiling apologetically. Beagle is slowly but surely learning to cope with the proximity of others and this select group of dogs and humans are becoming, familiar to him, albeit incrementally. Beagle is too stressed to actually greet anyone but Audrey makes up for it, saying hello to each person and dog in turn, remembering their names where she can, chastising herself internally where she cannot. She of course remembers more of the dogs' names than the humans'.

Charles raises an eyebrow and narrows his eyes, watching her. Audrey is rather too keen for his liking. *Not cool,* he thinks.

Lexi is still busy greeting the dogs and the humans one by one, methodically and enthusiastically, wiggling and waggling her broad white body, charmingly disregarding all notions of personal space. Except, that is, when it comes to Lily, towards whom she inclines her head politely, and Beagle, who she misses out almost entirely.

Lexi has a highly developed sense of emotional intelligence and she knows that Beagle will prefer this.

Lottie - tall, slight, and scruffily dressed all in grey - is there already with her grey, soft-curled, side-kick Piper, a Poodle without the Poodle cut. Piper's canine teeth are a little bluntened by the carrying of things, which Lottie doesn't have the heart to stop her doing. Lottie looks hip, although these days it's more by accident than design, she doesn't care about her appearance any more. Joyful and deft, pretty Piper casually greets humans and canines alike as they arrive; she doesn't particularly differentiate between the species and nudges body parts irrespective of which, or indeed if human or canine.

'Ready, Lex?' Piper asks, doing a play boy then jumping forward, spinning round and bumping Lexi with the back end of her body, roughly.

'Always, Piper!' Lexi replies, panting a little. It is getting muggy now, despite what had been a chilly start, and Lexi is a little overweight.

Their humans, Lottie and Sylvie, beam at each other and do a high five.

Piper and Lexi walk together often. They are somewhere around the same age but Lexi has more gravitas. Her nickname in the park is 'The Oracle' as the local dogs gravitate towards her for advice. Piper, by contrast, is frivolous and light-hearted. One wouldn't go to Piper for advice.

'The class' as Charles ironically refers to it, his disdain for teaching of any kind overt, has developed organically over time and is run, informally, by Lottie. She is a dog trainer by profession but seems unwilling to take on private clients just at the moment. Even Sylvie is unsure as to why. Piper is her demo dog and enjoys training, she is eager to start, but Lottie tells her that it's not time just yet. Piper goads the panting Lexi into a bit of wrestling.

Lily and Luke - attractive, liver-coloured German Shorthaired Pointers - leisurely approach with their human, Edward. Aunt and nephew, Lily and Luke live on Queens Gate Gardens near the park but spend long summers in a sprawling estate on the edge of the village of Lourmarin in Provence. Edward is a pleasant, unassuming chap in his 70s. Despite his slightly frazzled appearance and the perpetual carrying of an unbranded plastic bag, he is extremely rich. He copes well, phlegmatically, with the various and constant dramas of his five grown up children and his somewhat petulant second wife. Across the grass towards the bandstand the white-haired, rosy-cheeked Edward ambles bashfully, meeting the eye of no one in particular but mumbling some sort of vague, polite and archaic greeting. He has bright blue eyes, beady and intelligent. Lily and Luke are both collarless, unusually naked, for London. In Edward's bag, as well as a novel and his wallet, are two simple, good quality rope slipleads. His family have always had gundogs (Labradors or Pointers) and the way some of the dogs in Kensington Gardens are dressed baffles him.

Luke is a simple, unsophisticated dog. He sits down for a clumsy, half-hearted scratch, then proceeds to lick at his rear end but Lily nudges him crossly with her head, despairing to herself about his lack of social etiquette. She sighs, and glares at him. She finds it hard sometimes to believe that he is her blood relation, even though she knows it's irrefutable. Lily inclines her head towards Lexi, acknowledging her, and disdainfully ignores the rest of the crew. She is a formidable, intimidating, serious character and the other dogs skirt around her. Not as slim as she used to be, she wears a faint but definite air of disappointment and disapproval, which is sometimes mistaken for social awkwardness.

Harold strides over purposefully, imperiously, his sleek and biddable dog Rolf walking off lead perfectly to heel beside him. He nods curtly, efficiently at everyone, male and female alike, then discreetly gives a release command to Rolf, the subtlest movement of one finger and an almost imperceptible click of his tongue; he is prepared for later years, for if Rolf becomes blind or deaf. Rolf shoots away from his side and wiggles around happily in typical Working Cocker fashion, a compact package of health and vitality. He's rather shallow, but on the upside, friendly and well balanced, as well as exceedingly well trained; Harold can't cope mentally with chaos, so he arranges his life to avoid it as far as possible. He frowns, watching Lottie and Piper. He thinks that Lottie should be more disciplined with Piper and that it's a shame she isn't, as Piper is an intelligent dog with great potential to learn.

Lottie looks around for stragglers, checks her watch, and calls Piper to her in readiness to start. She wonders if Doggy Dog will show up today. The others gather round. Edward and Sylvie heckle her, saying that they don't want to learn anything serious today, that loose lead walking is 'boring' and 'far too worthy'. Harold raises his eyes to the sky, despairing. Audrey, caught between, laughs nervously. Charles reluctantly drags himself up into a slouching stand and stubs out his cigarette. He narrows his eyes and sighs, unsure how he's become part of this motley, random, friendly little crew but secretly quite liking it. Kip looks up at him and grins, poised, his eyes shining.

THANK YOU

Saša - for being you, for loving dogs as much as I do, and for loving me malgré moi

My mum, Margaret - for ploughing through early, rambling drafts - twice! - when no one else would; for that and for everything else

Katharine aka Eagle-Eyed Lewis - for knowing about stuff I didn't (grammar and otherwise!) and for being the best big sis

Eve - for such super kind encouragement and advice on the (too) early draft (I promise to plan and execute book two better!)

Chloe - for the beautiful book jacket, the perfectly pitched support, the typesetting, the precision on the final copy edit; for being lovely to work with and for helping me - finally! - get this over the line

My dad, Tom - for noticing the weird stuff and for the poetic, melancholy gene - I wouldn't be without it

My big bro, David - the talking birds are for you!

Meech – for pushing me to read out loud, for the easy-going flowy brainstorming email exchanges and for your artistic-hearted instincts and insights

Jo-Rosie, Nando & Dean of The School of Canine Science - for bringing together such a fun, smart, caring, inspiring and open-minded tribe of proper dog people, for being the voices of sanity and a massive force for good in the ever crazier human world that dogs have to live in. Am happy to be a part of it all

Cass Thomas, Nicky Grant and others in SOCS - for giving me feedback on early excerpts and helping me believe there are people who would enjoy reading this book as much as I enjoyed writing it

Anthony Brooks - for the illustrations even though they didn't make the cut (only because I wanted people to imagine the characters for themselves)

Scott Pack, Katie Espiner and Ed Docz - for taking time and effort to encourage aspiring writers, and for all being cool, kind and inspirational

All my park friends over the last 7 years in London and Belgrade

This project is self-funded and self-published. All proceeds will go to dogs in need, mainly to the following three charities who do even more than rescuing, sheltering and rehoming dogs in dire conditions.

Serbia's Forgotten Paws (Serbia) work with pounds to improve shelter conditions, run shelters and neutering campaigns and implement Catch/Neuter/Release programs for street dogs

www.serbias-forgotten-paws.com

Galgos del Sol (Spain) do education work with local schools, conduct neutering programs and raise awareness about the plight of the Galgos

www.galgosdelsol.org/about-gds

The Wild at Heart Foundation (London based but run projects globally) do neutering programs and education work as well as awareness building on many fronts

www.wildatheartfoundation.org

Details of funds being transferred to them as well as further information about the book and news about my next book will be posted regularly here:

www.nomadthief.com

If you liked this book please be so kind as to write a review on Amazon or Goodreads, pop me a message or share something about it on social media @dogsoflondon book or use #dogsoflondonbook

All details and links can be found here: www.nomadthief.com or by using the QR code on the back cover

If you are struggling with a reactive dog and feeling isolated, find the Reactive Dogs UK (RDUK) group on Facebook

The seed of the idea for the Rhett of this book came from a real dog called Rhett who was rehomed by a lady called Peta. You can see him here:

www.sadiesstraydogrescue.com/dog-rehoming-success-story.html

If you have been moved by Rhett's story and want to help dogs like him and Jessica, please consider fostering/adopting through SSDR, or donating to them. Every £ really does make a difference to dogs just like them.

If you are looking for good dog training courses or interested in becoming a dog trainer, check out the brilliant School of Canine Science

www.caninescience.online

This is obviously a work of fiction but please note that:

Park Rangers in The Royal Parks are nothing like those depicted in the book and they most certainly do not cull squirrels

Rescue centres in Serbia and the ladies visiting them are not true to the depictions in this book

BOOKS I LOVED

Spill Simmer Falter Wither, by Sara Baume

The Friend, by Sigrid Nunez

Fifteen Dogs, by Andre Alexis

Tomorrow, by Damien Dibben

Lost Dog, by Kate Spicer

Saving Missy, by Beth Morrey

Dog Days, by Ericka Waller

Fluke, by James Herbert

The Incredible Journey, by Sheila Burnford

Dog Stories, by various authors (edited by Diana Secker Tesdell)

Mountaintop School for Dogs & Other Second Chances, by Ellen Cooney

Elsewhere, by Gabrielle Zevin

The Education of Will, by Patricia McConnell

Sirius, by Jonathan Crown

Watership Down, by Richard Adams

The Crow Chronicles, by Ranjit Lal

Charlotte's Web, by E.B. White

Animal Farm, by George Orwell

Return Of The Wild, by O.L. West

WHAT PEOPLE ARE SAYING ABOUT DOGS OF LONDON

'Emma Lewis-Galić treats her canine characters with as much respect and dignity as her human ones. It is incredibly difficult to sustain an authentic voice of another species but she seems able to do it effortlessly. An adorable book, beautifully drawn and with real psychological depth, full of great characters both two and four-legged. Lewis-Galić writes with a heightened sense of observation and her work demands to be seen by a wide audience.'

Neil Norman, playwright and critic

'In Dogs of London Emma Lewis-Galić expresses the inner thoughts of our four-legged companions with uncanny empathy. In her heartwarming tales of friendship, escape and stick- fetching set in the leafy dog walking circuits of West London she reveals some of the abiding truths of life and portrays with great insight both how our doggy friends see us and how they relate to each other.'

Alex Michon, artist and writer

'Emma Lewis-Gali ́c shows an extensive knowledge of dog behaviour which is in itself interesting. Her writing is engaging - not prissy or overworked but with very well observed detail of characters and situations. I like the attribution of human traits and intellect to dogs.'

Eve Smith, author of The Waiting Rooms and Off Target

'A capital adventure through doggy eyes. Touching and thought provoking.'

Kate Spicer, journalist and writer

#dogsoflondonbook

ABOUT THE AUTHOR

Emma Lewis-Galić loves all creatures that inhabit the earth but not so many humans. She loves words, wild nature, walking, her home city London, theatre, clothes, interior design and crafts. She comes from Wales originally and is 47 although still doesn't feel very grown up. She lives with her husband and two German Wirehaired Pointers in London, Istria and Aix. Together they aspire to having a big pack of rescue dogs. Emma secretly hopes to also have chickens, goats, rescue cows, pet rats and semi-tame corvids.

This is her first book.

#dogsoflondonbook

WWW.NOMADTHIEF.COM

Use your smartphone camera to scan the QR code

Printed in Great Britain
by Amazon

71181697R00182